Quincey Morris, Vampire

P.N. Elrod

A Baen Books Original

Baen Publishing Enterprises
P.O. Box 1403
Riverdale, NY 10471
www.baen.com

ISBN: 0-671-31984-4

Cover art by Jamie Murray

First printing, May 2001

Distributed by Simon & Schuster
1230 Avenue of the Americas
New York, NY 10020

Typeset by Brilliant Press
Printed in the United States of America

My humble thanks to
Bram Stoker,
Fred Saberhagen,
and Clive Leatherdale.

Thanks also to
Eric Burce
and Shola Vyvial
for the high bids,
Teresa Patterson for the wolf talk,
and J. Kevin "S.I.K.O." Topham
for lending an ear over the beer.

Cheers all!

Much to my surprise, the story of the pursuit and execution of Dracula the vampire by my friends and myself that was published some three years after the event has remained in print and held its popularity with readers for over a hundred years. As it is so well known in the public mind, I shall not summarize it here, but will proceed straight into my own tale. At the time I wasn't the dedicated diarist as were my friends, but have endeavored to make up for it with this volume.

For them the story was ended; for me it began.

QUINCEY P. MORRIS

Chapter One

Transylvania, November, 1893

No single sense returned first. They mobbed me. The numbing cold, the soft whine of dogs, the rough jostling, all tumbled together in my dulled brain like seeds in a rattle. I slipped to and fro between awareness and nothing until a sharp lurch and bump caught my attention, holding me awake for longer than a few seconds. It was enough that I dimly comprehended something was very wrong. The next moment of consciousness I managed to keep hold of; the moments to follow had me wishing I'd done otherwise.

Things were strongly tugging at my feet and legs, which seemed to be bound up. So was the rest of my body. I was wrapped snug and tight in a blanket from head to toe, unable to move or see. It was right over

1

my face, which I never could abide. I groaned, trying
to get free of the annoyance.

At this feeble sound and movement the tugging
abruptly stopped, and the things—which I dazedly
grasped to be several dogs—snuffled at me. I couldn't
tell how many, but to judge by their sounds several at
the least seemed to hold me as the focus of their
attention. It made no sense until with a raw shock
tearing through my nerves I realized they weren't dogs,
but *wolves*.

In that instant full alertness returned, mind and body
hurtling awake. I froze utterly, in the full expectation
that the wolves would start ripping into me as I lay
helpless before them. After a few truly terrible
moments when nothing happened I tried to swallow
my heart back into place, but there wasn't spit enough
in my mouth for the job.

With whines and growls, their strong jaws clamped
firmly on my wrappings again, and they resumed dragging me along. I could only think that made bold by
hunger they'd entered our camp and picked me to pull
away to a safe distance where they could feed.

Panic would kill me. I dared not shout an alarm to
my friends. The noise might spark the wolves to attack
their prize. They'd held off—for the time being—so
I gritted my teeth and waited and listened in the frail
hope I might somehow find a way out of this alive.

There must have been dozens of them. I could hear
their eager panting and the click of their claws against
bare stone or crunching into the thick snow. Wolves
usually shy away from men—such had been my experience when Art and I had been trailed by that pack
in Siberia. Had they been more desperate they'd have
made a real feast for themselves on us. Being normal
wolves, they'd held off and we'd escaped. But this pack
seemed anything but normal. We were in the wild
deeps of Transylvania, a far different place, and I'd

already seen grim proof that a tall tale in one part of the world was God's own awful truth in another.

The wolves pulled me along another few yards. My weight, and I was aware of every solid pound of it going over those rocks, was nothing to them. Once they felt secure, they'd go through my all too thin blanket and clothes like taking the hide off a deer. I'd seen that happen once. The deer had been alive when they'd started in, and though quick enough, it hadn't been an easy death.

But all men have a limit to their self-control and that dark thought was enough to finally break mine; fear surged in my throat like vomit. It choked off any cry for help I might have made. I thrashed around like one of the madmen in Seward's asylum, fighting against my bindings. The wolves at my feet let go. One of them snarled, stirring up the others. They moved around me, excited, nipping at the blanket as though in play, their efforts ironically helping my struggles as they shredded the cloth. Fresh air suddenly slapped my face as the damned thing finally came loose.

Bright eyes catching the moonlight in green flashes, with lolling tongues and rows of white teeth, they scampered about like puppies. Some darted close to snap at me, wagging their tails at the sport of it. I wrested my hands free, but had no weapon to use. Some blurred memory told me I carried no knife or gun. I scrabbled in the inches-deep snow and found a piece of fist-sized rock. Better than nothing.

Then a big black fellow, one that was obviously the pack leader, lifted his head to the wild gray sky and howled. Ever an eerie sound, but to be so alone in the forest, to hear it so close and loud, to watch the very breath of it streaming from the animal's muzzle—had the hair on my neck not already been raised to its limit, it would have gone that much higher. The other wolves instantly abandoned their game and crowded near him, tails tucked like fawning supplicants seeking a favor. One after another joined him, blending and weaving their many voices into a triumphant song only they could fully understand.

The leader broke off and focused his huge green eyes upon me as the others continued their hell's chorus. It's a mistake to ascribe human attributes to an animal, but I couldn't help myself. The thing looked not just interested in what he saw, but curious, in the way that a human is curious.

He snarled and snapped at those nearest him. The pack stopped howling and obediently scattered. After a sharp, low bark from him they formed themselves into a wide circle like trained circus dogs. I was at its exact center. Some stood, others sat, but all watched me attentively. Though I'd had more contact with wolves than most men, I'd never seen or heard *anything* like this before.

A few of them growled, no doubt scenting my fear.

Clutching the nearly useless rock with one hand, I frantically tore at the bindings around my ankles with the other. It was desperate work, made slow by my reluctance to take my eyes from the pack. Despite the distraction of their presence, I saw that for some reason I'd been wrapped like a bundle for the mail, first in the blanket, then by ropes to hold it in place. Why? Who had tied me up so? I cursed whoever had done me such an ill turn, the burst of anger giving me the strength to get free.

I got clear of the blanket and staggered upright, half-expecting the wolves to close in. But they remained in their great circle, watching. There were no trees within it to climb to safety, and if I tried to break through the line at any point they'd be on me, so I kept still and stared back. One of the wolves sneezed; another shook himself. They knew they had me.

A gust of winter wind sent the dry ground snow

flying. Flakes skittered and drifted over the discarded blanket. I slowly picked it up and looped it around my left arm. The leader stepped forward, growling. I angled to face him, my powerless fear turning to fury that I should be brought to such a base fate.

"Come on, you big bastard. I'll take you first," I whispered, growling right back. I would sell myself dearly to them.

The wolf lowered his head and rocked back on his haunches, like a dog about to do a begging trick. A roiling darkness that seemed to come from within the thing's body blurred the details as bones and joints soundlessly shifted, muzzle and fur retreated, skin swelled. It rose on its hind legs and kept rising until it was a match for me in height. The crooked legs straightened, thickened, and became the legs of a man, a tall, lean man clothed all in black. Only his bright green eyes remained the same, and when his red lips thinned into a smile I clearly saw the hungry wolf lurking beneath the surface.

I knew his face. One can never forget such stern features. They were the stuff of nightmares, all the more so for my knowing, of my being *absolutely certain*, that he was *dead*—for I'd killed him myself.

Yet there he stood before me, stubbornly oblivious to the fact.

I was as afraid as I'd ever been in my life and could have expressed it, loudly, but there didn't seem much point. In a few minutes I'd either be dead or worse than dead, and making a lot of noise about it wouldn't help me one way or another.

"I can respect a brave man, Mr. Morris," said Vlad Dracula, pitching his deep voice to be heard above the wind. In it was the harsh tone I'd heard when he'd taunted us from the stable yard of his Piccadilly house. Now he clasped his hands behind him and continued to regard me with the same mixture of interest and curiosity that had manifested itself in his wolf form.

The wind buffeted against his body with little effect other than to whip at his dark clothes and gray-streaked hair. Black on white was the mark Harker had left on the pallid flesh of Dracula's brow; he bore the scar with little sign of healing, yet nearly a month had passed from the last time I'd seen that face. But since then, I'd . . . I'd . . .

Something very like the wind whirled sickeningly inside my skull. The creature before me, the circle of wolves, the snow, the cold, all faded for an instant of nothingness before asserting themselves again. It was like the focus of a poorly made telescope shifting in and out.

"I killed you," I said faintly. I recalled the impact of the strike going right up my arm when my Bowie knife slammed firmly into his chest.

"So you did," he admitted. "With some help from Jonathan Harker do not forget."

"Yes. . . ."

Harker had buried his Kukri knife in the monster's throat. We'd fought our way through the Szgany to get to the leiter-wagon and the great box on top of it. The Szgany had drawn their knives to defend it, and one of them had . . .

I looked down, my hand going to my side. The clothes there were thick and stiff with dried and frozen blood. I could smell it, sharp and compelling.

My blood. It had fairly poured from me as our enemies fled into the growing dusk. Harker caught me as I fell and sank back in his arms, my strength abruptly spent. Jack Seward and Van Helsing had tried their best to stop the flow, but the wound was too deep, the damage beyond any skill to heal. Thank God it hadn't been very painful. The last memory I had was of poor Mina Harker, her face twisted by bitter grief, but I'd been so happy, so at peace. The awful red mark on her own brow had vanished, and from that I knew I'd spared her soul from damnation. With such joy in my fast-beating heart did I slip contentedly away into what seemed like sleep.

Not sleep. Nothing so ordinary as that had taken me, changed me, turned me into . . .

"No need for such alarm, Mr. Morris," Dracula said, reading my face. "What you have become is not so dreadful as you've been led to believe."

Not knowing my own voice, a cry escaped me. Heedless of the wolves, I burst through their circle, running back down their trail. I crashed through snow-drifts, blundered against trees, and tripped on invisible snares, but kept going. Not far ahead would be the warm yellow light of our campfire. If I could just get there, if Van Helsing still had some of his Holy Wafer left, there might yet be some protection for us.

For *them*. At least for them.

I was close enough to make out their huddled forms far down in the clearing where they'd made camp: the Harkers lying together, Van Helsing and Seward each rolled up in their blankets, Art a little off from them by the horses, presumably taking his turn at watch. All were fast asleep, though, worn out by the hard travel and the chase, but just one shout from me would bring Art instantly awake—

A hand, colder and heavier than the ice, clapped over my mouth just as I drew breath. As though I were a child and not a grown man topping six feet, Dracula lifted me right from my tracks, hauling me swiftly back into the cover of the forest. I lashed out with the rock still in my hand, but couldn't connect solidly enough to slow him. He was quite indifferent to my struggles, though I managed a few solid kicks that made him grunt. Then he spun me suddenly, and cracked my head against one of the trees.

Lights brighter than the sun blinded me. Ungodly pain robbed me of speech. I collapsed. Quite helpless to stop him, he easily hoisted me over one shoulder like an old sack and hurried back up the way I'd run. The wolves had tagged along for the brief hunt and now bounded playfully all around us. I couldn't tell how far he went, only that it was beyond where I'd originally revived, and well out of the camp's earshot.

He eventually dropped me flat on my face into the snow, and all I could do was lie there for a time nearly paralyzed and miserably ill from the shock. It passed too slowly to suit, but did pass. When I felt ready for it I pushed the ground away and propped myself against a tree. Dracula loomed over me, his white face twisted with fury.

"Fool," he snarled. "Do you think they'll show you mercy once they know about you?"

"I'm counting on it," I snapped back. "I know what to expect and shall welcome it."

"Well, I do not. Give yourself away to them if you must, but not me. I've been to enough trouble over this matter and want no more."

"Go to hell."

I didn't think his eyes could hold more rage. I was wrong. He raised a hand as though to smash me like a fly. His anger beat against me, a physical thing like heat from a forge, but after a long and dreadful moment he lowered his arm, and visibly shook himself out of his threatening posture with a sneer.

"You're but an infant," he muttered with no little disgust. "You don't understand anything yet."

"I know enough."

"I think not. Come with me and I shall be of some help to that end."

"No."

"Stay behind and your friends will be food for my children." He gestured meaningfully at the forest around us. No need for him to explain who his "children" were; I could still hear and occasionally see them well enough as they ghosted in and out of the surrounding trees. "Come and your friends will be safe."

"For how long?"

"As long as you remain sensible. And that is entirely up to *you*."

He stepped back and waited, watching as his wolves had watched. He offered no help as I found my feet, leaning hard on the tree. Though dizzy, I was able to think straight, but no idea running through my mind could be remotely mistaken for a way out of this spot. I did not trust him, was utterly repulsed by him and all that he represented, but he was well in control of things and we both knew it.

"Where?" I asked grimly.

He pointed behind me. We were to go even deeper into the timber, climbing away from the camp. I didn't like that, but followed as he led the way along what looked like a deer trail. The wolves kept pace, panting and wagging their tails like dogs out for a walk. Glancing back, I saw more than a dozen of them padding almost at my heels and realized they were obliterating my tracks in the snow. Was it accidental or intentional? I made a step off to one side as a test and went on. The wolves sniffed the spot and blotted out my boot print as they swarmed over it, tongues lolling as if from laughter.

We began climbing in earnest. Rocks rose high on our left, forming a natural wall that cut the freezing wind. The snow underfoot thinned and vanished. Dracula waited until I was well upon this trackless surface and a little ahead. He turned toward the wolves, stretching his arms before him, then spreading them wide in a dismissive gesture. As though the pack were one animal and not many, his children silently retreated down the path into the trees below, and were lost to sight.

"Where are they going?" I demanded.

The question surprised him. "To hunt, to play, to run with the moon, whatever they desire. Your friends are quite safe from them, as are you. I have pledged my word."

"What do you want of me?"

"Nothing more than the answers to a few questions."

"What questions?"

He pointed to a knee-high boulder. "Please seat yourself, Mr. Morris."

He had a presence about him that could not be ignored. I sat. There was a similar rock not four feet away and he took it, facing me, and spent several minutes studying me intently.

"With your permission," he said, and held his hand out, palm upward, looking for all the world like some Gypsy ready to read my fortune if I but mirrored him. I hesitated only a little, for my own curiosity was awake and on the move by now. He minutely inspected my hands, finally comparing them to his own, which were broad and blunt. "Your fingers are of different lengths," he pronounced.

"What of it?"

"They are also quite bare, not at all like mine, as you see."

From Harker's journal I already knew about the sharp nails and the thin hair on his palms, so there was little need to gape in wonder.

"And when you speak, your teeth appear to be perfectly normal. The same may not be said for my own." He let them show in an almost wry smile. Not a pleasant sight.

"Have you a purpose to this?"

"To confirm to myself and prove to you that we are similar, but not too very alike."

"We are most certainly not alike!" I couldn't control my rising voice.

"I am so glad that we are in agreement," he said with a calm sarcasm that took all the wind out of me. "Such differences should reassure, rather than alarm you."

"What do you mean?"

"You know the truth of that well enough for yourself."

Indeed, but the agonizing terror inside made me consciously obtuse. To finally face the truth, to actually *speak* about what I'd hidden for so long. . . .

"As I told you," he said with a glimmer of sympathy I would have never otherwise ascribed to that hard, cruel face, "what we are is not as bad as you have been led to believe."

A short laugh burst from me, a laugh that might have turned to a sob had I not forcibly swallowed it back.

"You are *Nosferatu*, Mr. Morris, nothing more. I am *Nosferatu*, but much more, hence the visible differences." He opened his palms again, as though that explained everything. "I know how I became as I am, but I want to know your story. Who took your blood and gave it back? Who initiated the change in you? And when?"

I was speechless for many long moments as he waited expectantly for an answer. "Why do you want to know?"

"Those of *your* kind are rare. I would know more about you. You are the first I have ever met both before and after dying. Our encounters in London and in Seward's house were brief, but I sensed changes in you no one else could discern—not even yourself. For that I decided to spare you and consequently your friends. For that I planned a way to rid myself of their nuisance without killing them."

"You *spared* us?"

"Look not so surprised, Mr. Morris. At any time of

my choosing I could have destroyed the lot of you. Knowing what you do about me, could you doubt my ability?"

Van Helsing had been thorough in his lectures to us about the near-boundless powers of the Un-Dead, and of Dracula's genius in particular. I'd held serious reservations about just how even the six of us together—three being experienced hunters—could defeat such a formidable creature. Van Helsing had assured us again and again that God was on our side, which is always a help. My faith on that never shook for a moment, for it struck me we'd need an Old Testament kind of miracle to succeed.

"Why forbear then?" I asked.

"Your deaths were unnecessary. I could likely disassociate myself from the demise of five respectable people in the heart of England and be safe enough, but Harker is quite the diarist. So are the others, I discovered. Despite my efforts on the one occasion in that asylum study I knew I could never be certain of destroying all evidence linking them to me. And then there was Van Helsing. His knowledge of the *Nosferatu* is thorough, if short on wisdom, and he is highly respected within his academic circles. His sudden and mysterious passing along with the others would not go unnoticed. I also considered your reaction. If I killed all your friends you'd not be of a mind to freely speak with me, quite the contrary. It was far better to have my hunters believe in my own destruction than for me to deal with the inconvenient consequences of theirs."

"But I saw you die. We all did."

"You saw me vanish into dust," he corrected, "that was eventually whirled away by the wind into the darkness. A very excellent escape for me, was it not? It was a risk—things might not have gone so well had you used wood instead of metal weapons, but I am content with the results. Now you see why I had to stop you from waking your friends: to do so would have eventually meant their deaths and yours as well. You'd not let my actions pass, and I would defend myself from you. Larger parties have disappeared before in these mountains. Accidents are easily managed, and here I would *not* shirk the risk—but I chose to avoid such an extreme action lest you . . . take offense."

"You set all this to going just for a talk with me?"

"Had I a choice and an opportunity, I'd have found some way to speak with you in England and then quietly departed. No such opportunity presented itself, so I left, thinking to return some years hence. What I did not expect was for any of you to follow me to the very threshold of my own castle. You and your friends were possessed with such a grim determination to kill me that it needed to be dealt with first before I could indulge my curiosity. You may believe or not, as you will."

And I did believe him. He was the unopposed master of the night with the strength of ten, able to change shape or turn into mist at will, able to beguile anyone to do his bidding. Whatever gave us the idea we could fight anything like that? Van Helsing had been so confident, though, and had a way of instilling confidence in others. But seeing things from this direction put a whole new understanding in me. We'd been like children shaking our fists at a cyclone.

"You did all that, spared them, and yet caused my death?"

Now he had a turn at looking surprised, and a remarkable expression it was to be sure. "On the honor of all my sires, I swear that your being killed was not part of my plan of escape. I told the Szgany to resist but a little and then depart—to make it look well. Is that the phrase?"

I hung my head, staring at my snow-crusted boots. "Close enough."

"As with the others, your death was unnecessary, and not what I desired at all. Should you die, how would I then be able to speak with you?"

"Because I'd be a vampire." There. I managed to get the word out without choking on it.

He was silent long enough to make me look up. He shook his head. "Your ignorance again. You don't *know*?"

"Know what?" I couldn't keep the irritation from my voice.

"Though you carried the blood of change within you not all who have such rise from death."

"Draw that out a little more slowly," I said, giving him a narrow stare.

He understood my meaning if not the slang itself. "Those of your kind do not always transform after dying. They remain dead. To make the change is a rare thing. That is why I did *not* want you killed. What happened with the Szgany was . . . an unhappy accident."

"Is that what you call it? My life cut off? Me turned into a devil on earth . . ."

He assumed a look of vast patience and crossed his arms, apparently prepared to wait through a long tirade from me. I shut things down fast, scowling at him.

"You are *not* a devil, Mr. Morris," he murmured. "You will eventually come to learn that—if not from me, then from your own experiences and actions."

Which I did not care to consider just then. I was still mad as hell for what had happened to me, but there wasn't much I could do with my anger except push it aside for the moment. If I'd judged things right, then we still had a mighty big piece of talking to get through. I needed his knowledge.

"Now, as for your change . . ." Dracula prompted when he saw I'd mastered myself.

I gave a mental shrug, deciding no harm could come

from telling him. "It was a few years back, in South America," I said. "Arthur Holmwood—Lord Godalming now—and I were at an embassy ball. I met her there. I've traveled a fair part of this world and seen a thing or two, but hands down she was the most beautiful woman I'd ever clapped eyes on. She and I—"

"Her name?"

"Nora Jones. By her accent she was English, I think, though she had dark hair and eyes and that wonderful olive skin. . . ."

Which I'd been on fire to touch the moment I saw her. I hadn't been the only man trying to claim her attention at that gathering, but I was the one she picked as an escort for a walk in the embassy garden. I reveled in my good fortune and hoped to give her a favorable impression of myself in the short time we had, but it was she who took the lead in things. She'd made up her mind about me fast enough, though I wouldn't call her fast, just almighty charming and irresistible. That night, holding to a promise and plan made in the garden, she found her way to my room, and we fulfilled one another's expectations—exceeded them, I should say.

I'd been exhausted the next morning, of course, not from blood loss so much as the excess champagne and sheer physical activity. Her passionate biting into my throat had startled me only a little. It was different, but didn't trouble me much. Young as I was, I'd known more than one woman in my travels and came to know that each had her own path to pleasure, and it was my privilege to assist her there. It was always to my own advantage to be ready to learn something new, and Nora was a enchanting teacher. My body's explosive reaction to her lesson was like nothing I'd ever felt before.

I rested throughout the day, and the next night we resumed exploring mutual pleasures with one another.

It was then, caught up in the lust of the moment, that she feverishly opened a vein in her own throat and invited me to drink in turn. Brain clouded and body trembling for release, I gladly did so, taking us to a climax that left us both unconscious. I woke a little before dawn in time to see her throw on a dressing gown and leave, then dropped back into my sweet oblivion.

The word *vampire* was not unfamiliar, but its context for me then had to do with a species of blood-drinking bat that plagued the livestock of the land. In our drowsy love talk during later encounters, the subject came up, but Nora told me not to worry about it, and, lost in the warmth of her dark eyes, I forgot any and all misgivings . . . until that day years later in the Westenra dining room when I volunteered my blood to save poor dear Lucy.

I had no mind for Nora then—she was long behind me, an exquisite and happy memory—and put myself forward without another thought. It was afterward, when I began to hear more from Jack and Van Helsing about Lucy's alarming condition that the doubts crept in. The fact that her illness was so unique with her constant blood loss happening each night gave me my first qualm. I feared Lucy had fallen victim to someone like Nora, but a ravisher rather than a lover. From that point everything Van Helsing told us confirmed my growing fears. It was only after Lucy's death and the hideous proof of her return that I realized what horror was in store for me when I died.

Dracula took that moment to interject. "If by that you mean being staked through the heart by your well-meaning friends, then you have every right to be horrified."

"If it will free me to go to God, then so be it."

"I doubt that He would welcome such an enthusiastic suicide," he said dryly. "Do not look so amazed.

You are still one of His children—yet another difference you may rejoice in."

"How is that possible? I am . . . *Nosferatu*, one of the Un-Dead."

"Exactly. Un-Dead and nothing more. Do you not see?" I didn't, and he raised his hands in exasperation. "Your so-sweet Nora Jones has much to answer for. She should have told you all this and saved me the trouble and you your anguish. You *do* understand that she was, and probably still is, *Nosferatu*?"

"Yes."

"And you must know by now that she was not as *I* am. Her offspring, which includes you, will be like her. I have already had much proof that my offspring, no matter how lovingly taken, will never be so tame. Mine to hers are as the wolf to the hunting hound. *Now* do you see?"

"We're two different kinds of vampire," I whispered. "How is that possible?"

He gave an expressive shrug. "I know not, only that it is—for here you are and here I am, both hunters in the wide world. We have similar freedoms and strengths, but there are differences. Perhaps those will come to assure you that this life—or this Un-Death, if you will—is not so terrible as you've been told."

"Such as?"

"You will learn without doubt that your soul is still your own . . . and His," he added, with a quirk of his heavy brows toward the sky. "You will find the truth of it when next you walk into a church, which is something you are still very much able to do."

Well, time alone would tell on that one, if Dracula allowed me to test it.

"With some small changes you are free to live as before, but as *you* choose, for good or ill, as all things will be judged in the end. For me, it is not so simple."

"What do you mean?"

"I can do that which you cannot. The wolf, the bat, the curling mist are natural forms to me, but not for you. I prefer the shadows, but may walk in the sun if necessary; you would die from it and must sleep in darkness while it rules the sky. You can influence people and to some extent certain animals to your will, which makes the hunting easier, but can no more command the weather now than you could as a human, but that is of no matter. I've read in your heart and by your manner that you are a man who would refuse to pay the price for such powers. Long ago I paid and still do. My body bears the signs of that payment, marking me as different from other men. And as for *my* soul . . . I think you would be more comfortable to remain ignorant of such fearful things."

From the look that crossed his face I silently agreed with him. "And what of Lucy? Am I supposed to approve of what you did to her?"

"The matter of your approval is of no import to me. I did nothing with her that was not a part of my nature, a part of any man's nature. She was beautiful and willing—no, do not gainsay me for you were not there and never knew her true heart. I loved her in the only way left to me."

"Until she died."

"We all die, but I will allow that her time had not yet come."

"You kept taking her blood. I watched her weaken horribly with each passing day. You were killing her!"

"Her body was merely adjusting to what we shared. Another few nights and she would have gradually regained her strength with no harm done."

"I find that hard to believe."

He made a curt waving gesture, indication that my believing him on this was also of no import. "If you wish to fix a blame for her death, then you need look no farther than her attending physicians. Had they left

her alone she would still be walking in the sun. 'Twas
their ignorance that finished her, not my love. Doctors, bah!" His ruddy lips curled with contempt.

"And what about my own tainted blood going into
her—?"

"I do not know. The seeds of becoming Un-Dead
were within you, but you were not Un-Dead then. It
may have helped or made no difference to her health
or worsened things. That is beyond my knowledge. I
have heard of such transfusion operations, though, and
they fail more often than succeed. Some patients are
not able to tolerate anything put into their veins and
die from it. No one knows why as yet. In my own heart
I believe that is what really happened to her."

And were that to be true, then by trying to help her
Jack Seward and Van Helsing had . . .

"The poor, sweet child never had a chance," Dracula
said heavily.

A painful thing it was to hear him refer to her in
that manner, for I had loved her myself as truly as a
man could. I could not imagine a dark creature such
as he being able to love anyone. It angered and sickened me to think of her giving herself to the likes of
him, of his even touching her. He must have hypnotized or forced her, though it may have been as it had
with me and Nora, with her surrendering from honest innocence, unaware of the consequences. Were that
the case, then I certainly had not known Lucy's true
heart. With difficulty, I pushed all my emotions to one
side for later reflection. Right now I needed still more
information.

"So my blood might not have changed her?"

"It is barely possible, of course. I rather think it
more likely that to create your own offspring you must
first take blood from your lover, then return it, just as
Nora did with you."

"As you've done to Mrs. Harker."

His face went hard.

"What is to happen to her?" I demanded.

"Nothing. The miracle she prayed for"——he touched the mark on his forehead, for it nearly mirrored the one she'd carried—"came to pass. Seward and Van Helsing will not bother her now. That alone should suffice to guarantee her a long and fruitful life."

"But what you did to her—"

"As with Lucy, that which has passed between Mrs. Harker and myself is none of your business, Mr. Morris," he rumbled, his brows lowering.

"But that poor woman—"

"Is quite capable of making her own decisions. If you live long enough, you may come to see that women are far more formidable than you think. Like the rest of you gentlemen, I found myself quite enchanted by Madam Harker's grace, charm, heart, and mind. Unlike you, I decided to act upon my desires. I've lived long enough to have certain . . . perspectives on a few things, and so took the chance, knowing I'd regret passing it by. However, I came to see that which was once acceptable—or at least ignorable—behavior in my youth, was not so for an English lady in these times. All was sealed when the lot of you burst in on us, and I knew then it must end."

For a seducing adulterer he sounded quite smooth.

"I have since tendered my admittedly inadequate apologies to her, mind-to-mind, and severed all links between us. I would have also apologized to her husband, but given the circumstances it struck me as being inappropriate. Besides, he thinks he has killed me. That should be sufficient recompense for his wounded honor."

"What about the blood exchange you made with her?"

"That cannot be reversed."

"Then when she dies, she'll become like you."

"And to you that is yet a bad thing. Worry not. When her time comes she will have a . . . decision before her."

"Decision?"

"It—it is not an easy thing to make into words. My own memory of it is clear, but to describe in a way that you may understand is difficult. Let it suffice that she will have the choice to live as I live or to go to God. At death, each similarly touched soul has a moment of decision. I have told her as much, so did I tell Lucy, whose choice was to tarry on the earth."

"But I had no choice. I went to sleep and awoke to—" I spread my hands to indicate my situation.

"Another point of difference between us, between our kinds. And another question I have no adequate answer for. Why some of you rise and others do not is a mystery to me."

"Van Helsing said nothing of this choice of yours. Neither did Mrs. Harker."

"He may not know of it, and you can hardly blame the lady for such an omission. It is a most personal thing. But she has a noble heart, a great spirit, and her faith is so strong as to have done such to her—" again he lightly touched the scar on his forehead. "I have no doubt when her time comes she will fly to the angels to seek her rest."

"Are you sure of that?"

"Wait twenty or thirty years and see for yourself. For now, the subject of Mrs. Harker and myself is closed." By the finality of his tone I knew that to pursue the matter would result in unhappy consequences to myself. And he was right. It was none of my business. Besides, to be sincerely selfish about it, I had problems of my own to face. To judge by the miraculous healing of the burn she'd taken from the touch of the Host, Mina Harker was well recovered from her ordeal, and Dracula planned to leave her alone; I felt I could move forward with a fairly clear conscience.

Now that my eyes were opened a little wider than before, I looked out into the night. Though all would have been murky blacks and grays to my friends, it was as day to me. The faint moonlight put a silver gleam upon everything it touched, beautiful, but marred in my perception by my many troubling questions.

"Must I do as you—as Nora—to . . . to . . ." The words refused to emerge.

"Sustain yourself? Hardly. To drink from a lover is one matter, but you'll find that the blood of animals is your real food. One may live upon love alone for awhile, but sooner or later one must come down from the clouds and take more practical nourishment. This is as true for vampires as it is for humans."

That was a great relief. If it was true.

"Do you hunger yet?"

I continued to stare out at nothing in particular, giving no reply.

He shrugged. "When you're ready, then tell me. Your first feeding should be a pleasing experience."

He'd have a hard task of proving that to me. Separated so far from memories of Nora by time and new knowledge, the idea of my drinking blood of *any* kind like downing a cup of coffee sickened me to the core. I tried to hide my grimace as my belly turned over. "What about my friends? When they wake—"

"They will be shocked, of course. They will eventually conclude you have been dragged off in the night by a pack of ravenous wolves and will never recover your body. So very tidy, is it not?"

"It's monstrous!"

"Far better that than to see your footprints in the snow trailing away from the torn blanket that was your shroud. Then you would never be safe from them. I suspected you might revive and rise tonight, so I made sure my children and I were there to disguise your escape."

"But they're my *friends*. I cannot put them through such grief!"

His face went hard again, the change swift as lightning. "You will and must. It is part of my pledge of their safety to you. Leave them alone and they live."

"But—"

"You will leave them. Better that they suffer a little distress than for you to undo all I have done. I will not be moved on this. Accept it, or they will pay."

There would be no return to my comrades, not for the present, anyway, certainly not while his wolves were within call. "Very well," I murmured. Perhaps later I might be able to talk to Art or Jack and persuade them to reason as I had been persuaded, but in the meantime I was feeling very lost and miserable without them. And cold. The icy November air, something I'd been able to ignore because of my changed condition, had seeped well into my bones. It would take more than the long coat I wore to dispel it. I shook out the torn blanket I still had wrapped around my arm and threw it over my shoulders.

Dracula nodded. "Yes, it is time to go inside. My castle is not far from this place. Your friends thought to seal me from it, but there are entrances that they found not."

"What about *your* friends?"

"Mine?"

"Harker wrote of your three . . . companions." I nearly said "mistresses" and diplomatically changed the word at the last moment. I wondered how they would receive me. "The ladies."

His eyes flashed green, and his lips drew into a knife-cut of a line. He released a long hiss of breath. There was a strange blaze of madness in his stare that made me instinctively reach for my missing Colt revolver, for all the good it would have done.

Dracula rose tall and quickly turned away; one hand

shot out against the stone side of the mountain as though to steady himself. I'd stabbed right into a nerve it seemed, and couldn't guess what it might be.

With a terrible strength, his bare fingers curled right into the rock, ripping off a piece. I stood, readying myself in case he decided to make a problem, but he took no notice.

"Sir," I ventured after some moments. "What is it?"

His shoulders sagged. He slowly turned back to me. Now his eyes had gone dark, hooded over by those heavy brows. "They are no more," he said, his gaze dropping. "Van Helsing murdered them."

"Murdered?" Here was a shock. I'd long known that the professor had the idea of visiting the castle during the day, but it was news to me to learn he'd actually done so. But murder—?

"He served them as he served poor Lucy," Dracula said.

That told me all. Unbidden, the sight of her hideous second dying passed across my mind's eye as it had every day since. I'd been told—and had been thoroughly convinced—that what we'd done had freed her sweet soul from enslavement to pure evil. Now I was not so certain. God in heaven, had I helped to murder her?

Dracula flexed his fingers enough to let the stone fall, his voice a bleak drone. "Their deaths happened because Van Helsing was more careful and they too careless. In their minds, in their dreams, I gave them warning of what I knew must be his intent, but they would not heed. They thought him to be yet only a simple peasant, easily cowed by fear or seduced by lust for their beauty. I . . . felt each of them go and could do *nothing*." His face darkened, then cleared, like the shadow of a cloud running over the flanks of a mountain. He struck me as a man who felt things deep and felt things hard, but could hold control if he chose.

"What will you do to Van Helsing?"

"Nothing."

"How can you—I mean, if you cared for them—"

"I am pledged."

That simple statement took me aback.

He saw my disbelief. "My word, Mr. Morris, may be trusted."

"Sir, I—"

"There is more as well. You are not so old as I or you would understand the futility of certain kinds of retribution. To avenge my dear ones would put Van Helsing where he belongs—in hell!—but bring me no gain, and only reveal my deception to the others." He gave another shrug, this time with his hands. "What's done is done. I have pledged the lives of your friends to you on your sensible behavior. I will not recant."

I kept quiet, relieved, but still dealing with inner doubt. I had the suspicion that should my friends make themselves a nuisance to him again he might find a way of getting around his pledge.

He straightened, standing tall. "Come then, Quincey Morris. I will show you any number of dark places for you to shelter from the day, places much safer than that which my dear ones had."

"Won't I need my home earth as you do?" I suddenly felt frail and weary and very, very alone.

He turned slightly and motioned toward where the wolves had vanished, taking in the vast forest. "*This* land has become your home, Mr. Morris. When a brave man's blood strikes the ground where he fights he has purchased it for his own forever. You will find rest here and may carry away as much earth as you want when you are ready to depart."

Another surprise. Me being free to leave? I'd no notion he'd even suggest the idea that I could ever depart this oppressive place. It wouldn't be tonight. The hour was too late, to judge by the position of the stars.

Dawn was coming, but on top of all that, I needed help, which Dracula seemed willing to give. I'd be a fool not to accept, since I was still trying to get my brain to take in what had happened to me and how to deal with it. Back in Texas when a tenderfoot turned up on the ranch we'd guide him through things until he learned how to survive on his own. Now I was the tenderfoot.

"I'd appreciate that," I said.

Dracula grunted once and continued to stare away into the distance. His gaze and his mind must have been very much elsewhere, for he remained silent and unnaturally still for quite a long time.

I tried not to shiver, waiting, reluctant to intrude on whatever dark thoughts possessed him.

"But perhaps," he finally whispered, his voice so soft I barely heard, "perhaps you will tarry awhile? The wind breathes cold through the broken battlements and casements of my castle, but you will find more comfort there than in these wastes. We two have many griefs to settle in our hearts, and though I would be alone with my thoughts, in such a time of mourning it is better to have company."

My answer was to follow him. As we picked our way over the rocks and up the narrow path, his children began to sing again.

Chapter Two

Dracula stood behind and to the side of me, craning so he could see as I crouched in the stable straw. He pointed to a spot on the leg of one of his horses where the surface vein was quite visible.

"There," he said, touching it delicately, then withdrawing his hand.

I was supposed to bite deep into the flesh and drink, just like that, and I absolutely could not bring myself to do so.

"There," he firmly repeated.

Terrible hunger possessed me, hunger such as I'd never known could exist. My limbs trembled from it. Weakness fluttered throughout my whole body. I had to hold hard to the animal's leg to keep from falling over.

Hovering inches from this new source of life, aching for want of it, sickened by the thought of it, I stifled my overwhelming urge to vomit.

"Drink, Mr. Morris," he told me. "Drink . . . or die."

My appetite had come very much awake on my second night's stay in the castle, but I said nothing about it to Dracula. I had the faint hope that if I could avoid blood, then I wouldn't be a vampire after all. My plan was to put things off long enough so my craving might transmute itself to the point where I'd become so famished as to eat regular food instead.

If Dracula suspected what was on my mind, he never let on, and only politely inquired if I desired refreshment, abandoning the subject when I just as politely replied I did not. We passed the evening in conversation, he plying me with many eager questions about my life and adventures. I did my best to answer, all the while hiding the constant pain within.

On the third night he cocked one eyebrow at my disallowance and pursed his lips for some time before giving a mild challenge.

"My Szgany cook informs me that you sampled some of her soup earlier," he said.

Which was true. And yes, Dracula had servants about the place, just as he had when Jonathan Harker stayed with him, but now as then they kept themselves well out of sight. Harker had been unaware of them, thinking them completely absent, though he could have inferred their presence by his countless meals and clean bed linens. I'd known of their being about from the first moment I'd entered the castle. With my sharp new senses I could *hear* their subdued movements and voices echoing up along the stone corridors. I could hear the rats scuttling in the pantry, for God's sake. Little wonder Dracula sought solitude in the remote upper floors of his home if they offered isolation from such annoying distractions.

This third night, waking with the hunger burning with such intense pain that I could think of nothing else, I'd followed the sounds and soon the smells to a wide, low-raftered kitchen, startling the inhabitants there to silence by walking in. They were watchful, and certainly fearful. The men stood, their hands resting on the hilts of the great knives thrust in their wide belts; the women backed away a step or two from their washing and cookery to stare. There was no doubting that they were well aware I was like their master. Perhaps they saw my raw need stamped plain upon my face and thought I'd come to feed from them.

The place reeked of food smells. Boiling vegetables, roasting fowls, baking bread, and a vast cauldron of soup accounted for the moist stench. I wanted to run gagging from it, but made myself hold my ground and slowly come forward. Identifying an older and very solidly built woman as the most likely head of the pecking order I addressed her.

"I've a powerful appetite, ma'am. Would you oblige me with some of your fine soup?"

It was obvious that she didn't understand a word of it, but since I put a questioning tone to my voice and gestured at a stack of bowls and toward the cauldron, she eventually caught my meaning. She spoke rapidly at the others, probably making a translation to judge by their reaction. They eased up a bit, looking puzzled, and one of the men emitted a brief grunt that could have been a laugh. He said something back to her that I took to mean she should go ahead with my request.

A minute later and I was seated at a large and very old oaken table with a filled and steaming bowl before me and all their eyes fixed on my every move. I was skittish and didn't welcome an audience, but there was no helping it; I didn't have enough of the language yet to tell them to mind their own business. It would have been better for my peace of mind if they'd left. I could hear their very hearts drumming away, could scent the blood rushing beneath their flesh.

Ignoring its distraction, I picked up a spoon with shaking fingers and dipped a small swallow of liquid. I blew, then slowly forced it to my mouth. The smell of the stuff should have been toothsome and probably was, but to me it was like trying to sup off kerosene. I made myself take it in, though. It ran down my gullet like hot slime and hit my belly like a gunshot. I had to hold tight to the table to keep from doubling over from cramp. The others watched me close. From their murmurs I got the idea they thought my eating to be a most remarkable thing, indeed.

I tried a second spoonful, again taking in only the liquid. I couldn't bring myself to try chewing on any of the pieces floating in it. One thing at a time. It was still bad, but I got it down and kept it there. The same again for the next and the next. My poor belly roiled and twisted. Half a cup was about all it could manage. I put aside the spoon and stood, still holding to the table to keep upright. I bowed and thanked the cook in her own language, which pleased her mightily, gave a genial nod to the others, and made my way out, walking about as steady as a drunkard trying to hide his condition.

Mixed in with my nausea was grim triumph, the kind that goes with the accomplishment of a difficult and noxious task. I'd managed to consume normal food and get away with it. I'd been told otherwise. Dracula had been pretty resolute on that point; he'd said there was no way around it, but I wasn't ready to believe him. My nature is such that I generally like to see things for myself first if it seems a reasonable way to go.

It all seemed very reasonable indeed as I made my way along the empty passages, climbing toward my host's living area. Seemed, until I came to a window and the clean scent of fresh snow hit me. I'd found I had no need to breathe regularly, but wanted to clear my lungs of what they'd picked up in the kitchen. I opened the ancient shutters and leaned over the wide, bare stone sill. That was all it took. The soup I'd struggled so hard to consume now violently left me, those few feeble mouthfuls splattering on the cracked flags of the courtyard some twenty feet below.

How I hated it. Hated my body's betrayal of me, its rejection of such basic, normal nourishment. Most of all I hated the fact, that as I sat collapsed against the wall beneath the window and sweated out my recovery, I still desperately *hungered*.

It wasn't going to go away.

Groaning at the unfairness of it I gave in to true despair for a full five minutes, letting my tears flow, cursing the world, and feeling as sorry for myself as anyone has a right to be. None of which did me a damned bit of good at changing things. I finally woke out of it, not feeling better, but certain I could feel no worse.

I was half-blind from the craving. My legs trembled, and my head ached from having been sick, but I forced myself to totter up to the library and take a chair by the fire. It was well fueled and bright, filling the room with a warmth that had no effect at all on my shivering.

The only thing I'd gnawed on in all this time was my pride, my wish not to give in to what had happened to me. It kept me going, but did not satisfy or ease the pain. I determined that I would rest a few moments and warm up, then make myself try yet again. Next time I would take in simple water. Having had nothing in three nights I knew I'd need at least that to stay alive. I would *not* let this change take me over.

Dracula came in some little while later, though I didn't notice. Sharp as my hearing was the man could move quiet when he wanted to, though I wasn't paying mind to anything in my present state of misery.

"I said good evening, Mr. Morris," he intoned in such a way as to catch my attention.

I slowly crept up from the pit I'd dropped into and refrained at the last moment from pressing a protective hand across my always-hurting stomach. "G-good evening."

He'd paused by his work table, which was littered with many papers and books, then walked over to put his back to the fire, as though to seek its heat. He peered closely at me. "Do you desire some refreshment?"

"No, thank you," I replied.

Then did he make his statement about his cook.

"Yes, I was down to the kitchen just a little bit ago." No point in denying it.

"This was just after sunset?"

"That's right."

"Might I draw your attention to the mantel clock?" He nodded in its direction.

Finding difficulty focusing my eyes, I stared long at its face and finally worked out that it was nearly three in the morning. "It hasn't been wound," I said.

"The clock is quite correct, the problem is with yourself." He turned and got busy with building up the fire, which was now very low.

"I must have fallen asleep." It seemed the most natural way to account for the lost hours.

"Sleeping as others do is not something you may indulge in when the sun is down. You know that." He straightened and looked at me again.

"I'm sure I dozed off."

"You were in the thrall of a trance. When food is scarce in the winter certain animals do much the same thing. So it is with us."

That made a kind of sense, though it wasn't anything I wanted to hear.

"Mr. Morris, a good host allows his guest freedom, but also looks after his welfare. When I see someone under my protection trying to walk off a cliff, then it is my solemn duty to prevent him from harming himself."

"I'm all right," I muttered.

"I will risk giving offense and say to you that that is a complete lie."

I hadn't the strength to argue.

"Of course, you yourself are giving me much offense by your refusal to deal with a very simple matter. This denial of your need puts me in a position where I must either let you continue to injure yourself or force you to take action. Both would be unmannerly."

"This is not something I want," I whispered.

"Which is very obvious. You've shown a great will in fighting against it. A great will. Few would be capable of such and still be sane. But no matter how much you desire to have things back the way they were, it shall never be so. You are what you are. You must face that."

"But to drink . . ." I trailed off, shaking my head.

"Blood. Say it."

Damned if I will.

"You attach much importance to it, which can be a good thing, for blood is life to us. Attaching a negative importance is . . . destructive. To you. To anyone who crosses your path."

"What?"

"When your appetite finally exceeds your self-command you could kill. I'm sure you would not wish to murder."

I rallied enough to glare at him. "That will *never* happen."

"Never? You have not lived long enough to know the word has a most . . . flexible meaning." He clasped his hands behind his back and paced slowly up and down the room. "Does your head hurt? Is your vision clouded? Perhaps a decided weakness plagues your limbs?"

"Why? You got patent medicines to sell?"

His eyes narrowed. "These are serious manifestations, Mr. Morris, and jests are out of place. A *Nosferatu* of my breed may go without blood for long periods of time and not suffer. One of your kind cannot." He paused before me. "There is no point resisting this. It is only blood."

"Only?"

"Blood, Mr. Morris, not soul. And animal blood at that. A nourishing food they produce with their bodies. Like milk. If you think of it in such terms perhaps it will be easier for you."

"It's repulsive."

"Only in your mind. You must find your way past it."

"I will not give in."

"That is something outside your power. I've a responsibility toward you as my guest, but also toward those who serve me. I will not allow them to be endangered."

"I won't touch them. I swear it."

"You will come to a point where you won't be able to help yourself."

"No."

"It is an inevitability. You will lose control. I would prefer you sate yourself on an animal than on one of my servants. Would this not be preferable to you as well?"

"I'd rather try the cook's soup again."

"*This* is your broth now." He pushed back the sleeve on his arm, and turned up his wrist. The skin was whiter than bone. Beneath its thin surface the blue lines of his blood vessels were clearly visible. With the sharp nail of his index finger he dug deeply into the flesh, breaking it. His blood welled up, bright as a ruby.

"Don't," I whispered.

"You can smell it, can you not?"

I turned my head away, stopped my breath, but the insidious scent was already within me, ripping my self-mastery to shreds.

"You may wish to refuse it, but with good reason your body tells you otherwise."

Yes, its betrayal was well begun. I felt my corner teeth descending to their full extent. I could see nothing but the blood. Lurching from the chair, I stumbled toward the door, trying to escape the overwhelming temptation being offered. I made it halfway before my legs gave out.

Dracula stalked over, looking down from a great height it seemed. With me watching, he put his wrist to his mouth, sucking on the wound he'd made as one does to close a simple cut. He did it quite deliberately, his gaze on me the whole time.

Again, I smelled the blood. Cramp took me. I doubled over on my side, wishing for a knife so I could cut out the pain. A long time later it eased. Slightly. I could see again. Dracula was still there.

"Enough of this foolishness," he said, pushing his sleeve down. "I've better things to do with my time than look after your troubles."

"I'm not asking you to."

"Then you will look after them yourself? Excellent. I'm most delighted. Come, and I'll show you the way to the stables."

It wasn't as though I accompanied him by my own choice. He clapped one of his lean arms about me and hauled me up, walking slow so I more or less stayed on my feet. If I fell again he'd just carry me. That would have been too humiliating.

The journey seemed to take forever and at the same

time passed in an instant, such was the befuddled state
of my mind. I was no stranger to hunger and knew it
could do odd things to your thinking, but I'd never
experienced anything like this waking nightmare.

Dracula paused before one of the big black horses
in its stall. The animal was calm enough, probably well
used to its master's needs. It didn't budge a muscle
as I all but dropped at its feet. I managed to pull
myself up a bit, and there I was, in close proximity to
the vein on its leg.

I could hear the deep, regular thumping of its heart.
Smell the blood.

"This you *must* do to live," said Dracula, an edge
of impatience in his tone as I continued to hesitate.
"Take it now, before madness takes *you*."

Slumping, I finally gave in to the inevitable.

It was as bad as I'd anticipated, worse even. The
touching of the tough hide with my lips, my sharp teeth
working to cut the skin, finally breaking through. I
made a mess of it with the stuff flowing onto my face,
staining my hands and clothes—

Then the first taste of it struck my tongue.

Changing *everything*.

My realization that I'd been a fool would come later,
when I could think again. For now all was sensation
as the blood welled into my mouth and I swallowed
again and again. It was different from all the other
pleasures I'd ever known before, intense as any and
comparable to none. I was aware of the living heat
flooding through me, erasing the awful cold within. It
was better than a shot of the finest whiskey and far
more intoxicating. There seemed an unending supply,
and I drew on it greedily, a starved child whose hunger is at long last appeased.

I had no judgment over how long it took, having lost
all accounting of time, nor did I care. It mattered not.
I drank my fill and more.

When I finally took command of myself and drew away, I was quite alone except for the horse, which seemed none the worse for what I'd done. My host had departed, probably back to his library and whatever concerns he'd left there while dealing with me. I was glad of the privacy. It would give me the chance to organize my thoughts before seeing him again.

I owed him a profound apology.

He accepted it graciously enough, showing the sort of manners that would please even an Englishman.

"You had to discover for yourself," Dracula said with a slight wave of his blunt fingers. He was seated at his table before a drift of papers, pots of ink, and several goose quill pens. To see him, a deadly *Nosferatu*, amid such prosaic articles lent a bizarre note to my changing perception of what life was like for him. One moment he's urging me to drink blood, and the next he's working away at some dull-looking business task.

"I'll allow the truth of that, sir. You've been uncommonly patient."

"It is an acquired virtue for me, I fear. Happily you did not exhaust it before coming to your senses. May I now safely conclude that you've achieved an acceptance of your condition?"

I eased into the chair by the fire, opening my palms to its heat out of habit rather than need. Prior to coming up I'd washed away the blood from my hands and face and donned a clean shirt from a supply of clothing my host had provided. All proved to be of English make, and I could guess that it had been the stuff left behind by Harker when he'd made his escape from his prison of a room last summer.

"I accept that I must drink blood to live," I said.

Something like disappointment shimmered in his eyes. "Ah. Well. It is a beginning. Small steps are best when one is mastering a new thing."

"Providing one is willing to master it."

Dracula folded a sheet of paper up and sealed it, impressing the soft wax with a ring on his left forefinger. He added the finished document to a growing stack of similar items in an ornate metal box. "Until another dilemma makes a fever in your brain?"

He did have a point. "This takes some getting used to; I'm sorry to cause you inconvenience."

"Bah. You've done better than others I've seen. Some have gone mad from the change, but then they were of my breed. I was uncertain if you would adjust yourself, but this little progress is good."

"And if I'd gone mad?"

His heavy brows quirked and his mouth twitched. "Then I'd have dealt with you as with them. You may take some comfort in the knowledge that you would have not suffered."

His matter-of-fact manner on the subject of my death almost riled me, but I could see his side of things too well. If I'd gone mad, especially with my formidable new strengths and abilities, then I'd need killing. Best to leave that dog lie. Or wolf, as he might have referred to it.

I understood that I'd probably come up with other aspects of my change to object to, but feeding on blood had been the real cork in the bottle. It worried me now how I'd changed my mind so quick after such determination to starve. One taste of blood and suddenly I'm feeling right as rain, all my misgivings faded to nothing. Having seen how a syringe full of morphine could quiet the most violent lunatic in Jack Seward's asylum I wondered if the blood had done something similar to me, affecting my very thoughts. If I made myself go without again, would I return to the kind of thinking I'd had before?

Looking at the situation, with my head clear and the grinding pain in my belly vanished, I deemed it unlikely that I'd even try. Pure stubbornness had kept me going down that road. Since it hadn't led to anyplace good, I'd have to admit I could do nothing constructive for myself there and strike out in another direction. It just rankled that Dracula had been right about it all. At least he wasn't being smug.

"You're apparently well revived now, which is all that matters," he said. "Your color is better and your eyes are not so dull. What of your spirits?"

"Improved."

"Yes, a good meal is always a help there. You did enjoy it?"

What an inadequate word, enjoy. "Once I'd started. Yes."

"No more revulsion? Ah. So excellent. But for the future I must advise you not to become too lost in the pleasure of it as to be unaware of what is around you."

"What do you mean?"

"The time will come when you wish to leave my home, and the wide world is not so understanding of these things as are the people here. Should some stable lackey chance upon you while you are engaged in refreshing yourself his reaction may not be—ah—convenient to you."

"So I need to take care not to get caught."

"Exactly. A little caution will save you much trouble and probably your life."

His quill scratched over a fresh sheet of paper at irregular intervals as he made notes from an old book. I wondered why he did not avail himself of a modern steel pen, or even a typing machine like the one I'd gotten Mrs. Harker, but perhaps such items were scarce this far into Transylvania. Certainly I'd seen plenty of evidence that the advantages of living in the nineteenth century had not progressed far into this corner of the world. These days even in the wildest parts of Texas you could unexpectedly come upon a well-to-do household with a piano on proud display in the parlor, the whole family and the hired help having enough schooling to be able to read their Bible. Not so here. From the look of things the land and people hadn't changed much since the Dark Ages.

That was clearly in Dracula's favor. With everyone in the strong grasp of fear and superstition he had little need to worry about the peasants making trouble for him. He was fairly safe from any local sneaking up to the castle during the day with a stake and hammer.

Of course the same went for me, which was something to rejoice in, for I was far more vulnerable. Dracula could be up and about with the day if he chose or if necessity dictated. No such luxury for what I'd become. As soon as the sun made its first lance of light over the horizon I ceased to be aware of anything until it set again. Had I gone mad from my change, then that would have been the best time for Dracula to deal with the problem. At least then I'd have been oblivious, and as he'd said, I'd not suffer.

My thoughtful host had given me a secure enough place to retire. He'd provided me with the key to a windowless chamber high up in an otherwise abandoned tower. The oak door was a stout thing nearly a foot thick, and if the lock was very old then it was also quite formidably huge. There was also a heavy iron bar I could slip between two massive rings set in the stone on either side of the door. Even if someone got past the lock they'd still have to break through that obstacle, which would take hours, and the noise might draw attention from the other inhabitants of the castle.

I'd been rather curious on how Van Helsing had been able to enter this fortress so easily to make his executions of the three vampire women, until I got a look at their resting place on my first night. Dracula had led the way into his castle through a series of passages that he assured me Van Helsing had quite missed. Finally, my host pushed through a ponderous door that opened onto his family crypt.

The vault was so dismal and hideous, the air so fetid with the smell of sulfur, rot, and death that only a vampire with no need to breathe would dare penetrate such dreadful depths. Little wonder the Szgany servants avoided it even in the day, and little wonder they'd heard nothing of the violence that had taken place there.

We passed on to the old chapel. Dracula looked turn-on-turn into three empty tombs, but found naught there but dust.

And drying blood. The smell of it permeated the chamber. Butcher's work had been done here, brutal, audacious butcher's work. Even knowing the implacability of his nature, I could hardly attribute this horror to Van Helsing, but there were the man's own square-toed boot prints scuffed into the grime on the floor next to each resting place.

Dracula offered no comment, and apparently no prayer. He only heaved a great sigh, put his back to his sorrows, then guided me up into the castle proper and eventually to the tower room. After a brief discussion where he determined that I had absolutely no desire to lie in anything resembling a coffin, he saw to it that a supply of earth was brought up along with a simple pallet for a bed. As I still possessed the blanket that had wrapped my body, I lay it upon the dirt to spare my clothing.

Without irony he bade me goodnight and departed, pulling the door shut with a solid bump. The room became too silent and lonely for my peace of soul. I dropped to my knees and prayed as I'd not done since a child, pouring out my misgivings and terrors to a hopefully kind deity. Not knowing if I was heard or not did nothing to ease my low spirits. I remained on my knees until an awful sluggishness abruptly stole over me. Through the thick stones of the wall my body had sensed the risen sun. I crawled onto the pallet and for the first time assumed my portion of death for the day, unmindful of the discomfort of the hard floor.

My spirits were no better when I woke in pitch darkness. For a few moments panic overcame my hunger until I blundered my way to the door and hauled it open. The faint light that shone up the spiral passage helped steady me. I was ashamed of my fear, but did not know what to do about it, so I pushed it away for the time being.

Dracula had promised more agreeable amenities, and on the second night my room had a proper bed (with the earth spread between the linens and a fine feather mattress), a table, chair, oil lamp, and candles. No fire was possible, but that was of little concern to me since I now seemed to be fairly indifferent to the cold so long as I was out of the wind.

After inquiring, I learned that in ancient times the room was meant for use as a sort of final bolt hole should the castle be overrun by enemies. There would the women lock themselves away until they either greeted their triumphant defenders, surrendered to their conquerors, or killed themselves. Dracula made no mention which of those events might have happened in the castle's long history, only saying that I would be perfectly safe there. Certainly it was proof against anyone but my host, who could change himself into mist and slip through the cracks if he chose.

Of course, I could do pretty much the same, or so he maintained.

Though of different breeds, he vouched I could dematerialize and float about where I liked, except past running water. During our initial confrontation in the forest he said I'd lapsed into an incorporeal state for a few seconds without even knowing. At the time I thought I'd been about to give in to shock and collapse, when all along it had been my body responding to my heartfelt wish to escape.

I'd not attempted a repetition of it because of the pain and weariness of my self-imposed fast, but now made an inner promise to try to rediscover this new ability. It struck me that a proficiency for easy vanishing would spare me from being troubled by stray stable hands while dining.

"Why are you so concerned for my welfare?" I now asked Dracula after a good long study of the fire.

He paused with his writing. "Because the customs binding host and guest are sacred in this land."

"I accept that, but not many days past I was doing my all-out best to kill you."

"Such is the nature of war. As I have won, there is no reason for me to continue the fight. Besides, I had questions for you."

"Which I've long since answered."

"You have."

"So?"

He let the quill drop. "I have heard of how direct Americans can be. It is a most stimulating change from the so-polite British circumspection. Very well, my concern for you is tied to concern for me, for all others who share this life. I deem it a duty to see that you are able to look after yourself so that you may not draw attention to the fact we *Nosferatu* even exist. Our chief protection in these enlightened times of science is that most believe us to be a myth. It has not always been so, but now that it is, you will be wise to preserve the sham, to safeguard yourself and always keep others from being discovered."

"But I know no others of our kind. Except for Nora."

"That you are aware of. Recall that your lovely Miss Jones seemed a normal woman in all ways. Perhaps now that you know what to look for, you will find more than you would think."

"You make it seem like a secret society."

"Some may view it as such, though I find the idea of *Nosferatu* gathering themselves together quite absurd and dangerous. Such foolishness would only call attention to us. Those whom I've encountered had little in common with one another save their changed state. As with other people we each have our separate needs to look after."

"And maybe it's better for the predators to have plenty of hunting room."

"There's that," he admitted, apparently missing my sarcasm.

"So you do feed on people as well as animals."

"When moved by passion, of course. You will as well when the time comes. And do not make the face and begin to object. Did you not find great pleasure with Miss Jones?"

"Yes . . . but she should have said something to me."

He gave a little shrug. "Indeed, but that is something you must settle with her should you meet again. For your own future dalliances, it is up to you how much to convey to your mistresses. When it happens, make certain they are of a character that you may utterly trust them with your secret. By that you are trusting them with your very life. Few such exist, I promise. It has ever been so. It is best that you not even bother. So long as you only take blood and not exchange it with your mistresses, then—"

"But they'll know when I do that. I did."

"True, but you can make them think it unimportant. Did Miss Jones not impart such a request to you? Perhaps at the same time looking deep into your eyes? Such is the power of influence you now command. Use it sparingly, out of self-protection lest others notice."

"But I don't know how." I was wary of trying, too,

as it struck me as being almighty ill-mannered to press my will upon another person, especially a lady.

"It will come in the doing. Knowing that you are capable is all you need; the accomplishment will then be a most natural thing."

More like a most supernatural thing, I silently corrected.

"Any other questions?"

"Yes." I wondered if Dracula might shy away from this one. "I want to know about Renfield."

He looked honestly puzzled. "Who?"

"The wretch who helped you at Seward's asylum."

"That madman who attacked me? Yes, what of him?"

"You killed him."

"Indeed, I should very much hope so. He was useful to me for a short time, and then his insanity overtook him at last. He was a . . . liability."

"How can you say that?"

"Is it not the correct word? A danger then."

"A danger to *you*? That poor devil?"

"I suppose one may feel sorry for a mad dog, but—"

"You murdered him! I was there at his dying when he named you."

Dracula pursed his lips, regarding me with what seemed to be great patience. "I've no need to explain my actions to anyone. If you consider defense of myself against him to be murder, then so be it. You were *not* there to see how things were at the time."

"Then enlighten me."

He paused a long while, finally shrugging. "Yes, I used him to gain entry to the building. I used him and others in that house to help me discover what your friends were up to in regard to myself. My powers of influence worked well on the servants, but mad people are immune. Mad people and drunkards. That is something you need to remember."

"Why did you kill him?"

"You may believe or not, but he gave me no choice. He babbled of vengeance against those who had imprisoned him, and he included Mrs. Harker in his plans. I could not allow that. Seward was too kindly a keeper, and to my mind, too stupid to see what so obviously lay ahead. This Renfield was a disaster poised to overtake all of you. It was a fortunate circumstance he chose to attack me first."

"But he was trying to defend us against you."

"Ha. And you believed his ravings?"

"He was quite sane at the end. Completely lucid."

Dracula made a waving-away gesture with one hand. "I care not. Only his intentions prior to his death concerned me. In the days of my breathing youth I'd have had him removed from his misery, and it would have been more effective than confining him to an easily breached cell. Are all the lunatics under Seward's charge so adept at escape or was Seward simply incompetent?"

I bristled, wanting to defend John Seward, but quelled it. "You say Renfield might have tried to do us an injury?"

"It was a certainty to say the least. I was given to understand Mrs. Harker had taken to visiting him. Apparently she would sit with him with but one attendant for protection. Be that creature tied hand and foot, I would never have trusted to place her fate within twenty yards of him. Your friends have too much civilization. It overcomes honest sense. Bah!"

Once more I was placed in the position of trying to balance what I'd seen against what he was telling me. Both views made sense depending where I stood. Could we have all been so wrong?

"Is there anything else you wish to have clarified?" he asked.

"Indeed, sir. I wish now to know about Harker."

He did look mildly surprised, but not worried. "A most general request. Would you please more specific be?"

"I want to know why you treated him so harshly. He spent most of his time here with you in fear for his life."

"Is that what he told you and the others?"

"It's all in his journal, which I have read."

Dracula spared a regretful look at his papers, pushed his chair from the table, and stood. "I should be interested to hear a complete account of that, Mr. Morris."

"It is not complimentary."

"Evidently, since your friend was so anxious to kill me and was able to pass that desire onto others. Give me an honest reporting and spare no detail; I shall not take offense."

"But I want to hear what you have to say."

"In good time. Please." He made a gesture of invitation with his upturned palm.

As it didn't seem I'd get anywhere unless I went first, I did so, full well knowing that he'd have the chance to think up a ripe and reasonable explanation for each of his crimes against poor Harker. I plunged into things, from Harker's arrival in Munich to his desperate climb down the wall to freedom and his subsequent hospitalization in Buda-Pesth for brain fever. Dracula made no interruption, though once in a while his brows descended and he paced once or twice before the fireplace pulling at his graying mustache. He seemed more thoughtful than agitated, though, and continued in his silence for quite some time after I'd finished.

"This is Harker's exact story?" he finally asked. "That which he set down?"

"I've read it many times over. You've gotten a fairly short version, but everything's there that matters."

He shook his head and clasped his hands behind

him, stalking slowly up and down, his gaze on the floor. "No wonder all of you pursued me with such vigor and determination."

"Between what happened to him, what you did to Mrs. Harker, and—"

He froze in midstep at her name and snapped a dark look at me. "That subject, young sir, is closed, for now and evermore."

I smothered the rest of my utterance. It had to do with Lucy and was perhaps best left unsaid, lest I betray myself to him.

"Now shall I speak of Jonathan Harker's sojourn with me, nothing more," he stated in a manner that would brook no argument.

Pushing my nascent anger away for the moment, I leaned forward. "I'm listening."

"Then listen well, for now you will hear the truth of things."

Keeping a poker face is second nature with me when I choose to use it, and so I held to a neutral expression. I thought it would be to his advantage to lie, to make himself look better in my eyes, but I could not ignore the nagging instinct that he really didn't give a tinker's damn for my good opinion, or anyone else's for that matter. There was also the fact he seemed to be fairly annoyed about something, and if he was intending to lie then he'd be more prone to put on a pleasant manner in order to convince me of his sincerity.

"All that you told of his story was true—up to a certain point," he said. "Yes, I did hold him prisoner in his room, but it was for his own protection."

"To keep the—your three friends away from him?"

"Let me speak of it in order. You tell me that his real fear began when he saw me descending along the castle wall?"

I nodded. Certainly at that point Harker first

realized the true supernatural nature of his host. While reading that part of his journal I'll say without blush that my hair went straight up on the back of my neck and goose-flesh raced along my arms. I'd had to stop for a time to gather myself enough to finish it and needed a bracing drink afterwards.

Dracula snorted. "I shall state with certainty that the seeds of his fear were sown long before he arrived. His companions on the diligence he took here no doubt supplied him with many rumors about me, about the land. It must have quite slipped his mind how I'd gone to great pains to see that he arrived safely, and even saved his life when he insisted on an ill-advised walk and got caught in a snow storm, but that is nothing to the rest. Such is man's character to forget the good done for him. Harker is a most sensitive sort of fellow, is he not? I noticed that about him from the first."

"He was when I met him." He had good reason to be, after what he'd been put through.

"Which was after his return to England?"

"Yes."

"He must have always been so, but not allowed others to see, I think. When Harker first came here he was most anxious to be of service and so it seemed only . . . typical? . . . to me. I am accustomed to people behaving in such a manner; it was nothing to remark upon. I made him welcome, we conducted our business, and he soon became comfortable in my presence. He was helpful to answer my questions about the English law and customs. I found him a good listener, and the hours of evening passed quickly for his company. I thought all was well for him. What I'd not considered was the effect of the—" he gestured wide about us to take in the whole of the castle. "—atmosphere this place might have on one unused to it."

"I suppose he might have found it a little forbidding."

"Perhaps you are not as sensitive as he. You walk unafraid through passages that still ring with the thousand lives and deaths that have gone before. These stones have long memories—and I know Harker felt their oppression."

"Are you talking about ghosts?"

"Not in the ordinary sense."

I gave short chuckle. "I don't think a ghost is supposed to be ordinary, that's why people get all alarmed about them."

"I do not speak of crude figures in winding sheets rattling chains and locks. I speak of an essence left behind, an impression, a feeling one senses with the soul, not the eyes. This ancient land is steeped in blood and barbarity well beyond any savage imagining, and it can have an adverse effect on those unprepared. Harker was a soft man from the city, raised to civilized comforts, sheltered from the true terrors of the world past and present. Comes he then to a wild, dark country where he has not the instinct to listen to the wiser voice of his heart. When it says stay indoors at night and pull the covers over your head it is for a very good reason.

"I should have seen the *mal* power working away on him, but not knowing him well I could not judge what is normal or not for him, and he being English, he speaks nothing of his troubles to me. In a very short time the gloom of this place began to take its toll upon his mind."

"You're saying he got touched in the head just from being here?"

Dracula gave a little shrug. "A most interesting phrase. I must remember it. It seems right."

"And all that he wrote in his journal was a fiction?"

"Not all. Much there was true. He departs from the facts concerning my three companions. He departs very far."

I felt my heart sink. "In what way?"

"You say he wrote that I interrupted before my dear ones could kiss him, take his blood. That is not what happened."

"Then what did?"

"They were . . . playful and curious. And disobedient. I told them to leave him alone, but the temptation was too much for them, and when he fell into a doze in that part of the castle they did come upon him. What followed you may guess, for you are a man of the world."

"So they—"

"Oh, yes, They did indeed. Once he discovered the delights of their company he was a most willing participant. One can hardly blame the fellow. He is a lonely stranger far from the restraints of his own genteel society and has before him three most passionate, beautiful women. One cannot blame him at all."

"But he loves his wife, very deeply."

"She was not his wife then, and is it not the custom that young men are expected to, as I have heard said, 'sow oats' before settling down?"

"I wouldn't call it a custom. Besides, I can hardly see a steady fellow like Harker going on such a rip as you suggest. Are you sure?"

"My dear ones confessed as much to me when I did finally take notice of Harker's . . . deterioration."

"They were drinking blood from him?"

"Only a little, not enough to endanger him and there was no blood exchange. What I saw was a sharp decline in his spirits. At night he knew the heights of ecstasy, but during the day he wallowed in the depths of guilt. So much so that it began to show in his manner and speech. I do not understand why it is that some people suffer such distress and shame for doing what is so enjoyable. It is as though they must punish themselves for taking pleasure from life, as though they deserve it not. Why must joy be atoned for? There is no reason for it, but many persist in bringing harm to themselves when they should be thankful and accept. Harker was of that number.

"He felt guilt for his perceived betrayal of his fiancée and perhaps of myself, his unsuspecting host. Had I known I could have put his mind to rest on the latter. My dear ones were ever free to fulfill their desires with anyone they chose unless I bade them otherwise. Harker did not know that, of course, and because of things he'd observed as I went about my other business he was too afraid of me to speak. If he'd said but one word I might have prevented much anguish for him. By the time I discovered the truth he was already half mad with the brain fever and to stop him from harming himself I had to lock him up. I gave orders to my Szgany to free him and conduct him to a doctor after my departure for England."

"Why did you not take him yourself?"

"My arrangements of travel could not be altered to allow for it by then. Besides, toward the end the very sight of me was enough to send him into a terrible fit. It was most distressing to witness—and feel." He thoughtfully touched the scar on his forehead. "It seemed best to not be around him, though perhaps I should have tried otherwise. Then might I have found his journal."

"And destroyed it?"

"Of course, out of self-protection. As you've just realized, it contains some rather damaging untruths. He describes me as being a monster. If I am a great and so-terrible monster, then his little dalliance of the flesh is not so important."

"Like stubbing a toe to forget a toothache?"

"Ah . . . yes . . . I suppose. As for feeding a child to my dear ones and setting my wolves upon the grieving mother, or compelling them to attack Harker should he set a foot outside, those are fantasies from his fevered mind. He was indeed ill to invent such things."

I shook my head. "But he wrote so believably."

"Then perhaps he is misplaced in his vocation and should take up the writing of lurid romances instead. I have had to do many dread acts in my life, but torturing English solicitors—bah!"

And to hear it like that, it did seem absurd.

"What would be the point, Mr. Morris? I'd already obtained all that I required of him. No, young sir, the truth is that the very proper Mr. Harker could not bear to have his forbidden pleasures on his conscience and so buried them deep in his mind. That he made mention of them at all in his journal is what should be so surprising to you. The only way he could speak of his carnal encounter was to say that I stopped all before it could start, leaving him an innocent victim of the others' unfulfilled lust. Would that it were true, then none of this might have happened."

That was quite an assumption to say the least, for Dracula might not have preyed upon Lucy and everything would be . . . no, I could not continue on that trail. If I started thinking about her, then I'd start hurting again over the thousand might-have-beens. She was gone and there was no help for it.

"Any more questions?" he inquired.

"No. None for now," I said. My head was so stuffed full with all these new particulars I didn't think I was ready to add more without being in danger of splitting a seam.

"It is just as well. I feel the sun's soon arrival. You've just time to get to your place of rest."

I could feel it, too. Yet another link to him, to his kind. My kind now, damn it all. I huffed out some kind of quick farewell to him and hurried away, nearly running up the worn and narrow stairs to my high sanctuary. I didn't miss a step. It would have been like a coal mine to anyone else, but not to me, for enough ambient glow leaked up the passage for my eyes to use. When I got to the chamber and locked the door, though, I was cut off from all light except that of my own making. I wondered if Dracula's vision was similarly limited, or if he could see perfectly even in such a sealed place.

Hands out, I stumbled forward and fell onto my bed with its layer of hard-won Transylvanian earth, feeling it shift and pack under the weight of my body. It had a smell more of dry dust than of anything that could cause a seed to sprout. Dust and death, I thought. Dracula must have given me some of the stuff from his rotting chapel.

I wanted light. Wanted it very badly. Groping on the little table next to the bed for my packet of Vespas, I scraped one to life against the stone wall. The yellow radiance hurt my eyes for an instant, but my vision adjusted quickly.

The tiny match flame was more than sufficient for me to see by, but I still wanted my lamp and candles. It was foolish to need such reassurance. I pushed the notion away as best I could. I'd only have to put everything out again in a few more seconds.

What light I had gave no cheer to the forlorn room. The stones were a dreary gray, scarred by ancient marks and stains of unknown origin. Blood, perhaps, spilled by the ladies of the castle refusing to give up to invaders? Or had they surrendered only to be slaughtered?

That inspired a shudder.

I felt my inner change drag on my limbs as the heavy numbness stole over me. The sun had nearly arrived. I let the match drop to the bare floor where it died. Waiting with eyes shut against the confining blackness, I could understand how Harker's imagination might have given in to the morbid influences of this desolate place.

For that alone I was inclined to believe Dracula's account of things. All he'd said sounded very reasonable. He'd struck just the right note of exasperation and sympathetic regret to sound true, but I wasn't swallowing it whole hog just yet.

This would need a store of mulling over and then some before I made up my mind whether or not to kill him.

Chapter Three

The next night I blinked fully alert, though I had to put a hand to my face to be certain about the blinking. The smothering inkiness was absolute, and too much like my first waking wrapped head to toe in that blanket. I sat bolt upright to reassure myself I could still move about.

Such forced blindness didn't suit one bit and I quickly lighted a candle. As before, the little flame was too much of a comfort. I was a grown man of nine and twenty, and lying in the dark should not have disturbed me so. I'd either have to get used to it or find a way to have a light burning each evening when I woke. Perhaps a candle large enough to last through the whole of a day would do. Amid all this stonework there was little need to worry about a fire getting out of hand.

I stood and stretched, more out of habit than need. The instant I succumbed to the day-sleep I moved not a single muscle for the whole time, yet felt no crimp or cramp. It wasn't natural, but then I'd have to give up that kind of thinking.

Nothing much about me was a close cousin to natural, now.

I'd learned the truth of it well enough the night before with my first real taste of blood, and indeed it was my first. I could not count that which Nora had shared with me all those years past. Then I'd had only human-normal senses with which to appreciate the pleasure, but those limits were shattered forever. Part of me was delighted, part was dust-spitting angry for having had no choice in the matter, and a very great part was still afraid.

Just how afraid I didn't know until the moment when Dracula bared his arm and pierced it. The sight, the very *smell* of that blood had near-maddened me. Though I wore a human-appearing body, the changes within had enhanced everything. It was as though when I'd cast off that shroud of a blanket I'd shed a thick, unsuspected skin as well. All my senses were vibrantly aware, alive, and demanding stimulation. The absolute need to drink had near-overpowered me. The one thing to hold me back was knowing I'd be drinking from *him*, taking *his* blood into me. That, for reasons I dared not to think about, would have been unbearable, but still I nearly lost control and seized what was offered anyway. Only at the last second did I find the strength to turn away and run.

We all fear loss of control. Sometimes it's a rare, fine kind of fear you willingly challenge, like climbing onto a mustang that's never known a saddle. You either break him or he does his damnedest to break you with a wild bone-jarring ride as you settle up your differences. Falling off or not isn't as important as the fact that something else *is* in charge of things for a few moments.

But other times it's a sick-making kind of fear when disaster bushwhacks you, and no matter how hard you try you can't work things in your favor. That's what nearly happened last night. I'd gotten too close to the edge of giving in to mindless need.

And that just had to do with my hunger. What other ugly surprises awaited? I feared for myself and for others. Should I not master this change before leaving here, what harm might I bring to some innocent in my path?

The whole of the world was new again with fresh, cruel rules to learn. Whenever I ran up against a contrast between the old and the new it gave me something like an electrical jolt. I'd have to get past feeling so surprised and grim all the time or I'd not be able to do anything for myself.

The best way to stop being such a tenderfoot was to ply Dracula with as many questions as possible and absorb whatever advice he might care to hand me. Thinking over that which he'd already given, it made a load of sense, but I needed more from him. I was all too aware of my own desperate lack of knowledge.

One could adjust to anything, with enough time. Certainly Miss Nora Jones had done well for herself. Along with many other engaging attributes, she'd struck me as being a confident woman full of high spirits and happiness. There was nothing of the grave clinging to her that I could recall. If she could do it, then so could I, but I wondered how long it would take.

And . . . would I always be afraid of the dark?

Though the chill winter days sped swiftly by unmarked and unnoticed by me during my rests in the tower sanctuary, the nights were long and fully occupied as I set about learning how to be a vampire.

First and foremost I took special care never to let myself get hungry again. I could see now what a foolish risk I'd taken, so to avoid all possibility of losing control I kept myself well-stocked and full to the brim. As it turned out I didn't need all that much blood to be feeling my best. So far as I could judge, my first feeding had been the heaviest. A trip down to the stables every third evening seemed to suit my needs. The fine taste of horse blood was more than enough compensation for any lingering aversion I had about biting into the flesh of a living animal. For variation and to increase my skill I also fed from the Szgany's cattle. I thought I might sample one of the chickens, but decided against it. I could soothe and quiet the other animals, but none of the fowls. Besides, they really didn't look big enough to provide me a decent meal and still survive the experience.

That necessity seen to, I applied my energies toward getting used to other important particulars about my condition. I could move astonishingly quick when I wanted, but often with misjudgment, which made me clumsy. It was like being a boy again and going through a growing spurt. At about twelve I shot up a whole foot in height in one year and ate like any three field hands, and for all that time I seemed to be nothing but elbows, knees, and two left feet, forever bumping into things and knocking them over. Ma told me to be careful so often that I kept outside as much as possible for fear of breaking anything in the house.

I sought the same solution now, spending a good portion of the night exploring beyond the castle walls. There could I find the room to indulge my need for physical drill by clambering about the rugged country, testing my strength against the land. Running, climbing trees, scaling impossible cliffs, pushing myself beyond that which I'd known before helped me to reclaim command over my own body. It took a deal of concentration at first, same as when I'd grown out of my youthful awkwardness by learning to ride, rope, and shoot. There were moments back then when I thought I'd never get the art of it, but the hard realities of ranch life made such expertise needful for survival. To give up was not in the cards, so I'd kept at it until I forgot what it was like not to know how, until I was the best hand on the whole blessed range. So did I work myself once more.

Another, far less ordinary skill also required my most careful attention: learning to vanish—and, while bodiless, to move about in that state.

It took some powerful getting used to, I'll say that for the experience. Not that it was so difficult to disappear; the trick of it had to do with *believing* I was indeed capable of doing it. Dracula was of great assistance there, guiding me—in his own unique manner and method—through my first intentional attempt.

The lesson began in his library. One evening he traded all that writing for reading, giving me to understand he'd lost interest in it for the time being. When I once chanced to inquire about the nature of his labors, he simply replied he was making a memoir for himself about his life. The task had been somewhat inspired by the exhaustive diaries kept by my friends. He was more than willing to share additional details, for he quite enjoyed talking about the wartime exploits of his ancestors—or rather one-time contemporaries—and bent my ear for hours on end without running down. Tonight I thought it best not to raise the subject as I had the feeling I already knew more about him than was good for me.

He was very much at his ease in an old chair, his long legs stretched out before the fire and crossed at the ankles, hands steepled over the book on his chest, his head thrown back so he could stare at the wavering shadows on the ceiling. Though his face still retained some youth, his hair was quite gray now, becoming shot through with streaks of pure white, as was his lengthening mustache. It was trimmed away from his hard mouth, and I was fairly certain he'd used a touch of wax for neatness of appearance. How he could keep himself so well groomed without the use of a mirror was beyond me; perhaps one of his Szgany was a barber. The first time I tried to shave by touch was my last. After gaining a motley collection of nicks (which healed remarkably fast) I decided to just let my beard grow.

I bade him a good evening and mentioned my interest in learning how to vanish. He reminded me in turn that I'd already accomplished the task, which would make things easier.

"One can hope so," I said. "But you'll pardon me if I have some doubts. I don't know how I did it."

"You must believe that you can. Then will you master it."

"I'll allow the truth of that. What must I do?" I half-expected him to get up and give a demonstration, but he continued to stare at the ceiling.

"You must try to recall how it was for you in the forest," he said. "What were you thinking at the time?"

"I can't say that I was thinking of anything except getting away from you."

"A very understandable reaction given the circumstances. Immerse yourself in that moment again."

I tried, conjuring up as best I could the memory of being surrounded by wolves and facing their dread master, but nothing happened. "Maybe I'm not feeling as inspired now as I was then."

"Perhaps I could call on my wolves to come and chase you about the room until inspiration strikes you once more."

That raised a smile from me, until I realized he wasn't making a joke. "No, thank you."

He straightened slightly, directing his gaze toward one of the tall windows, his forehead puckering.

"What?"

"Listen."

I did, for he seemed to be entirely distracted by whatever he was hearing. Far below I only heard the servants going about their business, the soft scratch of cellar rats, the wind sighing outside, and the creak and tick of trees bending to it. All was normal. I shook my head. "What is it?"

"The wolves."

It didn't take much to catch on. "They're quiet."

He grunted agreement. "They've not hunted in the last few days and should be hungry. The moon is high, yet their song is silent. Something must be wrong."

He left the comfort of his chair and book and swept from the room with me right behind him. I'd grown so used to the nightly singing of his children that I'd ceased to note it. Its absence might mean nothing, but was worth checking. Back home when the wild things went hush it was generally for a good reason and best to be on guard.

I followed him up the stairs that led to my tower room, but we passed its entry and continued on until the ceiling pressed close. The stairs ended at a formidable trap door in the roof; he threw the inside latch and pushed. The hand-span thick oak slab boomed back on its hinges, and we climbed through.

Icy air stung all my exposed skin as we emerged onto the roof, but was not uncomfortable. If I chose to linger without sensible coverings, then might the cold wind begin to affect me, but all was well for now.

The sky was a rich dark blue such as I'd never been capable of seeing before my change, its vast field silvered with a dense net of bright stars. In my time I'd seen many sights that could be described as breathtaking, but this was the corker. I knew in my bones that no matter how long I lived I'd never get tired of it or lose the sense of wonder it inspired. This was decidedly one of the more agreeable aspects about my change.

The tower wall was low, extending itself only a foot above the roof's snow-dusted wood beams, which looked to be fairly recent compared to the rest of the castle. I would guess by their weathering they'd been put in place only in the last hundred years or so. The time of wars in this area was long past, else any sentry placed here would be too exposed to enemy fire. On the other hand it would take a rare shootist to accurately reach this far, though a good Sharps rifle would put things in his favor.

Dracula stood at the edge right next to the low wall, the strong wind at this height tearing at his clothes and whipping his hair flat along his skull. He faced into it, scenting the air. I did the same, breathing in and catching only the chill, clean snow, pine, wood smoke, and sometimes the earthy whiff of stale leaves that had escaped the last storm. His senses may have been sharper than mine or he knew better what to seek, for I took no clue from it. After a moment he gave up and walked slowly all around the limits of the wall to view the lands far below.

His castle stood proud on a high cone of rock. One side faced a terrible drop into a black valley where the pines stood guard like raised spears, the other a steep but less alarming descent which would still have been easy to defend from attack. From this vantage we had a fine broad view of the snow fields and dense stands of trees for miles in every direction. Clearly visible to my night-accustomed eyes was a thready depression marking the road my friends and I had used in the final stage of our hunt. I hoped they had a safe journey back to Galatz, and at the same time felt a deep twinge of guilt for their sorrow at my seeming loss. First my life taken away and then my body, the former bad enough, the latter making a sad situation all the more awful. At least with a body to bury one could make a true farewell and move on.

When I did return to civilization, it would have to be done with the greatest of care and doubtless be difficult, particularly in legal matters. Art, perhaps with Harker's help, would take upon himself the dismal task of notifying what kinfolk I had and my bankers. Due to cholera, the grippe, various wars, tornadoes, blizzards, summer heat, and other like incidents that were part and parcel of living in Texas I had no real relatives left, only some very distant cousins in the east. They'd had sense enough to stay put and thrived.

Seven years ago, when Pa passed on, the whole kit came to me, a vast ranch, more cattle than I could count, and more work than any one man needed in a lifetime. On advice from my Galveston bankers I leased the running of the place to some English investors— which was how I met Arthur Holmwood. His father had sent him as his agent to Texas to have a look at things; we struck up a fast friendship, and Art planted in me the temptation to see what the rest of the world was like. I turned the daily ranch business over to some trusty foremen to look after and the money counting to those who were good at it and took off. Because of the railroads and a new meat-packing plant, the old place kept turning a tidy profit even in bad years, leaving me free to roam.

That's how it enabled Art and me to circumnavigate the globe before my twenty-fifth year, hunting big game, paying our respects at various embassy parties, raising hell where and when it was appropriate, and otherwise having a good time. Whether sweltering in the Amazon or freezing in Siberia we collected enough experience for a dozen explorers in an astonishingly short time. That our tramping about together should come to an end here in the deeps of Transylvania was unthinkable, but end it did—this part of it, anyway. Going back promised to be uncommonly complicated.

But I'd worry about that later. Dracula was looking mighty annoyed as he glared out over the forest.

"Something is indeed wrong," he said in reply to my question. "There is no sign of them I can see or feel."

"Maybe the deer hunting wasn't so good and the pack moved on," I suggested.

"Were that true I would hear complaints from the peasants about missing sheep. Nay, but there is something else afoot. I know not what it could be, but I will find out."

"Tonight?"

"Why not? Ah, your promised lesson. Very well, we will continue, but not for long. First I will—wait a moment." He paused and stared intently into the night. "That should not be there."

"What?" He was rather closer to the edge than I, as I'm not overly fond of heights and the wind was a nuisance. Still, I took a pace or two forward as he extended one hand to point.

"There? Do you not see it?" he said. "A line of smoke about five or six miles distant."

I peered down the length of his arm, trying to see. Just as I was about to say no I felt something slap me smart and solid between the shoulders. The force of it launched me tumbling headfirst down the castle wall. I shrieked and clawed empty air, legs thrashing, sight blurring as the ground rushed up to smash me to pulp.

Then . . . nothing.

I still felt the sickening motion of falling, but not like before. This was strangely slow and suspended. I was lost, sightless and deaf in a void, with no sense of up or down, with no body at all.

He's killed me, I thought. This was death, true death, and this time I'd not be coming back.

Anger flooded me, or whatever wisp of consciousness remained that could be flooded. He'd gotten all that he'd wanted of me and in this way had disposed of an inconvenience. I'd never return home to carry the tale that he yet lived. The treachery of it was beyond comprehension. I wanted to scream my outrage, but had no mouth, no lungs; instead I seemed to roll in the nothingness like a stray piece of cloud at the mercy of the gales. Soon I'd be blown to shreds and drifting forever . . .

But another something blocked my way.

I was sensible of the wind buffeting me about, and now became aware of being pressed against a wide uneven surface. It was like swimming in murky water where you could only feel your way around things. Perhaps I'd found the bottom of the pond.

Only then did I dimly realize what had actually happened.

It did not mitigate my rush of anger, but I managed to push it aside for the moment, which was just as well for all concerned. The world came back to me, though it was more correct to say I came back to the world. My dulled senses reestablished themselves with such suddenness and painful clarity that it took a while before I sorted everything.

The black bulk of the castle loomed above me, for I lay flat on my back atop a drift of snow at its stony base. How I got there without injury I now fully understood. The method Dracula used to spark the process had been—no jest intended—Draconian to say the least.

Where in hell had the bastard gone?

Peering up, I made out a flurry of motion where he'd been standing on the tower. He was no longer there, but I did spy a bizarre, sinuous patch of darkness floating against the intense blue of the sky. This larger than man-sized patch was by no means opaque, for the stars were visible through it.

It drifted off the rampart and came spiraling lazily down toward me. As it got closer I saw it was made up of tiny specks like dust or a thick swarm of small insects. If you didn't know where to look it was nearly invisible. Only when certain bits caught the moonlight did it become easier to see and even then one might blink and find it gone.

This extraordinary cloud came to rest a few steps from me, collected together into a rough vertical column a yard or more across, then gradually compressed until there was more solid to it than space. Eventually it turned into his face and form and held that way. Dracula looked down at me, arms behind his back like a schoolmaster, one eyebrow raised.

"I gather you found your lost inspiration, Mr. Morris?"

"How—" I croaked, so mad I had to break off to work enough spit into my mouth to talk. "How *dare* you?"

He gave a small shrug. "As we stood together up there I had a childhood memory of how I was first taught to swim. My loving father picked me up and threw me into the water. It was . . . effective."

"It's—" Again I broke off.

He gave me an earnest, inquiring look. "Yes?"

"Nothing," I snarled and got busy picking myself up, not without difficulty for I kept sinking into the snowdrift. "It worked."

"Do you think you can repeat what you just did?"

"I reckon I'd better. There's too damn many cliffs around here."

"Ha!" he said, his eyes flashing briefly with much amusement.

Cursing under my breath, I struggled free of the drift, dusting snow from my backside and sleeves. "When it happened did I look like you do? All black specks?"

He thought it over. "More like a dark gray cloud. But understand that others would not be able to see you, only those of our kind. Animals will sense you as well, so—"

"I know, be careful not to get caught."

He grunted a short affirmation. "Do you require any more instruction tonight?"

"I think I've had more than enough. I'll get the hang of the rest on my own, if you don't mind."

"Then I will bid you good evening and good practice." So saying, he made another change in himself. I recognized the roiling darkness that spun within the outline of his body, only this time it was reversed. He seemed to shrink, his upright posture swiftly wilting, the bones of his face stretching even as those of his limbs shortened. He dropped forward, but not from injury. Four sturdy legs supported his wolf-form now. The only wonder of it was the fact that his action was now no more alarming to me than if he'd picked up a hat and cane to venture forth for a stroll.

His huge green eyes caught the moonlight and flashed again; then with little sound his shaggy black figure trotted briskly off between the trees. He was probably going to have a little hunt around for his missing children.

I slapped myself down to make sure everything was still there and intact and with some success managed to shrug off the remains of my anger. He'd surprised and scared the hell out of me, but I could see the purpose behind it. His memory about learning to swim had capped things.

Damnation, but if that wasn't *exactly* how my pa had taught me.

With such an alarming start to grease the wheels, I worked to avoid any threat of his repetition of the harrowing lesson. He'd been right; belief accounted for most of the effort required. Before the night was out I captured the skill of vanishing and happily experimented for hours until the cold finally drove me back to the shelter of the castle. I made my entry by means of the gap between the door and the stone threshold, re-forming inside by slow degrees so I could watch my hands gradually regain solidity. I'd once seen photographs with double images, the second image being fainter and more ghost-like; so now did I seem to imitate them. This was completely amusing to me, though exhausting. By the time I climbed up to my room to sleep for the day I felt like a wrung rag and instinctively knew I'd feed more heavily when next I woke.

I lighted candles for comfort, settled into my earth-layered bed, and tried to fill the remaining time before dawn by means of a book. It was one of the many works in English Dracula had in his vast collection, but failed to hold my interest for more than a line or two. His pushing me off the tower had set up a train of dark thought that needed pursuing.

You see, I'd not yet forgotten about that problem of whether or not to kill him.

Truly *kill* him.

Inarguably, this was bald-faced ingratitude on my part. He'd helped me—in his own way—was continuing to help me, and I owed him quite a lot for that. But on the other hand, even if it was with the unwitting aid of Jack Seward and Van Helsing, Dracula had still contributed to poor Lucy's death. There was no getting around it.

I'd deeply loved the girl, still loved her, though she'd chosen another over me. That sort of loss I could understand and accept, but to have her taken by a lingering and unnecessary passing was the height of unfairness. She'd been cheated from the joys of an ordinary life, and if Dracula was truthful about being

Nosferatu, she'd lost even that kind of existence as well. And there I'd been right in her tomb at her second death, in my ignorance helping them to kill her again.

If Dracula had only left her alone or if Jack had never called in the professor or if I'd known then what I knew now. . . .

It was a path straight to madness to think such things, but I had to get through it all. Sometimes I'd tramp my way along every inch of it, pausing now and then to crash a fist against the nearby wall whenever my feelings got the better of my self-control.

Because I could still hear her screams.

Throughout all these active nights I'd been mulling this over, which is a very long while for me. In the kind of rough and ready life I'd been born to in Texas you learn to think fast or else find yourself tipping your hat to old Saint Peter at the gate. Out of sheer stubbornness I'd taken my time with that forced fasting, but for just about any other troublesome situation or individual I had a talent for coming up with a quick plan to deal with the difficulty. Then would I swiftly carry it through without hesitation—but not for this one. The situation was complex, and I would not approach the obvious solution lightly.

Along with Lucy, foremost in my considerings was Mina Harker. I was still in a worry about her, being mighty fond and respectful of the lady. She'd once called me her true friend, and that had struck deep and stayed in my heart. She had been most kind to me when I poured out my grief about Lucy to her, not something I could ever forget. I didn't want to let her down if I could help it; honor alone forbade betrayal of that trust.

The subject of Mrs. Harker might be closed to my host but was wide open for me. Like it or not, I'd sworn to her face and before all the others that I'd see to Dracula's death, and her husband took my hand on it. Where I was raised a handshake's as sacred as any vow made in a church on a stack of Bibles. Though time had passed and my circumstances had changed, I still felt an obligation to fulfill my promise.

Van Helsing had been pretty clear that once Dracula was dead, Mrs. Harker would then be safe from becoming a vampire herself. At the time it made a lot of sense. But I wasn't so sure now after hearing what Dracula had to say about her being given a "choice" when she died. Though impossible to prove or disprove, it sounded reasonable. I'd learned that the professor had been sorely wrong about a lot of things concerning vampires, might he also be wrong on this?

The professor's version of vampires was dressed up with a lot of lore and what I would call superstition, and he and Jack Seward, both hardheaded scientists, seemed to have missed the main point of it all. If you looked at Mrs. Harker's blood-exchange with Dracula as being less like magic and more like passing on an illness, then the rules were different. Say a person with some fatal sickness infects you, then dies himself, does that mean you're safe from dying as well? Hardly. It struck me that whether he were destroyed or not, Dracula's blood was still in Mrs. Harker, his death would change nothing for her.

That rankled. We'd all done our best, and I'd willingly traded my life thinking to spare her soul from hell. In those moments when I drew my last living breath I'd wholly believed we'd saved her and had been profoundly thankful. All for naught, it seemed.

During one of our many talks in the library I'd raised the subject with Dracula about the terrible mark on her forehead, the burn she'd gotten when Van Helsing touched her with the Host. Its miraculous healing had been proof of our success, and thus had I slipped peacefully into the sleep of death. (Or so it seemed.)

Because of his link with Mrs. Harker Dracula had been aware of some awful injury befalling her, but knew nothing specific and pressed me for details. These I provided, completing my description of the incident with an obvious question.

"Was she indeed being shunned by God for her association with you?" I asked. "And if so, how could she be cured if you were not destroyed after all?"

He'd been silent for a very long time and finally shook his head. "How can I of all those who walk the earth answer you? Who am I to explain His works?" He twitched his fingers toward the ceiling. "Miracles are not so common as they once were, but they must still happen or faith would fade. She thought me dead, and perhaps it was enough for her healing. Beyond that I cannot say."

"But—"

"In truth, Mr. Morris, I cannot speak of such things. Long before your thrice-great-grandsire was born I gave part of myself to the Void. It is best you not know more of it, only understand that I am not one to consult on matters of faith."

For all that, I still wondered why it could be that he and his kind were able to sleep in hallowed ground yet must shun the cross, but I'd stirred him up enough with my questions and allowed that he would not welcome more for the time being. Perhaps he had no answer for that anyway.

The whole business was pretty complicated, and I wanted to be as impartial as possible, which is why I spent so much time sizing up the man to see how he compared with the monster I and the others had hunted.

Van Helsing had it nailed tight that Dracula was dangerous and resourceful as they come, but he'd missed on something he called the vampire's "child brain." I didn't quite catch the professor's meaning on that point at the time, for his accent and use of English took getting used to; I eventually worked out that he'd frozen himself on the idea that Dracula was missing a few bricks in his building when it came to new situations and worldly experience, giving us an advantage. He'd assumed that Dracula was all instinct, like an animal, and that his memory was flawed from lying around in his tomb for centuries on end. But I now saw this was pure lack of knowledge and perhaps wishfulness on the Dutchman's part, and we'd all foolishly fallen in with it.

The actuality was that Dracula was wily as anyone I'd ever met—which is saying a lot—and what I would call a long thinker. After all, he'd put years of preparation into his coming to England and would hardly let himself be thwarted by our little party. There was nothing amiss with his thinking or memory, and had he been of a different mind, he would certainly have found a way to kill us with ease.

We'd left ourselves wide open to him more times than we knew, as I learned when once he gave me the full tale of our hunt from his side of things, most of which I found to be irksome to hear because he drew such great amusement from it. But annoying or not, there was no denying that he could have picked us off one by one or all at once, such was his power.

We'd set our quarry on the run, but I came to realize he was never really in much danger from us. As the nights passed in his lonely castle, with me spending a good deal of it in his company listening to his apparently infinite hoard of stories, I soon saw that Van Helsing had severely underestimated our opponent.

If I did decide to finish the hunt, the task would not be easy.

Dracula wasn't in the library the next night, which was not unusual, for he frequently absented himself without a word. We weren't exactly roped together, so his comings and goings were none of my business, and it was a bit of a relief to be free of his company. I had plenty of distractions, such as taking the opportunity to steal a look at the papers he'd been writing on— only those on top, mind you, anything more would have been truly impolite. As it was he was safe from my curiosity since it was all written in his native tongue of which I had only the bare minimum of words. The stuff looked to be pretty heavy going, too, with many pages of closely written script. The books he had stacked round his writing area were, if I could judge by some of the Latin titles, histories of his country, which bore out his assertion he was writing a memoir of some sort. My curiosity satisfied, I turned my attention to a collection of month-old English, French, and German newspapers that had evidently arrived that day, along with a number of magazines. These items were obviously part of the research he'd done prior to traveling west to England.

Though out of date, I spent the evening delving into them all. My last weeks in England had been hectic, and I'd not had time to read much of what was happening in the world. Sadly, little had changed when it came to the general kinds of troubles like wars, and I knew that nothing ever would. Having talked so much about the past with my Un-Dead host it was quite clear to me that century after century people kept making the same mistakes, the only variation being in the details. The idea that I would come to see like blunders unfolding again and again over an equally long span of time was both daunting and disheartening.

Living beyond the usual three score and ten seemed a right good thing at first, a sort of compensation for the inconvenience of only being up and about at night. But after thinking the notion through I realized that along with the sad march of history I'd also be watching

friends not yet born age and die. Having spoken of it
to my host, his suggestion was simple and practical:
stay away from making close attachments to anyone.
He'd apparently done so, but I was from a place where
a man relies on his friends for his physical and spiritual survival. I wasn't sure I'd be able to harden my
heart in the same manner.

Dracula also assured me I wasn't immortal, so much
as ageless, and though extremely tough, I could yet be
killed by those who knew how, those like Van Helsing.
Certainly under *his* tutelage I'd learned all kinds of
ways of dispatching vampires, which understandably
horrified me now. Dracula's admonitions to keep my
true nature a secret did not fall on deaf ears, but I
wondered whether I'd be able to manage it all the time.
My temperament was such as to rankle against isolating
myself too much from the company of friends. I was
already feeling hemmed in by the remoteness of this
gloomy castle, and the more I read of the outside world
the more I thought about rejoining it.

But before that could happen, I'd have to decide
what to do about Dracula.

My instincts told me I still had to study him, and
as he wasn't available tonight, my need for action drove
me to borrow pen, paper, and a pot of ink from his
stock. After two drafts, I was finally satisfied with a
letter to be delivered to my London and Paris bankers, which would hopefully head off money troubles
for me when I rejoined civilization.

Knowing that Art would notify them of my prema-
ture death, and gambling that he'd not be forthcoming on the details, I informed them that I had, indeed,
suffered an accident that separated me from my friends.
In good faith Lord Godalming assumed I'd been killed,
which would account for any story he would pass on.
I told them to treat him kindly, but absolutely not
inform him of his mistake, as I planned to do it myself

as a happy surprise to him and my other friends. In the meantime, the banks were to take no action regarding my accounts until my return. As proof of my identity, they were welcome to compare the handwriting of my letter to past missives.

I prepared a similar letter to my Galveston bankers, again instructing them to take no action regarding my will since I still lived. Things would be in an almighty legal mess otherwise. I'd heard tell of a Galveston man who'd been declared dead and had suffered no end of trouble trying to prove himself otherwise so he could get his property back from his relatives. It must have been a bad day for him shouting himself hoarse before a judge trying to convince the court he was indeed alive. His family was no help, for by all accounts he was a bad sort, and they didn't mind him being dead, and in fact preferred it.

As I had no near kith or kin to worry over, such an alarming turn did not seem a possibility, but I patiently scratched lines on the paper all the same. Better to be safe than sorry, I thought as I folded and addressed them ready for mailing.

Before I knew it midnight was upon me, so I stretched and determined to take the air. The wind blew strong as it whistled around the shutters and set them to rattling. I wasn't familiar with the manners of the weather in this part of the world, but was willing to wager that a storm was brewing up, and I might not see the outside of the castle for awhile.

I found a long sheepskin coat and a fur cap to throw on as I intended to remain abroad for as long as possible to get some real exercise. A small side door in the courtyard opened onto a snow-choked trail leading down to the woods. The winds eased somewhat with my descent from the heights, but did not entirely depart. As I made the trees it continued to mourn through their tops, shaking pale flakes upon my shoulders. Except for its keening, the silence held complete rule here, and before I'd gone half a mile I felt the utter loneliness of the land closing over me like water on a downing man.

Shrugging it off as a fancy was useless, for the desolation kept circling back on me, refusing to leave. I thought of what Dracula had said of Harker succumbing to the dark atmosphere of the castle and wondered if it was finally working its way with me. Though alert enough to normal dangers, such subtleties of the spirit are usually lost to my perception. Until a few months ago my feet were planted square on the ground, no ghosts—or vampires—need apply to the world I knew.

That was the past, though, and this night world was crowded with far more things than I needed or wanted to know about. There wasn't much I could do to fix it back, either. The door had opened wide, and I'd been shoved right through, and like it or not would just have to get used to what I found there.

I stood for a long time with my back to one of the tall black trunks, listening to the forest. The heaviness in my heart lingered as I remembered other places where I'd taken watch in the late hours. This one reminded me sharply of the rare tough time Art and I had of it in Siberia being tracked by wolves. The pack had been so starved they'd not bothered wasting effort on howling themselves up for a hunt. I'd have preferred their noise, for then we'd have known where they were. Art had looked on the whole business as grim sport, keeping us morbidly cheered with a number of bad jokes mostly to do with welfare of the wolves. He maintained we had to keep moving to spare them from the indigestion they'd suffer should they eat us.

Where was he now? Back in England, probably, having brandy and a cigar at Ring or one of his clubs. He'd lift his glass in a toast to me. So much had happened to him, so many deaths in so short a time:

his much-loved father, dear Lucy . . . and myself. I hoped John Seward would stay with him. A man might not speak of his grief, but having a good friend around was often solace enough in bad times.

During these musings I became aware of a tantalizing scent on the air. It was not constant because I wasn't consciously breathing. Only when speaking or by the normal motion of my body did my lungs get exercise. Now that my attention was snagged, I tried to focus on the source. After a moment I had a general direction and identified the smell. My curiosity up, I began walking toward it.

After a quarter mile I got to thinking I'd made a mistake. For me to pick up such a trail like a hunting dog and track it so far seemed ludicrous, but as it was apparently true, my senses were far sharper than I'd estimated or imagined. That, or my nose was just highly responsive to one special scent in particular.

Bloodsmell, Dracula had called it, and so it turned out to be.

Lying in the middle of a wide patch of churned-up snow I found the carcass of a gray she-wolf. No other predators had gotten to it yet, so it was complete except for the tail having been lopped off. A trophy for the hunter. There was a hole in its chest that had gone clean through the beast, as I learned when I turned it over. There was quite a lot of blood on the snow, still very red and fresh-looking. That's what traveled on the wind to tantalize me, bringing me to the kill like a hungry buzzard. My corner teeth began to lengthen despite the fact I had no intention of touching the pitiful creature.

To get my mind off my belly, I made a long study of the area. There were wolf tracks aplenty here, a fairly large pack on the move. I also picked out two sets of men's boot prints in the snow superimposed over the wolves' tracks. One was unfamiliar, but the other belonged to my host. I'd spent enough time in his company to know his sign very well indeed.

So far as I could read things, the hunter had bagged his prize no more than two hours ago, approaching from the west. His shot and kill must have scared the pack, for their prints tore off to the east through the trees. He'd used a very sharp blade to take the tail, wiping it clean of blood on the wolf's coat. That done, he walked away, following them east. The prints Dracula left were on top of the rest and so recent the edges were still sharp. He'd just come through and also traveled east, but only for a few hundred yards when his boot tracks completely stopped. That flummoxed me for a bit until I found a fresh set of wolf prints larger than any of the rest. He'd swapped two legs for four, probably for better speed.

What his intention was toward the hunter I didn't want to think about. He was mighty fond of his wolves, and to hear him talk he had more regard for them than anyone or anything else. He would take this worse than bad, I was thinking, and I could understand him, too. To just shoot an animal down and take a mere trophy was wasteful to me. Where I'd been raised, we'd have skinned the body for the pelt and eaten the meat so as to get full use of it, especially during the winter when it was most needed. But I had the feeling Dracula would take grim exception to that as well.

I pressed forward, at times wishing I could turn into a wolf as well. Vanishing would have been convenient, but I needed to keep my eyes on the trail. A good thing it was, too, for the hunter's prints suddenly veered off to the north, and I might have missed them and the single set of wolf prints following. When both reached open ground the boot prints continued, but the wolf's ended. He'd not turned back, so he must have changed to mist or a bat so he wouldn't be seen by his quarry. I kept going, half in the expectation of finding the hunter's carcass next, lying dead and drained in the path. If so, then it might decide me about what to do concerning the life or death of Dracula.

The trail entered another stand of trees, and began slanting toward the east again. The hunter must have guessed the pack would turn at some point and thought to get in front of them and downwind. It was madness to hunt at night, but not impossible, for the moonlight was strong. The wolves would show up well enough against the snow for a good marksman to pick off one or two if he had a sharp eye. I ran through the trees, but made myself pause before crossing the next open field. The sky was empty of bats or cloudy swirls, but Dracula could be anywhere.

Then one of the shadows a good distance ahead of me unexpectedly shifted. Even with my improved night sight I discerned no detail. I'd have missed it completely if it hadn't moved against the wind just when my gaze fell on the right spot.

After a few moments I decided it was my hunter, and I was mighty interested in learning who he could be and why he chose such a strange hour to be out and about. My thought that he was trying to preserve the sheep population did not seem quite right. None of the locals, even the Szgany, ever came out after sunset. Generations of fear of the castle lord had been bred into them, along with a much more ancient fear of hungry wolves. What the man was doing slogging around in the snow this late for trophies I could not guess, but he was tempting fate in a bad way and would need to be warned away quick.

To get closer without being seen, I vanished and flowed swiftly over the snow for several minutes. It was not unpleasant, for I'd made myself get used to the change of sensation this form imparted. I was aware of shapes and slopes, and could hear to a limited degree, but was quite blind. This was less alarming than it might have been, for when like this I had no need to fear crashing into anything and causing injury to myself; I either coursed around or went through it.

I resumed solidity and got my bearings. The wind had affected my path, pushing me farther east than I'd wanted, but I was considerably closer and could see much better, spying my man again. He continued forward, his movements slow and cautious, his posture distinct and recognizable; he was stalking something. I watched to see what held his attention, and in the far distance saw yet more movement. Several dark forms showed themselves against the snow: wolves.

He reached a satisfactory spot where a thick branch came down low enough for him to rest his gun muzzle. He was less interested in sport than in bettering his chances to make a kill with careful aim. His figure went quite still, and I knew he'd be trying to match his sights up with his target, getting one to mesh with the other, and in between one heartbeat and the next he'd pull the trigger.

This did not happen, though.

After he settled in—and it was obvious his entire being was consumed by making his shot—a blur of black and white erupted from the snow just in front of him. It took a full second before I realized what it was and his awful danger. The great dark form of a wolf burst from where it had been hiding under a drift and leaped up at him, knocking him flat. His gun went off, the shot going wild. My belly turned over as I recognized the distinct sound of its flat crack in the emptiness.

That clinched everything. With a shout I pelted toward them as fast as I could.

The wolf, which I assumed was Dracula, since I'd never heard of wolves burying themselves in snow banks to wait for prey, paused its attack and looked right at me. I wasn't close enough to hear his growl, but saw a flash of white teeth against the black muzzle. He wasn't pleased by my interference. The man he loomed over twisted quick to face his danger. He still clutched his rifle and started to bring it around. The wolf went for it, strong jaws clamping down. I heard a thin cry as the gun was dragged from his fingers. The great wolf then seized his arm, held tight, and easily hauled him several yards over the ground like a child might drag a cloth doll. The man fought. His terror and rage combined and compressed themselves into a appalling shriek that tore right up my spine so hard I damn-near pitched headlong off my feet in my haste to reach him. The last time I'd heard a screech like that had been in India when a man-eating tiger had taken a pilgrim from the road not ten yards in front of me.

I doubled my speed and shouted again. The wolf broke off and started directly toward me, confirming his identity. A true wolf would have fled.

The man stopped his noise as soon as he was released. He yet moved, but was feeble about it.

At a run far faster than I could ever achieve on two legs, the black wolf pelted toward me and blocked my path, head lowered, fangs bared, and rumbling a deep growl of warning.

"I have to see if he's all right," I said, not feeling a bit foolish for addressing the animal. I knew he understood me.

He only growled, advancing slowly. By God, even knowing that this creature was my host in a different skin, I couldn't get past the fact he was a scarifying sight. I backed away a step before catching myself.

"Let me go to him," I insisted.

Another growl, but this time accompanied by a completely unexpected gesture. He shook his head, not as a dog, but as a man would, deliberately from side to side. The message was clear: if I took another step I'd be the one he'd tangle with next.

"I can't let you kill him and that's flat. Sir."

The growl ended, and damn me if I couldn't almost see Dracula's own lowered-brow expression on this thing's lupine face. He bounded forward and butted his body hard against me, forcing me back. He wanted us out of there, and since he was leaving his quarry be, I decided to agree to a retreat. I threw a last glance at the man, who was just starting to sit up and look our way, then hurried into the thick of the trees with the wolf at my heels. Hopefully, the hunter would miss seeing us in their stark gloom.

Once we were well into forest shelter, the wolf paused and made its change back into man-form again. As a human, he looked no less ferocious. Harker had once vividly described one of Dracula's rages; I could see now he'd made something of an understatement.

"You overstep yourself," Dracula whispered, his lips hardly moving, but the soft sound cut like a saw. He quivered all over as though barely holding himself back from tearing me apart.

"I could not let you kill him."

"Nor could I let him kill. Nor shall I allow him to do so again. *You* shall *not* interfere."

"I'll do whatever is necessary."

He made a half step toward me, fists raised, and I braced for whatever was to come. He held himself in check at the last instant, but it must have been taken a lot of effort. I could feel the heat of his anger washing over me. We glared at each other for I don't know how long, until my head began to ache from the strain of meeting his eye. He took another step forward, but as he did his body shimmered darkly and faded. The countless specks that took its place swarmed all around me, seemed to flow right *through* me. My very bones seemed to turn to ice as its touch brushed them. . . . Then it was gone.

I whirled and caught a passing glimpse of his

shapeless progress over the snow, like the shadow of a shadow. It moved quickly and with purpose, not in the direction of the fallen hunter, I noted with relief, but back the way I'd come.

A few seconds later the wind abruptly rose with a raging force that I'd only known standing on the castle tower. It clawed at me and sent dry surface snow skittering up in tiny cyclones. More snow came loose from the trees and rained down, creating an instant storm. I ignored it and walked to the edge of the stand so I could see how the man was doing.

He was trying to find his feet again and looking all about. His left arm hung straight at his side; he had to hold the rifle one-handed. I'd recognized the sound it made firing aright; it was a Winchester, one of the several I'd brought for our late expedition. I also belatedly recognized the man holding it: Lord Godalming—or as I knew him—Art Holmwood, and what the hell he was *still* doing traipsing around in Transylvania in the dead of winter was the devil's own guess.

Chapter Four

The last, the absolute *last* thing I expected in all the world was for my friend to be anywhere near. Certainly if our places were reversed I'd have departed this unfriendly land as soon as possible for home once the hunt for Dracula was finished.

Then it struck me that for Art, the hunt was not at all finished. I watched him from the shadows, my jaw all but scraping the ground as I realized *why* he'd remained behind. Though this proof of the depth of his friendship raised a lump in my throat fit to choke a horse, at the same time I was furious at him for taking such a risk. Dear God, but he had no idea what he was tempting—Dracula's limitless wrath.

And where had *he* gotten to? I glanced around, but saw no sign of him. That meant nothing, though.

He could be anywhere, including right next to my friend.

Poor battered Art finally struggled to his feet, holding his left arm close. From my vantage I could discern little more than that, though it was reassuring. If he could stand he was probably all right. We'd been in some tight spots in our time, and he was tough enough when he had to be.

He carefully scrutinized the surrounding forest, probably on guard for more wolfish ambushes. None jumped out at him. He followed the four-footed trail Dracula had left, but only a few paces before giving up and trudging back again, missing my tracks. Apparently he'd had ample excitement for one night. When he was well within the trees, I vanished, speeding noiselessly over the open ground after him.

A damned convenient way to travel this was, leaving no mark. Art was nearly as good at scout work as I, and for his sake I wanted no evidence of my presence around. I'd not forgotten Dracula's deadly intention toward his former hunters should his survival be discovered. I would have to keep my promise to him and remain dead to them as well.

This could go remarkably bad if I was not careful.

Sensing the bulk of a large tree in my path, I drifted close to use its cover, then materialized for a quick look.

Art was some twenty yards ahead, moving slowly.

Now I made myself like the second image on one of those double photographs. Even as I faded, the forest faded to me. I was faint enough to see through, yet could use my eyes, though it was like trying to peer through thick fog. The darkness hid what showed of me to normal human vision, leaving me nearly invisible, and I still had the advantage of leaving no prints in the snow. Thus did I follow him, drifting wraithlike just above the ground.

His was a dark gray figure against a gray background.

With all the tree trunks in the way I had to keep the space between us short lest I lose him and hurried, slowing when only ten yards off. To improve my vision I allowed myself to become just a bit more solid. Now was I able to see he was on a faint path, fighting against the rising wind.

It was becoming quite a nuisance. Little seemed to affect me in this form, except the force of a strong breeze. I had to struggle to maintain my course, yet keep far enough back to avoid Art discovering my presence. If he did, it would mean his certain death, but I wasn't sure my caution would make any difference. His shooting of the wolf had set Dracula off like ten kegs of gunpowder. I'd read in history books about how some old kings were so selfish of their range they'd kill anyone else who trespassed looking for venison. Maybe Dracula held the same views, though it did not seem likely. He had no use for deer meat. Besides, Art hadn't been after . . .

Uh-oh.

So *that* was why Dracula had taken it so badly. God knows I'd feel the same if some hunter got it into his head to use my ranch dogs for target practice. It was probably worse for Dracula considering how close he was to the pack that roamed this part of country. No wonder he'd been ready to rip Art's arm off.

He still could.

Art had slowed considerably. It was hard to tell whether his obvious weariness was from the hurt he'd taken, the press of the wind, or pure exhaustion. Bad going for him were it all three. I debated intruding myself. In my beard, borrowed coat, and with the hat pulled low I could pass for one of the Szgany in the dark. If need be I could approach and by gestures offer help. But Art knew me too well; there was a good chance he'd recognize me, which would seriously complicate things for us both. Yet I might have to try if he didn't find shelter soon. The storm was limbering up. Snow fairly rained down on us, thick, sticky flakes to blur one's sight and confuse direction. I hoped he knew where he was headed.

Then my problem happily solved itself when I spied a second figure, not quite as tall as Art and a bit more sturdy in frame, emerging from the grayness ahead. With a joyful shock I realized it was Jack Seward. Of course, he'd stayed as well, not being one to leave a friend to fend for himself in the wild. He lifted his arm and hailed loudly, and for an unpleasant instant I feared he'd seen me, but his greeting was meant for Art.

Art continued to trudge on, either not hearing, or too tired to respond. Jack got close enough to startle him from his stupor. I let myself go completely solid and peered at them from behind a tree.

"Arthur, what in heaven's name do you think you're doing out here?" Jack demanded, his tone expressive, balanced between angry exasperation and heartfelt relief—something I myself felt for them both.

Art mumbled something I didn't catch and indicated his injured arm.

"A wolf? Good God! How bad?"

More mumbling.

"I can't do anything about it in this murk. Come along so I can see to this and get some brandy into you, you're half frozen." He took the Winchester in one hand and threw his arm about Art, leading him back along the path. "Sweet heavens, what were you thinking going out at this hour?"

I heard Art's voice, but still could not distinguish the words.

Jack responded. "If you couldn't sleep, then you should have told me. I'd have given you something for it. Running about like this at night is suicidal. No, it's nothing to do with meeting vampires. You could have fallen into a crevasse or gotten lost or worse, you great blockhead. And look at you now, you're all in. If I hadn't heard your shot and come running . . . "

His words were harsh, but delivered as the sort of scolding an affectionate nurse might bestow on a mildly wayward child. The doctor in Jack could be fussy at times, but had never been so toward Art. There'd never before been a need.

Resuming wraith-form again, I tagged along until their track ended at a small windowless structure that must have served as a shepherd's hut in the summer. Smoke drifted up from its stone chimney, and firelight leaked from cracks and chinks in its crudely constructed walls. As a shelter, it looked only slightly better than being outdoors. Three horses were tethered on its lee side, heads hanging low, all looking miserable in the increasing cold.

Jack got Art in the hut, and I went solid, pressing close to one of the larger chinks for a look within. It was as primitive as could be expected, being a single bare room. The only beds were their sleeping rolls, the only comforts the supplies they'd brought and the blaze in the small fireplace. The sight of my two dearest friends settling in brought sharply back the memory of a hundred other nights when we three had made camp in similar rough places. Their being here gladdened my heart beyond measure, at the same time tearing it in two, for I longed to join them, to let them know I was all right.

Impossible, of course.

Jack got Arthur's coat off for a look at the injured arm, but the span of my view within was limited, and I could not hear them so well with the wind playing up. Chewing my lip for a second to think it through, I decided to take the chance. I vanished, located the chink, and flowed inside.

What a relief not to have to fight to hold myself in

one place. Until I was out of the wind I'd not appreciated how strong it had gotten. They were not the only ones needing shelter. I felt my sightless way to a far corner by the ceiling, held there, and listened. My need to hear their voices far overwhelmed any shred of caution left to me. I had to find out if Art was all right. After a moment, I (figuratively) breathed a sigh of relief.

"Nothing broken, just a bad bruising," Jack pronounced. "You can thank God for the thickness of your coat sleeve, for that's the only thing torn. If he'd bitten though . . . well, you need not worry about rabies, my foolish friend."

"Rabies?" Art queried in a rather flat voice. He sounded used up and little wonder.

"Indeed. No normal wild animal would attack a man, so it may well have been mad. There's a course of treatment for hydrophobia, but it's not at all pleasant, so thank God again that you've been spared."

"I do, but what if it had been one of those damned vampires? They can change themselves to wolves, can't they? So—"

"The professor said they were all destroyed, and we've no reason to believe otherwise. He told me he went through every room of the castle and sterilized it. Except for you shooting everything in the countryside, all has been perfectly quiet since, has it not? Here, have a sip of this and steady yourself. You're in sore need of rest."

Arthur was quiet for sufficient time to have a drink. When he spoke again, he sounded stronger. "I bagged another one of the brutes, at least," he announced. "Here's a fresh tail for our collection."

"A round half dozen, then. Excellent."

"It's a start."

"So you've been saying."

"I warned you. I said I'd not stop until the whole cursed pack was dead, even if it took all winter."

"As well it might. I hardly need point out to you that this is the first sighting you've had of any quarry for some time now."

"They're not stupid animals, Jack. Even if they aren't one of those damned monsters in disguise they've more intelligence than you give them credit for. That's the other reason why I went out at night."

"Meaning they were purposely hiding from us during the day?" Jack sounded skeptical.

"Yes! If you'd done more hunting you'd see it, too."

"What you see as cleverness probably has more to do with instinct than intellect. They know there's another predator in the area and are avoiding you."

"I tell you they understand more than they should. It's not natural. There's something about them, about this whole country that's not right, else we'd have found some sign of poor Quincey by now, but there's been nothing. Not one bone, not even a scrap of clothing."

"There's been plenty of snowfalls since that night. He's probably long covered."

"God, if only I'd stayed awake. To think of him lying abandoned and graveless—"

"Then don't. My comfort is thinking some peasant found him—or will find him—and do the decent thing. This place is so backward, we may never hear of it, but it *will* happen."

Art made a sort of refined snort, indication that he had little confidence in such chance. "Damned wolves. The one that attacked me was lying in wait. He'd buried himself in a drift of snow and—"

"*What?*"

Arthur found it necessary to provide full details of what had befallen him. Despite such earnestness, Dr. Jack Seward was reluctant to come around.

"You see it one way, I another," he said after some little discussion over the behavior of the wolf. "Did it not occur to you that the beast might have curled up under the snow to keep warm and you stepped on it while it slept?"

"That's not what happened! If I'd merely trod on it I should have known. I'm telling you the bloody thing *waited* and then came right up at me!"

"But it broke off and ran, which is what one might expect of an animal."

"No—there was something else as well. I heard a man shouting at the same time. Only when he yelled did the thing stop its attack."

"You're sure? You heard someone? Who?"

Art groaned. "That's the madness of it. My God, Jack, it was *Quincey!*"

Silence. For quite a long moment.

"You don't believe me?" Art demanded.

"I believe you heard a man shouting. But it had to be a peasant or some passing Gypsy."

"Shouting in *English*?"

"Really, Arthur!"

"Yes, really! I swear it. I can still hear his voice, and it was Quincey bellowing away in that unfortunate Texan accent of his."

"Arthur . . ."

"*What?* I'm not one of your pet lunatics, so don't give me that look."

"My dear fellow, I apologize for the look, but you can hardly blame me for it. Just listen to yourself."

A heavy sigh. "I know what I must sound like but it is the truth, I swear. Believe or not, as you please."

"Look, old man, you've had a nasty physical shock, and you're very tired, and I know for a fact that lack of sleep distorts one's perceptions."

"I'm not inventing this. I heard Quincey."

"And it could have been wishful thinking."

"Pah!"

Some moments went by, then: "Art, I miss him, too," Jack said in a much-subdued tone.

I gave a groan myself, silent, of course. It took all my resolve not to materialize right then and there before them in a foolish attempt to cure their grief and my own as well.

"Shall we have a drink to him?" suggested Art, his own tone much quieter now.

"Yes. Absolutely."

They made a simple toast to me, which I found powerfully affecting for its very restraint. With them being British and all, the less spoken the greater the meaning. Though nothing had been settled between them about what Art had heard, they'd found something to agree on and would hopefully leave it at that.

Jack the physican was still one for practicality, though. "You were very lucky tonight on many things, but I must insist you not repeat this hunting after dark ever again," he said.

"I'm no child."

"But you are being infernally discourteous. When that shot woke me and I saw you'd gone, I didn't know what to think and hardly dared to try. I can understand you being restless, but please have the decency to inform me of your intent and spare me undue worry."

"There's nothing hereabouts to cause concern—or so you insist."

"Nothing out of the ordinary, I'm sure, but mad wolves aside, those Szgany villains are doubtless still in the area and might harbor objections to our presence. After the fight we gave them I rather think they'd want to pay us back."

"Humph. They're the ones who owe us after what they did to poor Quincey. They're probably far away from here because of it. Believe me, were I to catch sight of any one of those murdering swine I'd serve him the same as I did this wolf."

"You don't mean that," said Jack, sounding shocked. Art fell silent, giving me to understand that he did mean it. While deeply moved by this declaration I was also quite appalled. Not for the world would I want my friend to have the deaths of others on his conscience resulting from his intent to avenge my demise. Something would have to be done, but I had no idea what.

"Let's get some sleep, Arthur—"

"And things will look different in the morning?"

"I should hope so."

"Nothing will change for me."

"No, but after some rest we'll both feel improved. Trust me, I am well trained on this."

"Yes, from those lunatics under your care. Were that true, then a bit of sleep would fix them up nicely and you'd lose your position."

"You're being unkind, which I forgive because the mangling you got has put you in a temper. In any case, I should be delighted if all my patients woke up restored. It would make my reputation in the field and be worth the loss of custom."

"Certainly there's no end of mad people in the world," Art grumbled. "I'm sure your asylum would fill itself again in no time."

This comment made Jack chuckle. "To sleep with you. I'll build the fire up. Damn me, but I think it's gotten colder."

"It *is* colder. Hear how the wind howls. Like those damned wolves."

I listened as best I could, then slipped outside and made myself solid again to hear better. My fears were thankfully for naught, for it was indeed only the wind and not wolves behind all the noise. The idea that Dracula had rounded up his pack to make some kind of assault on my friends had stabbed through my mind, but the absurdity of the notion soon asserted itself. He had no need to resort to anything like that so long as this storm continued to build.

The snow fell so thickly I could see no farther than a dozen feet. The wind drove it hard into my eyes and soon my face was coated white, forcing me to constantly brush it clean. I'd survived blizzards in my time, but this one promised to be worse than anything even Siberia had thrown at me. Van Helsing once said Dracula could command the weather, and I had the growing conviction that my missing host was behind this particular event.

If so, then Jack and Arthur stood little chance of surviving without help.

As they seemed to be all right for the present I made my way back to the castle, first following the fading tracks of my friends, then soon picking up my own. By the time I reached the point where I'd found the wolf's carcass nearly every trace was obliterated by snow, but from here I knew what direction to take to return.

It was something of a startlement, though, to discover the carcass was quite gone.

One set of faint tracks—of the two-legged variety—led away from the spot. I guessed that Dracula had retrieved the body, for what purpose I could hardly conjecture. A talk with him about this night's events was necessary; I might ask him then. The prospect of a showdown held no appeal for I knew he'd still be furious, but there was little point to postponement. I trudged in his wake, hoping to reach his destination before fresh snow filled in all trace of his passing. He'd headed straight back to the castle, but veered around its rocky base in a direction I'd not gone before.

This new path finally led to a very narrow opening, easily missed if one were not aware of it—or close on the trail of another who was familiar with the area. A vertical slab of rough stone, looking to be a normal part of the mountain, thrust out at a shallow angle in such a way as to appear to be haphazard rubble fallen from above. His tracks went right instead of left, bending toward the base rather than going around the outer side along the path. The stone acted as a massive shield to what appeared to be a natural cleft no more than a few feet deep and of no particular interest. I knew better than to trust such semblances around a structure of this age. Its ancient builders would have left nothing overlooked in the design of this fortress, and I pressed through, gratified to find I was correct in my suspicions. A sharp turn into a forbidding shadow revealed a narrow doorway and tunnel driving up into the mountain.

It might have once served as a secret escape route during a siege. The cramped passage zigged and zagged as it climbed, cutting off all outside light. I had no liking for blundering about in the dark and resorted to partially vanishing to spare my toes and shins. Feeling my way forward in this manner was only slightly less nerve-wracking. The familiar gray that my eyes could yet perceive in this form was now a profound and unrelieved black and so disorienting that I traveled close to the ground lest I lose all sense of what was up or down.

Again was I reminded of swimming in a murky pool, though I hadn't much experience at that since deep bodies of water of any kind are unknown in the part of Texas where I was raised. A trip to Galveston in my youth had given my pa the opportunity to provide me with that quick, unforgettable swimming lesson, but the green ocean was bright as a ballroom compared to this.

It occurred to me that it would be better to retrace my route and wait in the library for my host's return. Dracula might be as determined to speak with me as I with him. On the other hand, I had no way of knowing when he would turn up or whether he was finished with my friends for the night. If he took it into his head to seek them out again, then I was their only protection.

For what it was worth.

I could guard them after dark, but during the day . . .

They would still have their crucifixes with them, of that I was sure. As we'd all had ample proof of their effect against the Un-Dead—or at least Dracula's particular breed of Un-Dead—Art and Jack would hold fast to such defenses, even if the danger seemed past. For all they'd been through it would likely be a habit they'd retain for the rest of their lives; such would have been my intent had I not been so abruptly cut from the herd by a Szgany knife.

Of course, if he did not go himself, Dracula had servants who could ignore the cross to carry out their master's orders. Perhaps they were not armed with modern Winchesters, but a few had long rifles that were just as deadly given the right circumstances. But those were hardly necessary. One man sneaking up on the hut with a burning brand could set the poor structure afire in mere seconds.

With that terrible thought I decided I had entirely too much imagination and it was downright gruesome. Maybe the atmosphere of this place had gotten to me after all. No matter, I would speak to Dracula before the night was finished and try to head off further trouble.

The tunnel gradually leveled and widened, so I paused, allowing myself to become solid again. All was as black as before; I concentrated on listening. Naught came to me but a faint unidentifiable noise that might have been some trick of the wind except for the air being wholly still. I sniffed and determined that it was quite stale, being musty from bat droppings and the stench of old rot, indication that I was close to the tombs if not there already. I recognized it instantly from my initial visit that first waking night; it is not the sort of fetor one forgets.

Again, that faint sound came to me, like the catching of a breath. It lay ahead somewhere . . . in that unknown darkness.

Though part of the dread ranks of the Un-Dead I felt an awful chill settling over my whole being that had nothing to do with winter weather. This was the kind of basic fear that few ever really leave behind with their childhood. For me it was like my sunset wakings in that tower room, only a hundred times worse. There I knew where light might be found and should that fail I could always rush to open the door and seek escape from my inner terrors that way.

No such luxury here. I was in unrelieved blackness surrounded by the dead, the true dead. Little matter they were all gone to dust, their *essence* remained behind. Harker had sensed them, and now it was my turn.

My body, giving in to unvoiced desires, vanished away. I took foolish comfort for a few moments, before wondering if I might not now be even more vulnerable to whatever lay invisible about me. If I could float about like a wraith, could not a *real* ghost be able to . . .

To what? I finally asked myself in a surprisingly steady inner voice.

No answer presented itself, indication that I'd finally reached the limit of my idiocy.

I was in a dark tunnel, nothing more, and just because vampires existed was no reason to think the same was true for ghosts. And before my fear could make any argument against that point, I pressed forward.

My hearing was muffled, so if the sound repeated I did not notice. The way ahead occasionally rose, but remained more or less straight. Once I encountered a second opening to the left and farther down another to the right, but ignored them for the main path. After awhile I worked up sufficient courage to go solid again.

It was better this time. I perceived some extremely welcome light. The glow was far away and very faint, being a mere reflection off a turn in the walls ahead. As an ordinary man I'd have missed it. Now I rushed forward, eager as a dying sinner about to grasp unexpected salvation.

That is, I rushed for all of two steps before my shins caught against something hard and nearly sent me flying head over heels. A rock or a sarcophagus, it mattered not, and I didn't care to know, anyway. Before coming to grief I vanished once more and was spared a hard, noisy landing. When I stopped tumbling about, I gradually solidified to the point where I could see the light again and drifted toward it at a more dignified pace and in a much safer form.

It grew brighter with each turn until I knew one more would put me upon its source, so I slowed, curious as to what lay ahead, but not averse to caution. Going solid only at the last, I peered around the final corner and beheld that the tunnel opened into a proper chamber, very wide and long and low of ceiling. Stone columns supported the roof and were thick enough to hold up the whole of the castle above. The floor had been more or less leveled and smoothed, but was cluttered with many different kinds of funerary boxes, some of wood and rotted away, the pitiful bones within visible, other boxes of stone, both broken and whole. This was obviously another part of Dracula's family vault, and it had been well-filled over the centuries.

The death stench was thick enough to cut; I was glad of having no need to breathe.

A single candle that made more shadow than light rested on the end of a stone sarcophagus. Seated on the other end was Dracula. He was turned away from me and huddled over something in his lap. I couldn't make it out for a moment, then with a shock realized he held the body of the dead wolf—not merely held, but cradled it, gently, as a mother might enfold her sick child in her arms.

Then did I hear that strange sound again. It came in conjunction with a shudder that seized Dracula's whole body. The back hairs rose along my neck. I could scarce believe what I saw and heard, but it was unmistakable: this great master of the Un-Dead was entirely caught up in the throes of a profound grief.

He did not weep openly, but rather seemed to smother it within himself until it overtopped his control. Only then did his sorrow find release in a long-drawn keen of pain. He rocked back and forth, sometimes lifting his face high, sometimes burying it in the matted fur of the wolf.

How long I stood agape and stared I could not say, so great was my surprise, but eventually I woke from the astonishment and determined to quietly remove myself. Anything else would be an unthinkable intrusion. Our talk could wait.

I went nearly transparent and started to drift backwards, but my intent was headed off by the sudden appearance of his wolves coming up behind me. They'd made their way unerringly through the darkness, probably in response to some inner call he'd sent out. Dozens of them blocked the tunnel, their great eyes catching the feeble candlelight and throwing back green sparks. They were aware of me but paid little mind, simply rushing past to get to the chamber. Maybe Art was right and they were more intelligent than others of their kind.

Why are they here?

Again, to answer my curiosity, I had to risk resuming solid form—for holding a semi-transparent state was fatiguing—and waited several moments for things to resolve.

The animals milled about, whining. Ears flat and tails tucked under, they sniffed and licked at their fallen pack member, which Dracula yet held close. They swarmed around him when he finally stood. He stooped and gently laid the body into the open sarcophagus.

For some time he gazed down in silence, his stillness of manner spreading to the pack, to his children of the night. A few restlessly paced, but most sat gathered about him, watching his every move, waiting.

The transformation was swift and noiseless: one moment he was a tall man dressed in black, the next, a huge black wolf. This time I noticed that the fur on his muzzle was pure white, such as you might see on a very aged dog.

He roamed among the others, and they, with soft whines and tucked tails, greeted him. His movements were very like to theirs, but with my eye sharpened on what to look for I noticed subtleties marking him as being different from the rest. Where an ordinary animal might wander randomly, he was most deliberate, bestowing specific time and attention upon each of them turn-on-turn. Some he quickly nuzzled, others received lengthier, more elaborate welcomes. Throughout, there was from him an attitude of what I could only perceive as a sort of tender affection.

Caught up as I was in this strange spectacle, an errant thought began nagging me just then. It teased at the edge of my mind, and however dangerous it might prove to remain here I knew I must do so for the idea to come forth.

The wolves made a rough circle around the sarcophagus. Dracula sat in their midst and lifted his head high. From him came a full throated howl that turned my spine to ice. I winced, trembling head-to-toe, unable to help myself. The awful lament reverberated through the crypt, eerie beyond belief; I could scarce hold in place. My instinct was to turn and flee, but I fought it, needing to see more, to learn more. There was something important here I should *know*.

The truly terrifying part was how close this sound was to his earlier keening. Much louder, much more free in its expression of sorrow, but bizarrely similar. The others joined in his song of grief, their many voices rising and falling, interweaving, growing until the very walls seemed to shake from the clamor.

But this, all this for one dead wolf?

Not just one, though; there were six of them. Rites would doubtless follow for the rest when their bodies were found. The survivors would gather here with Dracula and mourn the loss, cleaving the dank air with their heartbreaking wails.

Never in my life had I ever experienced such a hellish chorus, yet it nearly made me weep to hear it. I'd stood strong at many a graveside service and held my peace, but this one was different. A man may go to his death with some understanding of the why of it, but not so for an animal. Within them lived a kind of sublime purity. That was what affected me so deeply now, their absolute innocence over matters that often troubled humans for the whole of their time on earth. The poor dumb brutes meet death knowing nothing of meanings and wherefores. But were things different and their perceptions raised, would they be any better off?

Perhaps this was why I'd stayed to watch, for seeing it all in this way was new to me. I lingered a little longer, testing the notion, then dismissed it. There was some other reason nagging me, if I could but grasp it.

The dirge continued, setting my teeth on edge. A mad desire seized me to join in their song. I pushed it away.

Dracula was no longer a participant. He threaded his way throughout their circle again, making contact with each, but finally stopping with a tightly gathered group of three. They were also black of coat and larger than the others, and though obviously very much of this pack there was a certain aloofness to them. The rest had deferred to them much as they did to Dracula. I thought they might be this year's crop of cubs, still benefiting from having been the center of lavish attention from their guardians.

But there was something more . . .

The look of them, their manner. *What* was I seeing?

Then all three stared right at me, their eyes flashing green. They stared . . . and I felt my legs go to jelly. Were my heart not already stilled forever it would have stopped in that instant as the realization struck home.

My God . . . they really ARE *his children!*

Chapter Five

Snow coated my shoulders and caked the thick muffler I'd wrapped snug around my head and hat, nearly blocking my sight. I brushed impatiently at it and pressed on against the wind. I kept moving steadily despite the drifts, not daring to go invisible yet lest the strength of the gale sweep me back to the castle. The storm was easier to fight in solid form, taking less out of me. When I got to the shepherd's hut I might need all my reserves for whatever I found there.

A whole inactive day had passed since I'd last seen my friends.

Anything could have happened to them.

I carried along such small items that they might need for survival: a dry box of Vespas, a flask containing the local plum brandy, and a freshly killed rabbit I'd acquired from the castle cook. How I might introduce these to my friends without revealing myself I did not know, but it seemed best to be prepared.

If they still lived.

For my own aid I had a compass and consulted it frequently to hold my direction straight. The hut lay exactly west of the castle, easy enough to find in good weather, but a needle in a haystack in this storm. A few yards left or right and I could completely miss it.

Once released from my daylight stupor, I'd hurriedly departed the castle without seeing my host. After last night's extraordinary revelation I did not feel up to talking with him yet. I'd stumbled across something that was doubtless extremely private that gave me much to think over.

Maybe far too much for my sanity.

That Dracula had bred with the wolves had shocked me to the core, but reason told me that it was not my place to make judgments. Though he had once been a man in centuries past and still retained a man's form and manner of thought he was yet something altogether different. He'd already stated that he'd given a part of himself—his soul, I would guess—to obtain powers beyond the mortal. The rules were different for him; I must never forget that.

The method of it I did not dwell on, but the why had me puzzled and full of furious speculation. How could he be fertile with wolves, yet not indulge in the equivalent of the same activity with a woman? He'd said that the sharing of blood with them was the only expression of love left to him, and I'd no reason to doubt his statement. But perhaps as a wolf he was able to embrace the fullness of living again, in all its aspects. That gave me a wry smile. I suppose if that was the only other outlet left to him, then of course he would take it.

As for his progeny . . . well, that would account for

their unnatural intelligence. It might also be the explanation for all those old legends about werewolves. If Dracula could make himself into a wolf, could they in turn become men? My mind reeled with the implications, but in my heart I knew these were questions I could never voice to him. Had he wanted me to know he'd have told me by now. I'd encroached enough.

At least now I understood why his grief for the dead she-wolf had been so great.

The cold wind drew false tears from my eyes which froze on my face under the muffler. I rubbed them away and tried to get my bearings. I'd found a clearing that seemed familiar, but no sign of a path. The snow covered all and changed all and continued to do so with every icy blast. Drifts filled in valleys and leveled hills. If I found Jack and Art in this it would be due more to luck than my skill as a woodsman.

The hut was not too very distant from the castle, but the hard going lengthened my journey fourfold. I took that into account for my reckoning, and after an hour of travel began to cast about in hope of spotting the structure. I cared nothing about leaving tracks at this point, the snow would cover them fast enough.

After another hour of it I was close to despair and feeling the cold creep into my bones with a vengeance. The changes within could not protect me forever.

I picked out an especially large tree for a landmark, paced fifty feet straight west, and trudged in a broad circle around it. When I found my own trail again, I walked another fifty feet out and made another circle, looking all the time for some sign of the hut.

Twice more I did this before finally stumbling upon it. The snow was piled so high on one side that it was nearly buried to the roof. I'd been looking for the three horses, but they were no longer there. That gave me a leap of hope for a second or two, thinking my friends might have left. Not possible, said the voice of common sense. By all the signs the storm had raged steadily through the day; they would never have been able to depart in it. My guess was they'd brought the horses in with them to add their body warmth to the shelter.

And so it proved when I vanished and sieved inside.

Again, I was grateful for the respite from the endless wind, but it was quite crowded within; I hardly knew where to carry myself to be out of the way. The animals quickly became aware of my presence and began to stir unhappily.

"What is it?" Art called out, his voice high with strain and louder than necessary for such small quarters.

"It's all right, the horses are just restless," Jack calmly replied. "Go back to sleep."

"With that row? I doubt it."

Thank God. They still lived.

"What's gotten into them?" complained Art, peevish.

"Not pleased with the cramped accommodations. A word to the management is in order."

"One good kick will bring the walls down on us."

Jack got up and made hushing noises at the horses while I floated toward the fireplace and hovered next to the ceiling to get away from them. It must have worked; they finally settled down. I kept utterly motionless and in silence rejoiced that all was well, or reasonably close to it.

"God, look at the time," said Art, still in a complaining tone. "I've slept all day."

"You needed it. Besides, we're neither of us going anywhere for awhile."

"Is it still snowing?"

"Yes, unfortunately. In all my life I've never been so bored with the weather. I hope to heaven it blows itself out soon."

"Our supplies—"

"I wasn't going to bring up that sore point, my boy, so don't bother yourself."

"This is my fault."

"The storm? Thank you, I was wondering who to blame."

"It's hardly a joking matter."

"We can do little else. Here, this will put you in a better mood and warm you up."

A pause as Art partook of what I presumed to be a sip from Jack's brandy flask. "We could be days here, you know."

"I know."

"Jack Seward, you can be damned annoying."

"So some of my patients have informed me in one way or another."

"Meaning I'm becoming a lunatic?"

"Well, it would give us both something to do to pass the time."

Art snorted.

"That's better. We've been in worse spots than this before and come out all right. Odds are we'll do it again."

"That, or we're overdue for a comeuppance."

"Are you hungry?"

"I can wait. We might need it later. I was a fool to just take the tails. Should have carved some meat from the last one."

If I'd been capable of such an expression, I'd have given a shudder just then. Knowing what I did now, had Art cut away a haunch of that she-wolf for his supper I had no doubt Dracula would have not let himself be distracted from killing him. He'd have torn Art to ribbons.

"We'll get along without," said Jack.

"I could probably find the body. It's not that far."

"It's on the other side of the world and hidden by drifts. Let it go."

"I've gotten us killed and there you sit—"

"We're not dead yet, Arthur, so hand me the brandy

and light yourself a cigarette. If we're going to die we might as well be civilized about it. Besides, we've still got the horses, so let's not worry about starvation for the time being."

Neither spoke for awhile. I conjectured they were most likely to be staring into the fire as men do when there's nothing else to occupy their attention. This seemed an appropriate moment to take a chance.

Carefully, so very, very carefully, I began to resume form, the barest whisper of form, just enough to allow me to see them. It seemed to take forever to emerge from the grayness. I held myself perfectly still, lest movement draw their eye or disturb the horses.

As gradual as the circuit of a minute hand, the inside of the hut took on shape and substance. I saw light from the fireplace first, then made out the figures of two men seated cross-legged before it directly below me. They were so near I could have reached out a ghostly hand and brushed the crowns of their hats. Once more did I feel a vast ache in my heart for these, my lost friends, so close and so far; yet the temptation to re-enter their lives remained firmly at bay. I was not in such desperate need of their company as to selfishly forget my responsibility toward them, but how I longed for a glimpse of their faces.

Tearing my gaze away, I surveyed the tiny interior. They'd organized everything neatly enough, out of habit and necessity. The horses took up nearly the whole of the room; not much space remained for anything else. I couldn't see what remained in the way of supplies, but noted that their store of firewood wouldn't last through the night. The presence of the animals might keep them from freezing or starving to death, but they would have a damned miserable time of it. If the storm continued on indefinitely—and I had no reason to think it would not, linked as it must be to Dracula's rage— they would surely die.

"I say, Art."

"Eh?"

"If we do get out of this, would you be averse to going home?"

"Home?"

"Yes, back to England, not just to the nearest village for more hardtack."

"But the hunt—"

"See here, I've been patient, but enough is enough. If we survive this, I would like to leave. The others must be worried sick about us with no word after all this time. You wouldn't want to cause Mrs. Harker any undue concern, would you?"

"Of course not, but I intend to finish what I've started."

"And I'm all for that. My suggestion is only that we break it off for now and come back in the spring for the finish."

"The wolves might be gone by then."

"Packs tend to stay in one area. Quincey told me so. Learned it from some red Indian he'd met once."

For the life of me I couldn't recall who Jack might be referring to, then it dawned that he was being less than truthful with Art in order to bring him around. Clever fellow.

"They'll all be here after the spring thaw, and we can pick up the trail then. Maybe hire some local help as guides. The herders here would probably be glad for the culling. It'll be like the old days when you and I and Quincey went tramping about. A more fitting memorial to him than freezing to death. What do you say?"

"You can leave if you like, I want to stay until I've got them all."

"I'm damned before I walk off and leave you on your own in this wasteland."

"I can look after myself."

"Yes, but—"

Art snarled something splenetic, obviously in one of his sulks.

Jack waited a moment, smoking. When he resumed, his manner was as serious and level as I'd ever known before. "Arthur. You know Quincey wouldn't want us to die on his account."

He got a short grunt for that one.

"What do you think he'd say if he knew of this? I'm sure he'd applaud the sentiment, but point out the impracticalities of our present circumstance."

I'd have said something more on the lines of them being crazier than a pair of drunk bedbugs for sticking it out, but Jack had come close enough.

"For the sake of his memory—" he continued.

"All right! I'll concede, but only until the spring."

Art sounded grudging, but I got the impression that his protests had been more about saving face than an unshakable determination to finish out his hunting. He could be stubborn when he wanted, but Jack invoking my name and likely wishes—which were indeed entirely correct—had allowed Art an honorable way to yield to sense.

With much relief, I made myself safely invisible again and went outside. I had to fight to hold in place long enough to materialize, and then the roaring wind was such as to scatter my thoughts as easily as the flying snow. God, but I was tired. I'd been in such a hurry to get away from the castle I'd neglected to feed before leaving. After the activities of the previous night and the strains of this one I was extremely weary, but it was less from hunger so much as a slowing of thought. I had to struggle to focus on my friends' plight.

Dealing directly with them was out of the question. Even muffled as I was and pretending not to understand English I could never pass as a Szgany close up, and returning to the castle to persuade one of the servants to act as my proxy Samaritan was impractical. Odds were he'd be shot for his trouble. I'd have to improvise something else for my friends.

First get them warmth. They could last days without food, but not fire. I cast about the surrounding trees, locating a dead one that would suit. Here did my extra-normal strength come in very handy as I broke off several whole branches, one as thick around as my leg. The wood was wet, but might dry out once inside the hut. I gathered enough to get them comfortably through the night and all the following day. Chopping it up was unnecessary; Jack was in the habit of carrying a hatchet for just such camp work.

I dragged the ungainly load around to the hut's door—only its top half was visible—and tried to arrange the wood to look as though it had been blown there by chance. Beneath the heaviest branch I placed the body of the rabbit. My friends could then give thanks to a thoughtful Providence Who not only sent them fuel, but had conveniently bludgeoned some dinner for them as well. I left behind tracks, but the wind was filling them in.

Hoping they would choose to accept the bounty without question or looking around too much, I grabbed one end of a branch and cracked it smartly against the side of the hut, making plenty of noise, then retreating a short distance upwind to hide behind a tree. With the snow blowing straight in their faces they'd be less likely to spot me.

Very shortly after the sudden commotion the door was pulled open and the both of them stood on the threshold, each holding a gun. Art had a Colt six-shooter I'd given him years back in Texas, and Jack held a Winchester at ready. As one they stared at the wood in disbelief and tried to pierce the darkness for an explanation. With a short, excited cry Art pointed out the dead rabbit.

Perfect. As I vanished and let the wind carry me east they were joyfully breaking off branches and tossing them inside. Even without the extra Vespas and plum brandy they could fend for themselves for the time being. Now it was up to me to see that they had a chance to get away for good.

With the wind tossing me like a tumbleweed, my trip back to the castle was considerably shortened if a bit wild. I concentrated on keeping myself low to the ground lest I be caught up and carried so high as to never come down again. The mad charge ended when I blundered one time too many against yet another tree trunk. Instead of flowing around it, I gave up, went solid, and had a look to see how far I'd come.

The tree turned out to be the rocky base of the castle, and it was just as well for me to stop there. Fifty yards farther and I'd have gone over the edge into that near-bottomless valley. I slogged through the drifts to the courtyard entry and took myself immediately to the stables to refresh my strength, for I was quite dizzy. Whether it was a result of that peculiar mode of travel or lack of nourishment I couldn't say, but a deep drink of a milk-cow's blood soon restored me.

Once inside, I went to the library, but Dracula was not there, nor had any of the kitchen servants seen him. This was not unusual, as they rarely crossed paths with their master if they could help it. Not that he was a cruel man to them; it had less to do with their natural fear of what he was than the fact he was a *boyar* and they his peasants. For all the enlightenment of a modern world, the ancient class barriers still held sway here. Democracy was something out of history that had to do with the long dead Greeks. Amid the expressive shrugs to my simplified question, one of the men paused at lighting his pipe and pointed upward expressively, rattling something off that was beyond my limited vocabulary. I thought I understood, thanked him, and left.

Emerging from the trap door in the high tower I found Dracula standing near the western edge of the roof, arms crossed, brooding over God knows what. Though the air was bitingly cold, there was no wind up here, which struck me as very strange until I reminded myself that the storm was not normal. The proof of this was driven forcefully home when I joined him at the edge. Above us the stars cut the deep blue sky in their bright, stately circle; below, thick dark clouds roiled, tormented by the moaning wind, completely hiding the ground. We stood on a small stony island suspended exactly between chaos and order.

Dracula barely acknowledged my presence and continued to gaze out over the clouds. There was a heaviness of manner about him, as though any movement would be too costly an effort. His hair and long mustache were pure white now, and he bore many more lines on his face than when I'd last seen him. A combination of grief and not feeding, I suspected. It imparted an unexpected humanity to him.

"This is my work," he murmured with a slight lift to his chin to indicate the storm.

"I thought it must be." The scent of fresh snow drifted up to freeze the inside of my throat.

"It seemed a good way to discourage your friends."

That he knew the man he'd attacked had a companion and the identities of both was no surprise. "I'm sorry about the deaths in your pack."

He favored me with a long, steady, and quite expressionless look. "You understand how . . . important they are to me."

"I do." He also apparently knew of my presence in

the crypt the night before, but I wasn't about to explore the subject. "If you sent the wolves far away—"

"That has been done."

"My friends thought they were avenging me, my disappearance. That's why they were hunting."

"So I presumed." There was a cold light in his eyes. "In using my wolves to save you I never thought they would be placed in danger. Though I can accept your friends' desire for revenge, it will stop now."

"I won't allow you to kill them."

Dracula made no reply, only continued to regard me steadily. I dared not look away. Do that with a wolf and he attacks.

"Allow," he said. His eyes narrowed slightly. He seemed . . . amused. And it was not at all reassuring.

I knew how to fight him and win. There were plenty of old but usable weapons scattered about the castle, mementos of past wars. Any one of the pole arms would serve as a stake, and the swords still looked sharp enough to easily remove a man's head. And though he might be nearly invulnerable at night, same as me, my advantage over him was the fact that I could yet hold a cross. Hanging from my neck on a long chain was a silver crucifix I'd worn since the beginning of this hunt. I had prayed much over it, asking again and again for guidance. It lay next to my skin even now, cold on my own chill flesh.

"The ploy with the storm worked," I said. "They're ready to leave."

His stare sharpened.

"I only looked in on them and listened. They never saw me."

He gave a short nod. "Most wise of you."

"Will you let them depart in peace?"

No reply. He turned back to the west, his features dropping into a frown.

"Will you?"

"A moment, Mr. Morris."

Dracula closed his eyes, lifting his head toward the clear sky. He let his arms relax to his sides, but raised his hands to waist level, fingers spread, as though holding an invisible ball close to his body. He held this pose for a very long time before gradually rotating his hands so his palms faced away from his body. Only then did I see he was under some kind of peculiar strain. Every inch of him trembled from it, though his hands were rock steady. There was an oddness about them, or rather the space between them.

It was like looking into a hole and finding another hole on top of it. I couldn't say that I saw anything, but *something* was there—or wasn't there. Maybe the more sensitive Harker would have been able to see what my eyes couldn't pin down. What I knew for certain was that all the hair on my scalp stood on end from whatever it was, and I wanted to put distance between us. I stayed, though, curiosity overcoming instinctual fear.

The wind below took on a deeper moan. Had I given myself over to fancy, I could have sworn there were words in it, not a language I spoke or ever wanted to learn, but words all the same.

Was he making the storm worse? That's what it looked like. Bad enough to start with, but if it became more violent the frail hut would certainly collapse.

I stepped toward Dracula and damn the consequences, but a blast of wind caught me in the chest like a giant's fist. It knocked me flat and sent me skidding on my back across the slick wood of the roof to fetch up against the low rise of the opposite wall. I half turned, throwing an arm around it to save myself and found I had a sick-making view of that black valley stretching straight down into hell. All was clear there, for the shrouding clouds parted around the tower and soared sharply upward to shred themselves to nothing in the high distance.

The force that struck me slacked off, allowing me to stand. Though still strong, this wind was bearable. Quite normal, in fact. No unearthly voices. I cautiously approached Dracula.

He was bent forward, hands resting on the wall to hold himself up, his head drooping with fatigue. He tiredly looked at me.

"Such elements," he murmured.

I ventured to cast an eye to the west. The clouds were gone. For as far as I could see the snow lay thick, silent, and trackless under the crystal bright stars. "What about the elements?"

"Easy to summon when you have the rage of ages to fuel it, not so easy to disperse."

He did seem utterly exhausted. The skin pressed close to his skull; his tiger-green eyes were now dark pits. Though I'd grown used to the age on his face this was the first time I truly perceived him to be *old*.

"Your friends shall find their going will improve some five miles away in whatever direction they choose to take when they depart."

Relief flooded me. "Thank you."

"You kept your word, I keep mine. What they have done was done in ignorance. I've stopped them. It will have to be enough."

I wisely did not enlighten him about their intent to return in the spring to finish the job. "The futility of retribution?" I asked, recalling what he'd said about the deaths of his mistresses.

His eyes sparked. "Indeed. For all my years . . . it is still the hardest of all wisdoms to grasp, for sometimes retribution is not always a futile action."

I grunted agreement; it seemed the right thing to do.

He slowly straightened. "Which gives me one question I will ask of you, Mr. Morris."

Only one? In our conversations he usually had dozens to ply.

"Have you decided whether or not you will conclude your own portion of the hunt and kill me?"

Did he know how to read hearts and minds as well as conjure up a storm? I tried to hide my startlement and alarm, but doubted my success. "I don't know wh—"

He made a throwing-away gesture. "Do not bother with such prevarication. I am not insulted by your intentions, whatever they might be. I assure you that I completely understand about such debts. You would take my life in payment for that of Lucy Westenra and the sullied honor of Mrs. Harker. Is that not true?"

There seemed no point in denying it. "Yes. How did you know?"

"Because you so carefully avoided such subjects throughout your stay here."

True. Partly because he didn't want to talk about either lady, but I also steered around any general mention of revenge whenever the topic surfaced. To him I must have been as clear as glass.

"By misadventure or on purpose, I have visited so much misery upon you and your friends, your desire to avenge them is not easily pushed aside. So I ask again: what will you do?"

Why did he wait until now for this? Having just shown mercy to Art and Jack did he think I'd look more kindly upon him? He was smart enough for that kind of manipulation, but I'd come to know him fairly well; such an obvious ploy was beneath his sense of honor.

Then there was his very evident weariness. Of all times, this was his most vulnerable, perhaps the best and only opportunity I would ever have of fighting him and winning. Why would he give me such an advantage?

Because this way he will get an honest answer from me.

He was taking a hell of a chance, courting an instant fight to the death or getting peace of mind. My reply would settle things forever with him, one way or another.

I could also respect a brave man. An honest answer he would get.

"We've both lost those whom we've loved," I said.

There was no need to mention the wolves. Or his three companions. They were here, anyway. They were all on the tower with us, along with Lucy's ghost, who hovered just over my left shoulder.

"Nothing will be served by more death," I continued. "The way I see it, things are even between us."

Though I'd made a sacred promise to Mina Harker, and another to myself to the memory of Lucy, I'd come to realize the heavy burden involved in the keeping of such oaths. In my heart I knew it was not one I was up to carrying for the rest of my life.

"My decision is to do nothing," I said.

I could not tell if he was relieved or disappointed. For the odd mood he seemed to be in either one would have equally suited him. Dracula gave a single slow nod, and that was that.

"The year is turning," he observed after awhile. "The solstice will soon be upon us, with its endings and beginnings."

Solstice? I'd been mulling over what to do about Christmas, having the idea it was a holiday he had reason not to observe. "I think my time here is ended as well."

He made no argument against it. "Indeed. You've learned all you need to survive and probably much more than you ever wanted to know."

That raised a rueful smile from me.

"Then fare you well, my so-young friend, if I might call you that. Our time together has been most . . . instructive to me."

"For us both, sir."

We stood for sometime after that, each looking out on the snow blanket, listening to the wind and trees whispering to themselves. Doubtless he understood more of their language than I . . . but that was all right with me.

It was one of those things I really didn't want to know about.

Chapter Six

Paris, January 1894

My return to western civilization was neither straightforward nor easy. Traveling is a difficult enough activity, but more so when one is unconscious during the day. I had to trust my inert, helpless body to the tender mercies of shipping clerks, baggage clerks, porters, and lord knows who else. Just getting to Buda-Pesth was such an ordeal that I was tempted to forgo the rigors of another train trip in favor of hiring a wagon and team and driving myself at night.

That would have been foolish, but I did consider it the evening I awoke to find the box I slept in smothered beneath a hoard of other boxes. The whole ungainly mess was locked into a railroad car left on a remote siding and apparently quite forgotten by those in charge.

Once I emerged to make my way to the station, it was no small task to sort things out, especially since I hadn't enough of the language to be understood. Fortunately, someone there knew French, and that helped to speed things, but I was told nothing could be done about my baggage until the morning, of course. It took some considerable persuasion on my part, along with a sizable bribe, to turn things in my favor.

No wonder Dracula had traveled by sea.

He'd suggested it from the first as being more convenient. I'd taken the opportunity to ask him about the deaths of the *Demeter's* crew. An interesting story *that* proved to be, for he managed to tell it in such a way as to cast him in a less villainous light. I wasn't sure if I believed him, but like everything else, the business was past and done. I had more pressing concerns.

I decided against a sea voyage because of the unpredictability of the winter weather, choosing instead to retrace the overland path Harker had taken last May. Dracula had one of his Szgany drivers take me as far as the Borgo Pass and from there I was put aboard the diligence that ran from Buknovina to Bistritz. In addition to a grip carrying such useful personal items as I might need, I was hampered by the necessity of keeping close watch on a three-foot-square box that was my daylight sanctuary. In it was a store of Transylvanian soil bundled up in canvas sacks. Heavy for the handlers and doubly so whenever I was asleep within. The accommodations were cramped for one of my height, but in this instance my daylight oblivion was a boon, sparing me from awareness of discomfort.

My chief worry was that while in this state some accident might befall that would cause my apparently lifeless body to be discovered. Dracula tried to assure me of its improbability, and even if something unto-ward happened, I would, with my new abilities, be able to easily talk my way out of it. Comforting thought, but for the fact I knew virtually no German.

After the delay in Buda-Pesth, things became thankfully less exciting. Harker had taken note of the irregularity of train schedules the farther east he traveled and had not exaggerated. I rejoiced the passing of each mile that took me west. The days were nothing, but the nights were wearying in their length. I avoided contact with people, easy to do when one is more or less confined to the baggage area.

I did venture forth in the early part of the evenings, using my new talent for vanishing to sieve my invisible way into the passenger areas. I was soon challenged by a conductor to produce a ticket, which forced me to test my command over hypnosis. As the man's English was nonexistent, his French dismal, and my German just as poor, I again fell back on the universal language of bribery to make my presence agreeable to him. It is amazing what miracles may be accomplished by cash in hand.

As for money, it was a happy discovery for me that my wallet had been left untouched on my person upon my death. My friends had apparently bundled me snug in that blanket without any thought of it, and I was very grateful for the omission. In our journeys across the continent I'd collected several kinds of paper currencies and I possessed a generous letter of credit, thus sparing me from having to further indebt myself to Dracula. My traveling papers were also there and in order, and I could trust that my name would raise no eyebrows on this side of the channel.

Once I reached England, that might change.

Dracula had plied me with questions about my plans, and I'd truthfully answered that I would anonymously pitch camp in Paris. Again, he admonished me to avoid contact with my friends. On that point—for the time being—we were in complete agreement. I had no wish to see anyone. I wanted to test my wings and get used to this new life first.

My arrival in that great city took place sometime in the afternoon, and by means of careful planning, my box was delivered to one of the better hotels. I awoke in a sort of cellar storage room. The box was on its side, leaving me in a jumble with the earth bags on top, but I slipped out easy enough and no harm done.

Taking a room, I arranged for the box to be moved upstairs. One of the young fellows who accomplished this task also inquired if I might wish to have feminine companionship. I thanked him and said maybe later and got rid of him before he could come up with further suggestions. The journey had tired me, mentally, if not physically. I wanted some settling-in time, and a parcel of solitude in a non-moving room was just the thing so I could recover and think.

I spent much of my first night simply standing before my tall window on the third floor looking down on the street. Unlike other cities, Paris is just as active after dark as in the daylight, but the sorts of business that thrive in the shadows are not considered respectable by most folks. I'm not most folks, though, and had always found Paris to be one of the more admirable of the world's metropolises. You can stroll its lanes and choose a wide variety of entertainments at the most ungodly hours.

You also have to be wary of the local predators, but they'd never bothered me much. Most ruffians think twice about going after a fellow of my size, especially when there's a shooter strapped to his hip. I was once stopped by a Parisian lawman who took exception to my Colt. As soon as he understood I was an American, though, he broke into a big grin and all but dragged me into some Frenchy saloon to toast my health. We had a fine jaw-wag about Buffalo Bill and

Kit Carson, whom he assumed I knew. Wonderful people, the French.

When I got tired of watching the street below, I ordered some English papers brought in and caught myself up on the world. Strangely, very little held my interest. I used to be as addicted to the news as any opium eater to his pipe, but now the parade of events seemed dull and pointless. Whether it had to do with my changed condition or the fact I'd been holed up in that Transylvanian backwater for over a month I did not know. Dracula possessed a distinct sort of aloofness from outside goings on; perhaps some of it had rubbed off on me. I did not share his passion for battles of the past, though. I didn't *have* much of a past yet. Maybe I'd partaken of a few little traveling adventures, but that wasn't much compared to being a prince and leading whole armies against invading hordes. Well, he'd never held the lack against me, so that made him all right. When he had a mind for it, he was a polite fellow.

I left instructions with the hotel clerk not to be disturbed during the day. My chief worry was that some curious chambermaid might discover me when she should be changing the linens. Against that possibility, my traveling box was firmly nailed shut. Upon awakening and slipping out, I was relieved to find all was as I'd left it upon retiring. I had picked the right place to camp.

My second night in Paris found me rousting out one of the bellmen to determine from him the location of a gentleman's haberdashery that was still open. I was told it was quite impossible to find any open so late, but I slipped him a few francs and smiled, and asked him to apply himself.

Have you ever noticed that poor people are crazy and rich people are eccentric? He decided I was yet another eccentric American and from that point on there wouldn't ever be enough that he could do for me.

It cost extra, but soon a tailor and his assistant marched up to my room with their books, measuring tapes, and fabric samples. I ordered several suits so as to be outfitted like a fine European gent. They were not so fancy in cut as those worn by some of the fellows strutting about, but would be of good quality, from boots to topper. No one on the ranch or perhaps even in London would recognize me, not at first glance, which was what I most wanted.

I had a hankering to get my face neatened, but having to do without a mirror was a powerful inconvenience. The hotel barber became the first man I tried my hypnotic talent upon.

Despite the lateness of the hour he cheerfully bustled in with his kit on a wheeled cart. I told him how I wanted my beard, namely clean off the scraggle under my jaw and trim the rest to be even, with just a little wax to train my mustaches. He went to work and not long after held a mirror up for me to inspect the results. We had a bit of a mild set-to when—standing as he was behind me with the glass—he saw only the reflection of the chair I was in but not me. It flustered him pretty bad until I gave him a good look in the eye and told him to calm down.

Damn if it didn't work like Dixie.

His eyes went a little dead, but he stopped jabbering and stood by quiet as a church on Monday.

So *this* was what Nora had done to me all those years past. I could see that it promised to be a very handy ability, but with a built-in temptation for abuse. I'm not the sort of man to take advantage of anyone, but the idea of being able to win every argument from now on was quite a pleasing one. I could also see that any lady I wanted to pass time with could be likewise persuaded to my will with just a look and a word or two. On the other hand, *that* was a talent I already possessed, if I can declare such without sounding boastful. Only poor, sweet Lucy had ever really turned me down, but then a marriage proposal is a serious enough step that a man wants a truthful answer. As for the rest of the ladies in the wide world, well, I'm not in the habit of forcing myself upon women. My Ma and Pa taught me better manners than that.

I wasn't wholly without a sense of mischief, though. I asked the barber to stand on one leg and cluck like a chicken—which he did without batting an eye— before telling him to ignore my lack of reflection. He readily agreed to that, too, then I woke him up to go about his business. I paid him generous enough for the liberty.

Feeling very well pleased with myself, I decided to stretch my legs. Fresh-shaved and in a fine mood for distraction, it would be a shame to keep so dandy a sight as myself hidden from the French ladies.

Walking stick in hand, I took a long, slow stroll that evening, tipping my hat to people along the way, and being likewise acknowledged in turn. I knew I cut a fine figure. My chief regret was being unable to sip coffee at one of the cafes or hoist a good whiskey at the infinite number of saloons. Nearly every kind of society the world over conducts its business and pleasures over food and drink. I'd always known that, but until now had never truly *realized* it. Everywhere I looked people seemed to be eating. I felt quite left out.

Yet there were places where I might go my unrefreshed way without drawing notice. Paris had plenty of entertainments where a man need only purchase a ticket without having a waiter hovering around. I would not want for amusement in this town, but I did long for company.

There were places for that as well. In the past, Art

and I had discovered a few of the high class establishments where a man might indulge himself. There was a price to pay, but seeing as how I wasn't spending any money on food, I would well afford the best.

And so I took myself to such a place. It was time I discovered the carnal side of my new nature.

Now there is a lot of talk about what a French whorehouse is like. Rumors tend to fall short of the reality with some; for others it's all they have to offer. There are as many different kinds of houses as there are restaurants. A man willing to look can find many to suit his taste and pocketbook. I have been to ones grander than any palace, loaded down with gilt, velvet, paintings, and mirrors, the women there dressed— or undressed—fancier and more beautiful than any empress. That's fine when one is in the mood for it, but this night I was more interested in plain home-cooking, if I might call it such.

I knew of a house that would do. It was located on one of the less traveled fares, a thin, modest building hunched between others of its kind, built some fifty years ago. The madam was a sensible woman and stern as a greengrocer about the care of her goods. Her charges were well-fed, cheerful, and healthy.

The big doorman, who might have been the madam's husband, answered my knock, and ushered me straight to a sitting room where I could have a look at the girls. That was something else I liked about this place, they didn't put up with time-wasting frills like a bar or gaming tables. They had a business to run and respected the fact that the single-minded customer might not want to be kept waiting.

The madam seemed not to remember me from past visits, but it had been awhile, and I'd changed a bit. She gave a friendly greeting and invited me to take my pick from the half dozen girls available. Here I hesitated. They all looked mighty fine to my starved sight, but I now had other particulars to consider. I quietly conveyed to the madam my preference for sobriety. Being a good woman of business, and having probably witnessed just about everything human nature had to offer, she gave no reaction to my modest request and readily pointed out two likely prospects. With their dark hair and pale eyes they looked enough alike to be sisters; I chose the sturdier looking of the two, paid my fee, and we went upstairs.

Things began well enough and in the usual manner. I'm a man of simple tastes when it comes to achieving my own satisfaction. When trying to please a lady, though, I'm more lavish in my attentions. In this instance I was free to indulge either way. The girl smiled, offering compliments and encouragement, but I could tell by the steady beat of her heart that she was just doing that which was expected. I could go ahead with matters for myself, and it would make no difference to her.

But something in me balked at that. I'd not been with a woman in a very long time. Maybe I was paying for a service, but if I could involve her more fully the enjoyment would be that much better. Toward that end I fixed my eye on hers and whispered a few words such as to send her heart racing.

Oh, my. What a difference it made to have her suddenly giggling and clutching me like a wildcat. Falsely induced her happy mood might be, but it certainly broke the dam for my own passion to come forth. How we made that bed creak and groan.

My own excitement took over; I was aware my corner teeth were extended, responding to a different kind of body hunger. My desire now was how to culminate things to accommodate my new nature. Memories of Nora guided me there as I nuzzled this sweet little gal's pale skin. I was in her and plowing away, with her holding on for dear life, gasping in time to our dance. She was caught up in it, of that I had no doubt, and verging on fulfillment. I was more than ready myself, and when the time came it seemed the most natural thing in the world for me to bite down on that pulse-spot in her throat.

She let out a suppressed shriek and bucked under me, legs kicking and thrashing. For an instant I feared it was from pain, but she held me all the tighter as her blood welled onto my mouth. With its first taste I felt an explosion of pleasure such as I'd never known before, and rather than fading, it only built up more intense as I fed. It was different from when I'd been on the giving side of things, better, darker, more solid. I could stay here for hours and not find its end. Nothing I'd ever experienced could match this.

Her breath came fast and short, and in between she whispered endearments. Her reactions gradually slowed, though. I understood what that meant, knowing it well enough. Her body could take only so much before the pleasure exhausted her. Nora had been kind to me and had drawn away at such times. I did the same, shifting my weight from the girl, and allowing us both a good long interval to rest.

Not moving a muscle, she went straight to sleep. When I recovered enough to take notice of things I made a careful examination of my partner's throat. The damage was alarmingly visible: two seeping wounds, the surrounding skin blotched and red. Not good. Nora had been much more careful. I was going to have to practice at this, it seemed. Not that I was in any way averse to more of the same.

Except for the blood, my sign on this girl might be mistaken for an overly enthusiastic love bite. Well, I could instruct her to hide the damage with a scarf or something. As for the remaining seepage, I found myself kissing it away, and that was enough to make me want her all over again.

She woke up, and from her expression, she'd fallen in love with me. An unwise thing for a whore to do with a customer. I once more fixed her with a look and managed to ease things back to normal business again, at the same time telling her not to remember my drinking her blood. Sweet as pie, she accepted it without demur along with a bit of extra money that I felt she deserved for the extra service. We parted company on very good terms.

I dropped back in the tangled sheets, stretching wide, feeling mighty pleased with myself, and suddenly grateful to the incomparable Nora Jones. She'd not warned me of what lay ahead, but hands down, lying here all sated in a French whorehouse sure beat the hell out of a cold grave in the Transylvanian earth. Perhaps when I got to England I would make an effort to find her again and thank her.

Someone knocked softly on the door. The other sober gal, the one who looked like the first one's sister, entered, smiling. I'd asked for her to be sent up.

I grinned in turn, anticipating what was to come, and invited her into the bed.

As I said, it had been a *very* long time.

My stay in Paris continued for several weeks, during which I managed to adjust quite well to the limits of my condition and did my utmost to fully enjoy its advantages. Most of the latter had to do with frequent visits to professional establishments. I'd never been such a hedonist before, but it struck me that now would be my best opportunity to perfect my skills in the fleshly pleasures available on this side of my empty grave. It cost a pretty penny, but as I wasn't spending my money on meals three times a day, the expenditures at these houses worked out to be nearly the same amount.

Dracula had said I couldn't live on love for very long,

and certainly focusing on one lady all the time would make that true. One woman could not supply enough sustenance for me without danger to her health, but I was supping from many women on a nearly nightly basis. My need for animal blood remarkably decreased. In all that time I'd fed, truly fed, only twice.

As for the reports of my death, I had quite a tangle to unsnarl. The letters I'd written from Transylvania had arrived only just ahead of me. Unfortunately, Jonathan Harker had been at work a month earlier, conveying the sad news of my demise in a distant land to my lawyers and banks. I was forced to send a number of cables to Galveston and eventually make an appointment with one of the local bank officers, hoping to provide myself with an agent to look after my day-time concerns. The man was a stuffy sort and unimpressed with my accounts. He took no pains to hide the fact that my odd wish to speak with him well after business hours was most inconvenient.

As the fellow had imbibed in some cognac prior to my arrival at his home, hypnotizing him turned out to be difficult. Had I been in a hurry, it might well have been impossible, but I kept at it, and brought him around to my side of things before an hour had passed. The effort made my head hurt like the morning after a Fourth of July rip, but was worth it. I had created a valuable ally whom I could utterly trust to carry out my orders without question. Over the weeks he proved his worth sorting out my affairs and getting me declared alive without letting on to Harker or any of the others.

At last I was ready and able to go to England.

Chapter Seven

England, February 1894

As with Paris, my arrival in London took place during the day, but this time the porters managed to keep my box upright. I should say boxes, as I now had a separate trunk holding all my new continental clothing and a few other souvenirs. I had instructions for both to be left until called for. Claim ticket in hand, I wafted from my small sanctuary to solidify in the dim recesses of yet another huge storeroom full of similar shipments. To my right came the clamor of great activity and the smell of the river. I struck off in that direction, eventually finding the right office and arranging to have my property delivered to my hotel.

As it was very bitter out, I hired a coach. For all the snow I fought in Transylvania and even Siberia, there is nothing quite like England for true winter cold.

It's got damp in it, which burrows down into your bones and even in the warmest room it is reluctant to depart. Though fairly immune to the low temperature, I felt it, mostly because of the sharp wind tearing through the bleak streets, making things more miserable.

For all that, there was no shortage of people out and about. It was yet early in the evening; the gas lamps glowed steadily, and brave crowds bustled in and out of shops and public houses. The constant traffic slowed my carriage's progress, but that was to be expected. I'd never once seen a main thoroughfare in London that wasn't always choked with conveyances. Their noise and that of the people within and without was a welcome assault to my sensitive ears. Loud they may have been, but it was in my own language, albeit with all those distinct accents, some of them nearly as hard to understand as German.

The visual cacophony was just as welcome as I was carried past street vendors of all kinds, shouting their wares to a largely deaf multitude. Those buildings that were not given over to residences—and some that were—sported broad advertisements for everything from tooth-pulling to hot cocoa the Queen herself favored.

And there were ladies, my God, but this city was *full* of women of every description. Why had I never noticed them before?

Because of Lucy, a soft inner voice told me.

Abruptly, I sat back from the coach window onto the chill leather seat, sharply reminded of why I'd come to leave England the first place. My mourning for her had by no means ended. Perhaps it never would. I had loved her. Her bright smile, her utter sweetness and honesty of spirit and so much more had captivated me in a way I'd never known was possible. I had done my best to woo her with charm and humor, telling tales of my life on the ranch and of my travels, but throughout it all I had the dark feeling that none of it had really touched her. It had been a grievous day for me when she turned down my proposal.

Jack Seward—also rejected—and I had drowned our sorrows somewhat and played the good sports in congratulating Art on his luck, but there was a sad sting to it. Art barely noticed, being too stunned with his own happiness. We made a good party of it, though, the last we had together before she took sick. The last we would ever have, apparently.

Arriving at the hotel in a dour mood, I paid my driver, and went in to confirm the reservation I'd made by cable. They'd received it in good time so all was well. I went straight up, literally, by means of a new elevator, to the fourth floor. These digs were on the fancy side, but I could indulge myself. Later, after I figured out a few things, I might find a flat or a house to rent. Until then, I wanted the sort of privacy one achieves by being lost in a great crowd.

Once my baggage arrived and one of the hotel men had unpacked the trunk and put everything away, I found myself at a loose end. I'd been pretty engrossed in the getting here, and had only a vague idea of what to do next. At some point I would seek out my friends and see how they fared, but tonight seemed too soon to begin such business, yet sitting in my room held no appeal.

I changed into one of my evening suits, determined to track down some entertainment. Perhaps London was not as lively a town as Paris, but was still full of distraction, even on so cold a night.

Top hat in place, stick in hand, I ventured forth into the turmoil.

I'd hardly gone fifty steps before a youngish woman caught my eye and gave me a regal little nod and wink. For an instant I thought I might know her, then

realized she was merely looking for custom. Some of
her Parisian sisters were more obvious in their
approach; I'd have to adjust myself to the change.

As it seemed only polite to return her greeting, I
did so. From there, things proceeded as one might
expect, but more slowly than on the Continent. The
English can be mighty roundabout in their ways, so it
took a while before we determined what sort of
arrangement to agree upon. She dressed up what should
have been a fairly simple business into something fancier with all her pretty flirting, but I wasn't so impa-
tient as to not enjoy playing along. Keep the lady happy,
and the gent always benefits a thousand-fold.

She said she had a room just around the corner,
which struck me as odd. This was not the East End,
after all, with bedroom doors opening right onto the
street. Curious but eager, I escorted her as she
directed, finding myself in a narrow byway off the main
thoroughfare.

Now I may yet be young, but in these matters I'm
no greenhorn. The instant I left the gaslit walk I suspected I might be in for something disagreeable.

The lady did not disappoint. Had my eyes not been
so well suited to the dark, I might have taken a bad
turn then and there when her partner darted out of
the shadows, club in hand.

A few months back and I'd have given him a first-
hand show of my boxing skills. You don't grow up
where I did and not learn how to account well for
yourself. But that was changed. With hardly any
thought behind it, I vanished quick as a music hall
magician. And just in the nick. I felt the rushing intrusion as his club came down, whistling harmlessly
through what had once been my solid body. To him
it was empty air, and the force he'd put behind the
blow must have overbalanced him; from the sound of
it, he stumbled.

The woman let loose with a good hollering screech. Up to a second ago I had firm hold of her arm, so I couldn't blame her for getting spooked. I was none too happy with either of them, but the fear-filled questions they shot at each other over what had just happened had me laughing, or close to it. In this form, without breath to draw or lungs to put it in, it's a little difficult to express oneself, but the feeling was strong.

Funny as they were I didn't feel right in just letting them go. There would likely soon be another gent come into their clutches, and he'd not do so well by himself as I.

While I thought things over, they searched the area, arguing the whole time over the impossibility of my strange escape. When the woman suggested ghosts I got my idea.

Floating some three feet off the ground, I began to cautiously resume form. It was by no means easy to keep myself light enough to float, yet dense enough to speak. I wavered, like a tightrope walker having difficulty with his balance, slowly rising and falling as I swam in the air.

"Gor, Prudy, lookit that," said the man, staring at me.

She blurted another shriek, clutching him.

I pointed at them both in a grand way, summoning up my memories of a fire and brimstone preacher who had been a great favorite of my mother's.

Prudy shrieked again, but was too rooted in place to think of running.

"I serve the Angel of Death!" I boomed, loud as I could manage. My voice came out all hollow, though in this case it seemed to be an advantage. "Change your ways or suffer the Wrath of Hell for Eternity!" How that preacher man had scared me as a boy.

"Bosh," said the man, nonplused. "Yer jus' one o' them stage fellers swingin' on a wire."

He must have been drunk, making such a sight as myself normal. Though his reaction was disappointing, I had a ready answer and swooped right at him, arms spread wide. I passed through them both, with Prudy screaming her head off. She was now of a mind to escape, but her man had a good grip on her.

"Never you mind 'im, old girl. If 'e's nowt but a ghost, 'e can't 'arm us."

I had an answer for that as well and went fully solid, landing light on my feet. The man turned around to face me, but not as fast as he should. I dropped my cane hard on his lower arm. He released his club with a howl. Next I put a fist into his belly. He doubled over, staggered back, and fell on his seat. So much for my being a ghost.

Rounding on the woman, I let myself shoot up in the air again to tower above her. She fair cowered, her eyes fit to pop. I pointed right at her face. "Repent, sinner! Repent or be damned to the Lake of Fire forever!"

"Eeeee!" she cried.

"Repent or be doomed! Go thy way as an honest whore and never thieve again so help you God!"

"Aaaaaah!" she screamed, covering her face as I dove upon her, vanishing at the last instant. I wrapped about her like a blanket, knowing she could feel my cold touch. Dracula had once said the effect for them was like being in an ice bath. She lurched up and stampeded toward the main street, still making a fine hysterical racket. I let her go, having made my point.

"Repent!" I bellowed.

Her partner gave one hell of a jump, for I'd materialized right behind him to deliver this order. He now looked ready to abandon his theories about magicians and ghosts.

"Repent or be damned!"

Whether he'd come around to my way of thinking

I could not tell. What he *did* show was a remarkable fleetness of foot in his own howling retreat.

I laughed myself into a coughing fit after that. Once I'd settled down my chief regret was not having Art or Jack around to have seen the show. How they would have loved it.

Perhaps in time, I thought, as I followed the path my would-be attackers took and resumed my explorations. Henceforth, I promised myself to seek fleshly entertainment only at whorehouses and ignore the temptations of the street. I might not be so lucky again. I was no coward, but I'd turned into enough of a dandy to not want my fine new suit ruined by common roughhouse on its first wearing.

The rest of the evening I wiled away at one of the city's many musical theaters. Art had first introduced me to them years ago, and a rare treat they were and remained. Back in Texas we had nothing to compare with them, and rarely had enough acts to properly fill up the whole evening. Here they had dozens of performers doing all manner of highjinks, from little songbird gals in pink tights to jugglers to dancing dogs that could count out your age by barking. Paris had similar halls, but naturally I enjoyed myself more hearing the jokes in English.

I sat in one of the upper boxes and roared laughter, applauded, or sang along with the rest of the audience until the last curtain, then purchased a new ticket to see the second show. In the interval I studied the program, picking out familiar names of favorites I'd not seen since last summer.

What a long while since then. Lifetimes. I'd lost a good-sized parcel of living for my sojourns in Transylvania and France, and I felt vaguely cheated for the gap. I wanted the time back to do things over, to change things for the better.

That put me in another slump. Lucy had been alive

then, engaged to my best friend, but still smiling and happy despite her mysterious "illness." Throughout all those weeks she'd shown a loving face to him . . . and yet at night she allowed Dracula to pay his special kind of court to her. I couldn't see it. It was almighty indecent. How could she have done that and been the same sweet, innocent girl?

Dracula's words about none of us knowing her true heart came back to me yet again, and I wondered at the truth of them. He'd had no reason to lie. From the first he'd been in charge and could have killed me whenever he wished for he had no need to curry my favor. He was a man—and I could just about call him that now—who absolutely did *not* give a tinker's damn what anyone thought of him. I'd met that kind many times, and had ever found them to be truthful, often brutally so.

The orchestra began its overture, then the curtain came up again. I was able to lose myself in the show and was thankful for it. I had troubling questions for which there were no satisfying answers this side of the grave. Best to leave them alone.

One of the presentations was a bit of what I would call serious acting, being the dueling scene from *Hamlet*. The otherwise rowdy audience in the stalls held still for it, too, which astonished me. I thought it a wonderful thing how Shakespeare could reach just about anybody, until I took a closer look at the actors. They were all women.

Well, that sat me back in the box, and got me to paying attention. What a remarkable performance it was, and once I got over the shock, I came to see that they were doing a rare good job of acting, female or not. The girl playing Hamlet was more full of fire than even the great Henry Irving, or so I imagined. I could judge that this lady looked better in leg tights than he ever would. She sure knew how to dance around on stage with that sword, as though she'd been born a duelist.

The program book listed them as the Ring Players. It sounded vaguely familiar, but only because Ring was the name of Art's family estate.

I looked more closely at the woman playing Hamlet. Her voice and form struck me anew, but I still couldn't place her. The program did not list the names of the actors, only their company.

At the end of the scene, after they bore Prince Hamlet away, the curtains drew shut to great applause and a certain amount of hooting. It seemed half approved of the novelty of an all-female company and half did not. I was for it, so I cheered.

The curtain rippled as someone behind it tried to find the middle opening, then Hamlet stepped out and bowed—not curtsied—to more mixed reaction. She held her hand up for silence, and by God she got it. The lady was small but had a tremendous commanding presence. She loudly thanked them for their kind reception (hoots and cheers), then announced that a performance of the entire play would take place as a matinee next Saturday. I resolved to attend, then grimaced as I remembered the impossibility. This was the first time I had reason to regret the limits of my condition. Determined to find out more about the Ring players, hoping there might possibly be an evening show sometime, I quit my box.

Outside by the stage door I found I wasn't the only one wanting to pay my respects to the ladies of the theater. The narrow alley was crowded with other men like myself in evening dress along with more ordinary johnnies in less formal attire. Some hopefuls carried flowers and boxes of chocolates. I pushed my way past them to present my card to a weary doorman.

"I hain't 'ere to run no herrands," he said, by way of a rebuff.

"Nonetheless, sir, I'd be much obliged if you would take this to whoever is in charge of the Ring Company." Along with the calling card, I put a shilling in his hand, and fixed him with a look. It was enough. To the astonishment of those next to me the man went inside.

"Bloody Americans," someone muttered. I shouldn't have been able to hear but for my changed condition. I pretended to be ignorant of his feelings, and waited.

More astonishment when the doorman returned and told me I alone was welcome to enter. Amid additional jealous mutterings, I pushed my way up the steps into the cavernous dark of the backstage area.

We were separated from the stage by at least one wall, but I could clearly hear the orchestra merrily booming away. The doorman signed for quiet and led me along a dim passage to the dressing rooms. Here things were still somewhat hushed, but there was a great deal of activity as people bustled to and fro, fanatically urgent to make their cues. The brightly costumed players were a strange contrast to the chilly, drab surroundings.

Our trek ended at an open door where women in various stages, types, and eras of fantastical dress were gathered. Some were changing clothes right in the hall, despite the presence of a number of stage hands walking about. From the sound of things, the room itself was too crowded. I tried not to stare, but none of them seemed to mind and a few called greetings and endearments to me as though we were old friends. When gathered together in such a pack women can get downright *bold*.

The doorman was apparently well used to the sight of half-naked females and went inside, calling for "Miss Bertie." I wondered if that was the name of the lady I sought. Moments later he emerged.

"She's on 'er way," he said, then left.

I thanked his back, thinking it was the best shilling

I'd ever spent. Of course it helped to be able to get my suggestions across so well. What a wonderful thing is was to have people truly *listen* and do as they're asked.

"Mr. Morris?"

I recognized the voice of Hamlet and turned, hat in hand. A pretty lady she was indeed, of an age with me. She'd worn a short blond wig on stage, but had removed it, revealing a heavy knot of dark hair.

"Mr. Quincey P. Morris?" she said, holding my card. She fair gaped at me for some reason. "You've a beard now, but how the devil . . . ?"

I was all set to bow a greeting, then got a good *close* look at her and froze awkwardly in mid-motion. "Oh, my God. Lady B—"

Her eyes—and they were remarkable orbs, all green fire—flared hot. "Not here, you muggins! Not one more word or I'll murder you."

"Uh . . . but L—"

She clapped a hand over my mouth. It smelled of greasepaint and some sort of rare spice. "I said not one word!"

She grabbed my arm and dragged me away. I was yet too startled to think to resist.

Thus did I unexpectedly renew my acquaintance with Lady Bertrice, Art Holmwood's black sheep sister.

Chapter Eight

She was the elder child by exactly one year to the day. Until Art was sent off to public school they'd been raised close as twins, and he told me that therein lay the beginnings of her defiance to the Holmwood family and the rest of the world.

Upon learning that her brother would go off to school but she was not allowed to go as well, Bertrice had pitched a conniption fit that nearly brought the house down. No amount of orders, argument, scolding, cajoling, or spanking could persuade her from her rage. She bitterly railed against the unfairness of being separated from her beloved brother and playmate by the mere fact that she was not a boy. Art said she'd rushed up to his room, donned some of his clothes, and brutally attacked her hair with dressmaking shears, then presented herself, small traveling case in hand, ready to go to the train station with him. He'd been all for it, but their outraged parents had other ideas. She was locked in her room, and he was packed off to Eton, both children in tears.

From that point on it was Bertrice against all of society. She'd have done well in Texas, where women with high spirits and gumption were welcome. In England, and especially in the class to which she'd been born, those qualities were considered Deadly Sins number Eight and Nine.

I'd met her at Lord Godalming's funeral. They were his only surviving children and rode in the carriage behind the coffin. Jack and I had been there, too, at Art's request. Bertrice had been alone, with no friend for support. He'd quietly introduced us, and I'd bowed over the hand of a veiled lady in a dress somber enough to please even the still-mourning Queen, but apparently not the rest of the Holmwood kinfolk. As we stood around the grave I noticed the whole pack—especially the women—staring at Bertrice as though she carried the typhoid. Some of the men either looked poker-faced blank or nudged each other with sly smiles that I didn't like.

This sort of manner was long familiar to me, having experienced a certain amount of disparaging patronization from the English. It started the moment they found out I was American. Some of them liked me for it, the rest would have drowned in a rain storm from holding their noses so high. I was raised in a place where if you looked wrongwise at a fellow you could get that nose blown right off. None of these fancy britches would have lasted two minutes with my hired hands back home, so I always smiled and let it slide.

The exceptions to this snobbery were Art and his father, who were true gentlemen when it came to respecting a man for who he was, not who society thought he should be. It was too bad there weren't more like them in the world.

After the service, the crowd lined up to give words of condolence to Arthur, but said nothing to Bertrice, who stood right next to him. Though she was suffering just as much in her grief they simply moved on like she wasn't there, which I thought damned bad manners. It made no mind to me that this was the cream of British aristocracy, I was ready to dust my knuckles on the next one to cut her short, male or female.

To my surprise, Bertrice touched my arm and gave it a squeeze.

"Miss?" I said in response.

"Never mind them, Mr. Morris," she whispered through the folds of her thick veil. "They're not worth the trouble."

How she knew what I was winding myself up for still mystified, but it was just as well she'd headed me off. Fist fights at funerals aren't unheard of, but best that everyone be in agreement for their necessity or it can get almighty embarrassing.

Later, in that draughty old stone pile that their great-grandfather had built and named Ring, the gathering took tea or breakfast or whatever meal one has after an English funeral. Arthur again got all the attention and Bertrice nothing, though she remained fast by his side. He made a point to include her in all the conversational exchanges. No one took him up on any of it except me and Jack Seward, but just the three of us against all those black crows of nobility made it hard going.

Then an old grandaunt called for the ladies to come along with her to a distant parlor. She looked right at Bertrice and said, "Not you." Everyone within hearing stopped talking with a near-audible gasp.

I saw the younger woman, who had held herself

straight and unmoved all this time, flinch in reaction. Art stared, his mouth gaping.

"Oh, I say, Aunt Honoria—" he began, unhappily.

That was all she wanted for an opening. "Arthur, your sainted father may have allowed her to indulge in her disgraceful conduct, but I've never tolerated it and never will. This *creature* is an unnatural example of her sex. If you've any respect for the peace of your dead parents, you will have her locked away where decent people need not soil their sight on her."

Now everyone really did gasp. In the back, some narrow-faced crones murmured smug agreement. Art was too shocked and too well mannered to give short response to this outburst. I understood that Bertrice had a number of Bohemian friends the family did not approve of, but what she'd done to raise such acrimony I could not imagine.

Aunt Honoria turned away from us with stiff-backed dignity, heading for the door.

But Bertrice had a parting shot and made it in a very clear voice that penetrated the whole of the room.

"Dear me, Dr. Seward, I believe poor Honoria is ripe for your lunatic asylum. It's a shame what extreme ravages age inflicts on the brain. What a pity it is to witness such terrible senility. I know I should not be pleased to have anyone behold me in such a feeble-minded state. Death would be a merciful release from the constant self-humiliation."

Both Art and Jack drained white. Honoria kept going as though she'd not heard, but of course she had. There was a collective silence in the room, and it seemed as though no one wanted to be the first to break it. Bertrice put herself forward, addressing them.

"I hope you've enjoyed yourselves. My thanks to you, my good family and friends, for the condolences you've all wished upon me. Dear Father would have been so pleased with your compassion."

That turned a number of shocked stares into shame-faced abashment. No one would meet her eye.

Bertrice smiled graciously at us. She'd taken off her veiled bonnet, showing a remarkable braid of thick, dark hair shot through with glints of mahogany. She looked very tired. "Arthur, I'm sorry to have made a scene at this of all times."

"You weren't the one to start it."

"Nor is it finished. I'm sure that wretched gorgon is planning out another attack even now."

"Well, piffle to her. I've a mind to demand she apologize to you."

"You're very sweet, but there's no point to the exercise unless she honestly regrets her behavior. Besides, she'd only become angry with you."

"She's angry with everyone."

She nodded, commiserating. "Dr. Seward, I apologize to you as well for dragging your name into things."

Jack stood a bit straighter. "Lady Bertrice, I am ever at your service in whatever way you deem fit."

"Thank you, sir. Would that there were more like you three in the world."

I'd not had any real participation in the business, but felt a warm glow to have been included in her praise.

"If you gentlemen will excuse me, I'm a bit fatigued. Best that I leave now so the relatives may exercise the opportunity to freely talk behind my back."

"May I escort you upstairs, Lady Bertrice?" I asked. Art shot me a grateful look, but I'd have made the offer anyway.

"I should be most obliged, Mr. Morris." She took my arm, and I led her out.

We climbed the main stairs slowly. Some of the gathering had lingered to watch her progress and whisper. She kept her head high, not appearing to be overly troubled by them or showing the least evidence that she was in any way retreating.

"Quite a harrowing gauntlet," I said, as we reached the landing.

"They're insects," she intoned. "Can't see beyond their tiny little antennae to the larger world."

"A rare turn of phrase."

"Thank you. I'm glad Arthur has such friends around him, but then one may choose friends; with family one is not always so fortunate."

"Yes, miss, I mean, Lady Bertrice. May I offer you *my* condolences?"

"Indeed you may, sir. And I thank you for your great kindness."

I bowed over her hand. She gave my fingers a little squeeze, then wafted away, heavy black skirts and petticoats rustling.

Now she stood before me in the remnants of her Hamlet costume, an open black doublet and tights that bagged some at the knees as though too large for her. I made myself not look at her rather shapely legs. On stage it's one thing to stare, but backstage it was quite another. She still had that presence going for her. It sparked off her small form like a constant tingle of electricity. At the funeral I'd been subtly aware of its potential lurking under the surface. She'd let some of it blaze out when she broadsided her aunt. This was my first chance to actually have its focus aimed at me. I wasn't sure if I liked it or not, but it was impossible to ignore.

We were no longer in the building as she'd drawn me up several flights of stairs and through a door. I found myself suddenly outside in the February cold, standing on the theater's roof. The wind was still sharp, but Bertrice seemed not to notice.

"All right," she said. "We may speak freely here."

"Why the secrecy? If you don't mind my asking."

"Because the Ring Players only know me as Bertrice Wood, and I want to keep it that way. My title would be a terrible drawback in the company."

"Why so?"

She laughed a little. "You Americans. I adore your innocence. Let it suffice that you must never address me as Lady Bertrice, or make any mention of my connection to the Godalming title. Not here, anyway."

"Very well." I supposed she also didn't want her relatives to know she was running around in leg tights in a music hall, even if it was to do with Shakespeare. Aunt Honoria would have had cats. Full grown ones.

"What are you doing here, Mr. Morris?"

"I just came to see the show. All I wanted was to find out more about the *Hamlet* performances. I had no idea you were involved."

"How amusing. At least now it is. When I got your card I thought it was some disgusting joke. Aren't you supposed to be dead?"

"Uh—hm—ah . . ."

Hands on hips, she gave me a piercing head-to-toe scrutiny as though uncertain of my condition. "Arthur came dragging back from the Continent months ago with an incurable case of the mopes. He said you'd been killed and refused to give particulars. Even that nice Dr. Seward refused to speak of it. I was ready to strangle both of them. Would *you* please enlighten me?"

"Uhm—ah. It's a long story."

"I'm sure it must be. Did you three have a falling out?"

"No, nothing of the sort."

"You *are* allowed to be more forthcoming with details, Mr. Morris." She looked ready to strangle *me*, now.

"In good time, I promise. Tell me how Art's doing."

"The last I was at Ring he was in a terrifically low state."

"When was that?" While in Paris I'd verified that he and Jack had made it safely home, but I was eager for fresher news, even if it promised to grieve me.

"A few weeks ago. Why the devil does he think you're dead?"

"I had an accident that separated me from them, and they assumed the worst. It's a *very* long story. Might I ask how you came to be here?"

"Have you objections to female players?" Her eyes flared dangerously.

"Not at all, but I was curious—"

"As to how a member of the aristocracy could demean herself by taking to the stage?"

"Lord, no, Lady Bertrice!"

She eased off, settling back a little. "Forgive me, Mr. Morris. I forget how you are. I've grown so used to defending myself against all in my path that I don't recognize a friend when I see him."

It was rare-pleasing to my heart that she thought to consider me a friend. "You've no need to worry about my good opinion, Miss. I thought you looked to be having a grand time of things while you were doing all that acting."

"And you really didn't recognize me? I hardly knew you with that beard and the French suit."

"Well, I *thought* you seemed familiar, but for the life of me I couldn't place you. You can take that as a tribute to your acting talent."

She looked mighty happy. "Thank you, sir. Your open-mindedness is most refreshing. At our matinees most people catcall or throw rotten food."

"It's their loss, then. I am unable to come to your show at that time of day. Will there be any evening performances?"

"Not unless the receipts improve. The manager here makes more money from the regular fare he stages— dancing dogs and sing-alongs. He's certain he'll be ruined if he allows *us* to play in the evening. And I'm sure he's right. The music hall crowd will sit still for one portion of an act, but not the whole play."

"Perhaps another theater?"

"If I could find one that would have us. The instant they find out it's an all-female company they discover they're booked for the next five years."

"They just want getting used to the idea. Where *did* the idea come from, anyway?"

"Mr. Morris, I should be delighted to tell you all about it, but at the moment I'm having second thoughts about my choice of setting for a private conversation. I've gotten bloody cold."

We retreated inside. Through chattering teeth she reminded me once more to exclude her title from my speech, entreating me to call her by her first name. That well-pleased me, and I insisted she return the honor.

She and Art were very alike in many ways, but apparently worlds apart in others. Disguised under a blond Hamlet wig or not, he'd have *never* stepped onto a stage and spouted out Shakespeare even at the Lyceum, much less this humble music hall. He was a stouthearted fellow and brave as a bulldog, but he had his limits. His good sister, on the other hand, seemed to revel in it. Of all the players in that scene she did show the most forthright fire.

Back on the ground floor she found most of her company had already departed, either to their various homes or to seek out late dinners. When I determined she was herself feeling hollow around the ribs, I offered to escort her to any place she liked.

"Actually, I was planning to attend a gathering near Grosvenor Square," she said. "They always have a substantial collation on the board."

"A party? This late?"

"For many of them it's yet early. Most of the guests won't even think of going home until the milk wagons start clattering around. Have you any objection to Bohemian society?"

"I've some decent French, but bless me if I can wrap my head around German speech."

She blinked, then burst into a laugh at the joke, grasping that I was, in fact, aware of what she meant by "Bohemian." "You shall fit right in, then. Let me change and we'll go."

"Will any of Art's friends be there?" I was worried about encountering further unanswerable questions about my death.

"My God, I should hope not." She dove back into the dressing room.

Kicking my heels in the hall, I pondered what she meant by that. I could guess that her theatrical doings would scandalize her family if word got back to them by way of Art's other cronies. It might be different if Lady Bertrice was a staid and distant patron of the thespian arts, but her actual participation on a stage would put the relatives into six kinds of fits. I always thought it strange how attending a play was respectable, but being *in* one—especially for a female—was not. I couldn't get around it.

I also considered what, precisely, to do about Bertrice. She could not be allowed to speak to Art about my turning up miraculously alive, not until I was ready to deal with him, anyway. That meeting would require careful planning. I had no wish to terrify him, nor send him hurtling for the nearest weapon under the misapprehension that by dispatching me he would be saving my soul. Given the shortage of good choices, I could consider that Dracula might well be right in his recommendation that I should cut ties to my former life.

But poor Art was apparently in a bad state. If I could just get him past the first shock and make him *listen* . . .

"All done, Mr. Quincey," said Bertrice, emerging. She was just fixing her bonnet in place with a hat pin. "We can get a hansom. There are usually a few dawdling about at the front of the theater."

I made no reply, being too stunned. She was all in black velvet, the top part something like a riding habit with touches of pale lace at the throat and wrists. It nipped in to a trim little waist and was wholly admirable to my eye, but the lower half of her costume would cause a traffic snarl even in a desert. I'd seen bloomers now and again and not really liked them, neither a dress nor trousers—comparable to being neither fish nor fowl. Lady Bertrice's were cut very stingy, fitting shockingly close to her form like a boy's knickerbockers, ending just below the knees with silver buckles on the banded cuffs. On her lower legs— and they were still most shapely—she wore black silk stockings and short boots with riding heels.

I've beheld much in the world in the way of women's costume, from the saris of India to the mud daubed on by South American Indians, but here and now in the heart of London, I found myself scandalized.

My feelings must have escaped onto my face. Those bright green eyes of hers blazed up again, and she lifted her chin. She looked ready to go fisticuffs with me and all my ranch hands.

"Is there a problem, Mr. Morris?" What an arch tone was in her voice. And she was back to using my last name.

"No, miss." I cleared my throat and straightened. "I'm just admiring the view."

For a second I thought she might dispute this, then she smiled and nodded. Apparently she'd cottoned on to the fact that I was trying my best. "It is a bit of a turn for a few, but the world shall have to get used to my ways. I'll not change."

"Nor should you," I said, for something to say.

A sharp look from her. Then another, approving, smile. "What a refreshing thing to hear. Thank you."

She had a long velvet cloak to match, which I helped her into. To my relief, it covered everything.

"I should have a proper coat made," she said, sweeping toward the stage door with me in tow. "But this is ever so much more dramatic, don't you think?"

"Yes, L—Miss Bertrice. Indeed it is."

"And perhaps more ladylike," she continued. "When I'm in these, my walking clothes, the cab drivers won't stop, thinking I'm a lunatic or a woman of easy virtue. You know, that phrase never made sense to me, for virtue should come easily to people. Instead they tend towards being judgmental. I'm always guilty, of course, sans the benefit of a proper legal trial. What insects people can be."

I was well aware she was passing on a light warning. If I didn't like what she did or wore, I could go hang myself.

She made a wonderful exit. The man who had let me in held the door wide for her like she was royalty, and she was just as gracious. A couple dozen johnnies were still clustered around the steps, hopeful in the cold.

"Come on, Miss 'Amlet, show us a bit a' leg!" called one of them. Offensively, I thought, and prepared myself to flatten him.

"Come to my matinee on Saturday and you will see much more than a bit!" she called in return, all good nature. This garnered her a roar of approving laughter. "And not just mine, but the *rest* of the Ring Players!" Another roar. She stepped down into them, and they magically parted for her like the bow wave of a graceful schooner.

As she predicted, we had no trouble finding a hansom. Cold it was to have the wind press on our faces as we rolled through the streets, but I prefered this conveyance to a four-wheeler. There, I'd have had to sit opposite. Here I was close by her, shoulder-to-shoulder, and that felt very fine.

"How did you come to be an actress?" I asked, wanting to forstall inquiries about my mysterious resurrection.

"I'm not really an actress, I'm a painter. The family disapproves of that quite enough."

"Why ever for?"

"Because instead of doing pleasant little watercolor sketches of the gardens at Ring, then taking tea, I insist on smearing oils over canvas, showing them in galleries, then selling the results. It smacks too much of Trade. Far too common, you know."

"If the recollection is not too painful, is that what your Aunt Honoria was so unhappy about the day of the funeral?"

"She's disapproves of everything, including the very air she breathes. I daresay it's the result of a demonic childhood and a sour marriage, but one cannot forgive such relentless stupidity. But to answer you, no, that is not her quarrel with me."

"What is it then? Unless—"

She raised a delicately gloved hand. "It's to do with *her* absolute and unmoveable stupidity. A disease that is too easily passed on, for she tends to call the note for the rest of the family. What a horrid lot of old bores they are. Father was different from them, he being well-mannered and intelligent. How Arthur and I turned out so well is largely due to Father's indulgent side. He saw to it that I got some education, though the curriculum was rather too limited. They put more emphasis on the proper way to curtsy and flirt behind one's fan than how to manage household accounts. Blockheads."

I took the descriptive as having to do with the governors of her school and not the gaggle of drunken pedestrians who were momentarily hampering our progress.

"But to return to my aunt," she continued. "Honoria heard some rumors about me, and being the charming person she is, chose to believe them. The more I denied them, the greater her belief. So one day I thought, to the devil with her. She seems to derive a twisted enjoyment from her loathing; who am I to take it away?"

"My God, what sort of rumors could they be?"

"That, sir, I may confide to you when I know you a great deal better."

I liked the sound of that happy possibility, though I had to wonder what the rumors were about. I couldn't imagine her doing anything seriously untoward, like robbing a bank. "I am ever at your service, Miss Bertrice."

"You are most kind, Mr. Quincey."

"How did you end up as ramrod to the Ring Players?"

"Through a series of chances and missteps. Looking back I wonder if it was less those than Fate itself drawing me down paths I might never have trod. Because of my painting I have many friends in the artistic community. They know me only as Bertrice Wood."

"Why is that?"

"If I signed my paintings as 'Lady Bertrice' they would be judged on the basis of my title, not my talent. As it is, they are already being judged on the basis of my being female, and in this world that is quite enough of a handicap. Most of the reviews were very favorable at first, before the critics discovered my sex, then they became harsh indeed or detestably patronizing. 'For a woman, Miss Wood shows a certain modicum of promise.' A week earlier, the reviewer was wildly enthusiastic over the 'rising star of B. Wood.' Bloody Philistine."

God help him if she ever meets the fellow, I thought.

She rounded on me. "Do you know that until I was twenty I had no idea that there were *any* female artists?"

Until this moment, I could have said the same for myself.

"All the art history books—*all* of them!—make *no* mention of female artists. You'd think we were born without talent at all, but not so. We were simply *ignored*!"

Once more I felt the blaze of her inner electricity. Thankfully it was not directed against me or I'd have been smoked to a cinder. No doubt but I was in the company of an English wildcat. And I liked it. She was wonderful. "Perhaps you will be the one to change that, Miss Bertrice."

"I can make a start. I'm already compiling a book on women artists through the ages, but it's going to be damnably thin."

Artist, actress, and writer. She certainly possessed a boundless energy for such pursuits, but where did she find the time? "It sounds like it could be mighty interesting reading."

"It will be. But finding a publisher, I fear, will be something of a nuisance. I may have to fall back on the generous patronage of 'Lady Godalming' to influence things in my favor. Oh—you don't know about her connection to me."

"But you're the same."

"Not in these artistic circles I'm not. But this has to do with the Ring Players and wants explaining."

" 'Speak; I am bound to hear.' " I intoned, raising a flash of amusement in her eyes. What a smile she had. Made me want to see her happy like that all the time.

"That drawl of yours brings out a whole different nuance," she said. "I should try it some night. No, perhaps not. You might make an interesting Hamlet, though."

"No, thank you. I'd rather watch someone who knows what they're doing. Just how did you come to be on the stage? What's this 'Lady Godalming' connection?"

"Yes. That. Well, one evening at a party some of the actors there wanted to stage a reading of a new play, and being short by one they asked me to fill in. Afterward, they insisted I join their company, thinking I had potential. It was there I did my apprenticeship. When I was not in my studio I was in the theater."

"Having the time of your life?"

A laugh. "You are most perceptive. I was indeed. My studio, or a portion of it, soon became a rehearsal hall. It was at that time I got the idea of the Ring Players. We always had far too many actresses and too few roles to cast them in. The material that is available for women is dismal and sparse."

"Even Shakespeare?"

"Especially Shakespeare. It is well and good to play Lady MacBeth or Juliet, but nearly all the rest of the characters are men. How boring for us, so I formed the Ring Players, after having secured the patronage of a certain Lady Godalming."

"So you are playing the angel for them. Does Art know?"

"Not at all! I've not even told him I'm acting yet."

"Why not?"

"Because he might be tiresome and mention it to someone in the family who would duly pass it on to Aunt Honoria. He doesn't need the complication of her roaring into his study insisting he do something to stop me. She plagued poor Father like that when she discovered I was living like a Bohemian artist and—horrors!—*selling* my art. What an awful row she made. Weary months of it. I'll not put my good brother through such purgatory."

"I'm sure if you insist he keep shut, he will."

"Yes, but not just yet. I'm far too busy at the moment. Anyway, concerning my secret patronage: I told the girls this 'Lady Godalming' wished to remain anonymous lest she offend her stiff-necked family—

which is perfectly true! I act as general manager and go-between, and hired a clerk for all the real work of balancing the accounts and issuing the pay packets. When time permits, I have the fellow instructing me in his bookkeeping methods as my deportment school fell short on certain practicalities. I'm sure Father would not have approved of this undertaking, thinking I should save my inheritance for a dowry, but since I shall never marry I might as well enjoy myself."

"*Never* marry?" Not unheard of, but surprising to me. She sure didn't look like a spinster. "A fine filly like yourself? You must have had a hundred offers."

"Oh, at least," she said lightly. "But none of those moonstruck fools were worth ten minutes of my attention, much less a whole lifetime. The sort of man I find even remotely interesting is very rare. When I do find one he's either not interested in me or already married."

"Poor fellows. If any of the unmarried ones truly had sense, they would have done the same as that merchant who'd found his pearl of great price."

"You're very kind, Mr. Morris," she said, after a pause.

Damnation. She'd gone back to my last name again. Had I been too enthusiastic? She had fine spirit about her that I found more fascinating with each passing moment, but was also skittish. It would take a bit of doing, but I'd have to slow myself down if I wanted to continue keeping company with her. There was never any mention in the Bible about how *long* it took the merchant to sell all he had so he could get his pearl.

Something like a glint returned to her eyes, hardening them. "I hope you don't mean that, like the pearl, I may be bought?"

The air suddenly got all thick between us. Where the devil had *that* come from? "No. Miss." I said it with feeling.

She pursed her lips. "I'm sorry. That was extremely rude of me. You did not deserve that."

Unique as she was, maybe she was more trouble than I wanted to tackle.

"I was trying to be clever, and instead I was insulting. I have a tendency to babble and say the most awful things. I don't mean any harm, but harm happens. I *am* sorry, Mr. Morris."

A handsome apology. But I couldn't help but get the idea that she'd done it all on purpose, the purpose being to show me the door. Was this what she did to the men she wasn't interested in? I hated to think she viewed me as yet another moonstruck fool not worth ten minutes of her time. "No harm done, Miss Bertrice. I think we can forget it. Why don't you tell me about this gathering?"

She accepted the distraction, and launched into a description of the host and possible guests. Artistic types they seemed to be. I didn't catch more than one word in five, and none of the names were familiar. Much of my mind was still turning over that last odd exchange. A man with a shorter temper would have probably made an excuse and found a way to leave. Was she testing me?

"Here at last," she announced. Before I could do anything about it, she quickly hopped out, paid the driver, and bade him a good night.

That fair flummoxed me. I'd heard of such a thing, but never experienced it for myself. What an infuriating female she could be. I resolved to make a point of paying for the return trip.

"Do hurry, Mr. Quincey, I'm half frozen," she urged, tugging her vast cloak more tightly about her.

I had half a notion to vanish from the hansom and reappear right next to her. Maybe she'd think that was quick enough. Pushing the idea to one side, I escaped the seat and offered her my arm the way a gentleman should. She took it the way a lady should, and we walked up the steps to the house.

There was a footman just within the door who opened it for us before I could try the bell. He was a young fellow and looked rather foolish, for his head was wreathed round with a garland of flowers. He seemed unaware of this fantastical addition to his otherwise sober garb. In fact, as soon as he took charge of our outer garments he held forth a tray stacked high with similar crowns.

"No, thank you," said Bertrice, with a quick side-long look at me. "Let's get our feet wet slowly."

"Flowers? In February?" I asked.

"Lord Burce has a huge greenhouse on the grounds. I don't know how he does it. Claims that a few drops of whiskey is his fertilizing secret, but that has to be nonsense. I should think the alcohol would burn the roots up."

I recalled her mentioning Lord Burce as being the host. I'd never heard of him, which was strange, since Art had an extensive circle of friends in the nobility to whom he'd introduced me. This part of Grovesnor Square was familiar, though I'd never been inside this particular house. It was a grand one, even compared to Ring, but much more modern, boasting the installation of electricity. As we passed from the entry hall to the inner rooms I saw each one ablaze with its own bright white light. It took some getting used to having so much of it around. I liked it, though. There was none of the usual smell of gas, nor the constant hiss that a person had to learn how to ignore.

The place was lavish on the decoration, maybe even overdone, indication that Lord Burce had no money worries. We strolled into a very large parlor where dozens of guests were gathered. Things were noisy, for they were all talking at once, trying to be heard over the play of music. The rich ornamentation touching the

eye at every turn was appropriate once one got an
eyeful of the guests, who seemed to be in competition with the house.

And here I'd thought the players at the music hall
were exaggerated with their various costumes. The
people here would make a pack of circus clowns look
like Quakers. Indeed, there was a white-faced clown
amongst them, along with various Romans, Indians—
both east and west, Gypsies, a sultan and his harem,
and others I could not readily identify.

"Oh, rot," said Bertrice frowning at the gaudy company. "I forgot it was fancy dress tonight."

Chapter Nine

"Bertie! Darling girl!" A very large, full-blown woman in a white powdered wig and red ball gown swooped toward us. She swept Bertrice right off the floor in a bear's hug. Then I got a closer look under the heavy face paint she affected and realized the woman was a man. That gave me a turn.

"Wyndon, how lovely, now put me down, you great oaf," Bertrice cheerfully ordered.

"Your wish is my command," he boomed. He looked at me. "My word, but that *is* an original. You must be the only Frenchman here who is *not* dressed as Napoleon."

"He's not a Frenchman, Wyndon—"

"You're absolutely right, dear girl. Bonaparte was from Corsica. My apologies, sir." He curtsied at

169

me, and I almost bowed back before catching myself.

She patted his arm and had to reach up to do so, for he was very tall. "Wyndon Price, may I introduce you to Mr. Quincey P.—"

"Quinn," I hastily finished, thrusting out my hand to him. Bertrice only blinked at my interruption, not giving away any startlement. She understood the value of anonymity, even if she didn't know my particular reasons for wanting it.

"How do you do, Mr. Quinn," said Wyndon Price. "Were your parents at a loss for a name?" Anyone else might have sounded rude, but this fellow seemed only innocently curious.

"I could not rightly say, Mr. Price, but people always remember me for the repetition."

"He's delightful, Bertie. Where did you find him?"

"He found me—that is, he's an old friend of the family. He saw the scene my company did at the hall tonight and came backstage." She watched me for a reaction, probably mindful that I might object to what she said, but I only nodded agreement. It was the truth, after all.

"Yes, she and all her ladies did a real corker of a job," I added. "I am filled with admiration for their effort."

"That makes one for your side, Bertie, out of . . . what *is* the population of London again?"

"Hush, Wyndon, or you shall annoy Mr. Quinn. He thinks you're serious."

"How gallant. You've found yourself a knight-errant, albeit an American in French clothes. There's a story, I'm sure." He looked at me expectantly.

"A dull one, Mr. Price. I spent some time on the Continent looking after my businesses, is all. Nothing nearly as interesting as this."

"Oh, but this is dull as ditch-water, sir. You should come 'round the place when Burce really gives a show. Puts the old Roman emperors to shame."

"That I should like to see. May I ask what prompted this occasion?"

"Just a little birthday party for one of the crowd. I forget whose, but you know Burce, any excuse to have people over. He hates getting drunk alone."

As there seemed no proper way to respond to that, I gave what I hoped was an amused smile.

"Speaking of refreshment," said Bertrice. "I'm famished. Is the feed trough in the usual place?"

Price pointed. "Right through there. Mind you don't trip on the fallen. Some of the revelers arrived early and the servants haven't cleared them away yet."

He was not exaggerating. Bertrice bade him goodbye for the moment, then threaded a path through the crowds of guests, several of whom were asleep or passed out on the floors and stairways. With no pause in their conversations people stepped over them as though nothing were amiss.

"What was that about with your name?" she asked. "I know why I'm incognito, what's your excuse?"

"It has to do with rumors of my untimely passing. I want to keep my head down for awhile yet."

"Why?"

"It's pretty complicated."

"I'm an excellent listener." But she saw my reluctance. "Oh, very well. Be secretive, but tell me why you even bother with it here. No one knows you."

"That you're aware. I'd just rather be safe than sorry."

"Is it connected with Arthur?"

"Pretty much. He is my best friend. Of all people he should be the first to know of my return. I don't want to make a big to-do until I've had a chance to talk with him."

"Why haven't you? Why haven't you rushed up to Ring and let him know you're all right? He's all miserable and moping while you're out having a night at a music hall."

My face fell. She'd hit the bulls-eye, and I said as much. "I will see him as soon as may be. I don't like the idea of his misery either, but I wanted a chance to settle in and think how best to approach him."

"There's nothing to think about, you just go."

"Miss Bertrice, no one in the world admires your directness more than I, but this situation needs a little more subtlety. I don't want to walk into his study like some ghost and scare him out of his wits."

"Then let me go in first and prepare him."

I started to object, then caught myself. "You might have something there. Maybe I could write out a message for you to give to him."

"Anything to speed you along. When are you going?"

"Tomorrow night—if he's still at Ring."

"I'm sure he will be. Since he and Dr. Seward came back from their hunting trip, he can't be budged. Last I was there he spent most of his time in his room. Seward comes often to see him, else I should be worried that Arthur might give himself a fit of brain fever. Between losing Father, Lucy, and you in so short a space of time . . ."

"Yes, Miss Bertrice, I understand." *No more delays,* I thought. "He's been carrying a burden, three of them. I want to lighten the load by one, I hope."

"So do I. Unlike me, he's not had work or other distractions to help ease his grief. What family that is at Ring is of no help. They're all too old or too distant from him to be able to truly give comfort. God knows I've urged him time and again to come stay in town to give himself a change. He just puts on a ghastly thin smile and says he'll think about it. You speak of a ghost, I think he's turning into one."

I made surrendering motions. "All right, you're preaching to the choir. I'll go tomorrow for sure."

She seemed about to argue that, then relaxed into a smile. "There I am again. When I feel strongly about something I get like an overwound clock: ticking along too loud and fast to hear anything. Forgive me, Mr. Quincey. I shall be much better after I've had a bite of food."

"Let's see to it, then."

We entered another vast room where long tables groaning with victuals of every description had been set up. A small army of servants tended to the needs of the hungry. I was not among them and felt my belly turn over at the stench.

"Are you all right?" she asked. "You look very green all of a sudden."

"I . . . think I had a bad—uh—biscuit with my tea this afternoon. The butter must have gone rancid."

"You put butter on your biscuits?"

I'd forgotten about the Yankee-British language barrier. She thought I was talking about cookies. "Toast, then. You go ahead, and I'll take in the sights."

"You'll not mind?"

I did very much mind being deprived of her company. But if I stayed with her I'd be talking, and that meant breathing in the cooked-food stink. It was very irritating. "There seems plenty to look at. Maybe Mr. Price will be kind enough to give me a tour."

Her gaze darted longingly toward the tables. "All right, if you're sure."

One thing I have learned in my travels is never get between artists and food. I bowed her into the room and retreated.

Wyndon Price wasn't difficult to find, not wearing that get-up. He seemed strangely comfortable in it, causing me to wonder just how artistic he might be.

"Mr. Quinn!" he said, laying a friendly hand on my arm. "Lost her already?"

"She's busy filling up a hollow leg."

"Yes, trodding the boards is famishing work. How long have you known her?"

"I'm more of a friend of the family. Business connections. Could have knocked me over with a feather seeing her tonight doing that show."

"Ah, but did you *really* like the Ring Player's feminine twist on the Melancholy Prince?"

"Very much, once I got used to things. I don't think even Mr. Irving could have done a better job than Miss Bertrice."

"Dear heavens! Don't speak too loudly. I think that odious manager of his might be lurking about. If you see a big, bearded Irishman stalking the halls give him a wide berth."

"Sounds as though you have a story there, too, sir."

"Not much of one. I was in Irving's company for a month. Thank God it wasn't any longer. Between Henry Irving playing the generous perfectionist tyrant and Mama Stoker's maniacal fussiness I was quite put out. I'm in theater to enjoy myself, but for them it's an obsession. It got quite boring for me, really. *Much* too serious."

I wasn't too surprised to hear he was an actor. "Are you doing something more to your satisfaction now?"

"Oh, just some this-and-that, and I sometimes take a part—you should *see* my Falstaff—and write reviews for the papers and magazines to keep heart and soul together. I was favorable to Bertrice's production, of course. And to her paintings, too. I didn't have to lie one bit, either. She's a lovely girl, very talented but full of thorns, if you know what I mean."

"I'm not sure I do, sir."

"Then you don't know her well at all."

"I think I should like to, though."

"Ah." Price favored me with a thoughtful look. "Be very careful, my boy."

"In what way?"

He glanced around and leaned in close, his tone low. "Well, I don't care to give away confidences, so I shall tell you a story instead. Once upon a time a handsome prince stole away a beautiful princess to Bohemia-land. There they lived for a time, where she blossomed into greater beauty that delighted all who met her. Jealous of her success, the selfish prince proceeded to cruelly break her loving heart into tiny little pieces, then smash those pieces into dust. The princess bravely threw him into the street, but was so scarred by his betrayal as to be cured of all thoughts of love forever."

I frowned. "Who was this rascal?"

"Long dead, thank God. He indulged in the pleasures of cocaine one time too many. No one mourned his passing. None of it was Bertie's fault. We're all entitled to fall in love with the wrong person once in a while. She's just determined never to repeat her mistake ever again, so it's made her rather prickly—especially to those gentlemen she finds attractive. She does not trust her own judgment. Oh, dear, now I've put you in a sour mood. Bertie will never forgive me."

"No, sir, but I do have strong feelings against such scoundrels as abuse womenfolk. Miss Bertrice is a fine lady and anyone showing her disrespect will have to answer to me."

"Providing they survive *her* response," he said. "She's a little thing, but quite able to take care of herself. Don't try protecting her unless she asks for help. Otherwise . . ." Price lifted his hand, palm up in a giving-away gesture. "And you need not mention my fairy tale to her, either. She hates having the past stirred up like mud in a pond. The future is something else again. She loves talking about possibilities. I think she has too many to choose from with all her talents; it keeps her from concentrating on any one thing."

Just then a sparely built young man in an elaborate highlander's kilt lurched toward us. "Wyndon, where the devil have you been all night?" he demanded, but in a humorous manner.

"Playing hostess, of course. Did you just wake up?"

"I've been here for hours, I think." He favored me with a sharp look. "Who's the Frenchy? Why ain't he dressed up as Napoleon?"

"Because he was not French, he was from Corsica," said Price, again referring to Bonaparte.

The man thrust a hand at me, speaking slowly and loud. "Wel-come-to-Eng-land-sir."

"Burce, don't play the fool this early in the evening. You'll give your guests the right impression. Let me present to you Mr. Quincey P. Quinn. He's a family friend of Bertie Wood. Mr. Quinn, this is Lord Eric Burce."

"How-do, sir," he said, squinting with very startling blue eyes. He didn't look drunk to me.

"How do you do?" I responded.

"Very well, thank you. You squiring our Bertie around now?"

Price answered for me. "Burce, don't be annoying."

"Why not? It's my party, I can annoy whomever I please except the cook and wine steward."

"Very well, that's reasonable."

"Where is little Bertie, anyway?" Burce looked about, trying to spot her.

"Feeding a hollow leg, I'm told."

"Good, she wants fattening up. What about you?" He fixed a still-squinty eye on me. "You look in need of some food."

"I'm fine, Lord Burce, thank you for asking. You sure know how to throw down a red carpet for your guests. This is one of the grandest parties I've been to in a very long while."

He frowned at me, then at Price. "He's American, ain't he? That's no Corsican accent."

Price rolled his eyes. "You need a keeper, Burce."

"The devil I do."

"I shall put an ad in the *Times* tomorrow, I swear."

"Don't you be swearing. It ain't becoming in a lady." Burce then slapped a hand across Price's broad backside. Price mimed a jump and little scream, producing a laugh from those nearby. Burce hooked an arm around mine. "Come on, Yankee-Doodle, let's go look for Bertie. I want to see what she's wearing tonight."

I allowed myself to be dragged off. Wyndon Price waved good-bye with a red lace fan.

"Miss Bertrice called them her 'walking clothes.'" I said to Lord Burce. "She didn't know it was a fancy dress party."

"Humph. Hardly matters for her, then. I think she's in secret league with Oscar Wilde's tailor to produce those whatever-they-ares. You need some help, though. Here it is, just the thing." He'd spied a discarded black half-mask on a table and plucked it up, passing it to me. "There, put that on. You can be a gentleman burglar from France or Corsica or something."

I readily accepted the gift and donned it. Perhaps Bertrice and Art moved in different society circles, but there was a small chance that a common acquaintance might be in this great crowd and someone would know me. With the mask, my beard, and the foreign cut of my evening clothes, I would be safe enough from instant recognition.

"Now for some amusement." His destination for amusement proved to be a wine and spirits table where he supplied himself with a glass of whiskey large enough to see most men through a Siberian winter. "What will you have, Mr. Quinn?"

To avoid an argument—and I knew I'd get one by refusing his hospitality—I accepted a glass of champagne.

"I thought all you colonial types went in for bourbon," said Lord Burce.

"It being a party, I thought to enjoy a little change." Actually, I did not want to waste a good bourbon since

I'd not be able to imbibe. Though champagne had a kick that sneaked up on you, it had always tasted thin to me, like soda water, so it seemed less of a crime.

"You know anyone here?"

"Just yourself, Mr. Price, and Miss Bertrice."

"Have to fix that." So saying, he immediately got the attention of several people in a nearby group and introduced me before moving on himself. As they all seemed as drunk as my host pretended to be, I knew they'd not remember much of the encounter. Contrariwise, I would not likely forget it.

All manner of artistic devotees populated the floors, some in a most literal sense. A few of these were moved to more restful areas by the staff. Burce seemed to employ two strong fellows whose only duty was to carry off overly drunk guests.

Those still standing had an endless supply of talk loosened up by their drinking. Their costumes ranged from being as elaborate as Price's to a modest half-mask like mine. The people wearing them were anything from utterly seedy to nose-in-the-air aristocracy. Not many of the latter, though. By some standards—such as Aunt Honoria's—this was one of those dens of iniquity that you always hear about but never can find when you want one. For someone like myself, it was as interesting as anyplace else I'd visited in the world, just folk of a like mind gathered to play. A few, I observed as another drunk was hauled off, might play very hard indeed.

Judging that Bertrice had had enough time to eat her fill and go back for seconds I returned to the dining room. She was gone, but as she seemed to be pretty well-known, I asked around and finally tracked her to the billiards room, where a number of the men had retreated to enjoy their tobacco.

The air was choked with pipe, cigar, and cigarette smoke, almost too thick for the electric light to penetrate. Despite this, a close game was going on, Bertrice against a fellow in a pirate costume. He'd pushed his eye patch back, and his crepe hair was askew. He made his shot, but the ball just missed the pocket. There was a general groan, then Bertrice stepped forward. She looked hard-pressed not to smirk.

She lined herself up and shot with more success. In the space of two minutes she sank the remaining balls on the felt and collected not only applause, but some shillings.

"Another game, Bertie," they called.

"Another night, if you please, after you've aired out this room." She handed her cue to the next player and came to take my arm.

"Mighty fine playing," I said as we strolled out.

"I should hope so. I spent hours practicing with Arthur at Ring. How have you been faring, Mr. 'Quinn'?"

"I've met a lot of fine folks. There's a conversation to please everyone here. If you don't want politics, just turn around and someone's going on about religion. If that's not your taste, then it's books or plays or anything else."

"You're enjoying yourself?"

"I am. It's good to be back with normal people again."

"Heavens. Where have you been that you consider this lot to be normal?"

"France."

Now I wasn't meaning to be funny, but she threw her head back in a full-throated laugh. No half measures for this lady, she put her entire self into it. A few of the women turned their heads, giving her a disapproving eye, but Bertrice didn't give a hang for their good opinion. I suppose after having dealt with a big bullfrog like Honoria these were no more than tadpoles.

Bertrice recovered and we roved through the rooms in a most pleasant way, her on my arm and giving greetings and introductions as needed.

"Do you dance?" she asked, for there was now music drifting over the buzz of talk.

The thought of dancing with her made me want to do handsprings. I could probably get away with such antics in this place and with my abilities, but it might scare her off. "A little waltzing and maybe a polka. It'd be my pure pleasure to squire you 'round the floor, Miss Bertrice."

"Good enough, there's not a man in this whole house who's brave enough to dance with me."

I chose not to ask her why, only laughed, taking it for a pleasantry.

We found the ballroom, and wasn't it the most jim-dandy thing I'd ever seen with those electric lights turning it to bright day all over again. A whole string of them had been connected up to the crystal chandeliers, making them blaze like diamonds on fire. They were almost too bright, but I got used to it. The players obligingly started up a slow waltz as we walked in.

She was perfect. I'd forgotten what a delight it was to have a pretty lady floating in my arms. Bertrice kept in step as though we'd practiced together for years. She seemed to truly relax just then; it wasn't something I could see, but I sure felt it.

"Miss Bertrice, if you don't mind my asking, that fragrance you're wearing—is it from India?"

She was surprised. "Yes, it is. However did you know?"

"I remember the day Art bought it for you in a marketplace in Calcutta. It was hotter than Beelzebub's boots and so sultry you could dip the air with a soup spoon, but Art stood it out, arguing away with this merchant about the price. He wasn't sure what you'd like better, perfume or a shawl, so he got both."

She laughed. "I have the shawl still. I draped it over the piano at my studio."

"A red silk thing with tassels?"

"Fringes. You've a remarkable memory."

"It just stuck in my mind for some reason. At the time I thought Art must have a very special sister for him to put so much effort into all that bargaining."

"Do you still think so?"

"Indeed I do." I hoped that wasn't putting myself too far forward, too fast for her, but hang me if any other man could have been in my place and lied.

"Ah," was all she said for a time. "Even a sister who does what I do?"

"That just makes you all the more interesting."

"Ah." And she got quiet again for longer.

I wondered if she might be working up to another attack of prickles. Time to head them off. "Speaking about Art . . ."

"Yes, what time were you planning to be at Ring?"

"Around eight."

"Drat, can you not make it earlier? I'm going to be engaged at the music hall by then."

"I'm afraid it's impossible." I was hoping she'd be busy. I had the idea that my return from the dead would be too much the terrific shock for Art and like that Frenchy barber, he'd need calming. Hypnotizing him while his sister looked on just didn't seem right. Besides, he and I would have a lot to talk about and over things that she didn't need to hear.

"Very well, if it can't be helped," she said. "Then what message would you like me to take to him?"

"None, though I very much appreciate the offer. I got to thinking that you're right, and it's best that I just go straight in and grab the bull by the horns. Art's a stout fellow, I'm sure he'll be able to handle it."

"As am I, but I *did* want to see the look on his face."

"I shall be pleased to give you a full description of

events at any time of your choosing. Perhaps I might
call on you again after one of your performances."
There. Skittish and prickly as she was she could not
find fault with that offering. Any decision to see me
would be hers.

"That would be lovely," she said.

Hallelujah.

"What about after you've visited Arthur?"

Oh, but didn't my heart give a lift? Maybe she just
wanted to hear about her brother, but the thought of
seeing her so soon again set my head to buzzing. "Well,
I can't rightly say how long we'll be. Once we get to
jawing about things we could be all night."

"Of course. The next evening then?"

"I'd be delighted, Miss Bertrice. If you should have
a change of plan, though, you may telegram me here."
I paused our dance long enough to find a pencil and
write the name of my hotel on the back of another
calling card. There was a hope in me that she might
return the favor so I'd have her address, but she only
tucked the card away in a pocket. For the first time
I noticed that she did not carry a reticule like most
of the other ladies. There was a decided advantage to
male costume.

Once more I struggled not to stare at her legs,
alluring though they were. A change of subject was in
order again.

"May I ask what galleries are showing your paintings? I've enjoyed your acting, seems only fair to have
a look at what else you do."

"If you like, I can take you 'round to one tomorrow in the forenoon. Not too early, though. I need my
sleep."

Damnation. More daytime pleasures to miss. "It
pains me to say this, but I'm going to be prisoner to
my business until the evening."

"How tiresome. Another time then?"

"I hope so." This condition of mine was infernally inconvenient. "Are any of them open at night?"

"Art galleries? Hardly. Candles and gas distort a painting's colors to a viewer. One should view such art by indirect sunlight."

"But what if a body buys a painting and hangs it in his house? Half the time it will be seen at night by candle or gas. Will the piece be any less beautiful?"

She almost stopped dancing. "What an excellent point. Perhaps I should experiment and paint something after dark."

"Bertie! Where have you been hiding?" Our host, Lord Burce, staggered across the floor toward us.

"I've been here and there, Eric."

We'd have had to stop dancing anyway for the orchestra had finished the waltz. I tried not to show chagrin as Burce got between us and bowed over her hand. Was he going to ask her for a turn or two? In his condition? His huge glass was nearly empty.

"Showing this Yankee-Doodle around?" He eyed me once more. "Why don't we see what he's made of, hm?"

"What do you mean?"

His reply was to put his finger on the side of his nose. "Come along, my dear, and find out."

He snagged her arm and led her away. I followed, as he took us to another, smaller room where a knot was gathered around a table. The electrics were off in here; candelabra on the table provided the only light, the soft glow falling upon the delicate features of a young woman seated there. She appeared to be playing cards, but with a very odd-looking oversized deck, each one bearing pictures instead of suit markings.

She was at the head of the table; seated to her right so he might easily view the cards was a very tall, imperious-looking blond man dressed like a crusader. He was one of the few people here who looked comfortable in his costume, wearing it like ordinary clothing. She turned a card face up between them and smiled. "The six of wands, a victory next to the Ace of Swords. Very good. I'd say that your venture will be highly successful, Lord Richard."

The man smiled his amusement while the surrounding group applauded. "You've quite a gift," he said gravely. "I hope it always brings you happiness."

"Not always, but when a reading comes out like yours I'm glad." The woman was dressed like a side-show Gypsy fortune-teller, but with blond hair flowing from under her head-kerchief. It was a sharp contrast to the bright colors of her costume, but there was an exotic cast in the angles of her face and tilt of her blue eyes, suggesting Slavic ancestry.

"Sholenka, you darling witch," said Lord Burce, coming close to put an arm around her shoulders. "What sort of spells are you casting tonight?"

"Really, Eric, do be quiet or you'll get me arrested and hanged."

"That was my relations up in Scotland who were so tiresome, nothing to do with me; they're all dead."

She shook her head and spied Bertrice. "Good evening, Miss Wood. Are you enjoying yourself?"

Bertrice smiled, arching an eyebrow. "You tell me."

They both laughed; evidently this was an old joke for them.

"Sholenka, what can you tell us about this fellow?" Burce nodded in my direction.

"My dear man, I'm not one of those automaton machines at the seaside that points to slogans for a penny. At least introduce us."

Burce did so. Her name was Shola Vyvial; she was also an actress, and everyone called her Sholenka.

"Russian?" I asked, after giving her a proper greeting.

"Czech," she replied. "A long time ago for the family. You, I perceive, are from America."

"She's amazing," said Burce to the audience, all pleased confidence.

"I've an ear for accents, you silly drunkard."

He pretended offense. "And you are a fraud."

"Of course I am, aren't we all?"

Laughter from the crowd as she shuffled her strange, oversized cards. "Would you like your fortune told, Mr. Quinn?"

"I don't rightly know, miss. Seems to me that the future is best when left as a surprise."

"What a refreshing opinion. There are many here who would fanatically disagree with you." She put down her deck and smiled at the man in the crusading gear. Damn, if that sword on his hip wasn't real, and it had the look of an antique. "Lord Richard, you may become scarce now, your success is assured for many years to come."

The tall man vacated the chair, pausing to bow over her hand and brush his lips against her fingertips. "It's been a pleasure. I am ever your servant, lady." He straightened and paused, his gaze fastening on me as though in recognition.

I tried to place him, but was fairly certain he was a stranger. Still, I was glad of my mask.

Burce stepped in. "Lord Richard d'Orleans, Mr. Quincey P. Quinn, an American businessman, if you will allow me to commit a tautology. I've yet to meet an American who was *not* a dedicated entrepreneur."

"An honor, Mr. Quinn," said d'Orleans as we shook hands. He had the most remarkable piercing blue eyes, and I got the feeling that should we ever meet again, he'd remember me despite my mask. "Welcome to the circle, young one."

"Sir?" I didn't quite understand what he meant.

"You are wise not to be overly curious about the future," he continued, as if he'd not heard. "It's a dangerous place. Even for us."

He didn't explain that cryptic statement, either, and moved off. He had a walk like a panther. Bertrice, along with all the other women in the room, marked his progress until he was gone from sight.

"What was that about?" I asked no one in particular.

"Who knows?" said Burce. "He sometimes mutters the most fascinating nonsense. Abandon all hope, ye who banter here."

"Eric, you're an evil man," said Sholenka.

"I adore you, too, witch."

"Please take the chair, Mr. Quinn."

I spared a glance at the others present. "You've plenty here waiting ahead of me."

"Nonsense, Eric wants me to look you over."

"Uh . . ."

"Oh, nothing untoward, Mr. Quinn. It's not that sort of party, leastwise not in this room. Now remove your mask and put down your drink."

Setting the still-full champagne glass to one side, I stuffed the attempted disguise into my pocket. She stared long into my eyes. I didn't know what to expect. In my travels I'd encountered a number of native fortune-tellers, shamans, and what-not. I won't say if I believed or disbelieved any of their doings, but understood that it was always wise to respect them.

Sholenka's expression went all puzzled.

"Something wrong?" I asked.

She gave no reply and began shuffling the cards. "Cut them," she ordered.

I did so.

She then cut them herself in to six short piles. She turned the first two cards over, her mouth drawing into a serious line. "Three of Swords and the Five of Cups are in your past. You've known terrible sorrow. A very sharp grief, perhaps from an unexpected death."

I felt my belly give a sickening twist. Bertrice, who stood just behind Sholenka, frowned at me as though

thinking this might be a bad idea. Obviously she'd
known that, like her brother and Jack Seward, I had
also proposed to Lucy Westenra and endured the pain
of her loss. I couldn't help but stare at the card showing
a heart pierced by three swords, one for each of us.
Unbidden to my mind came the terrible image of Lucy
thrashing and shrieking in her coffin as Art drove the
stake into her. Her heart. I'd stood by with Jack and
Van Helsing, reading the prayer for the dead.

Dear God, what had we done?

What terrible irony lay before me on the table.
"Those pictures t-tell you that?"

She made no reply and turned over two more cards.
"The Tower of Destruction and Strength. You've
recently known sudden, dire transformation, or a collapse of something in your life, but you weathered it.
It has made you better and stronger."

A chill seized my spine, as though a breath of winter
straight from Transylvania had invaded the room and
sought me out. Was she also a reader of minds?

"The last two are your future. Do you want to see
them?"

Dry-mouthed, I nodded.

"The Moon. Beware of deception, either deceiving
yourself or believing lies from others."

Well, that was ever a good idea.

The last card. She shifted in her seat, uneasy. "The
Fool, reversed."

"What's it mean?"

"You must beware of a risk or of taking risks."

"I always try."

"You don't understand. Four of these six cards are
of the Major Arcana. That means there are *very* powerful forces at work around you. This is no ordinary
warning to be cautious. Deception and risk could truly
be in your future."

"That possibility holds for us all, ma'am."

"One last card," she said. "You must turn it your-self. Cut it from any of the six stacks before you."

"Does it matter which one?"

"No. Let your feelings guide you."

My feelings were that of puzzlement and fearful dread. She'd bulls-eyed too much already for my com-fort, but I could not bring myself to stop. I chose from the thickest deck of those remaining, cutting and turn-ing as she had done.

A little murmur went through the crowd. The card needed no interpretation for me, depicting as it did a skeleton with a scythe cutting away at the tiny fig-ures of people.

"The death card," said Lord Burce.

"Major Arcana, five out of seven," Bertrice muttered.

"This isn't exactly cheering, is it?" I asked.

Sholenka recovered from her own disconcertion. "This doesn't always symbolize a physical death. It can mean change, like the death of a way of life, the passing from the old to the new. These first two cards indicate that a physical death has already occurred and is behind you. These others are only warning you to either be cautious or to prepare yourself for the change to come."

From the reaction of the others, I wasn't so sure. It seemed to me that she was trying to ease the bad news so as not to scare me. "I fear I am no wiser for the warning. Is there any way you might be more clear about just what the change might be?"

Bertrice had watched the exchange with great inter-est. "Shola, he's all worried now, and who can blame him? Mr. Quinn, perhaps you'd best not attach too much importance to this. Think of them as nothing more than bits of pasteboard with pictures that tell a story with no end."

Sholenka smiled sympathetically. "The cards can be vague at times. I'm sorry if I've upset you."

And here I thought I had been covering it up well.

"I confess that I am greatly stirred around for not knowing the nature of what may lie ahead."

She nodded. "All right, there might be a way of getting a hint. Let me see your hands."

For an instant I recalled that moment in the stony wilderness when Dracula made the same request. I extended my hands toward her, palms up on the table. She took them in both of hers. For a moment she only studied the lines.

"You've lived very deeply, an intense life, but there's a sudden break in its flow. There's a resumption here, but it's very strange . . . I don't quite see what . . . oh, *God!*"

She released me as though my touch burned her.

"What *is* that?" she demanded. She stood up so quick her chair fell over. She backed away, staring at me. "What *are* you?"

"Miss?"

Sholenka's eyelids were peeled wide and her expression was wild. "You're here and beyond. It's black with death!"

The others gaped at her, then at me. I didn't know what to think or do. She'd gone plumb crazy.

"The colors, like an empty grave," she went on. She grabbed up her cards, shaking so much she could hardly hold onto anything. "A swirling pit of fire, black fire under the moon!"

Burce stepped next to her. "Shola? Control yourself! It's all right."

"*Get me out of here!*" Without waiting for him, she bolted.

Chapter Ten

Everyone, myself very much included, gaped at her as she retreated, wailing, with Lord Burce trying to catch up. No one moved for a long moment.

I was stunned as you can get and still be awake. I didn't know what to think.

It seemed best to stay put, though I was well aware of all the people starting to turn their shocked attention on me, particularly Bertrice. I felt just about the same as they must, but more of it. How had Sholenka picked up on my being a vampire? There was no other explanation for her pitching such a fit. I looked at my hands, but they were the same as ever. Not in the least like Dracula's. Now if she'd acted that way over *him* it would make sense. Given the right circumstances, he could set most anyone off like a box of dynamite.

"What's wrong with her? What did she see?" several asked, peering at me, suspicious. The good humor filling the room moments before had quite vanished. I could tell they were blaming me for it, too.

"Excuse us, ladies, gentlemen." Bertrice seized my arm. We made an ignominious retreat. People in our path got out of the way. As we left the dim room, I heard them starting to talk.

Bertrice didn't stop until we were nearly to the foyer, then rounded on me. "What the devil was *that* about?" she demanded.

By now I was fairly shaken too, like descending a staircase too quick and finding there's one less step than you expected. "Blamed if I know. Was she joshin' me with an act?"

"Shola is a very steady sort. She saves the hysterics for the stage, and she's not that good at them. That was real fear. Why was she babbling about death and graves?"

I shook my head, very troubled and uncomfortable. "I can't say. That was the dam—well, I've never seen anything to beat her. I'd apologize, but I don't think she'd welcome it."

"Maybe I should go see her."

Wyndon Price, drawn by the commotion, rushed past, holding the skirts of his ball gown high. He did not notice us.

"Seems to me things are under control. Or will be," I said. I wanted to get clear of this homestead before Sholenka talked too much more. "They'll likely give her smelling salts and brandy, and she'll be right as rain."

"I hope so." Bertrice's eyes went narrow. "What did she *see* about you?"

I spread my hands. "I couldn't say that either."

"Really?" She expected an answer, one I dared not give.

"Maybe I should be heading out, if you don't mind.

Seems like my continuing to be here might spoil things for some, and I wouldn't want to do that."

She seemed about to ask me more, then swallowed it back. "What an excellent idea. I'll go as well."

"Please don't deprive yourself of staying on my account."

"It's for me. I've said hello to those who needed it, eaten a good meal, and know when to make a proper exit. What a surprising evening this turned out to be."

I could wholly agree with her. Damnation, but *why* did it have to end this way?

Bertrice found another guest who was also about to leave and skillfully arranged a ride for us in his four-wheeler. He was tottery from drink and dozed on his bench, while she and I sat opposite and made sure he didn't entirely fall off. I wondered why she did not maintain a carriage in town for herself, since she could well afford it. Perhaps it would not be in keeping with her pretense as a struggling artist and actress.

She didn't say much during the ride, and I could tell the woman was simmering herself up for something. She was likely angry that I wouldn't answer her, maybe having seen through my lie. It made for a very chilly journey.

The driver paused at my hotel. I got out, bade Bertrice a simple goodnight with a chaste kiss on her hand. She responded with a regal nod and a piercing look. I trudged inside, weary in heart. The palm-reading incident had had a decided cooling effect on our once-easy conversation. I wondered if she'd ever want to see me again.

Such were my glum thoughts just before dawn when, divested of my evening clothes, I sieved inside the traveling crate and settled on top of the bags of earth there. Dracula had said I could pretty much resume the same life I'd had before—with some changes. Did those changes include forsaking Bertrice?

I very much wanted to become much better acquainted with her, but how to do that without explaining myself? I'd been warned not to trust my secret with just anyone. If I hypnotized a lady into acceptance of my condition and instructed her to keep quiet about it, then would I be fairly safe. But making so free with Bertrice just wasn't honorable. This wanted sleeping on, though simple sleep I could not achieve.

Between one thought and the next the sun had come and gone. My only clue of its passage was a subtle feeling of having rested and a change in the sounds of activity around me. Instead of the early morning staff quietly placing the guests' cleaned boots outside doors, I heard the modest bustle and conversation of those guests going about their business. To have such excellent hearing was a mixed blessing, as I'd learned during my stay in Paris, but I'd also learned to ignore such jabbering.

My own room was quiet, meaning it was safe for me to slip clear of the crate, which I did. The maid had been and gone, for the bed was made up. I'd taken the trouble to lie in it to make things appear normal, and that's as much as was needed here for my safe-keeping. So long as I maintained such simple ruses and drew no undue attention all would be well for me. With strangers, anyway. Despite my rest, I was no closer to a decision concerning what to say to Bertrice, and it would have to wait.

The night before I'd written a telegram to Art at Ring, instructing the hotel's night man to see to its delivery. I'd done this to assure that Art would be home when I came calling, careful to give no clue to my identity:

"My dear friend, it's been too long since we've shared

conversation. Please be home tonight after dinner that we may catch up on past adventures. I wish to surprise you, so I will sign myself only as—An Old Comrade."

I'd wanted to intrigue him and knew this would turn the trick. If he was still feeling low, then would this spark his curiosity, hopefully in a pleasant way.

When I had readied myself for the trip to Ring, I went downstairs to find a reply had come that afternoon, left in care of the hotel. It warmed my heart enormously.

"Dear Old Comrade, whoever you are, you are most welcome to my home. Will be waiting. Arthur, Lord Godalming."

The train schedules in England being vastly more reliable than those on the Continent, I was able to board my car in the full confidence of arriving just after the dinner hour. I carried a small travel case, heavy with a quantity of the earth so necessary to my rest. There would be no return trains until the following night, so I'd have to find a place to shelter for the day. Once Art and I had had our talk, though, I was sure he would provide one for me.

If all went well.

It had taken Dracula an astonishingly short time to bring me around to a different way of thinking about vampires. But then I'd become one, so that did have a powerful influence over the quickness of my conversion. Art would be a tougher nut to crack, but there was a good possibility he would see reason, once I got him past the first awful hurdle. I'd decided to take the least unpleasant path and hypnotize him from the start.

It was cowardly, but I saw it as a way of sparing him from needless distress. He might eventually forgive me, for we were old friends.

As a small salve to my conscience, I determined

never to take any such liberty with Bertrice. In this instance with her brother I had a tolerable excuse, but she would ever be spared from my lack of resource. How things would unfold between us, if they were there for the unfolding, was up to the Fates, and thus I prayed that those capricious sisters would be kind to me.

My arrival at the little station went unmarked. No one met me, which was satisfactory. If I'd wanted a carriage and driver waiting, I'd have requested it in the telegram, knowing Art would oblige and likely be there himself. That would never do.

Valise in hand, I walked from the station to Ring, it being a half-hour's leisurely stroll away, and the countryside was pleasant—in the summer. At this time of year, though the land was strangely green from winter wet, the charms of a walk were less appealing, but the wind was not so bad, and it was not raining or cold enough for snow. My thoughts were more on the coming interview than anything else, even Bertrice.

Art and I were as close as any two men who were not born as brothers. Even though we'd had vastly different upbringings, back in Texas we'd formed that kind of instant bond that sometimes happens between people. We thought alike on many things, disagreed on others, but respected our differences and celebrated our similarities.

How long ago it seemed to me, those days, those years of tramping all over the world, testing ourselves against its countless obstacles and winning. It seemed as though nothing could stop us then. How changed was our world now that our view was tempered by so many sorrows, one sorrow in particular. As much as I mourned Lucy, Art had the greater grief, for he had been the one she'd chosen. I'd seen his love for her bring about a nobility of spirit in him that ran beyond the limits of his inherited title, but at what price?

That I was about to discover.

I passed through the great gates of the estate. They were always open, England being long past the days when such defenses were needed. A curving graveled drive led to the huge old house. It looked bleak, for the surrounding trees were bereft of their foliage except for a stand of evergreens off to the west. There I took myself, seeking their shadows.

On this side of the gray stone pile was Art's study on the second floor. The windows were shut, of course, but the curtains were open. He usually forgot to draw them unless one of the maids chanced to do it.

Had my heart been beating it would have given a leap, for a figure now appeared at one of the windows. I could not make out his features, but guessed it to be Art himself. A servant would not have stood there looking out for so long. I wanted to rush forward, shouting, but firmly held back. I had a plan on how to go about this reunion and would stick to it.

I concealed my valise under the low branches of a fir that had grown crooked, marking it in my memory. Should the evening go badly and I found it necessary to retreat, I wanted my earth in a safe, easily found place. Not that I expected trouble, but damn me if Sholenka's strange card reading hadn't left me thoroughly unsettled. It is all well to discount such things as superstitious nonsense, but I'd seen too much. There was more to the world than most of us are aware, and having experienced—if not become a part of—that hidden side, I'd be a fool to ignore it.

Leaving the fir stand, my eyes peeled for stray gardeners making rounds, I walked straight to the west side of the house to stand beneath the study window. From here it was only about twenty feet up. That had not seemed so much from a distance, now it looked impossible, though I'd scaled taller cliffs in Transylvania.

On the other hand, those had not been composed of smooth, mortared stone.

Very well, I had another way of gaining entry. I wanted to avoid the front door. The servants knew me too well. Instead, I vanished and lifted my incorporeal self higher and higher, using the hard face of the house as a guide. When I sensed a change of its surface, I went just solid enough to see I was level with the window. Art, thankfully, had drawn the curtains by now. What he'd have done seeing me floating ghostlike against the sky did not bear thinking about.

Vanishing utterly, I sought and found my way through the cracks in the casing until I was fully within the room. So much for Van Helsing's lore that a vampire could not gain entry to a house without invitation. Then again, perhaps my original welcome to Ring made when I still breathed was yet in effect. No, but that lore was false as well. I'd had no trouble walking into Lord Burce's home. Maybe the restriction only applied to Dracula's breed.

I dismissed speculations in favor of acquainting myself with the lay of the land. I knew it well, having spent many hours here yarning away with Art over a bottle or two from his rich cellars. Over there was the big fireplace; he would have it blazing in anticipation of his guest's arrival. Near his desk stood his drinks cabinet, probably open for the same reason.

Well, I mustn't keep him waiting.

I felt my way across the large room, and yes, sensed Art's nearby presence. He was in his favorite chair by the fire, no doubt filling the time by reading the papers or some book as he was wont to do. I brushed rather too close to him, for he made a sudden exclamation and left his chair. At first, I couldn't apprehend what he was up to, but muffled sounds soon explained his actions. He'd piled more wood onto the blaze. How his servants would be scandalized, with their master looking after his own comfort, but he'd picked up some very bad habits from his travels.

This reminded me that my coming too close had given him a profound chill, which I'd not meant to do. I backed away, trying to find the door leading to the hall. That accomplished, I passed beneath it, finally becoming solid again on the other side.

The hall was very dim, even for me. There was only a faint glow from the stairs at the far end where lamp light seeped up from the front entry. Had I come in by that means, a butler or footman would have guided me up here with a candle.

The darkness suited me fine. I was covered by a good heavy Inverness cape I'd bought to disguise my form if not my height. Now I took a moment to deal with my face, donning the half-mask I'd thrust in my pocket the night before. Over the lower part of my features I wrapped a woolen muffler, for Art would know me in a beard. On top I perched a low traveling cap. It was all highly dramatic, but necessary.

I softly tapped on the door, as a servant might, and received permission to come in.

He was back in his chair again and just turning 'round. Possibly he expected it to be a footman sent to announce the arrival of his guest. Certainly by Art's expression he did not expect the guest himself, nor a guest done up in so fantastical a manner. He quickly stood, his face a mix of guarded expectation fighting with amusement.

"Well, old comrade," he said after a moment to look me over, "you've flummoxed me. I give up. Who are you?"

Hearing his voice again, sounding the same as always brought me close to choking on the sudden lump in my throat. How I wanted to tear away the disguise and rush forward to seize him up in a back-thumping bear's hug. I made myself go slowly, my hand outstretched to take his. We shook, formally, like gentlemen.

"Will you not speak?" he asked, still with a smile hovering about his lips but puzzlement in his expression.

I shook my head, then went to light the lamps. He'd not been reading, for the only other light came from the fire, which was not enough for my purposes. I recalled what Bertrice had said about his moping about. This could not be good.

He watched my every move. I could tell he was holding himself back, allowing me to have my own way until I had things arranged to my satisfaction. One aspect of his character I could always count on was his ingrained politeness, but it could not be pushed too far.

"Sir, I have been eaten up with curiosity all the day, will you not ease it?" There was the faintest edge of exasperation beginning to creep into his tone.

To this I made a calming gesture, and motioned that he should seat himself again. In turn I pulled a chair close to his, that I could look him right in the eye. When I sat, he sat, but was barely able hold himself in place. I could hear his heart thumping away.

He was much thinner than when I'd last seen him, almost gaunt; the change was alarming, unhealthy. His face was very pale and drawn, with lines of care beginning to etch themselves into his otherwise youthful flesh. The intervening months had not been kind to him, and little wonder. Why had not Jack Seward done anything?

Catching Art's gaze with my own, I extended all of my will toward him until he seemed to relax. His eyes bore only the faintest glazing, though.

I put my hand over his. "Please," I whispered. "Do not be afraid of me."

"What . . . why . . . ?" He was stout of spirit and will, not one to easily surrender to suggestion.

"Art, remember that I am your true friend. I won't hurt you."

A flickering in his features, and I heard his heartbeat suddenly quicken. Aside from Jack Seward, I was the only one who ever called him "Art."

"Be at ease, all is well. I swear it."

He made a long, awful exhalation of breath such as you only hear from the dying.

This was more difficult than it should be, but the explanation stood on the table next to his chair: a brandy bottle and two glasses. He'd apparently been imbibing prior to my arrival.

He began to recoil, trying to pull his hand from my grasp.

"Don't move," I ordered, and it wrung at me to use so sharp a voice with him, but I'd learned that the more emotional I was while working hypnosis, the more telling the results.

His movements ceased, but his heart yet boomed away fit to burst.

"You're not afraid," I said, feeling desperate. "You must not fear me."

"No . . ."

"Art, it's all right. I came a long way to talk with you, so please don't collapse. I wouldn't know what to say to that old snob you have for a butler."

He gave a short gasp, almost like a laugh; it lacked mirth, but served its purpose. It had pulled his thoughts sideways to something out of our past, something normal. "Q-Quincey?"

"Yes, my friend. It's me. And everything's all right." I held tight to his hand with both of mine now. He trembled like a fever victim. "You just settle yourself, and I'll explain everything."

"You're a ghost," he said in a thin, lost voice.

"Oh, lord help us, no. Be sensible, Art, there're no such things."

"There are, I've seen them."

"Yes, well, enough of this stuff will make you see all kinds of whatnot. I'll take the risk and give you a bit more, though, as you look to be in sore need." I let him go and gave him his brandy glass. Thank goodness, he didn't bolt from the room.

He finished it off in one swallow and coughed, staring at me the whole time as though I might vanish if his attention wavered. Slowly, so as not to affright him further, I undid my muffler and removed the cap and mask, piling them on the table. If he'd had any shred of disbelief left, this ripped it fully away. He groaned as if in great pain, his eyes rolled up, and he started to pitch forward.

I caught him in time and pushed him back in his chair. "No, you don't, Art Holmwood! You wake up this instant and face me. Come on, man!"

It took a few moments to fully bring him to again. I'd not thought any of this would be easy and was sorry it was living down to my expectations. He clutched at my arm.

"You seem solid enough," he allowed. "Not a ghost? Then tell me how you recovered, for the two of them pronounced you dead on the spot that awful night."

For an instant, I thought how easy it would be to give him a lie. To say that Jack Seward and Van Helsing had both been mistaken and that I'd somehow recovered from the knife wound. How much easier it would be on him. On us both.

But I'd been raised to be truthful, which made me a very poor liar to those who mattered to me. I could *make* him believe whatever I wanted, but that would set up a whole other passel of problems. One of the good points about speaking the truth is you never have to work to remember what you've said.

"It's a long story," I told him. "And I won't say word one of it until you've gathered all your wits."

"What a weary wait that shall be, I-I think they've fled the country."

That was what I wanted to see: his old humor coming back again. He sounded frail, but it was a beginning. "Tell you what, you catch your breath and look at me all you want until you finally believe your eyes."

So saying, I quit my chair and shrugged out of the Inverness, throwing it onto a nearby settee. As I expected, his gaze never left me, giving me an idea of what a zoo animal's life must be like.

"Nothing's changed here, I'm glad to see," I said, making a slow round of the room. "I feel like I've returned to my second home."

One thing was new: there was a photographic portrait of Lucy on his desk. It must have been taken shortly after announcing their engagement. I remembered that particular dress and how radiant she'd looked in it at the celebratory dinner party. Some of her sweet beauty shone out even from this meager memory of her true self. I had to turn away. It hurt too much.

"You look well—for a dead man," said Art. He was not smiling.

"I reckon I do."

"How did you . . . survive? Recover? For God's sake, Quincey, speak to me or I shall go mad!"

"Don't go flying off the handle, this isn't exactly an easy thing for me, either. I've much to tell and you may not believe any of it. What you must believe is that I am the same old Quincey and your true friend."

"What *happened* to you?" His voice rose, tight with nerves. He stood and came toward me. He walked almost like a puppet, arms and legs jerking, barely under control, unsteady.

My heart sank. He would not be able to deal with the truth. Not now. I would have to draw him into a

deep sleep and convince him my intrusion had been
only a dream.

Then he wasn't looking at me, but at something over
the fireplace. All the color drained from him, and he
seemed ready to faint again.

"Dear God Almighty," he whispered, and though his
family was and always had been strictly Church of
England, he crossed himself.

"Dear God, indeed," I said, and felt myself go pale
as well. Over the mantle, so much a part of the study
that I'd forgotten its presence, was a large mirror in
an ornate gold-leafed frame. It showed him to be alone
in the room.

He fumbled at his neck. His fingers twitched almost
too much to work properly. His collar button popped
off, then suddenly he produced a crucifix on a chain.
No, by God, it was a real rosary, the very one he'd
worn all during our hunt for Dracula.

Holding it before him seemed to bolster his courage. He stood straight, and determination returned to
his expression. I was very glad that he did not have a
weapon just then.

"Stay back," he said, his voice firm.

"Art . . . it's all right. I'll not hurt you. I'm not like
he was, I swear it on Lucy's soul."

Rage flooded him. "How *dare* you speak her name!"

Damn, that had been ill-considered. "You'll understand when you've heard me out."

He shook his head. "No. You will leave. In the name
of God I command you! Depart! Now!"

"And in the name of God I ask that you listen! I
am *not* like that fiend we killed. If I were, would I
be able to wear this?" I slipped my fingers under my
own collar. I drew forth a silver crucifix on a long chain,
the one that *I'd* worn during and since that fateful
hunt. The same as Art, I could not bear to part with
its comfort. "See? I am *different*!"

The truth took a while sinking into his brain, and when it did it made an ugly job of twisting his whole world around. I could almost read the mix of feelings as they marched over his face, for certainly I'd gone through them all as well.

"You died," he insisted. "You *did* die. You're one of them."

"Yes. But another breed."

"Breed?"

"That's the only word I have for it." A memory flickered. "Think of it this way: if Dracula was like a wolf of his kind, then I'm more of a hunting dog."

"You're a vampire, you kill."

"No! Never—I swear on this." I held up the crucifix.

"Impossible!"

"It is."

"You drink blood! Damn it, Quincey, you drink blood from the living!"

"Animal blood."

"But—"

"Animal. Blood. That's all. Please, believe me, Art. I would never for the world hurt anyone."

He said nothing for a long time, only stared, his face gone blank.

I used his stillness, fixing on him. "Art, listen to me. Calm yourself and don't be afraid, not of me."

There may have been too much brandy in him for me to have any luck getting past his agitation, but he did ease a little. "I'm not afraid. I am horrified. Sickened."

"So was I at first. Took a while to get over the shock. But this is *not* what you . . . Oh, hell, sit down and let me tell my story. Then if you still feel the same I'll leave." It wrung my heart to say that, and from his reaction he must have seen it; he suddenly looked awkward.

"All right."

I wanted to help him to his chair, for he was in need, but it was better to keep my distance. He sank into it jerkily, like an old man with bad bones. I took my seat across from him, sparing a glance at the brandy bottle.

He followed my thought and shook his head. "No. No more for now."

Probably just as well. He had to have his head clear, but dear heavens, how I wished I could have some for myself.

"It was pretty danged cold that night, wasn't it?" I said.

"Yes." He nodded. "I remember."

"That's about all I remember of it. That and the fight."

"What about your wounding?"

"Some of it. Didn't hurt all that much, sort of like a fist in the belly from a good roundhouse punch. I only knew how bad it was from the way the rest of you were acting, but my heart was light, truly it was, for I could see that we'd saved Miss Mina."

"Yes . . . but lost you."

I shook my head. "No. Not the way you think. Not to *him*. What happened to me goes much farther back. . . ."

And so I came to remind him of that embassy party years ago in South America and of Nora Jones.

"You're saying that that charming girl was one of *them*?" he asked.

"Well, a different kind of 'them,' but yes, she was."

"Why did you not say anything?"

"Art, you of all people know that a gentleman never speaks of such things."

He looked like I'd just popped him one square between the eyes. Then he thought a little more. "She had you under some sort of enchantment."

"Only that of her beauty."

"But for you to become . . . she'd have had to . . ."

I touched my throat. "Yes, she did, and I did. And, yes, it was odd that I didn't think much about it at the time. I will say that the experience was profound, but I took no harm from it that I noticed. Quite the contrary."

Some color flooded his cheeks. It was more of a blush. "She did not . . . force you?"

Evidently he was recalling that awful tableau when we broke into the Harker's room to find Dracula and Miss Mina in such a compromising embrace. "No. I guess you could say I was caught up in the moment. It's hard to allow, especially here, thousands of miles away and years in the past, but at the time it was the right thing to do. I had no idea it would have so strange a consequence. She never told me. I wish I knew why."

"I never suspected she was . . ."

"That made two of us. Until I met Van Helsing and listened to his tales I hadn't thought twice about what she did. Then when I started thinking about her, I got scared."

"Why did you not say anything?"

"It would have done no good and the time was wrong. We were all busy with more important matters. My idea was to first see the hunt through to the end, then talk to the professor in private about my dilemma. Only that never happened."

"No . . . you died."

I heaved a great sigh, mixed with a soft snort of a chuckle. "Yes, I did. And I came back."

"You're dead. A dead man that lives."

"Art, I pledge to you, I'm the same as I ever was, and I *feel* alive."

"But the blood . . ."

"Animals provide my food, like a cow gives milk. It's same as you eating a pheasant for your dinner. It's what I have to do to stay alive."

"But to *drink* it?"

"Think now, my friend, think of all the strange things we've dined on in our travels. You once raised a small objection when I offered you fried rattlesnake, but you changed your mind once you tasted it. What about that raw fish we had in the Orient? Or those fellows on the steppes who mixed horse blood with their rice?"

"You make my head whirl."

"Then maybe you should not worry about it. I don't."

"All that and yet . . ." He touched the cross that dangled from my neck. "Will you kneel and say the Lord's Prayer with me?"

The power of speech departed from me for an instant, swept away by surprise, which I hoped I concealed. I nodded, understanding why he needed this. When we hunted Dracula it was truly a quest of good against evil, where we all witnessed incontestable proof of the existence of both. "Yes, of course I will," I answered.

So there before his fire Art and I knelt. I said the words of that old prayer and found solace in it as I always did. In my heart I hoped that Art would also feel the same. When we came to the *amen* we paused, looking at each other, silent a moment, then on my own and without thought behind it, I began to say the Twenty-third Psalm. Halfway through it, tears rolled down Art's cheeks. He quickly stood and lurched blindly away. He stumbled against his desk and held onto it, needing its support to stay afoot. I continued until the end, then got up.

His weeping was silent, for men are not free to wail out their grief as are women, though the pain is just as piercing. Directly before him was the portrait of Lucy. I recalled we'd all recited the psalm at her service.

"I'm sorry, Art. I shouldn't have—"

"*No.* It's all right, really it is. I know it's all right now. You've convinced me. I just need a little time."

I stepped away and went to the window, drawing the curtain aside. The grounds were also as I remembered them from this vantage, gently rolling away from the house to a small tangle of woods, beyond which lay cultivated fields. Not far in the distance was an old eyesore of a stable that had been around since the queen was a young girl. It was long deserted, a roost for stray birds and other animals. I'd considered it as a daytime sanctuary should it become necessary. That possibility seemed lessened, but I had reservations. Maybe Art had accepted my changed condition, but I had to face the ugly possibility that he might later reject it in the brightness of day. I had trusted him on countless adventures with my life as he had trusted his with me, but this was different. I had no desire to test the strength of his acceptance just yet. Not until I saw a return of his old free and easy manner with me.

He blew his nose, cleared his throat, and in an almost normal voice invited me to sit again. I relinquished my post and gladly returned to the warmth of the fire. Maybe I didn't feel the miseries of extreme heat and cold as before, but there's a comfort in stretching your hands forth and feeling the glow soak into your bones.

"I want to offer you a drink," he said. There was a tinge of bleak chagrin in his tone.

"As God is my witness, I wish I could accept it." I gave a small shrug, shaking my head. "I do appreciate the thought, though."

"This is damned awkward, isn't it?"

"I reckon so, but we'll probably get over that hill when we stop thinking so much."

His eyes flickered in a familiar way, and I suddenly saw how alike he and Bertrice were on certain subtle mannerisms. I wanted to mention renewing my acquaintance with her, but this was absolutely not the time.

"I imagine things were also pretty awkward in the camp when I turned up missing," I said.

He drew his lips back in a brief grimace. "You still retain your gift for understatement."

"Everyone in a tizzy?"

"God, it was dreadful. We'd come so far and done so much and were in shock from your d—well . . ."

"I am that sorry, but it wasn't exactly my idea to get dragged away."

"Certainly not. We were appalled beyond words. Poor Mrs. Harker broke down completely. Harker and the professor saw to her while Jack and I tracked the wolves' trail, but they had climbed to some rocks and we lost it. I couldn't imagine why they'd taken your b-body so far a distance."

"Wolves are strange varmints, maybe even more so in that part of the world," I said dismissively. "What did you next do?"

"We got back to the camp around noon, tired and famished. The others had recovered somewhat, but we were all in a terrible state of mind and sick at heart. That was when Jack and I resolved to stay and continue the search for you. It was a wrench for the others. They wanted to stay, too, but Mrs. Harker was in need of a proper place to rest and recover from her ordeal. The professor would have stayed, but Jack sensibly pointed out to him that the lady might later require his professional help. I knew it was all a sham on Jack's part, for he could see Van Helsing was also in need of rest. He has a lion's heart, but isn't as young as he was. He must have seen through the sham, but accepted it as an honorable way out. Harker was willing to stay, but the professor took charge and insisted that his place was with Mrs. Harker, which was something of a relief to her."

"I thought that's how it might have worked itself."

"What do you mean?"

"I'll explain."

"I rather think you should. Immediately. How did you escape those wolves?"

"That I don't recall too well. I didn't really become aware of anything until they were gone, chased off by this old hermit who found me."

"A hermit? All the way out there?"

"I think that's the whole point of being a hermit."

"Was he one of the Szgany?"

"I'm not rightly sure who he was as he had no English and I didn't have but a few words of his speech. We each knew enough Latin to get by on a few things and the rest had to be acted out. Near as I could understand him, he saw the wolves dragging me along and scared them away before they could start in on me. He thought me dead at first, then I began to come around, so he carried me to this cave where he'd been living for years. He was mighty curious about me, and what a trial it must have been for him to hold it in seeing as how we couldn't talk much."

Art was riveted. Yes, I am a poor liar to those who matter to me, but I'd been rehearsing this story since before leaving Transylvania. I could now flatter myself that I was telling it well.

"He took care of me for awhile until I was on my feet again—"

"But was he not aware of your . . . your . . ."

"Condition? Yes, from the first. My clothes were all covered with my blood, so he was quick to figure I was not some ordinary lost traveler he'd rescued from hungry wolves. Soon as I was sitting up and asking questions he thrust a big crucifix into my hands and gave me a hard look. When nothing happened he tried an old Bible on me. I think it was a Bible, he treated it with a lot of reverence and signed for me to kiss it. I did, and after that we got along just fine."

"What an amazing man."

"He was indeed. Near as I could tell, he'd been living alone up there for maybe twenty years. I think he'd gone into the forest to get away from a war and decided he liked being on his own. He'd trap animals for their fur and trade the skins in some village for supplies."

"And he had no difficulty with your . . . condition?"

"Not that I noticed, just seemed to accept me like a beach does a shipwrecked sailor."

"What did you do for—?"

"Food? He kept some cows for milk and meat. They served."

"But how did you—no, I don't think I want to ask about that just yet."

Judging by the green cast to his skin he was wondering how I obtained the blood. "Perhaps not. He didn't seem to mind, and I did what I could to assure him I wasn't taking any samples from him. It was . . . an interesting time. Besides, he knew I'd be moving on, which I did a month or so after."

"Why so long? Why did you not immediately return to us?"

"You just hit on the rough part. When I woke and figured out what had happened I thought myself damned to hell then and there. I thought I should give myself up to the professor so one of you might free my soul, but what held me back was the old hermit and his crucifix and his Bible. They not only proved to him that I was not evil, but me as well. I was mighty confused, though, for the professor had drummed a lot of tall tales into our heads like they were pure gospel. Until then it hadn't occurred to me that there might be different breeds of vampires like there's different breeds of dogs, some more dangerous than others. I had to do some long thinking. I concluded that if I walked in on the camp you all would keel over from failed hearts or shoot me to hell and gone and then keel over."

"Or we might have heard you out."

"Art, what did we just go through in this very room?"

He chewed it over, then reluctantly nodded. "I begin to see what you mean."

"Now multiply that by five and put it in the wilds of the Transylvanian woods during the middle of the night. When it came down to it, my nerve failed me. I was in a pretty terrible state of mind as well, and I just couldn't face the rest of you. Not like that, not until I'd gotten square with myself about what had happened. So I stayed with the hermit, assuming you'd all soon go home again. Imagine my surprise when I found you and Jack Seward were still roaming around."

"You saw us? When?"

"Do you recall being attacked one night by a wolf lying under the snow?"

His jaw nearly brushed the floor. "My God . . . then it *was* you! I *heard* your shouting! Jack thought I'd gone mad and imagined it all. After a time I thought so, too."

I grinned. "That was me all right. Could have knocked me flat with a feather I was so surprised seeing the both of you there. I worked out the why of it, and it fair choked me up."

"Why did you not come to us?"

"I still wasn't ready. On the other hand, I was afraid you'd get yourselves froze to death. Me and the hermit were well set up, but all the two of you had was an old shack ready to fall down any minute."

"You spied on us?"

"Kept watch is more close. Then that blizzard hit, and I was sure you'd be trading calling cards with Saint Peter. I did what I could to help out, but so as to not get caught. Did the rabbit cook up good?"

He burst into a short delighted laugh. "*You* all along! We were thanking the wrong guardian angel for those miracles. Yes, it cooked wonderfully, the best rabbit I'd ever had, and the warmest fire. You truly saved us."

"I'm glad."

"If only we'd known."

I shook my head. "It wasn't the time."

"Yes, I suppose not. We left the next day. What did you do?"

"Said good-bye to my new friend the hermit and left soon after as well."

"That was ages ago, Quincey. Where did you take yourself?"

"I had a hankering to see Paris again and wound up there."

"Paris? What did you do?"

Here was I finally able to impart some real truth to my story, but I did leave out all the time I spent in the brothels. A gentleman doesn't talk, after all. For now Art was overwound just getting used to having me back and didn't need anything else added to the heap. Speculations about how I now enjoyed pleasures of the flesh could be put off for the moment. Instead, I answered his questions about more mundane pursuits, like how I got my bankers cooperating. I did have to mention my ability to hypnotize, for he was very familiar with the ways of bankers and how pigheaded they can be without the right persuasion. In turn, that led to him asking if I could turn myself into a mist or a bat. I said no, but explained the business about being able to disappear, finally giving a demonstration. Lots of them. He was fascinated, but as the hands spun around on the mantel clock into the wee hours I could see he was near-exhausted.

"I'll ring for some *cafe noir*," he said, when I suggested it was time I go. "There's so much more I must hear."

"Art, your poor skull must be ready to burst from

what you've already got tonight. Give yourself a good night's sleep to sort it out."

He sensibly gave in, sinking back in his chair. "Yes, you're right. But you must stay, I'll have Foster turn out your old room—"

"No," I said, maybe a touch too sharpish. "I can't stay. I have reasons, good ones. I must ask you to trust me on this."

His disappointment was almost like that of a child, but he quickly recovered himself. "Very well, of course I will respect your wishes."

"That's all I want. I'll be able to explain more later."

He visibly brightened. "Then you'll return here tomorrow?"

"The day after. I mean night after. Tomorrow evening I've an appointment to meet someone."

"May I ask who?"

"Another friend I ran into in London. Doesn't know I was killed, and there's no need to let 'em in on the secret. Wants to do a little yarning and catch up on old times is all."

"So you're not in hiding?"

"Why should I?"

"Well, because . . . oh, damn. I don't know. This is so strange."

"Art, I've done nothing wrong, and I do nothing wrong so there's no reason for me to skulk around like a thief. I have an ordinary room at a respectable hotel, and keep to myself, which is pretty much how I've always dealt with things."

"But don't you need a box to rest in and consecrated earth?"

"I did trouble to pack along some earth in a shipping crate, but don't know if it's been consecrated or not."

"Then you do need something of the grave with you."

"Yes. I am its prisoner during the whole of the day, completely unconscious until the sun is gone. And that can be damned inconvenient, let me tell you."

He made a helpless little gesture. "You speak of it all so normally."

"Because for me it *is* normal. Now. But I've had months to get used to it, you've had but a few hours."

"I'm not sure I ever shall."

"You will. Sleep on it and I'll see you night after tomorrow."

"What about Jack Seward? Are you going to see him?"

"I plan t—"

"And the professor? And the Harkers?"

"Whoa, there and slow down. One at a time! You're not the only man in need of a rest. I'll get around to them all, but you must let me handle it my own way. If you should see them, you mustn't say anything about me."

"Then I'd best play the hermit myself, especially where Jack is concerned. Once he sees me he'll know something's up. He can read people like a book, comes from dealing with all those lunatics."

"So he's back running that place again?"

"Yes. Keeps himself busy. Van Helsing looked after the asylum while Jack and I were in Transylvania, but things are as they ever were before. The professor is on a sabbatical from Amsterdam, though, and staying at Purfleet with Jack. They're working on some sort of paper together, I think. He doesn't talk about it, so I imagine it has to do with Dracula."

"In what way?"

"You'll have to ask them. I don't wish to know or be reminded. For myself, I would give anything to get through a single day without thinking of that monster and what he did to us all."

"I feel the same. Truly I do." I meant it. Though in a strange way I'd forgiven Dracula for Lucy, Miss

Mina, and even poor old Renfield, I could not let it go. The horrors of that time still clung to me.

"Who will you speak to next?" he asked.

"I was thinking Jack, but perhaps I should speak sooner with the professor. If I can convince him as I have you, then he will make things easier for the others. But . . ."

"What? Tell me."

"Look, it's been very hard on you tonight, much harder than I ever imagined. I don't wish to cast more sorrows on our friends. For me to reappear again, and bring up a load of old griefs they may have finally buried—"

"Don't you dare think that! Yes, you've given me a hellish turn tonight, but I'm over it. Once they get past the shock, they will be overjoyed."

"But will they accept me like this? Returned as an incarnation not unlike our worst enemy?"

"Quincey, it won't matter. I'll make them see reason and so will you. We *will* make it all right for them, I promise. Just swear to me you won't go off without a word, I couldn't bear it!"

"Very well. If you're behind me on this, then I'll see the business through."

"Absolutely."

How relieved I was to have my friend back. The gladness of the moment was sweet, but how long would it last? I went to his desk, drawing forth pen, ink, and paper and wrote a short note. After blotting, I gave it to Art.

He read: " 'Yes, I really was here, and all will be well, Quincey,' What means this?"

"Just in case when you wake up and in the cold light of day think you had more brandy than was good for you."

Then he laughed, a real one. Perhaps the first he'd enjoyed in months.

Chapter Eleven

Though things were easier between us, I chose to leave Art and find a sanctuary for myself in some deserted place, rather than reconsider his invitation to have my old room back. Ironically, there was no need for me to depart Ring at all, though I must appear to do so. When one is utterly helpless for hours at a time, one becomes very anxious in regard to securing complete privacy.

As the servants were all long abed, Art ushered me down to the front door himself. He offered the use of his dog cart and horse, but I declined, saying I wanted to stretch my legs. He saw me off, standing in the doorway for a long time, as though still not quite believing I was back and reluctant to lose sight of me. But the curve of the drive took me away, and when that happened I struck off west over the property, heading for that stand of fir trees.

My bag was where I'd left it, not that I was too worried it would walk off on its own. That retrieved, I turned my steps toward that old deserted stables in the near distance.

The place was in a very bad state, with the roof bearing more holes than slate shingles. The brick walls were fairly solid, as was the stone floor. At one time it must have served very well as shelter, but not now. I found a possible sanctuary in an isolated corner stall. The roof over this part of the building would shield me from the sun, but it chafed not having a proper door to close. Suppose some playful child should chance across my inert body during the course of the day, or worse, one of Art's servants? A quick investigation of the hayloft also proved futile. The rotted wood floor there would not support my weight, and it was open to the sky. No, I would have to seek shelter elsewhere.

I returned to the fir stand by the main house and waited, hidden by the black shadows, going over in my mind all I'd said this evening. It had been rough, but now I felt I'd done the right thing by coming back. Art had been in a poorly state and now, hopefully, was past it, and I'd kept my pledge to Dracula, maintaining the fiction of his death. Back in Transylvania I'd promised him my silence, but hadn't been all that specific about keeping away from my friends. That was some sharp hairsplitting on my part, I know, but damn it all, I'd missed them and given the choice I'd do it the same way again.

The lights in Art's study had been turned down. A half-hour later—I timed it by the quarter chimes of a distant church bell—I felt it safe enough to return to the house, again going in by means of the study window.

The fire had died out and all was dim and silent but for the usual creaks of an old house. I listened most carefully and decided that Art had turned in for the night.

Vanishing, I flowed under the study door, partially re-forming on the other side. From there I floated down the long hall, my feet inches above the floor, truly looking like a ghost, albeit one in an Inverness and cap, clutching his bag like a misplaced traveler. At the far end were stairs, which I ascended. The upper areas were servants' quarters. I meant to go higher still, but could not recall where the attic stairway was; Ring was quite huge, and Art had shown me the way only once years back on a search for some forgotten relic. I'd been impressed that so large an area topped the house and that it was unused except for storage.

"I suppose we'll have to clean it out someday," he'd said, "but there's no need for the time being." Though the household was large, the lower floors were more than sufficient for their wants.

Giving up on finding the stairs, I vanished fully again and drifted upward, encountering the vague resistance of the ceiling and pushing into it. Such a disturbing feeling it was to pass oneself *through* a solid object. I cannot say that it was pleasant or unpleasant, only that I felt better once I was done.

Solid again, I found myself in a very dark, dusty chamber. Light filtered in by way of some narrow windows, but not much of it. The attic was divided up into a series of small rooms that opened one upon another. Long ago, servant girls made their miserable homes here, taking what rest they could in the winter cold and summer heat. I suppose they had it better than most of their class back then, but I couldn't help but feel sorry for them.

Some of their furnishings remained along with the cast off flotsam and jetsam of the house: narrow little beds, too short for my frame and no mattresses. Those had likely been removed to keep mice from nesting within. Well, I'd had worse accommodations.

I consulted my *Bradshaw's Guide* to make sure of the train schedules. Once awake, an easy walk would get me to the station in plenty of time to catch the last train for London. Excellent.

After a little quiet searching, I found a suitable closet-like berth bereft of windows that would serve. I shut its one door and blocked it with a heavy old trunk to further insure the preservation of my privacy. Of course, I was quite without light of any kind until I fumbled out matches and a candle from one of my pockets. I'd still not yet lost my distaste for utter darkness and took much comfort from the tiny yellow flame.

I put the candle on the trunk lid, settled in on a bare floor with the valise for a pillow, and amused myself for the remaining hours until dawn with a copy of last December's *Strand Magazine* borrowed from the hotel's reading room. To my delight it had a Sherlock Holmes story in it. I had ever been a great admirer of his adventures. What a bitter disappointment to discover that this, "The Final Problem," truly was final. For all the terrible things I'd been through in recent times I was quite aggrieved to read of the awful end of Sherlock Holmes. He'd gone as a hero, yet was he still gone. Unlike me, he would not be returning. I felt cheated. Damnation, but I wanted to write to that Conan Doyle fellow and give him a piece of my mind. There was *no* reason for it that I could see. *Why* did he do it?

I still had that righteous anger, or at least irritation, in my head when I woke the next night in thick blackness. In one hand I had a match, in the other the stub of the candle. Both had remained firm within my grasp through the whole of the day, for I never moved during my rest. In an instant I'd struck the match and lighted the candle, hardly before my eyes had fully opened. Childish, I know, but let anyone waken as I did that first night with a blanket swathing his face and wolves milling around and confess himself unafraid of the dark, and I'll take my hat off to him in humble admiration.

The house was more active at this earlier hour, but I made my escape with no one the wiser for it, using one of the attic windows. Hunger plucked at me this night, so I made my invisible way to the stables. Art had quite a collection of fine horses, including a matched pair for his carriage and several big hunters he'd brought from Ireland for the foxing season. I had to be careful, as the stable lads lived just above their charges, but it was dinner time and most were up at the house with their noses in their own kind of feedbag.

Since that first reluctant lesson with Dracula peering over my shoulder, I'd gotten better at drawing off blood, teaching myself to be neat and fast. Most of the time the animal just didn't notice, but I'd also learned to size up which were more likely to hold for me latching onto one of their veins with my mouth. Picking out a dozing hunter I saw to my needs quicker than Dixie and got clear, feeling much refreshed for it.

My return to London was just as uneventful, though anticipation of seeing Bertrice again made the journey seem longer. I hoped that the two busy days since the party would have softened the oddness of the fortune-telling incident in her memory. Tonight I would do my best to make her forget it—not by any hypnotic means—but by being as amusing as possible in the tale of my meeting with her brother. Perhaps that would redeem me in her eyes, and she would continue to allow me to pursue my acquaintance with her.

After a stop at my hotel to change clothes and otherwise prepare myself, I strolled to the music hall, this time without any encounters with would-be robbers. I could hope my "suggestions" to the hapless couple to find another kind of work had taken root. At any event, they were not lurking in the alley tonight.

With a different audience for company I watched the various entertainments again, joining in when there was a sing-along and marveling anew at the cleverness of the trained animal acts. With more appreciation than ever, I once more enjoyed the dueling scene from *Hamlet* and applauded until my hands stung. My, but Bertrice was wonderful to watch. This time I fully indulged myself in admiration for her legs, and all the rest of her. She cut a *very* trim figure, even in a doublet and waving a sword around.

During this, I heard some derogatory whispering from a few people. Seems they didn't approve of an all-girl troupe of players. One of the men opined that he thought the lot of them were the sort of women who preferred the company of other women. I'd never heard of such a thing back in Texas—coming to England had done wonders in certain areas of my worldly education. I *had* given some thought to that possibility, but did not consider the notion to apply to Bertrice in particular. Her manner at the party led me to understand that she very much welcomed the company of men, she was just particular about who she allowed to get close. From the story that Wyndon Price had related, I could not blame the lady one bit for being cautious. In fact, I heartily approved of her wariness, for the world is full of knaves.

Now, if I could but convince her I was not one of them.

After the *Hamlet* scene was done, I went out and around to the stage door, there to gather with the hopeful johnnies and wait. One of them recognized me from the other night and asked how I'd fared with "Miz 'Amlet."

I thought it was no business of his and let him know—in the politest possible terms, of course.

"Har! 'E 'ad 'er all right!" the man crowed. He had liberally fortified himself against the cold from a flask he carried.

"Sir, the lady *is* a lady and deserving of a gentleman's respect. Being drunk you seem unable to grasp that, so I would recommend you make yourself scarce."

"Drunk, am I?"

"Indeed, else I should be pleased to defend the lady's honor by punching your nose out the other side of your face for your insult. As you are in no condition to defend yourself, I will allow you a chance to leave."

"Damn Yankee toff!"

I expected a set-to, having met his type countless times before in my travels. The fighting words are always the same no matter what the language, and a fool is always a fool no matter what the country. This one charged forward ready to grapple, but I easily stepped to the side so all he encountered was the unforgiving brick wall of the theater. He turned in time to avoid smashing his face, but his shoulder hit hard. That put him in an even more unpleasant humor.

A few of his comrades then decided to help him out. Things got very warm and busy for the next few minutes as we traded swings and blows. There was a shrill whistling somewhere above us by the backstage door.

I kicked a backside, put a fist into a belly, and sent my original attacker reeling toward the alley entrance— straight into the arms of a very large, red-faced constable.

" 'Er, now! Wot's all this then?" he demanded, though it was very obvious what was going on. Holding his captive by the scruff of his neck like a cat with a kitten, he glared at me as a possible source of the trouble. The rest of the johnnies broke off their fighting.

I quickly put my clothing in order and retrieved my hat from where it had fallen. "It's nothing, officer, just a little roughhousing and high spirits."

He gave a mighty sniff of his man. "Hit's spirits, roit enuff. I fink you'd best come along wif me, sir, an' we'll sort it out at the station."

The unfairness stung. "But I cannot leave, I'm waiting for someone!"

"You may wait at the station, come along naow."

I looked around for support, but the johnnies had all fled. Only the doorman remained, still clutching the whistle he'd used to summon the law. I appealed to him. "Sir, tell this officer that the fight was none of my doing."

"Would if I could, but I didn't see 'ow it started, only 'ow it ended."

Damnation. "I was here just the other night. Miss Wood will vouch for me."

"I'll let 'er know where you are, then. 'Ave a good e'n." And he went back inside the theater, apparently having forgotten the consideration he'd originally collected from me or that I could be the source for more of the same.

"Roit along, sir," said the constable, pleasantly. "This way."

"Very well." I sighed and went quietly, biding my time until we reached the sidewalk and were under a gaslight. "There's just one thing, officer . . ."

"Naow nonsense, sir."

"Of course not, but I seem to have something in my eye. Please have a look, as it is paining me."

Being no fool, he must have sensed I was up to no good, for he dropped one hand to the truncheon on his belt, perhaps anticipating a physical attack.

"I must ask that you listen to me for just a moment . . ." I began, staring hard to reach his mind. As he was stony sober and I was annoyed, this did not take long. The slight pain between my eyes was nothing to the satisfaction I got when he marched onward with no memory of me at all, only his oblivious, drunken captive in tow.

My satisfaction lasted until I turned toward the music hall and all but collided with Bertrice. She was in her walking clothes, her cape thrown over one shoulder as though she'd not had time to put it on. She held a furled umbrella ready in her hand like her stage sword. "Mr. Morris," she said, guardedly. "How nice to see you again. What *was* your business with that constable?"

She was back to using my last name again. Drat. "Just a minor misunderstanding." How long had she been there? How much had she seen?

"He was cooperating with you most wonderfully. Hanging on your every word, in fact."

"I can be persuasive when necessary, miss."

"Above and beyond the call of necessity, it would seem."

"It's nothing."

"If you say so. The doorman said I'd be in court all night because of you, so I came to the rescue. How nice that you took care of things yourself."

She was willing to rescue me? My heart lifted. "I appreciate your willingness to help, Miss Bertrice. May I thank you by offering you a late dinner?"

"Yes," she said after a moment of watching the still-retreating officer. She handed me her umbrella for a moment as she unshouldered her cape and gracefully wrapped up in it. "You may."

She knew of a nearby pub that catered to the theatrical crowd and guided us there. Several of her cronies from the hall had already taken it over and tossed familial greetings at her while giving me a look-see as we picked out a table. It was a big, jostling, friendly place, but seemed to have no separate area for ladies, and I remarked on it to her.

"They do during the day, when ladies are out and about, but at this hour there's little point," she said. "Those of us in the business, for the most part, are all one together, male and female. This pub understands that and allows for it, though many may see our innocent camaraderie as scandalous. Those on the outside don't always understand and make assumptions that theaters are dens of iniquity. Some of them are, I'm sure, but I've yet to encounter one. As with any little society it is the sins of a few outstanding failures who paint the picture for the rest of us. Hence we have the larger world assuming that all actors are drunken buffoons and all actresses are prostitutes."

"I've never thought that."

"I'm glad to hear it. You can imagine that having such a stigma attached to this profession causes its members to become even more insular to themselves, thus increasing the mystery, thus increasing the dark rumors. The more one denies them, the more people believe them to be true. Yet for all that condemnation, the crowds still come to see us perform."

"Hopefully the experience will enrich them. I certainly felt such again tonight. You were in fine form up there, if you don't mind hearing me say so."

"One never grows tired of sincere praise."

I was about to heap on more of it for her, but a waiter came to take our order. Bertrice asked for sausages, eggs, and an ale. I settled for a half pint of the latter.

"You're not hungry?" she asked.

"I ate earlier." The stink of cooked food was bad, but if I kept her talking then I had no need to breathe. "Have the shows been going well for you?"

"Very well, indeed. No one threw rotten vegetables at us, and the catcalls were not so loud that we couldn't speak our lines over them. But never mind that, tell me about Arthur. How did your Lazarus impersonation go over?"

I narrated a highly expurgated version of the truth, adding in as much humorous comment as I could, wishing to lighten what had been a most serious situation. "He was in quite a state, and it would be hard to say which of us was the more shaken, him seeing me again or me rushing to catch him before he fainted."

"He fainted?" This alarmed her.

"Not quite, but he was dozy for a moment or two from the shock. Poor fellow thought me to be a ghost for awhile, but a little brandy and pinching on my arm put him right again soon enough."

"Good. How I wish I could have been there. Arthur's a strong man, but lately I've been worried for his health. He's not been the same since . . . since last summer."

"No one of us has been. It was a terrible ordeal."

"I didn't know Lucy all that well, but she struck me as being a very sweet, loving girl."

"She was that and more."

"Just what did take her away? Arthur never said anything specific."

I hesitated, not knowing how much to relate. "Jack Seward said it was some kind of pernicious anemia. He dressed it up in a lot of medical words, but I think it had something to do with her blood not being right. You'll have to get him to explain it properly."

"I will. You never told me the circumstances of how he and Dr. Seward came to think *you* were dead in the first place."

The waiter brought our ales just then and offered her and then me a curious stare before hastening away.

"We were on a hunting trip—"

"Where?"

"Transylvania."

"Where on earth is that?"

"Eastern side of Europe; it's pretty out of the way."

"Sounds it. What were you hunting?"

"Wolves."

"Did you shoot any?"

"We took one big fellow before being attacked by some local bandits."

"What? Arthur in the middle of a fight?"

Damn, perhaps I should have expurgated this story as well, even if it was made up. "We were all in the middle of it, but the size of our party told in our favor and the bandits soon retreated. I fear I got caught up in the excitement and gave chase when I should have stayed with the rest. We became so far separated that I lost my way. Then—and I hate to admit it as I regard myself as a good rider—my horse threw me."

"Heavens."

"That's what I think happened. I'm sure I struck my head when I landed, my memory is very thin on that part. I woke at night, stiff and cold and surrounded by wolves."

Her eyes went wide. "You're joking! Wolves?"

"The very pack we were hunting. They had a mind to return the favor upon my person, but I managed to fight them off, then this old hermit came to my rescue . . ."

From that point my story was the same as the one I'd given her brother, but without the vampire element. Bertrice was hard pressed to believe any of it, which said a lot to me about her sharpness of perception. I wouldn't have easily believed me, either, but the truth was much too fantastical.

"Well, Art and Jack found my horse running loose, but not me. They spent more than a month scouring the area for sign of me or my body, and had I been there to be found I might be telling you a different story now. But the hermit's lodgings were some miles distance, and I'd gotten feverish, so we none of us ever hooked up. Assuming the bandits or the wolves had killed me they went home—for which I don't blame them one bit, as I'd have done the same. It was the worst of the winter by then and they were close to perishing themselves from the cold. By the time I got back to civilization I was surprised to discover I'd been declared dead by my friends. I didn't know if I should be horrified or laugh my head off."

"One is allowed to do both."

"I reckon I did. I stayed in Paris awhile straightening out the mess, then finally ended up in London, in need of some music hall amusement spoken in English. You know the rest."

Her food had come during the telling of my tale, but she'd hardly touched it. She was spellbound, and it felt mighty good to have captured her attention so well.

"That's quite amazing," she said. "You should write it up and post it to a magazine catering to adventure stories."

"Oh, it's not good enough for that. Besides, I'd have to dress it more fancy and put in a villain and a chest of treasure for everyone to find."

"Don't forget to include a lost princess to rescue and restore to her throne and at least one duel to the death atop the castle turret."

"Of course." I smiled, basking in the spark that now lighted her eyes. She seemed to be relaxed with me again, the other night's incident forgotten.

"What was Arthur's reaction to all this?" she asked.

"He held a view similar to yours, but tempered by his memories of the experience. We spent most of the night yarning about the whole thing. I will say that I agree with you about him looking poorly, as I almost didn't know him. He's gotten so thin and pale. Has Jack not noticed the change?"

"I don't know. He's never there when I chance to drop in."

"I shall have words with him, then. Maybe we can persuade Art to come out of his lair now. He seemed much improved in spirits when I left."

"Thank God for that. I'm glad you've returned." She made a move as though to put her hand on mine, but instead drew back and picked up her forgotten fork. "I'd best eat this before it's too cold to enjoy. Tell me about Paris. It's been some years since my last visit. Do they still have that awful tower up in the Champ-de-Mars?"

"They do, and they may be keeping it. Seems people like the view from it, even if they don't care to look at the tower itself."

"It is such a pretentious thing and quite ugly, all that bare metal, like a skeleton."

"Kinda grows on you though. I didn't know it until I went there, but that Eiffel fellow also did the frame for our own Liberty Statue in New York, so I suppose his tower can't be all bad."

"So speaks an American." She gave me a mock toast with her glass of ale.

"And a Texan. We were a separate country before hitching up with the United States, you know. There's some say we should have passed the honor and just kept to ourselves."

"Just how big is Texas for it to have been a whole country?"

That stumped me and I said as much. "Might as well ask how big is the sky. You could drop a hundred cities the size of London into Texas and lose 'em faster than a penny at a sideshow for all the space we've got to spread 'em around in."

"My! I've heard Arthur speak of our holdings there, but I had no idea."

"There is plenty of room for a man to stretch and

not find his limit, but it's not for everyone. We've a story of how the devil came to Texas to live but gave up and moved back to hell a few days later because the heat got to be too much for him."

"Our cold English climate must be a trial for you, then."

"The winters are a caution, but for all the places I've traveled, it comes up pretty even with the rest of the world. Maybe you get more rain than an Indian monsoon, but it sure makes for a green and pleasant land."

"You're most kind, Mr. Quincey."

I felt like a ring-tailed fool. I was sitting across from this wonderful, beautiful woman with a laugh sweet as a nightingale's song, and here we were talking about the damned weather. She was back to my first name again, though, which was good, but I wanted to get that spark in her green eyes to burn even brighter. "When I was in Paris I was able to see some of their theatricals . . ."

That helped, touching on one of her enthusiasms. "Yes, what are they doing there, these days?"

"Some of it was a bit above me. They seem to like the brooding, philosophical stuff with people looking at each other and not saying much. My preferences are for a lot of yelling, fighting, and laughing. I like to see an actor work for his applause and enjoy the work."

"The Shakespeare is definitely to your taste. He has something for everyone."

"Indeed, though I've not seen all that much of what you would call proper theater, but I do like watching actors who know their business."

"What a pity you cannot come to our matinee and see the whole play. Is there not some way you can forgo your business for a few hours?"

"It's impossible. I very much regret that it must be so."

"As do I." She sounded like she really meant it. "My company will eventually secure an evening performance. I'm sure of it."

"I certainly hope so."

"By then it might be a different play. What think you of an all-female version of *MacBeth*?"

"It is beyond my poor imagination, but I'm sure you'll do just as fine a job on it as you're doing on this one."

"We try. You have a most liberal attitude. Most who hear of us treat the company as though we were a gaggle of giddy schoolgirls out on a lark, not serious actresses. Some accuse us of being 'adventuresses,' a fine word that has fallen in its meaning. It once stood for a brave woman out to make her way alone in the world, not unlike the male hero of many a fairy tale. Now it would seem all adventuresses are women of questionable repute if not low morals."

"I would never think that, Miss Bertrice. Anyone with eyes can see you are a lady through and through."

"But that is my point. It should not matter if a woman is a 'lady,' for the strict standards of such are those burdened onto her by a highly judgmental society. She must adhere to each of them or be an outcast. But standards are more lax and forgiving in regards to a 'gentleman.' So long as he pays his gambling debts and doesn't beat his wife in public he may plunge himself into all manner of iniquity and be admired for it."

I had to laugh. "You've hit the nail on that. Why don't you write it up for *The Times*?"

"I have until they're weary of hearing from me. I'd join with the suffragettes, but apparently actresses and artists are rather too shady for them. Hence, they are themselves still carrying the burden of societal judgment, when they should cast away such trifles and unite with all their sisters in the quest for freedom."

"You'd make a rare speech writer."

"Or barrister. I have a mind to play Portia some-day, which is as close as I'll get to it. Between the acting and my painting I'm busy from morning to midnight so I've no time to study for the bar. Which reminds me—" She consulted a small watch pinned like a brooch to the lapel of her velvet jacket. "Heavens. I'd no idea how late it was. You've not even touched your ale."

"I must not be thirsty. It's gone flat anyway. No matter. May I escort you home?"

"Yes," she said, gathering up her cape and umbrella. "You may."

This time I was quick enough to pay for the cab fare.

Her studio, as she referred to it, also served as her lodgings, and frequently a rehearsal hall for the Ring Players. The neighborhood was on the seedy side, not wholly decrepit, but neither did it appear to be especially safe for an unescorted lady at night. Bertrice must have read my expression, for she smiled as we walked the few steps to her door.

"I'm perfectly able to defend myself, Mr. Quincey. Those fencing moves I do on stage are based on real training. Hours of it, as it is a passion of mine."

"All well and good, if you have a sword."

"But I do." She did something to the handle of her furled umbrella and drew forth a long, wicked-sharp blade that threw out gleams caught from the distant gaslights.

"But what if your opponent has a pistol?"

"Then I am prepared for that as well." She neatly sheathed the sword blade and from her jacket pocket produced a very handy little two-shot derringer. "There. As you see I am well able to defend myself against most calamities. And should the odds be very ill against me I have my most effective line of defense to employ at the first sign of danger."

"Which is—?"

"I run like the devil and scream 'fire' at the top of my lungs. Few people will respond to a call for help, but everyone pays attention to an alarm for fire."

She was a devil herself, and I liked her for it. "Well, I'm most glad to see you taking such good care of yourself." I took her hand, bowing low to kiss it, but she stayed me, lightly touching my face, before drawing her hand away as though surprised by the gesture.

"Oh, I hope you won't leave just yet," she said, her voice softening.

That took me aback. "Well, I . . ."

"I am so enjoying our conversation, and I thought you'd like a quick look at some of my paintings."

"I would, indeed, but for you to have a visitor at so late an hour—"

"Is entirely my business and none of my neighbors'. Do come in, I won't bite."

Nonplused by the irregularity, but pleased at the opportunity to spend more time with her, I signed for the hansom driver to go on.

The front door opened to a tiny, bare entry that was very dark. She kept a candle on a little table there and lighted it, then led the way in. The next room was of considerable size and length, bigger than the music hall stage, with rows of high windows along the outer wall.

"My congratulations on finding a place with such conveniently placed lighting," I said, for the windows all faced north.

"I was very fortunate, though it gets miserably cold here in winter. I've had a coal heater put in, but it's not always up to the task, especially when I forget to stoke it."

She'd had gas laid in as well and went from sconce to sconce with the candle until the room glowed.

She had several easels set up, all with paintings in progress, or finished and drying; some were shrouded with drop cloths. The smells of linseed oil and turpentine were in the chill air, but not so heavy as to be sick-making. Two of the windows were cracked open an inch or so for ventilation, and I could see her breath hang in the air.

"Lately I've had some success with portraiture," she said, indicating one of the uncovered canvases. "I'm not up to National Gallery level, but I flatter myself that I may provide some competition to James Whistler. Here's a nice one, I'm rather proud of most of it."

The portrait was of a young woman in a garden surrounded by flowers. Her pensive face had been captured in such a way that I was sure I would know her if I passed her on the street. "This is marvelous. You've a most remarkable talent."

She gave me a long look, as though to ascertain that I was not spouting empty flattery, and seemed pleased. "Thank you. I think I worked too hard on her hands, though, I may have to cover them with a bouquet to conceal my mistake. You do not think the background is overdone, do you?"

"Not at all, she stands out from it, and it complements, but does not overwhelm."

"You've an understanding of composition and balance." That pleased her, too.

"I've learned a few things in my travels."

She turned toward the painting, her eye critical. "Backgrounds can be very difficult. I paint the background first, then the figure. There are whole schools that vehemently argue for and against it. I've tried both ways. It's a terrible disappointment to put so much work in on the figure, only to botch the background. Once I had to burn the final result lest someone see it and think me terribly incompetent."

"Every artist must find what best works for him or her, there is no right way for all."

"You are most perceptive."

"Well, I did spend a lot of time in Paris. You can't help but pick up ideas talking to people. Artists with strong opinions are thick on the ground over there."

"As are art critics. The French are very particular in their tastes."

"And the English?"

"I wasn't aware we had any taste at all. The Queen's preferences can be most mundane."

"I hope that observation does not border on treason," I joked.

"It does in some circles, but not the ones in which I orbit. Of course, *they* have their own strict standards, which shift and change in a most whimsical way, so I pay them no attention. I paint what I like and to the devil with what they think."

"You apply that philosophy to the rest of your life, Miss Bertrice. You have my admiration for it."

She paused, favoring me with the sun of her smile, warming me. "What a sweet thing to say. Thank you. But I'm a poor hostess; I must offer you a brandy against this cold."

"Oh, I'm fine. What are these chalk marks on the floor?" I pointed toward a large area clear of furnishings except for two mismatched chairs set next to each other. I was becoming quite adept at distracting her.

"That's our stage." She strode over, her arms out as though to conjure up curtains and footlights. "Here are the thrones for Claudius and Gertrude. The chalk lines mark the bounds of the music hall stage area. It is somewhat smaller than this room, so we must make certain the action for the duel stays well within them. Elsewise I or Laertes might tumble into the orchestra."

"That would be inconvenient."

"It's been known to happen. Well, if you are not cold, then I am. I've a sitting room within. Let me build up the fire while you have a study of my other paintings. I'd show you 'round, but it's best not to have the artist peering over your shoulder."

So saying, she excused herself and went through an arched doorway, taking her candle along. It surprised me that she did not have any servants, or perhaps they resided off the premises. I listened most carefully and could hear no other stirrings within the building. Certainly it bespoke strongly for her sense of independence that she looked after her own needs, especially since she was raised from the cradle to take privilege for granted. The other ladies of her class would not even know how to make a fire for themselves, much less see to the practicalities of earning their living. I hoped that at some point, when she would not think me too forward to inquire, Bertrice would tell me of how she came to be a successful "adventuress" in her own right.

For the present, I amused myself looking at the rest of the uncovered paintings, and found my esteem for her growing by the minute. She was a rare actress, but outshone herself as an artist. She had some dandy landscapes and still lifes, but it was the portraits that truly mesmerized. She had some trick of capturing the most fleeting expression in such a way as to expose the very soul. One in particular was almost disturbing, that of a very delicately featured young woman. She was beautiful, nearly ethereal, but seemed to bear the weight of a thousand years in her dark eyes, yet they were warm with compassion for all they saw.

"One of my more successful commissions," said Bertrice, coming up. She'd divested herself of hat and cloak and had dabbed on a fresh touch of that spice perfume. "I hope it will be well received, anyway."

"I think the lady will be most pleased with your work."

"Yes, but it's her gentleman friend who hired me that I have to please first. Nice fellow, but sometimes a bit exacting, especially in regard to her. You met him briefly at the gathering. Lord Richard d'Orleans? The fellow was dressed like a crusader and had the card reading just before you."

Damn. And I'd wanted to avoid that topic altogether. "He should be very happy with what you've done here, I know I would."

"You are most kind. I've wondered if you've thought more about that little ruffling of Sholenka's psychic feathers."

"Erm . . . not really." I needed to distract her again. "I've since been more concerned with your brother. He was in very good spirits when I left. Quite brought his color up, though that may have been the brandy . . ."

"So you've told me, and I'm glad. Sholenka is also feeling more improved. I later called on her, and we had a very nice chat."

"I'm sorry that I distressed her. It still puzzles me."

"Does it?" She cocked an eyebrow. "Come to my sitting room. Perhaps I can remove some of your puzzlement."

That sounded ominous.

She had a way about her, polite, but nothing that would brook refusal. To do so would be rude, so I followed her into a much smaller room. It was quite a surprise. Where the outer hall had the look of a railway station, this inner apartment seemed to have been lifted *en toto* from Ring. Its decor was that of a proper and quite comfortable home ready to receive guests, with oak wainscoting, flocked wallpaper, and a number of chairs and settees scattered about. The walls sported paintings, the style of which I recognized as her own, and a merry fire blazed away in a generously sized fireplace.

"This is very nice," I exclaimed.

"Yes, and a bit of a shock, too. Most people expect an artist to subsist in a dreary garret, but I've never cared for the Spartan philosophy. Besides, the damp is bad for the canvases. Please do let me take your coat and have a seat by the fire."

After we disposed ourselves, me on a settee and she in a basket chair opposite, she again offered me refreshment, and seemed amused when I told her not to trouble herself.

"You're a very interesting man, Quincey," she said.

She'd left off the "mister" I noted. "I'm just an ordinary sort of fellow. You're the one here who is truly interesting."

"I think not. Especially after my talk with dear Shola. I also had a brief chat with Lord Richard and a few others who had been at the party. They were . . . helpful to me."

"In what way?" I spoke lightly, but she regarded me in such a focused manner that I felt a prickling crawl along my spine like spider tracks. She was leading up to something, that was obvious. I wasn't sure I would like it, either.

"What did you think of the people there?" she asked.

It seemed an abrupt change of subject, but my instincts told me there would eventually be a point to this. "I'm not sure what you mean."

"Did not a few of them strike you as being somewhat unusual?"

"Certainly Mr. Price did. But I put all that down to it being a fancy dress party and everyone having a connection to the theater. Most of them seemed to be artistic types, and they never come out of the same mold as the rest of the world."

"How diplomatically put. Let me speak of Lord Richard in particular. Did you not sense anything different about him?"

"Only that his outfit seemed to suit him more than most."

"And what about what he said to you? As though you two were part of some secret club or society?"

I spread my hands in a shrug. "I've no explanation. Drink, perhaps?"

She gave me a most winning smile. "Oh, dear, I must stop teasing you. You deserve better."

"Again, I don't know what you mean."

"Oh, but you do." She leaned forward, laying her soft hand on mine and looking into my eyes. Her voice dropped to a very warm, comforting tone. "You see, Quincey, I *know* what you are."

Speech fled me for an instant. Ice seized my heart. "I'm sure I don't know—"

"But you *do*. And it's all right. You're safe with me. I understand." She stood and went around her chair. Behind it was another cloth-shrouded easel. Smiling down at me, she stripped the cloth away in one sweeping motion.

Beneath it was a mirror.

Chapter Twelve

I sat as one stricken, turned to stone. This was like some horrible repetition of what happened the night before in Art's study. Even her words were nearly the same as my own had been.

"Please, Quincey, don't be alarmed," she was saying, as if from a great distance. "You may trust me."

Only this time, *I* was the one afraid.

Had to turn away from the mirror. It was awful, not being able to see myself.

She hastily covered it again. "I'm sorry, I've no wish to offend you."

I abruptly stood, but couldn't bring my feet to hasten me toward the door. One look at her and I knew I dared not leave. Not yet. "You . . . you have forced a confidence, Miss Holmwood."

Her face fell. "I only wanted you to see that I understood, and that it is all right. I'm sorry."

"No, you are not."

"Then I'm sorry for pressing so hard. This was overly theatrical, but it seemed a quick way of cutting past your guards, of allowing us to speak honestly with each other. Your prevarications are charming and clever, but it is obvious to me that you are not altogether comfortable with them."

"If I have offended you with my lies, I ask forgiveness," I said stiffly. "I was trying to preserve an illusion of normalcy about myself."

"As you rightly should. But you may trust me. Have you not trusted Arthur with your secret?"

"How do you even *know* of such matters?" I cried.

Bertrice flinched at my tone. I had to struggle to master myself.

"How?" I asked, more gently.

Her face was somber. "One hears things. Especially at Lord Burce's house. I'm there nearly every week. One hears rumors, and occasionally sees something. Did you not notice there were no mirrors in his home?"

I shook my head.

"*He's* aware and sympathetic. In him a few of your kind have found a friend."

My kind. "Does everyone in London know of this?" Alarm made my voice rise again.

"No. Only a very, very few. Those like you make sure of that by means of their strange . . . 'influence' over people. Everyone else is absolutely ignorant or regards the fact as being simple myth—which is almost as safe."

I felt as though I'd stepped off a curb into a puddle, but dropped instead into a deep sinkhole with black water closing above. There were more vampires like me in London? How many? Were they of my breed or of Dracula's? How much did she know? "Who are they? Who else?"

She shook her head. "I only know there are others. If I've met any, then I've no memory of it. Lord Richard spoke for himself—or hinted at it, but I think he's something of a special case, different from any of you."

"How so?"

She shrugged. "Burce once said that d'Orleans moved in high government circles and even had the blessing and patronage of the Crown. That's all I could get from him."

I sat down. Rather heavily. Now did I fully comprehend what Art had gone through last night. And me unable to partake of brandy to blunt it. "So one fortune-teller has a fit of hysterics and you suddenly know all."

"Between her and Lord Richard's reactions to you, yes, after I'd given it much thought. But my first inklings began before we went there. From the start you interested me very much."

"Did I?"

"And still do. I had clues. I followed them, and came to a logical, if a bit unexpected, conclusion. Hearing rumors of something so fantastical is a long way from finding proof enough to believe in them. *Here* was my final proof." She gestured toward the mirror.

I snorted, without derision. "Just my blamed luck that of all the people in this blessed city I should run into a female Sherlock Holmes."

"More of a 'Loveday Brooke, Lady Detective.' She also has stories in *The Strand*. I'll loan you my issues if you wish."

This was absurd, but I could see she was trying to put me at ease. "May I ask what clues?"

Cautiously, as if fearing I might bolt like a shy mustang, Bertrice resumed her seat in the basket chair. "The first was the great mystery of your return from the grave months ago. I had a brief opportunity to observe Arthur's reaction of mourning. It was deep and genuine and I felt very helpless to comfort him. Remembering that and comparing it to the story you told this night of becoming separated from the hunting party struck me as most curious. If you had merely disappeared, leaving the remotest hope that you yet lived, Arthur would *never* have left Transylvania. He's resolute and loyal as a bulldog when the fit's upon him. His grief was that of a man who had seen unmitigated proof of his friend's passing. What that proof might be I am not sure. Perhaps you will enlighten me?"

"Perhaps." Still in no state to speak coherently, I wanted to hear her out first and asked that she continue.

She was pleased to do so. "There was the minor matter of your not eating or drinking at the party. That might be excused, but twice in a row when we went to that public house and later here. I've yet to meet a gentleman who turned down the offer of a brandy on a winter night. Again—curious."

"Go on."

She'd fair warmed into it now. "That little interview we had on the theater roof was the most telling—I noticed you seemed to have an uncanny habit of not breathing unless you spoke. Cold as it was, no vapor flowed from your lips as one might expect. Not many people would notice that, but since taking up acting I've trained myself to observe all sorts of little quirks that people possess. A quirk is one thing, but what you were *not* doing was quite impossible. I suspected something then, and so invited you to the gathering to see what might happen. My thought was that you would encounter others who would confirm or deny my speculations. The results were remarkable, beyond anything I'd hoped. Afterward I gave you the chance to explain yourself to me, but you were not yet ready. The reason why I was so closed-mouthed in the carriage was to keep from bursting forth with a flood of questions then and there. You might have fled away forever."

"Did everyone there know about me?"

"I doubt it. It's not as though you walk about with a sandwich board hanging from your shoulders. Even others such as yourself would not instantly recognize you as one of their number, nor, I think, would you know them. But special people, like d'Orleans and those with Shola's abilities, might."

"Is she really a witch, as Burce said?"

"That's only his pet name for her, but she has certain . . . gifts."

"What, like that Madam Blavatsky or that Hume fellow?" I'd read a few tall tales about them in the papers, but had otherwise paid no mind to their antics.

"Hardly; Sholenka is genuine. She's no confidence trickster preying upon people's griefs to attain money and fame, her living comes from stage work. Many's the time Shola's expressed the wish she'd not been so psychically gifted."

"Just what is it she does?"

"It's hard to describe. She gives ordinary card readings to amuse, but beyond that she is able to see colors around people, the glowing of their souls, she calls it."

"Colors?" I'd never heard the like before, but tried to keep the skepticism from my tone. Not so long back I'd not believed in vampires, either.

"Yours shocked her, once she took the time to look. I think it was the first time she'd ever touched one like you. She said you were surrounded by the cold of the grave, yet there was light within. The shock of your death yet held sway over your soul."

"I have a soul?" Dracula had told me as much, but I'd not been all that prepared to trust him. In low moments the questions ate at me.

"Of course you do, and a good one, she maintained, once she recovered from her fright."

"How reassuring," I said, faintly.

"Why would you think otherwise?"

"It's another long story. What else do you know? Of me? Of my . . . 'kind'?"

"I know that like actors and actresses, they have acquired a tainted reputation."

She spoke so ingenuously that I gave a short laugh in spite of myself. "Very gently put, miss. How can you just sit there like that, knowing what I am?"

Her mouth pursed and eyebrows arched. "Is there something *wrong* with what you are?"

"Can you not see it?"

"What I *see* is a good-hearted gentleman who seems to be bearing some sort of guilt. Are you ashamed of what's happened to you?"

"I am shamed by what it forces me to do, to lie to people who don't deserve it."

"There is no lie when it is to preserve one's privacy."

"But I've lied to *you*."

"Out of what you deemed to be a necessity, I should hazard, and they were most entertaining. Beyond those, you've likely done little more than omitted information about yourself, which we all do when we wish to make a good impression. A harmless sham for any casual acquaintance. But I perceived that you were interested in deepening our acquaintance. Was I mistaken?"

My face went all hot. "No."

Some of the sun returned to her smile. "Then were you ever planning to inform me of your nature?"

"I . . . don't know."

"Honestly answered," she murmured. "And as you've said, I've forced things. If you've not discerned it already you have just learned that I tend to knock my way through walls. Sometimes it turns out badly and they come down about my ears, other times a clear path is made. Which is it tonight?"

I took a while replying. It had been difficult confiding to Art, for he'd had to overcome all the terrible things we'd been taught about vampires. Here was his sister, as fine a woman as I'd ever met, and apparently lacking any qualm or caution against them. Was she reckless or just misinformed? Was she even to be trusted? For that I had a hypnotic solution, and it seemed the easiest. I could make her forget this whole evening, forget she'd even met me and never so much as think my name again.

But in turn I would have to forget her. Never see her again.

My heart sank at such a dismal prospect.

"Which do *you* prefer?" I asked, doing my best to sound neutral.

"I should like a clear path that may lead to our becoming very good friends. Unless I am much off the mark, you need one."

How right she was on that. How I longed to be able to speak without having to worry over each word, to not be on guard all the time.

To not have to lie.

"A man can't have too many friends," I hazarded.

Her eyes fair sparkled. "Then I should be most pleased to oblige you, sir, and will call you Quincey from now on if you will call me Bertrice without the 'Miss.' "

I took her hand and damn if I wasn't having to fight a lump in my throat. "It would be an honor, Bertrice."

"That wasn't too awfully hard, was it?"

"Well . . . yes it was."

Laughter. "I suppose so. But now that we are friends, perhaps you will tell me the *real* story about your death and return. And I should like to hear how things turned out for my brother last night. You told him the truth of yourself?"

"I did, and a rare burden it was, too."

"Why is that?"

"It's a long tale. I shouldn't want to keep you from your rest."

"Oh, no you don't. If you left now I would not sleep a wink. Or do you have another appointment?"

I sighed. "No, I do not. The early hours of an evening pass by quick enough, but after nine or ten, they drag, and after midnight they can come to a complete halt." Not so back in Transylvania, where time was arranged to suit the count's convenience. I always had company when I chose no matter what the lateness of the hour. "The world is set up for day people."

"Most of it, but in the theatrical world no one thinks twice about making calls at three in the morning."

"Especially at Lord Burce's house?"

"Particularly there."

"I'd like to know more about him."

"And so you shall, but my turn first with you. It is yet early for me, so please, tell me everything, leave out no detail, however small." She curled herself up in the basket chair, arms clasped around her shins, chin resting on her knees, a picture of alert interest.

I didn't need a second invitation, so I started talking. It turned out to be easier than I thought, even when telling about my encounter with Nora Jones in South America. I left out the more intimate details in favor of decorum, but the necessary facts were left intact so Bertrice understood how I gained the potential for drastic change.

This time it was different from talking to Art, for Bertrice had no disagreeable associations with vampirism, nothing to be unlearned. I found it a great relief to finally speak to someone not afraid of or disgusted by my new nature. She was fascinated.

Then I necessarily had to tell her about Lucy and of Dracula and all the rest of that sad, horrible story.

It took some time, for Bertrice had heard nothing of it from Art.

"Good God," she exclaimed. "He's been marching around, all brave-faced, with *that* weighing on his soul?"

"I fear so. He's able to talk to Jack and the others, but—"

"My poor brother! And when they are not around he is all alone with it. No wonder he's been a walking ghost since his return. I shall have to go to him."

"Not just now. Please. He doesn't know our paths have crossed yet. Last night he had more than enough new notions to fever his brain up for days to come."

"Have you some objection to Arthur knowing we are friends?"

"Not one whit, but let him first get used to the idea of just having me back. Then *later* we'll give him a chance to get used to the idea of you knowing all about me."

She thought a moment, then relented with a nod. Then she frowned. "What I don't understand is *why* he said nothing of any of this. We used to confide everything to each other."

I spread my hands. "I suppose it was too unbelievable. If he'd started telling you this when it was happening you'd have bundled him off to Jack Seward's asylum in a strait-waistcoat."

She bristled. "I would not. I'd have asked for proof and seeing poor Lucy would have been proof enough. He should have said something to me!"

"But at the time your dear father was ill as well. I'm thinking Art would have held back because of that, too. You were all going through a terrible time. You didn't need any more grief laid on top."

Again, she nodded. "Yes, that must have been it, but for him to carry such a dreadful weight alone . . . and it is because of what this professor told you about vampires that you felt so badly about becoming one yourself?"

"At the time what he said made a lot of sense. I believed Van Helsing with my whole heart, for there was no doubt that Dracula was evil. We were on a holy crusade to destroy him."

"For killing Lucy, yes, of course, the same as one would hunt down any murderer."

My voice dropped. "Bertrice, there's more. It's pretty bad."

"How bad?"

"It's to do with what happened to Lucy *after* she died."

"Dear God, you mean she . . . came back?" The color left Bertrice's face. She uncoiled from her chair to put her feet on the floor, looking suddenly fragile.

When I got through that part of the story, about what we found in the Westenra vault and what we had to do about it, Bertrice was pale enough to faint, but fought it. I found her drinks cabinet and poured her a brandy. She could manage only a sip, then hiccuped into a near sob. I gave her my handkerchief and felt almighty helpless.

"Damn, I hate when I get like this," she said. "Give me a moment. That is the m-most appalling thing I've ever heard."

I gave her a moment and more, my respect for her growing even greater as she fought to overcome her shock. She erupted from her seat and paced around, eventually excusing herself to go through to the outer room for awhile. The cold air would help her, that, and looking at the familiar sight of her paintings. I'd opened a door to a dark and wholly frightful world; she needed to get her bearings before I could say more of it.

But her response when she came back surprised me. Her eyes were positively blazing.

"That *bastard!* That consciousless, cowardly *bastard!*"

Her anger was like a physical thing. I'd not felt its like since facing down Dracula. "He's gone, now. We—"

"He is? I thought he was at Purfleet."

"Who? Dracula?"

"No! That craven, cruel, bloody *bastard* of a professor!"

"Van Helsing?"

"Yes! How *dare* he put my brother through such a nightmare? To force him to kill his own fiancée? It's obscene! My God, poor Arthur!"

She wasn't too coherent, stalking around the room and using language that would shame a sailor. I was very shocked by it, then flooded with shame of a different kind. Shame for my part in the . . . execution. I abruptly saw things from her view of them and went cold inside.

"How *dare* he!" she raged.

During these last months I'd always made myself push the dreadful image of Lucy's second death from my mind's eye. Each time it appeared, I'd dodge away and distract myself. Even in the cold fastness of that tower in Dracula's castle, while I debated on whether to kill him or not, I had avoided thinking about what we'd done to Lucy. At the time, Van Helsing had us convinced we'd freed her soul to go to God. At the time, we'd had no doubts. I still had no doubt of it, for she'd truly become a monster, preying on helpless children. She had to be stopped. There was no other way around it, which was cold comfort at best.

But for Art to be the one to do the deed . . . and that *had* been the professor's idea. He'd made it seem like an honor, a holy duty. How Art had steeled himself, responding as he was expected to, assuming so heavy a millstone and later kissing Van Helsing's hand in gratitude, blessing him for the privilege.

I felt sick.

Staring at the floor, not seeing it, I sensed something above. Bertrice stood over me, high color in her face now from her anger, but she'd gone quite still.

"Oh, Quincey, I'm sorry. I wasn't thinking. How wretched it must have been for you, too."

"For us all," I murmured.

She put her hand on my shoulder, then was sitting next to me, arms around me. It happened all of a sudden, and it seemed the most natural thing in the world to catch her up and pull her in close and hard. There we stayed for a long while just fiercely clinging to each other. I felt safe yet recklessly protective all at once, as though all the problems of the world could be solved just by holding her.

Then we were kissing. I wasn't sure who started it. It just happened and swept us along, two entwined leaves spinning on a fast tide.

Too fast. My corner teeth were out. And I wanted her.

Still kissing me, she began to undo the buttons of my coat, slipping her hand inside to attack those of my shirt.

Wrenching as it was, I gently pulled away, hating the action.

She was startled a moment, then gathered herself, trying to calm her breathing. There was a lovely flush on her cheek, but if things continued, I'd drain that rosiness from her quick enough.

"Don't you want to?" she asked.

"Too much."

"And perhaps this is the wrong time."

"We can't. Ever."

"Why not?"

I shook my head and went to stand by the mantel. More than just the glow from the fire heated me. "We just can't."

"I've been given to understand that such congress

can be most . . . stimulating, You find me attractive, do you not?"

I'd heard that question before on the lips of many women, and woe to me if I ever answered it wrong. Sometimes I've had to lie, but this was not one of them. "I do indeed. In a respectful way."

She quirked her mouth. "Just what does that mean?"

"I admire you very much."

"Admiration and attraction need not be mutually exclusive—and I see that I've made you uncomfortable again. I'm a direct woman, Quincey; respect that I would like an honest and direct reply. Are you attracted to me?"

"Yes, I am, but—"

She held her hand up. "Let's stop here. I know that 'but' means you're trying to be a gentleman."

"Uh . . ."

"Because you consider me to be a lady."

"Yes, miss. Bertrice."

"Then I will make a suggestion: let us eschew 'gentleman and lady,' in favor of 'man and woman.' Would that not be more agreeable?"

"To what end?"

"A physical union," she stated, as though it were the most obvious thing in the world. "What? Is there anything wrong with two healthy adults consenting to enjoy one another?"

"But . . . we're . . ."

"Not married? Not engaged?"

I nodded.

She waved her hand. "I no longer believe in marriage so you may omit that objection."

"But you . . . you're . . ."

"What? Not a woman of easy repute?"

"No! You're my best friend's sister!"

That took her aback. "What on earth has Arthur to do with us?"

"How could I look him in the eye, if I—if we—"

"Quincey, anything that *I* choose to do in my private life is none of Arthur's business. Were I not related to him, what might your reaction then be to my suggestion of an intimacy between us?"

Well, that put a new face on things, but still . . . "You don't know what it's like with me. I—I go about things differently than I did before."

"Because of your change?"

"Yes. I am well able to . . . but I'm . . . that is, I'm not . . . fertile in the usual sense." Though everything worked nearly the same, I did not throw off seed during my crisis. The strangeness lay in the fact I did not miss it, for I was more than amply compensated elsewhere.

She shrugged. "I've no complaint against that. On the contrary, I find it a relief not to have to worry about conceiving."

Such brutally honest speech on such a subject should have shocked me, but I think I was getting used to her way of speaking her mind. Very well, honesty she would get in return. "My achievement of pleasure requires that I drink your blood."

"Obviously you had no objection when Miss Jones did this to you. Apparently you found her way to be . . . satisfying?"

I felt myself going red to my roots. Then I was suddenly smiling. Couldn't help it. "Yes. It was. Very."

Bertrice smiled back. "I'm only asking if you would like to share that experience with me."

"I don't know." God knows I wanted to, but Art would not be pleased. You don't take advantage of a man's sister. It just wasn't done. But what to do when the sister is trying to seduce you?

She continued. "If you were unchanged, would you accept my invitation?"

"If I were unchanged, would you invite me?"

Her eyes sparked. "Oh, yes. Absolutely. I found you to be a most singularly attractive man from the moment I met you."

My turn to be taken aback. "Really?"

"Of course, I could say nothing at the time. It would not have been right. The funeral, you know. I'd rather hoped to meet you again later, but it never worked out. And then to hear you'd died . . . I did cry for you, you know."

"You did?"

"It was a shock, after all. But had you returned, none the different from your journey, I think we would have had this conversation regardless." She came to me, standing close. She turned her head just a little, lifting to me.

What a lot of words are in a single kiss. She gave me a week's worth of talk in that brief touching.

How incredibly good it was to be with a woman eager for me, but how much better that the woman was Bertrice. I felt myself the luckiest man in the wide world to know the taste of her mouth, to know the heat of her flesh under my hands. We took our time, getting acquainted with each other's wants, which happily were in accord. She wasn't shy about telling me what she liked, which sharply reminded me of Nora. I told her my likes in turn, murmuring in the darkness.

She was different from any woman I'd been with since my change. I thought it would ever be my lot to pay for my pleasure and then influence the girl into forgetting what I'd done to her to achieve it. No such necessity here with Bertrice. She understood what was coming and teased me into it, drawing my head low to kiss her throat, pressing my lips against the pulse point there, moaning when I teased her to greater excitement by only nipping lightly, or lapping her smooth flesh with my tongue.

It's always better to wait, I'd found. She grew feverish from it, from the anticipation, urging me on, but I delayed things until her heart pounded fit to burst. By then I was inside her, pressing things in that manner until she could no longer hold herself off. She clawed at my back, pulling me close and hard. Her strong body arched in one vast spasm, her cries echoed off the walls in time to my thrusts. I reveled in her reaction, in a strange manner caught up in its rapture as well. Gradually she subsided, until she lay relaxed, breathless, and exhausted, hardly able to move.

I breathed myself, to embrace her many scents, that rare spice of her perfume, the deeper musk of her womanhood, the sweat drying on her. I was still enfevered, having delayed my sating. But it hovered close, very close.

"Why didn't you . . . take from me?" she asked. "Why? I thought . . ."

I lightly touched my fingers to her lips, hushing her. "Because I wanted you to know what I've always done to please a lady. May I inquire if you're satisfied?"

"God, yes. But—"

"Now you just hold onto that feeling. There's more to come."

"How? I mean—that is . . . you . . ."

"Just proving to you I'm yet a man in the traditional sense. But now . . ." I kissed her long and sweet, then went lower, nuzzling her dear flesh. Her heartbeat pounded heavy in my ears, quickening at this delicate touch. We were yet joined together, and I felt her reaction down there as well.

"Now?" she asked, wonderingly. "Will you now?"

"Yes . . . just be very still."

I lingered long over her pulse point. Savoring. Holding the moment. She was so precious.

"Please, Quincey."

"Yes . . ."

I bit into her throat. Cleanly. Hard. My corner teeth cutting painlessly.

Her cry was faint, hardly more than a long sigh, then it became a short, sharp gasp. She spasmed under me all over again as it seized her, seized us both. She shuddered the length of her body, as did I at this taste of her blood. After that first glorious swell of outpour I sipped slow, pulling away to kiss her soft mouth, then returning to those small, flowing wounds again and again. Her life was hot and vital, filling me to the brim with her unique fire.

"How much . . . more?" she whispered. "I-I'm still . . . it's still . . ."

"For as long as you wish it to last," I whispered back, then wholly buried myself in her essence.

"Oh, *God* . . . !"

And then she was beyond speech.

Chapter Thirteen

When I returned to my hotel a scant quarter hour before dawn a telegram from Art Holmwood awaited me, almost as though he'd found out what had occurred between Bertrice and myself.

I experienced a very strong twinge, if not of guilt, then of high discomfort. Of course, it was impossible he should know, but the foolish notion galled until I opened and read his message.

"*Professor and Jack visit tomorrow to stay overnight. Excellent time for your talk. Please advise if you're free. Holmwood.*"

This was damned annoying.

I scribbled a reply, cursing mildly.

"*Expect me in study after dinner. Q.*"

The world and its mundane concerns still existed.

For a time I'd quite happily forgotten such dreary
worries as I lay next to Bertrice, watching her sleep.
She'd roused a little as the approach of sunrise forced
me from her side to dress. She watched, her eyes heavy
with drowse, a smile on her lips. We shared a loving
farewell kiss, then she slipped back into deep slum-
ber. I wanted to ask her to marry me right then and
there, but it would have to wait. She'd want to be full
awake when I proposed.

Yes—she had stated that she never wanted to
marry, didn't even believe in marriage, but women can
change their minds easy enough. I was wildly in love
with her, and that fact must and would count for
much.

Tomorrow night I had hoped to find a late-closing
jewelers where I could order a suitable engagement
ring. I'd already composed in my head a telegram to
Art to excuse a delay for my second visit. Instead, I
had to write to Bertrice care of the music hall—as I'd
foolishly taken no note of her street address—and
hoped she would receive it and understand.

*"Very much regret that wretched duty calls me away
to Ring. May we please meet the following evening?
Your true and devoted friend, Quincey."*

I also wrote instructions for a bouquet of roses to
be delivered along with the telegram and paid over a
suitable amount of cash. The night clerk who would
see to the task seemed less than enthused, giving me
to doubt he was up to the job. I forced my influence
upon him to make sure he would remember and carry
things out to the letter even if he had to take the
telegram and flowers to the theater himself. Then I
had to dash upstairs, racing against the sun, but confident of winning. So enthralled was I in good feeling that I forgot my dislike for absolute darkness when
materializing inside my box. A pleasant hum had
manifested itself between my ears. It meant I was in

love, and that nothing else really mattered. I could deal with *all* obstacles. Easily.

The hum was yet there when I awoke and slipped out again. I gave in to a hedonistic stretch, resisting the urge to run up the walls and do handsprings on the ceiling. How alive I felt, far more so than when I walked in the sun. All was right with the universe or would be after I'd spared a few light moments to deal with it. Once finished with my meeting at Ring I could turn my entire focus upon Bertrice—happy prospect.

I readied myself for the train ride, again donning the fore-and-aft traveling cap and Inverness, the half-mask in my valise of earth along with the wool scarf. While I did not think such a disguise would be necessary this time, it seemed wise to be prepared.

Thoughts of Bertrice filled my mind and heart during the trip, seeming to shorten the time. It's amazing how love can make a clock's hour hand spin fast as a top or slow the minute hand to a complete halt. I would have much preferred to be waiting by the stage door for her, but could not shirk my friendship and obligation to Art. He'd obviously gone to some effort to bring Jack and Van Helsing to Ring, the least I could do was turn up and provide a bit of postprandial entertainment.

My humor darkened, though, the closer I got to my goal. By the time I'd left the local station and walked through the gates of Ring, my mood was quite sober regarding what was to come. The professor would be a tough nut to crack. He was utterly set in his ideas about vampires, and those had been right—insofar as our pursuit of Dracula had been concerned. Where *I* stood in his view of things promised to be on most shaky ground. He had years of learning and research on his side, I had only myself and who I was, and somehow that would have to be enough to convince him that not all vampires were evil incarnate.

Also sharp in my mind was Bertrice's reaction to what I'd told her of the professor. His work that terrible night in the Westenra crypt now seemed to be subtle and ugly manipulation. I'd been right there, and part of me knew that he had acted in good faith, but another part was horrified at what he'd put Art through. There was no taking it back, nor was there anything I could do about it since all was past and over.

Bertrice might give the professor a piece of her mind, about it though, should she ever meet him. After the way she flew off the handle last night I wouldn't put it past her to do more than that. She possessed a powerful temper and an acid tongue when it came to the righteous defense of her brother. Woe to anyone who crossed her concerning him.

The lamps in Art's study were on, the curtains open. I took that as an invitation and, leaving the valise hidden in the fir stand, covered the open ground to the window. In less than a quarter minute I'd gone up the stone flanks of the great old house and made my entry through the tiny cracks in the framing around the glass.

I floated for a moment, listening as best I could with my muffled hearing for signs of occupancy, finally determining the room was safely empty. Going solid again, I found the place generally unchanged from my last visit. Brandy, whiskey, and sherry bottles awaited on the table, along with the gasogene and several glasses. A carved humidor Art brought from India was also there, a souvenir of our tiger hunt with the reckless Colonel Sebastian Moran. What a time that had been. While everyone else sensibly stayed atop their elephants, Moran had descended to the ground to track his quarry, which is the most dangerous way of going after tiger.

Of course, Art and I could not resist the urge to follow. How the mahouts had stared, eyes huge in their dark faces as they called on their gods to spare us from our foolishness. Things had turned out well, though. Moran bagged a twelve-foot man-eater with one shot and our celebration had gone on well into the wee hours. He'd given us each a humidor as a remembrance of the occasion. Mine was still in a shipping crate somewhere in Galveston.

Van Helsing was no tiger in that sense, though to me he was every bit as dangerous. But this confrontation also *must* end in a celebration—I fervently hoped. I summoned up every shred of optimism in my being to square myself for the task. After all, things had gone well enough with Art. Van Helsing and I did not have so long a friendship to draw upon, but he was a man of science and trained in logic. By presenting my case to him properly, he would have to accept me as harmless.

Should that fail, I'd hypnotize him.

If he'd not drunk too much wine with dinner.

I regarded the bottles on the table with a raised eyebrow and considered moving them elsewhere for the time being.

A noise down the hallway arrested my attention before I could act, and I slipped quickly toward the windows. They were of the bay type, their curtains hung before them in such as way as to create a private alcove when pulled closed. I unhitched the holding ropes on each side of both and drew them shut, sheltering behind the one nearest the table.

Though it was not honorable to hide like this and eavesdrop, I wanted to get a feel for how the land lay before making my appearance. I could simply vanish and hover close, but did not want to chance missing a single word due to the muffling effect on my hearing when in that non-solid condition.

The study door was thrust open and two people rushed noisily in. I ventured a peek through a sliver of a gap in the curtains. It was Van Helsing, looking to be in a hell of a hurry and in charge of one of Art's female servants.

"Lose not a moment!" His voice fairly whip-cracked with authority.

The sound flooded me with an unsettling mix of strong emotions and memories for which I'd not adequately prepared. The force of it took the strength from my legs and I sat, rather too quickly, upon the window seat.

"Seal these as you did the others," he said. "Be haste! Be haste!"

What the devil was going on here? I tried for a better look, but in that instant the maidservant threw aside the curtain of my hiding place. We gaped in horrified disbelief at each other, then she let out a scream that would peel paint off a wall. She backed up until she all but fell against Van Helsing.

"It's 'im!" she screeched, pointing at me. Clutched in her fist was a good-sized clove of garlic. All at once I understood.

Damnation, this was *not* how I'd planned for things to proceed. Art must have let the cat out of the bag somehow.

I stood and raised a placatory hand. "It's all right, Professor. I can explain—"

But he wasn't interested. From his frock coat he drew forth a familiar-looking metal container and quickly opened it. He reverently produced a Holy Wafer and held it before him like a weapon. The maid slipped past him and ran howling for help.

"Depart from this house!" he boomed. "I command it in the name of God!"

I hesitated; for the life of me this was one time I just didn't know what to do. "Professor Van Helsing, there has been a mistake. I am not what you think—"

"Trouble this house no more, depart!"

"Will you calm down and hear me out? I'm not leaving until we've talked. Where's Art?"

"In a safe place." If he was nonplused at my lack of response to his orders, he didn't show it. "You will never harm him, this I have sworn."

"What are you on about?"

"Depart in the name of God!" Then he repeated those same words in Latin, making the sign of the cross.

"When I'm damned good and ready! Professor, I am *not* in the least like Dracula, so have the kindness to give me a listen before you pop a blood vessel."

"Your words are the devil's lies."

This wasn't going to go well, not unless I could get his attention. Right now he was too wound up to hear anything. "If that were so, then I'd not be able to do this . . ." I stepped forward and gently closed my hand over the Host.

That struck him speechless. For good measure I began saying the Lord's Prayer as loud as I could.

"*Blasphemy!*" he whispered, going white with shock. He released the Host and backed toward the door.

I hurried to get behind him and closed it with a bang, turning the key with my free hand. There was some commotion going on down the hall. The maid's cries must have drawn a crowd.

"Professor, if I was what you think me to be, I'd be howling in pain now. Instead I stand before you with this—" I held up the Wafer. For good measure I kissed it. "Does that not make you the least bit curious to find out why?"

"I will have no trade in your lies and tricks, be gone, image of our dear friend."

"No!"

And so we stood at an impasse, me trying to make him see sense and him with his eyes squeezed shut against it.

I stepped forward, holding the Wafer toward him as he had done to me. "Doesn't this prove that I am not an evil thing?"

He snorted and gestured at the mirror that overlooked the room. As before with Art, it showed the professor to be alone. "Soulless wretch. You mesmerize, you deceive us, you *make* what we see in our minds, and we believe the false words. You are the falsest of the false, using the form of poor Quincey Morris to trick our better nature. I know you, devil. I am not to believe the hell's game you try to play. Depart."

Well, if he thought I was already doing some hypnotizing, then perhaps I should not disappoint him. "Professor, I want you to listen to me. Listen very closely to my words . . ."

I got a reaction, but not the one I expected. Instead of his eyes glazing, he came all over in a rage. He cast about, spied a Bible on a table, and grabbed it up, holding it out. It must have turned into straw-plucking time for him. How he thought that might help when the Host Itself failed I could not imagine, but two could play at this.

I took out my crucifix from beneath my clothes and made sure he saw it.

He looked baffled, but the anger returned to him quick enough. "Deceiver!"

"Van Helsing, for God's sake settle down! Believe what your eyes tell you. I am the same Quincey Morris you knew before. Open up your mind, you hard-headed Dutchman, and *think*!"

He got quiet a minute and did some thinking, or perhaps it was more like calculation. "If you are the true Quincey Morris, you would not hold me here a prisoner."

"You're no prisoner, I just want some privacy. What has happened? Where's Art? What did he tell you about me that got you so het up?"

"You exist, that is what hets me up."

"But you think I'm like Dracula?"

"A young one, with not so many sins upon your head, so the holy things do not work as they should."

"They should all work equally well no matter what. They worked well enough on poor Lucy." What bitter words those were to speak.

"Because she was defiled from the hurting of the children."

"But—oh, never mind. Use your common sense, Professor. All the things you told us about vampires means that this should send me running for the hills. But here I am with no harm done. If this stuff doesn't affect me, it means I am not anyone you need fear."

"I do not fear you. I have the sorry for you, and swear I will end your imprisoned soul's suffering as soon as may be."

"Like hell you will!" But I knew he would do just that unless I could turn him aside. "My soul is the same as it ever was, and if you can think of a way for me to prove it to you, then I'll take any test you care to hand out. I've tried saying the Lord's Prayer, you want me to sing a hymn? That you may regret as I've no voice for it. I'll march into church and read whatever Bible passage you please or—"

"Stop!"

I stopped. And waited. "Well?"

Anger still clouded his face. "Your games will not work on me, vampire. Be gone and trouble us not."

"Just what in tarnation did Art *tell* you?"

"You deceived Arthur, for he wants to believe. The tricks you did to gain his trust will not work on me."

"How did he even come to tell you? I swore him to silence." That's what really troubled. Art had ever been a man of his word.

"Knowledge is power, and I will not empower you more. Be gone."

"Where is he? Get him up here—"

A frantic banging at the door and rattling of the knob interrupted him.

"Professor? Are you there?" With a thrill I recognized Jack Seward's voice.

"Yes!" cried the professor. "And so is *he*! He has locked us in."

I yelled louder. "Jack? It's me, Quincey. I'll let you in if you'll talk some sense into this—"

"Quincey? Oh, God." Even muffled by the intervening door I heard the pain in his voice. "Then it *is* true."

More banging on the door, then he tried the lock. "Professor, I can't open it, the key is still in it on your side."

"Jack? Did you hear me?"

"Listen to him not!"

"Professor!"

We were all shouting at once and not any of us doing a damn bit of good to straighten out the situation. It would have been laughable but for the fact that Van Helsing posed a truly serious threat. If he came across me during the day he would show no mercy. Indeed, he thought putting a stake through my heart to be the height of compassion. He might even get Art to do his dirty work for him again.

I slammed the flat of my hand against the door, which made a hellish racket and brought a pause to theirs. "Jack Seward!"

Blessed silence for a moment as I glared at the professor, daring him to speak again. He held his peace, but still simmered hot.

I tried again. "Jack?"

"Yes? What do you want?"

"For you to calm down and hear me out, dammit. The professor is too set in his ways to listen, I hope you will be . . . be more obliging."

"If you are truly Quincey, then open this door."

"I am Quincey, and I'll open the door, but I want you to keep a cool head when I do."

He made no reply. Maybe he was thinking it over, not wanting to make a promise he couldn't keep, but I was willing to trust him over my present company. Besides, I was getting almighty tired of looking at Van Helsing's scowl.

I turned the key and moved quickly to the side to allow the door a clear swing. In my hand I still held the Host, and my crucifix yet hung from my neck. Such was the sight greeting Jack Seward when he cautiously entered the room.

He looked older, more careworn. How that last adventure of ours had taken its toll on us. He was dressed in evening clothes, come to Ring with the professor for one of Art's excellent dinners.

"Quincey?" His lips trembled.

I nodded. "It is I, as you can see. You see this, too?" I lifted the Host and his eyes widened.

"Impossible!" he whispered.

Van Helsing stepped between us. "It is a lie, friend John. Do not let him beguile you as he did Arthur."

My patience was thin as it could get, and it made me rude to the point of bellowing. "Professor, shut the hell up and let the man make up his own mind!"

The explosion was sufficient to hush him a moment. I turned to Jack. "Now *look* at me, for God's sake! If you believe in the power of this Wafer, then you must believe that I am harmless."

"I—I . . ."

"Jack, what has happened? Did Art tell you about my visit?"

He shook his head. "Not in so many words."

"What, then? Mind reading? I asked him to keep quiet to *prevent* everyone throwing six kinds of conniption fits and going off in all directions. Where is he?"

"Tell him not!" said the professor.

Jack stood flatfooted, and from the agonized look on his face he didn't know which way to jump. I hated putting him in such a fix. It was hard enough on him to have to deal with my return from the grave, let alone choosing sides.

"All right," I said. "Never you mind, let's just get this saddle over the horse first, then worry about where to ride. The professor thinks I've come back from hell itself, but as you can see that's not a place I've been to yet. He doesn't—"

"Do not let him fool you, friend John. In all other things have you not trusted me? For the sake of your soul—"

I cut him off again. "Professor, I've seen men shot dead for less lip than what you're flapping at me now. If you want to end up with your head thumping the floor like a rubber ball, you just keep interrupting. How can you look at me and not—no, just forget it. Your mind's all made up. You know you're the smartest man in the world when it comes to vampires. Jack . . ." I appealed to my friend. "You gonna believe your own eyes or not?"

He made one mirthless laugh. "I can believe my ears. Only Quincey P. Morris of Texas would speak like that. Professor, it is clear to me that he's not like poor Lucy. She was dreadfully changed, turned into that . . . that monster. Quincey is the same as ever he was."

The professor was reproachful. "Did not Lucy tempt Arthur with the bond of their love? So does this devil tempt you with the memory of old friendship."

"I can't believe that. That thing we saw in the grave-yard filled me with horror and disgust. I have no such feeling now. Let us hear him out. There may be truth to Art's rav—to what Art said."

"What's wrong with Art that he's not here?" I demanded. "Did he take sick?"

"He's not . . . feeling well." Jack wouldn't meet my eye.

"What do you mean?"

"He's been under a great strain these months. It finally overburdened him, and he collapsed."

"But he was *fine* the other night! When I left he was cheerful and chipper as ever."

"I'm afraid that your visit might well have been the very thing that sent him over."

"How can that be? If anything he was—take me to him, I must see for myself how he's doing."

"Quincey, he's in no fit state for visitors. We think he's fallen into a raving fit of brain fever, and there's nothing to be done until he pulls himself out of it."

My sails ran out of wind. I backed off a little. "That doesn't sound right. Art can get nerved up about some things, but when the hammer falls, he's more steady than any anvil."

"This time the anvil broke, not the hammer."

"Just how bad off is he?"

"I can't say, not without more—"

"Enough!" snapped Van Helsing. "Do you dice with the devil for your friend?"

Jack was shocked. "Really, sir!"

"Have done with this. He uses your affection against you."

"It seems to me that he's showing a great concern for Art. What possible evil motive can he have in that?"

"One you may perceive not as yet, but in time he would all to his favor turn."

"Forgive me, Professor, no one holds you in greater esteem than I, but that is utter nonsense."

"Hold your horses," I said. "Both of you stop before you say too much you don't mean. We were all friends together once, and may be so again—"

Van Helsing gave a derisive snort.

"But that won't happen if we're all fighting like a

pack of coyotes over who howls last. Nothing good ever
came of such squabbling. Jack, you got a job ahead of
you convincing him to listen, but don't you ever forget how far you two go back. Professor, you'll think
what you want about me and toss common sense out
the window, but remember the respect you've always
given Jack not only as a friend but as a colleague. He
just might know what he's talking about."

Jack took it well enough, but none of this sat too
well with Van Helsing. His face went so red I thought
steam would blow from his ears. I could not understand why he was being so pigheaded. He was a smart
man, but here he was, just paces away from me, and
absolutely refusing to accept what his eyes told him.

"Professor . . ." began Jack.

"*Nein!* This no more will I hear. No more either
should you hear. Even this little of his lying words
much damage has done. You doubt me, but you will
see. You must! But pray God that none others shall
die by his hand while you swim in the doubting sea."

"Who's died?" I wanted to know.

"Those wretches from which you slake your unholy
thirst, devil."

"Oh, good God! Didn't Art tell you I only ever feed
from animals?"

"You do?" asked Jack, surprised. "But I thought—"

"I know what you thought, but you can cut that idea
from the herd. Jack, I am a different *breed* from
Dracula. If he was a war-horse in full armor, then I'm
a no more than a Sunday riding pony."

"But this is fascinating. Professor, there is sense in
this! We can—"

But Van Helsing had given up on talk. He'd sidled
over to a wall display of Comanche war lances Art had
acquired while in Texas. He grabbed one up, and came
at me. Jack let out with a cry and jumped on him,
trying to take it away. I had enough presence of mind

to put down the Host before stepping in as well. The three of us danced this way and that, each trying to gain control of the lance, all grunting and cursing like mad.

I managed to get a solid grip on the professor's wrists and pulled his hands off; Jack staggered away in startled triumph, holding the lance high. It had a stone head bound to it, the edges chipped wickedly sharp, and could have sliced any of us open as easily as a modern metal blade.

Van Helsing and I wrestled around; he shouted a lot of words that were far outside my very narrow German vocabulary. I used some choice American terms as I struggled to get behind him and pull his elbows together. My strength was greater, but I was trying to avoid injuring him. He wasn't making any of this easy on himself.

"Hold still, carn-sarn it, or I'll hog-tie you with the curtain rope!"

Another stream of bad-tempered German or Dutch. His collar popped open, his shirt pulled nearly out of his trousers, and his jalousies had snapped clear of their buttons, threatening the proper placement of those trousers.

"Quincey! Professor! Stop it! Stop this instant!" Jack hovered just out of reach of the struggle, clutching the lance.

I was willing to leave off, but Van Helsing was stubborn, fighting like his life depended on it. Sooner or later he'd tire out, but I worried for his heart lasting the course.

Jack Seward quit shouting and took action. He went to the desk where stood a vase of greenhouse flowers next to Lucy's photograph. He tore the flowers clear and dashed the water square into his former teacher's face. I got a good splashing as well, but it was worth it. The professor sputtered and ceased to struggle. I dragged him over to a chair by the fire and pushed him down onto it.

"Damn, Jack," I said, ineffectually swabbing my face with a handkerchief. From the open doorway I heard a nervous titter. The maid, along with what seemed to be most of the household staff was there, the whole herd clustered close together to watch. I scowled and slammed the door in their faces. "Now we *will* be the talk of the county. I hope your reputation can stand it."

Jack stared at me, mouth opened, then snapped it shut and put the lance back up on the wall. "My *God!*" he said, rounding on us. "Professor, what in heaven's name were you *thinking?*"

Van Helsing—for once—had nothing to say for himself. He glared defiance, after he rubbed the water from his eyes.

I put some distance between us, going over to Jack. He seemed to have caught his breath, but nothing more; there was a lost look to him. Well did I understand the feeling. I clapped a hand on his shoulder.

"It'll be all right, old partner, some things just take a passel of time to get through."

He gave me a sharp eye, searching my features, for what I could not say. I gave him a wink, grinning. Then all of a sudden, his face twisted, and he threw his arms about me in a bear's hug. "It *is* you!"

"None other, I swear," I said, pounding his back and laughing. Relief surged over me. My other friend had returned.

"But how? Did Dracula—" He pulled away to check my face again.

"No, he's got nothing to do with it. Didn't Art tell you?"

"He was in no condition. He babbled bits and pieces, enough to put the wind up myself and the professor. He took charge and had the servants here running about rubbing garlic on all the windows."

I shook my head. "Guess I can't blame him, seeing the confines of his experience. You have a tangle with a vampire as wicked as Dracula, it kind of colors your view. But as God is my witness, Jack, I am *not* like him."

"Then what are you? And how did you come to be this way? I've a thousand questions."

"So did Art. Where is he? No, don't answer, it might set *him* off again." I gestured toward Van Helsing, but his chair was empty, the study door just closing. Jack started after him, but I held him back. "Where will he go?"

"Back to the asylum, I expect. I hope he'll speak to me again. Everything just got so out of control . . ."

"You did right, but he's gonna be mighty angry. He's not the kind to forgive too quick, if at all, and now he may think you've gone over to the devil's own side."

He groaned. "What am I to do?"

"I don't rightly know, but these things have a way of working out. After he's cooled down some you'll be able to talk to him. He might not listen to you, though. He sure as hell wasn't hearing me."

"But why? He's the most logical reasoner I've ever known."

"Mend your fence first, and figure the rest out later. What about Art? Did you take him to the asylum?" I was only making a guess, but it was a good one.

Jack went very sober. "Not yet, but we plan to; it's the best place for me to care for him. He's still here in the house."

"He is? Then I want to see him."

"I'd advise against it. When we arrived here this afternoon he was very agitated. His eyes were so bright I thought he'd caught a fever, but he was in a very merry, happy mood, as though he'd finally broken free of the grief that's held him all these months. He'd invited the professor down for supper, you see, and I

decided to tag along and make a party of it. All was
well, until just after dinner. Art kept running to the
windows and peering out. Then he excused himself and
went upstairs for a bit. He never returned. Just when
I was curious enough to go find out why we heard such
an awful shrieking laughter from his room."

"What happened?"

"That's the devil of it, we don't know. We ran up
to him and found him collapsed, laughing his head off,
and raving about your having come back from the
dead."

I felt cold inside. What had I done to my friend?
"And you believed him?"

"We did when I pried a piece of crumpled note
paper from his fist. My heart all but stopped when I
recognized your handwriting. He stuttered out enough
for us to piece things together, then drifted off into
a heavy doze. The professor went very grim and took
charge of the house. You know the rest."

"I wish I didn't." Suddenly weary, I found my way
to one of the fireside chairs and dropped into it, rubbing the back of my neck. "My return must have
brought on his attack, but why? If anything, it should
have made him better."

"The mind is capable of reacting in any number of
unexpected ways from that which we'd prefer. I think
the strain was too much and he simply gave in."

"I can't believe that. I'm going to see him."

Jack looked ready to object, then shrugged. "Very
well. But I would not be too optimistic."

He opened the door. Waiting on the other side were
a dozen or so of the house's male servants, each one
armed with some deadly implement ranging from golf
clubs to fireplace pokers. Jack gave out an exclamation at the sight, half-jumping out of his skin.

"What is the meaning of this?" he demanded, quite
outraged. "Foster?"

Art's butler, a formidable old snob, lifted his chin, the better to look down his nose. "If you please, Dr. Seward, the foreign *gentleman*"—his emphasis was more indication of sarcasm than respect—"insisted we take up arms against this other foreign gentleman. We none of us wants any trouble, sir, but we are placed in a very difficult position."

"I'm sure he did not mean to, but you may be assured that all the trouble has been sorted out. Mr. Morris is not to be assaulted, is that clear?"

Foster nodded and the rest of the rag-tag army of footmen looked highly relieved. "Very well, sir. May I inquire if this is the same Mr. Morris who was killed in foreign parts?"

"Yes, but it was all . . . a mistake."

He sniffed. "Then may I offer my congratulations on your recovery, Mr. Morris?"

"Thank you, Foster," I said, doing my damnedest to keep a sober face on.

"Are there any other orders, Dr. Seward?"

"Just go about your usual business, Foster."

"Very good, sir." Regally, he turned and surveyed his troops, and dismissed them with a word. They shuffled away slow, reluctant to leave, and obviously full of questions, but they'd just have to do without. God knows what answers they'd supply to themselves once they reached the servants' hall.

As soon as they were out of earshot Jack and I fell into a quiet fit of laughter. We were like two school-boys who had just put one over on a strict teacher. It was absolutely the wrong time and place for it, but we just couldn't help ourselves. If Van Helsing reappeared brandishing a stake and hammer, I'd have not been able to fend him off.

"God, but I needed that," confessed Jack, wiping his eyes. "Hysterics has a place in one's recovery, it seems. Come on, then."

He led the way to Art's room, which was toward the end of the hall. Some few of the household lingered about the stairway, pretending to work. Jack knocked twice on Art's door, then carefully opened it.

"Professor?" he asked, holding to this side of the threshold. Perhaps he expected Van Helsing to be standing just out of sight with another Comanche lance.

"Let me," I said, moving past him, my senses all alert. If there was a piece of bushwhacking at hand, I'd be able to react quick enough to head it off.

But the room was empty.

No sign of Van Helsing, no sign of Art.

"He's taken him away," whispered Jack in disbelief, as shocked as I'd ever seen him.

Chapter Fourteen

"What's his game?" I cast about the room, trying to find a sign of what had happened. The bedcoverings were tossed around; other than that the place was in good order.

Jack's face was a prairie thunderstorm ready to cut loose. He crossed over to the bed and yanked on the bell pull next to it. Presently, Foster came up.

"Sir?"

"Where is Lord Godalming?" he demanded.

"The foreign doctor took him away, sir. While the rest of us were arming, he had two of the footmen carry his lordship down to your carriage, then he had the driver whip up the horses."

"While Mr. Morris and I were—oh, for heaven's sake, this is quite too much! Why did you not tell me?"

"I was given to understand that you already knew, sir."

"You should have stopped him!"

"It wasn't my place, sir, seeing as how he'd taken charge of things earlier, and though a foreign chap, he is still a doctor. I had the understanding that it was an emergency on behalf of his lordship and it seemed best not to hinder him. He promised he would see to his lordship's recovery."

"What else did he say?"

"I could not even guess, sir, as it was not in the Queen's English. He was most excited, though. In a great hurry."

"I expect he's taken off for Purfleet, then."

"Sir, may I ask if his lordship's relations should be notified of his condition?"

An exclamation broke from my lips. "Tarnation, yes! Someone needs to tell Ber—Lady Bertrice. I'll do it."

Jack stared at me. "You? But she heard you're—that is, she thinks you're—"

"Well . . . no, she doesn't. We sort of ran across each other in London; I'll explain later. But maybe it's best if you sent her the telegram, just make it quick, we have to get cracking to Purfleet."

"Quincey, it may be better for me to go alone. If I can talk to Van Helsing under less . . . upsetting circumstances I might persuade him to reason."

I could see the sense of it. "I'll want to be close by, though. I'll come along, but will keep out of sight."

"Of course. Foster? Telegram forms?"

"His lordship keeps them in his desk in the study, I believe."

"Fine. I'm going to have to borrow Lord Godalming's carriage for a day or so. Could you have it made ready?"

"I will have it seen to, sir." Foster left, and though his face was frozen as an old fish, I got the idea he was pleased to have Jack giving the orders now. He returned to the study, while I went after Foster.

"Did you see his lordship?" I asked. "What condition was he in?"

"Sir, it is not my place to make judgments on his lordship."

"If you don't tell me I'll gossip with the footmen instead."

That absolutely appalled him. "Sir, it—that is—"

"Just say it."

"Well, sir, to put it charitably, I believe his lordship was drunk. He was in a very good mood, but the doctors . . . they seemed to read something sinister into his behavior."

With all their dealings with lunatics I could see how they could make such a mistake. I *hoped* it was a mistake. Nodding a thanks to Foster, I went to the study. Jack was writing out the telegram to Bertrice. I browsed through the drawers and found a small leather-bound diary.

Nothing of note was in it, just addresses—including Bertrice's—and brief entries to remind Art of social appointments. My visit was one of them, written as *Guest—?!—after dinner. Drinks.* For tonight he had: *Dinner, J. & V.H. Q. Later. Long talk!!!* His handwriting for both was a little hard to decipher, wandering and uneven. His fist was usually very strong and readable, but I suppose when a man writes to himself he can be as careless as he likes.

When Jack had finished, I composed my own message to Bertrice. *"Regret another unavoidable delay, must be in Purfleet with Seward to look after Art. Will write you from there soonest. Your faithful friend, Quincey."*

After I'd quietly retrieved my valise of earth from the fir stand, Jack Seward and I got into Art's closed carriage and off we went. The ride to Purfleet proved to be long and uncomfortable compared to covering the same distance by train. The roads in England weren't much better than the tracks and trails in the wild back country of Texas, just a little less bumpy and with no prairie dog holes or bandits. Jack and I had shared rougher transportation on some of our travels with Art, but never passed the time with a yarn more strange than the one I spun now. It was more or less identical to what I'd told Art, with me being careful to leave out any hint about Dracula's survival, focusing instead on my helpful mythical hermit. The difference between this telling and the last was Jack's inability to keep from interrupting with dozens of questions, mostly of a medical nature, concerning my changed condition.

"I shall have to get a blood sample from you," he said at the end. "It's not my specialty, but I'm sure I can find someone conversant in—"

"But isn't Van Helsing a specialist?"

"I don't think he will be especially amenable at this present time. He's in quite a state to make him resort to kidnapping Art. I'm sure he thinks he has the best of reasons, but . . ." Jack left off with a shrug. "Van Helsing can be an eccentric fellow. This is very disappointing to me that he should go to such an extreme, but perhaps later we can bring him around. If I propose your case to him as something to be treated as a rare disease in need of a cure, *that* might turn the trick with him."

"How can you cure death?" I asked.

"You did," he pointed out, with a meaningful look that shut me down for some time. "There must be some taint in your blood that has the capacity to . . ." His face screwed up from some hard thinking.

"What?"

"Well, I could speculate that whatever was

introduced into your blood by Miss Jones brought about a drastic change in your entire physiology. Obviously it was very subtle, else you'd have noticed something odd in the years since. It may lie dormant, then during the ordeal of your wounding it kindled to activity. The effect of it dropped you into a profound trance while you were on the brink of death. You lay in this state until your injury healed. To us you had passed on, but instead you were in a coma so deep as to be indistinguishable from complete expiration."

"That's a possibility, but for my own admittedly nonmedical judgment, I'm positive I died."

"How can you be sure?"

"You were there. You saw how much I bled out after the fight. Have you ever seen anyone recover from the kind of cut I got? I haven't, and I've been around and seen some pretty awful things in this world. When I felt the cold take hold of my feet and legs and start creeping up my chest I knew I was gone. All that was left was a quick prayer and sing a hymn over the body. But I had no regrets, not after seeing the good we did for Miss Mina." I tapped my brow to remind him of the burn that she had taken when Van Helsing had touched her there with the Host. Only when she thought Dracula had died had it vanished. "How does science explain that?"

Chagrined, Jack shook his head, spreading his hands. "It was a matter of faith, something beyond science."

"So maybe there are other things around as inexplicable as faith. Meaning myself."

"Well, whatever is behind this, the price you paid for your . . . recovery—once awake—is this terrible addiction to blood-drinking."

I took exception to that. "It's not terrible to me!"

"Neither is the pipe to an opium slave."

There were several more objections I could make to his assumptions, but held them in. He'd have to run with his theories first before being ready to hear the facts. I was certain my condition was quite supernatural and modern science would not stand. How else to explain the lack of a reflection and my ability to vanish? Those were well outside the natural order of things.

He looked all earnest. "Will you let me help you, Quincey?"

"I'm in no need of help. I'm just as fine as I was before, better even." Especially in regard to fleshly pleasures, one of the advantageous facets of my state I'd not confided to him. I'd distracted him with the vanishing business and that had been fascinating enough—if tiring to me.

Jack seemed almost hurt. "But you must surely want to be free of this affliction."

"You think of it as an affliction. I don't."

This was a new notion to him. A troubling one. Enough to give him second thoughts to Van Helsing's warnings?

"This isn't a disease, Jack." I did my best to sound reassuring. "And if it is, then it's a benevolent one. I'm more hale and hearty than I've ever been in my life. The only drawback is how it shuts me away from dawn to dusk. Dracula could get out and about during the day. For some reason, I don't have that freedom. If you can find a way to restore the day to me, *then* I should be much obliged for your help."

"I can but try. We'll make a start as soon as may be."

He wanted to conduct an examination right there in the rolling carriage, but I persuaded him against it, as it was really too dark for him to see anything. We'd have to go through the whole business again later. I did allow him to take my pulse, and since I had none he was fair flummoxed.

"You *must* have a heartbeat," he said, very unhappy. "You simply *must*."

"Well, maybe that's why we're called 'Un-Dead.'"

"But it is physically impossible for you to be walking about with no heart to pump your blood or respiration to—it's not *natural*."

I had to chuckle, which annoyed him. "In the scientific world, that must be so. But the professor introduced us to a different kind of world, a hidden one that should be impossible, but is not. Took him a long time to do it, too, which he did by showing, not talking, to you about it. He sets a great store over giving you something to look at, then asking you to draw a conclusion, doesn't he?"

"That is his very method of teaching, yes."

"Well, I tried it on him tonight, so why didn't it work?"

"I cannot say."

"Then I will. Van Helsing's a stubborn old coot who can't bear to be proved wrong."

"Quincey! Really now!"

"Then what else would you call it? I was standing there big as life holding the Host itself and bellering out the Lord's Prayer without one hitch and he accuses me of blasphemy and calls me a devil."

"I'd no idea. That's so unlike him. I've never seen him that way before. And attacking you with that lance, like one of my patients gone berserk."

"He's a smart fellow, I've never seen his match when it comes to his kind of book learning, but he's got himself a little too set on being right all the time. In this case he doesn't dare allow that he might be wrong about me."

"Why is that? If you're a different breed . . . what harm could there be for him to be wrong? I should think he would delight in the research possibilities."

I gave out a heavy sigh, taking my time before drawing breath to answer. It was an ugly answer, painful to me, and would be doubly so for Jack. He'd not had

time to walk along next to the idea and get used to
it.

"Quincey?"

"All right. I won't dress it up in varnish, but the plain
fact is he *has* to have me as foul as Dracula . . .
because of Lucy."

His face fell at mention of her name. He puzzled
a moment, trying to work out the connection, then
shook his head. "What about Lucy?"

"You saw the terrible change Dracula's touch
wrought on her, and how she was freed afterward. Well,
Van Helsing has to believe that I am in the same devil's
thrall as she was. If he admits that I am different, that
I am truly a safe sort to be around, then he might have
to admit he was wrong about *her*."

Jack went white to his lips. *"No . . ."*

"But he *wasn't*! He was not wrong, neither were we.
If not for our intervention she'd have gone on hurting those innocent little mites, and possibly killed one
or more of them. What we did was *necessary*, and don't
you *ever* think otherwise!"

He took a flask from his coat pocket and drained
off a healthy swig. He tilted it toward me; I declined
with a shake of my head. He put the flask away, oblivious. This told me much about his acceptance of me.

"Poor Lucy," he said. "If we'd waited. Talked to her
as I'm talking to you—"

"No!" I snapped. I had to be sharp to pull him out
of that pit. I'd been there too many times myself.
"That . . . *creature* was *not* Lucy! Not the gentle little
girl we loved. It was all that was left of her, like that
photograph on Art's desk. It wore her face and form,
but the sweetness of her soul was gone or held prisoner. We freed her."

"Yes . . . I know. Truly I know that. But sometimes
I doubt. Then I see that awful scene all over again,
her sufferings . . ." He bowed his head.

"Then don't look at it any more, old partner. Remember instead the peace on her beautiful face when it was all done." I was having trouble speaking, now. My throat was trying to choke up. How I wished I could have the use of a jigger's worth of Jack's liquor.

He straightened up a bit. "You're right. I should not dwell on the darkness. I tell that to my patients often enough; far be it from me to ignore my own advice."

"That's the right trail to take. You've a tough time ahead with the professor. I hope he sees sense, but you've got to be mighty careful."

"What are you on about? He wouldn't hurt *me*."

"He could—if he thinks I've got you under my influence. Just don't back him into a corner of any kind. Always give his sort a way out. If a man thinks he's got no escape he gives up all and drags anyone next to him down as well."

"Quincey, he's a highly-educated, well-respected scholar who wouldn't hur—"

"He did his damnedest to skewer me like a chicken not two hours past! Don't ever forget that. You talk to him, but keep a distance between you. I know you set a store by him, but so long as he's this het up he could do you some serious mischief."

Jack was none too pleased by my talk, but he needed to hear it. Maybe he'd forgotten that it was Van Helsing who had gone into Dracula's sanctuary and driven stakes through the hearts of his three mistresses. He it was who had then severed their heads. Dreadful task, but he *had* done it. Jack would be cautious, but I worried that the high regard he held for his mentor might work against him. Van Helsing could be persuasive and was as dangerous as any man I'd run up against, and that included Dracula himself.

Until the professor was won over, I would never be safe.

❖   ❖   ❖

We could not have been too far behind Van Helsing. At each turning we'd half-expected to catch up with him. Riding singly on a couple of Art's fast hunters, we might have done so, but had chosen the carriage in case we needed to remove Art home again. Purfleet was mostly asleep by the time we arrived. We rattled over the deserted roads before finding the even quieter lane that a few miles later led to Jack's asylum.

The building, with its tree-shaded grounds, was nearly as big and rambling as Ring, but more plain. Once it had been a grand country house for someone with more money than sense at the gambling tables. Sold off to pay the debt, it was eventually converted into its present state as a haven for lunatics, and Dr. John Seward put in charge.

He was very young for the job, I understood, but no one could find fault with him on his energy or abilities. There was also the consideration that perhaps no one else wanted the position, but that was unfair to my friend. Taking care of mad people wasn't nearly as prestigious as purchasing a fine practice on Harley Street, but such things didn't matter to Jack. He was ever a student, ever a researcher, more devoted to his patients than his social position. This was the perfect post for him.

Jack had some very modern ideas about how to deal with mad people. Rather than just keeping them shut away as hopeless cases, he was willing to listen to their ravings to find clues to their delusions and hope for a cure. He was a kindly keeper, which sometimes worked against him as in the case of Renfield, who had on occasion been very violent. Fortunately most of the other charges were of gentler temperament.

The place had a sinister reputation locally, though, which was only to be expected. Few people could welcome the placement of a madhouse in their midst. The necessity of high walls, barred windows, and isolation from the rest of the world gave rise to all manner of rumors, from ghostly hauntings by dead patients to human vivisection with bodies stacked like cordwood in the cellars.

Jack's reaction was that of distress tempered by amusement. In an effort to quell local fears he once opened the doors to a select group of the town elders inviting them to inspect the facilities. Of course, they were far more interested in gaping at the lunatics than anything else, but Jack would not indulge their morbid curiosity, citing the necessity of respecting the patients' privacy. If somewhat disappointed, they departed, full of sweet-cakes and good feeling from the sumptuous tea Jack provided instead.

That helped his relations with the neighbors, but mothers and nannies would still point him out on the street to their children with the cheering warning: "If you're not good, he'll lock you away with the loonies." He felt badly about that and opined that such maternal manipulations were likely to supply him with more patients in the future once the terrorized infants were grown.

Like some of his Continental colleagues, he leaned (quietly) toward the radical idea that how we're treated when very young dictated the kind of adult we'd become. It made sense to me. A drunken wife-beater usually fathered another drunken wife-beater. Jack said that was what the Bible really meant about the sins of the father being passed down through many generations, in terms of spiritual and emotional punishment.

That also made powerful sense, as I wasn't one to believe that God would have much use for holding a grudge for so long. If my great-grand pap had robbed a bank, what was that to me that I should suffer for his crime? But if he decided to take a buggy whip to his wife and kids, that was something else to consider.

There are some family traditions that should never be passed down.

The patients' wing was dark, but the central area where Jack and others of his staff had living quarters was lighted up and active. We peered through the carriage windows, curious, at the goings on. Two orderlies were posted at the outside of the entry, holding clubs. A number of other staff members within were busy at the windows, vigorously scrubbing at them.

"What do want to wager that that is garlic being rubbed around the frames?" Jack asked with a sigh.

"Not one penny," I replied. "Did I mention to you that garlic doesn't hurt me?"

"I suppose it wouldn't, if you don't breathe except to speak. My poor asylum will smell like a French kitchen for weeks."

"Considering the cook you've got it might be an improvement."

"What's wrong with my cook?" He was suddenly querulous.

"It's not my place to say a word against her, but why do you think Art always takes you out to the local hotel to eat whenever he comes for a visit?"

"He was just being—well, really! I've never complained about *his* cook."

"That's 'cause she knows what she's doing."

"But—oh, the devil with it!" He leaned out the window and called for our driver to stop before reaching the front door, then turned back to me. "I think it's best that you stay out here for the time being."

"I'm for that, but you might be jawing with the professor all night. If that happens, I will have to find a safe place to lay out my roll for the day."

"The hotel in town," he suggested.

"I'll wait a half-hour, then skedaddle. Don't tell the professor that I'm here. If there's any news leave a

message for me at the town telegraph office. I'll come
by after sunset tomorrow."

"Good."

We shook hands for luck, then he opened the carriage door himself and went stalking off to the entry.
He spoke calmly to the two men there, who were a
lot more animated, pointing this way and that as they
answered his questions. The impression they conveyed
to me over the distance was vast relief at Jack's arrival.

After some head-shaking, Jack gestured toward the
building, and all three went inside.

"Sir?" The driver called down to me.

"Yes? What is it?"

"Beg pardon, sir, but the horses are steaming and will
need a cooling-down walk after that long road . . ."

"You're right on that, old partner. I'll get out and
you take them along to the stables and look after
things."

"Thank you, sir."

I emerged from the carriage on the side facing away
from the building. "The stables are around the back."

"Yes, sir. May I inquire if his lordship is planning
to return home tonight?"

"I doubt it, being so late. Someone in the house will
look after you, though."

"Yes, sir. My old mum said I'd end up in one of
these lunatical places. Never took her serious." He
shook the reins and urged the blowing horses forward.

I stood alone in the ensuing quiet, travel valise full
of my hard-earned Transylvanian soil secure in hand.
I'd not informed Jack what I carried. Another evening
would suit to tell him about this other supernatural link
of mine to the grave. Maybe.

After finding a place to stow my earth, I slowly made
my way around to Jack's study, keeping to the shadows. It was on the ground floor, and light showed
through the curtains. Pressing my ear to the window,

I heard nothing within, though I expected to, shortly. When a man is being social, he takes his guests to the drawing or billiards room; when a man has business, they go to his study.

Van Helsing would have a study of his own. That's where Jack would likely find him. Where would it be? This was too a big place to go searching around haphazardly.

Recalling that Van Helsing had chambers on the second floor, I vanished and floated up, reappearing inside an empty guest room. No sound came from the hall without, so I chanced remaining solid and tiptoed along, trying to remember which of the many identical doors might be the right one.

Then I heard their voices, Van Helsing and Jack, both sounding very heated. And after I'd warned Jack to caution.

I went to that door and shamelessly listened. The argument was about me, and neither of them giving an inch either way at this stage. Van Helsing had taken full charge of the asylum and set everyone to work with the garlic to prevent my entry, particularly in the patient's wing. Any one of the poor wretches there might be seduced into inviting me inside as Renfield had with Dracula. Thankfully, Jack did not disabuse Van Helsing of the notion that I required an invitation to enter a home.

The professor was in high form, apparently having had plenty of time to think out his arguments on the journey from Ring. He had answers for every objection, and good ones. I'd not want to face him in a debate. Jack could be stubborn, too, though, and would not be swayed.

"If he was as evil as you maintain, then why did he avoid harming us when you were trying to attack him?" he demanded.

"He will have aims yet of which we know not," the

professor countered. "Like him who must have created him, he makes long plans. His child-brain is most clever, we must not let our affection from the past allow him to do present mischief."

"What mischief? What could he possibly want from us?"

"I know not for sure, but it will be to no good for the world."

"Professor, you have only vague assumptions that fly in the face of fact. With my own eyes I saw Quincey holding the Host and coming to no harm. He is not the evil creature you—"

"He is Un-Dead! There is no such thing as harmless Un-Dead! Can you not see? They use *any* means they might to beguile us to good feeling, to pity, thus do they always find more souls to feed from, who then rise in turn to march ghastly in the night. He must be stopped!"

This outburst rang through the room. Jack was silent for a long time. Lord knows what he was thinking, but it could not have been pleasant.

"How do you propose to stop him, sir?" His tone was very mild. I did not sense that he'd given in, though.

"That will come to me in time. He knows you here have arrived?"

"He was with me when the butler reported you'd gone. I guessed that you would return here."

"What did Quincey do after? What did he say?"

"He was as astonished as I. He wanted to come along, but I persuaded him to leave things to me."

Very neatly done, I thought. Jack had managed to avoid a direct lie.

"Where now could he be?" asked the professor.

"Obviously not within these walls. You seem to have safeguarded all the entrances."

"For now, for this night if God is with us, and we

know He is. If the Un-Dead try to make the assault, then for him we are prepared to rebuff."

"I am not going to do Quincey any harm. You, however, should sit down and think things through."

"Ha! Still you believe not, my young friend. Did I teach you nothing? Or does the Un-Dead already have him a hold upon you?"

"Don't be ridiculous, of course not . . ."

This sounded like they'd be worrying over that bone for a good while to come. Easing away, I continued down the hall to another guest room where Art usually hung his hat when he stayed on overnight visits. I listened and determined that someone was within and softly knocked on the door.

"Who is it?" asked an unfamiliar man's voice.

"Dr. Seward asked me to check on the patient," I replied in a low tone, aiming for an English accent and probably mangling it. I could have sieved under the door, but wanted to conserve my strength.

"We're fine here."

"I also brought you tea. You'll want it before it gets cold."

Had I offered a bag of money the ruse would not have worked better. I was rewarded with the sound of the key turning. The door swung open, showing me the startled face of one of the larger orderlies. His mouth popped wide in surprise; he had no time for anything else. I focused all my will upon him, fully capturing his attention.

"Be quiet and *listen* to me . . ."

He did just that, obeying my request that he back into the room and not do anything. I closed us in and turned. Art was fast asleep on his bed. He still wore evening clothes, but his collar and coat were off, his dress-shirt partly open, his shoes neatly tucked under a chair.

I went to him. His brow was dry and cool, his

heartbeat slow. I didn't know if that was good or not. At least his face had relaxed, smoothing out the lines of care. His breathing was labored and sodden, as if he struggled in some dream. I hoped he'd not been given a sleeping draught on top of his drink. There was a coverlet folded up at the foot of the bed. I pulled it over him. I wanted to do more, but Jack would be along soon to look him over, and I'd informed him that our friend was more likely to be in his cups than out of his mind.

The orderly yet stood by, his eyes dull. He was a massive fellow, hired on to deal with the more cantankerous patients. Art was in no condition to give trouble, but perhaps Van Helsing thought he needed protection from me in case the garlic permeating the room did not work. Sure enough, there was a sturdy walking stick propped against the wall by the door. A good wooden weapon that would knock me senseless; not all of Van Helsing's lore was erroneous.

I questioned the man, confirming my assumptions. Instructed to guard Lord Godalming, he was to invite no one in. Strictly speaking, he'd been faithful to his duties, having only opened the door to me. No formal invitation had been spoken.

He knew nothing of Van Helsing's plans.

A disappointment, but not unexpected. I told him to resume his guard duty and to completely forget my intrusion. He did so, and by then I was back out in the hall.

The argument in the study had not progressed in either direction. Jack was a fair hand at debate himself and trying to pin the professor down onto what specific threat I posed. Of course, he could not get a proper answer. Van Helsing did launch into one of his lengthy call-and-response lessons, though, where he'd ask a question about some unrelated subject, and Jack's replies would lead through to a meaningful conclusion.

That conclusion would somehow relate to the current situation, and require Jack's agreement in the end.

Such manipulation worked fine when Van Helsing was in the right. When he was in the wrong it was just blamed annoying.

I'd heard its like before. Soon after I'd inherited the ranch a fellow came by there to get me to invest in some sort of shares he was selling in a new business. He was quite good at painting a picture of the huge profits I would reap, but less than clear on the exact nature of his merchandise. Every time I tried to get him to spit it out, he'd slide away onto the profit potential and the shortness of time the opportunity would be available. As I was in a kindly mood that day, I only set the dogs on him to chase him off and did not play target practice with his toes.

Not that I was tempted to do the same toward the professor, but the idea did make me smile.

As they would probably still be fighting until sunup, I decided I'd best go looking for a safe place to bunk for the day.

I awoke, unperforated by wooden stakes, but chilled to the bone. I had to force myself to stretch the warmth of movement into my arms and legs. My chosen shelter was an empty house bearing a worn "To Let" sign propped in a dusty window. No fire had been lighted inside for years, and the winter air had done a good day's work on my inert body. A hotel would have been more comfortable, but too much a risk. If Van Helsing had gotten Jack to change his mind, or struck off on his own, he'd scour every inn, hostel, and pub for miles around trying to find me.

As before at Ring, I picked the attic over the basement, though I'd checked out the latter. It possessed a stale, moldy reek that reminded me of Dracula's burial vaults. Not wanting that clinging to my clothes,

I went for the higher ground. The small dormer windows here were so begrimed with soot as to make midnight of noon, so I was very safe from the sun.

The town was more active at this earlier hour, but showing signs of slowing down for the night. No one marked my materialization outside the house or my stroll up the high street to the telegraph office. There I ascertained that a number of messages had been delivered to Seward's asylum that day. With no twinge of guilt I extended my influence over the clerk to inquire on the nature of their contents, but he knew nothing, and the man who had taken them down had already gone home.

I could guess that Bertrice had likely sent some reply or other to Jack and, hopefully, me. Knowing her devotion to Art she might have come up to see him. She could even be here. That gave a lift to my spirits. They had not been in the best of form while I lay in the cold attic waiting for the dawn. I had much to worry over what would be happening with my friends during the day. Thoughts of Bertrice were cheering, but I was concerned that she would be aggravated with me for absenting myself. True, I had been dragged off for an excellent reason, but she might not see it that way. When a man's been with a woman as we had been together, she's like to take it very amiss when he doesn't make a point to see her again as soon as possible.

With this in mind I hurried along the lane toward the asylum, passing no one, meeting no one. The miles went under me quick enough, even at the last where I had to go by Carfax Abbey. The decaying old pile still seemed to emanate an evil atmosphere. All in my head, of course, all dark memories. Dracula's presence was long gone, if not the boxes of Transylvanian earth we'd sterilized. Those were still scattered about, ownerless at the present time. It occurred to me that I could make use of such a huge cache of soil. I had a very adequate supply of my own, but more might be handy. Dracula was unlikely to return for them.

I'd easily rejected Carfax as a resting place. If he took it into his head to hunt me down, Van Helsing would certainly look there first. The same went for all the outbuildings surrounding the asylum. They might have been more convenient to me in terms of travel, but too dangerous to my health. When one is so absolutely helpless for so many long hours, one has a perfect right to be particular about accommodations.

I marched just a little more quickly, eager to find out how Jack had fared and to see if Art was feeling better.

The asylum was beginning to settle for the night. Lights showed in the patients' wing, but not many. Their waking hours were regulated by the sun, as many of them were not to be trusted with candles. Everything seemed normal, or as normal as could be expected for such a place. Still, I wasn't about to ring the front bell without a little scouting around as someone had been doing a passel of extra work that day.

Every blessed window on the whole of the building had had a cross whitewashed onto it from the inside.

Each door had likewise been embellished on the outside and was wreathed with strings of garlic.

I had no doubt that holy water had been sprinkled everywhere.

This did *not* bode well.

It took only a moment to slip up to the window of Jack's study and sieve inside. The chamber was empty. I sniffed. The air was still and stale, except for the taint of garlic from the window frames, and no fire burned in the grate. The unswept ashes there were at least two days old.

That wasn't right. Jack was a dogged worker. Even in the midst of the worst of all our troubles with Dracula he'd be in here scratching away on patient histories, or speaking reports into that phonograph machine that was his pride. It wasn't like him to be away. Maybe he'd taken Art back to Ring, but if so, then he'd left no note here for me to find.

I went next to Van Helsing's rooms, listening outside a moment, but no one was there either. Going in—it was unlocked—I found ample signs of recent occupancy, but not the professor himself. It was a liberty, but I searched through his desk, rooting out a journal. I recognized dates and time notations at intervals on the closely written pages but nothing else as it was all in Dutch.

The latest entry was for this morning at ten o'clock. He had a strong hand, but spiky to the point of illegibility, as though he'd been in a hurry. He'd had time for only a few paragraphs. From them I picked out Jack's and Art's names, and then mine. I felt suddenly uncomfortable, wondering what he'd written about us. The last line was just a few words beginning with "*Gott,*" which I did know, and ending on three exclamation points. It was short enough that I could guess it translated as "God help us!!!" or something like that.

So . . . at that hour of the morning he was still in a fearful, hell-raising conniption fit about me. Jack hadn't turned him around. Damnation.

Next, I visited Art's room. Also empty. This was unsettling, but I quelled my worry with the hope that he'd simply gone home. The staff here would know for sure; I had to isolate one of them and ask a few quick questions.

If I could find anyone.

It was the dinner hour, most all of them would be gathered just off the kitchen in their own dining hall. Jack and the other doctors took their meals in a separate area from the nurses, who ate separately from the orderlies, who ate separately from the house servants, who ate separately from Lord knows who else. I'd never known anyone like the English for dividing themselves up into so many groups. They were dedicated zealots to that eccentricity. Not that Americans were much different, with us basing our divisions on how much money a body had, rather than social class, though that was there as well.

The doctors' dining room was empty and dark. Again, no sign of a fire in the grate, so no one had eaten here.

With awful suspicion, I yanked on the bell rope. I could hear it in the distance, but no response. With all the stir the professor must have created to get the cross-painting done, more than one person should have come to investigate.

Nothing and no one. The place was deserted.

I made my way to the patients' wing. Surely someone would be there. It would be too much a disruption for Van Helsing to move all those wretches. At night only one man usually held vigil in a little alcove in its main hall. He had access to a bell rope and an actual bell stood ready on his table in case there was an emergency with one of the inmates.

This part of the original country house had been the most altered by the transformation to an asylum. The doors were made of metal with very stout bolts and grillwork fitted over small windows. They gave the long passage a jail-like appearance, very grim, very bleak.

One such door was the line of demarcation between the two sides of the house, and it was firmly locked. I had no key, but did not need one as I poured through the grid to the other side. Damn, but it was a truly handy talent, if tiring.

I was perversely relieved to hear the sounds of activity, those being the muted groans and wandering talk of the more restless souls.

The hall to which their cells opened was dim, but not wholly dark, and partway along was the alcove. The young man on duty there was probably a medical student of some sort to judge by the books stacked before him on his table. He had a lamp to read by and a plate with the remains of his dinner shoved to one side. He pored over one volume so closely that he did not notice me until I was quite close.

A good thing too. By his startled reaction, he obviously took me for an escapee. However, I managed to stay him as he reached for his bell. It was hard going to get past his burst of fear. My head was fair pinched from the pain of effort, but it was better than physically grappling with him.

"Just ease yourself, partner, I'm not here to hurt anyone." Just like calming a skittish horse. You talk slow and easy and don't make any sudden moves. Of course, a sugar lump or a piece of carrot always helps for them. "You just settle down so's we can have a little talk."

I was very thankful that Jack ran a sober establishment. The man's racing heart slowed, and his wide eyes went blank. He sat quiet and freely answered my questions without a hitch.

Professor Van Helsing was still running the place. He'd given the staff an unexpected holiday, providing they entirely quit the house and grounds for the whole night. It was inconvenient to them and highly mystifying, but he'd slipped them all an extra bit of wages to smooth things over. The fellow before me was the one exception, being the volunteer the professor required to remain behind to look after the inmates. He was paid extra as well, and did not mind having some quiet place to pursue his book-learning. He knew nothing about the crosses and garlic adorning the house. Apparently he was content to let the Dutch doctor have his fads so long as they had the blessing of Dr. Seward, who was apparently indisposed with a digestive upset.

Van Helsing certainly was ambitious and hopeful, and very misguided. This utterly contradicted what he'd witnessed the night before with my immunity to holy symbols, and made me wonder if *he* should not be confined to the asylum instead of running it.

The man had no idea where the professor or Jack Seward were, only that they were in the house.

"Where's Lord Godalming?"

"Here," he replied, his voice flat from his trance.

"Where?"

"Here."

"What? In one of these cells?"

"Yes."

"Take me to him! Now!"

He got his ring of keys and led the way. He paused in front of a door with a cloth flap hung inside its window. It could be lifted from the outside by means of a cord sewn into the material that was threaded through the grid. I pulled on the cord and peered in. High up on the wall, beyond the reach of even the tallest of madmen, a dim gaslamp lighted the room.

The sight meeting my eyes left me too flabbergasted to think straight.

"Did Professor Van Helsing order this?" I demanded, fighting down a sudden tide of rage.

"Yes."

Such unconscionable audacity left me stunned. How *dare* he?

Bertrice had said the exact same thing. And she'd not even met him.

Horrified, I stepped back and directed that the door be instantly unlocked. The man obeyed and I pushed into the cell. There was no other name for such a room. It was about six feet square, and the walls and floor were covered with a very thick, tough canvas padding, meant to keep violent patients from injuring themselves.

On the floor lay Art Holmwood, bound up tight as a tick, immobile in a strait-waistcoat.

Chapter Fifteen

I rushed in and began tugging to unbuckle the stiff leather strap that held his arms wrapped around his body.

Art mumbled, struggling to stir himself.

"It's Quincey," I said in a low, reassuring tone that I did not feel. In fact, I was mad enough to spit rattlers. "I'll get you out of here, old partner. Don't you worry about a thing."

"Quincey?" He sounded very weak.

"What has that devil done to you?" I demanded.

"Mm . . . ?"

"Wake up, damn it! Come on!"

I got the strap parted clear and dragged the canvas restraint from him. Beneath he wore the rumpled remains of his evening clothes. He lay like a beached fish, limbs flapping randomly. I helped him sit up. Under a long day's growth of beard he was a dreadful green color, and I feared he'd go sick on me. His coat was missing, along with his shoes. I told the student to go fetch some spirits.

"That must have been . . ." Art rubbed his eyes with the heels of his hands.

"What must have been?"

He blinked sleepily.

"Art?"

He stared blearily at me, gulping a deep draught of air. "God, my head's bursting. What a sleep I've had. Nightmares too. Dreamt I was shut away in a box like Lucy. Awful stuff."

"Look around, it's not much better."

He did, his thoughts making a visible progression over his features. "What in the world . . . ?"

"Tell me about Van Helsing. What do you remember about last night?"

"I'm . . . last night?"

"You had dinner with Jack and Van Helsing."

"Don't know. My mind's too muzzy. I must have some coffee."

I grimaced. "All right, then, don't trouble yourself just now. We'll get you out of here first."

The student returned with a small bottle of brandy and I gave Art a good sample from it. He was having a hard fight to bring himself back, but looked to be winning. After a few moments he was on his feet, swaying a little, but able to walk under his own power. We got him outside and seated at the student's table. Art availed himself of the contents of a carafe of water there. Some of the green cast left his face.

"God, but I was thirsty." He sounded much more awake.

"You hungry?"

"Dear heavens, no!" Some of his old manner had

returned, which was a relief. Beyond an expected state of confusion, there was no sign of the collapse such as Jack had described, only the usual ailing from too much drink. "I'm trying to remember. All I can see is the professor's face. *He* did this. He put me here this morning I think. Had those bullies of his shove me into that coat. Too many to fight. Kept calling for you. Thought you'd come bursting in like that time on the waterfront in Marseilles. . . . How the devil did I get here? Where's Jack?"

"Someplace in the asylum. Van Helsing took you from Ring last night."

"I don't remember. God, I was so *drunk* . . ."

That explained his "collapse" of last night. Staid and sober as they come, Art could put on a hell of a rip when the mood struck him. A couple of doctors used to the antics of lunatics might think him in need of restraint, but Jack should have known better. This had to be Van Helsing's doing, though why he saw fit to lock Art up and hog-tie him, I couldn't say. "What *do* you recall?

"Um . . . dinner. I was too nerved up to eat. Every noise made me think you'd arrived. I wanted to tell them the good news about your being back, but couldn't, so I kept pacing. And drinking. I fear I had more brandy than was good for their peace of mind. Jack kept watching me like I was one of his patients. He knew something was up."

"What about the professor?"

"Yes, he had that same look. Asked me if I was anxious about anything for God's sake. He was just a shade too nonchalant for my taste, for I could see he was hanging a lot on my reply. I finally told them that we were to have another guest as a surprise and that I'd promised not to reveal his identity. That held them for awhile, but it irked me that they were still watching. Put the wind up me, I tell you. I thought to shift the subject and asked them about that paper they were writing. They weren't forthcoming, but I kept at it. Jack deferred to the professor, and he said they were putting together the record of our hunt for Dracula, trying to get everything into order."

"They must have thought talking of it would upset you. Did it?"

"No more than usual. But while the topic was open they asked me for some details on my side of it, and got me to thinking things out again. Then I started asking about Lucy. I couldn't help myself. I had to *know.*"

"Know what?"

"If . . . if I'd murdered her."

Oh, dear God.

"Y-you're back, you and she *both* came back. Why did she have to die again? Were we too swift to judge her?"

My heart ached for his anguish. "Art . . ."

"Quincey, you returned without bringing harm to others, why not Lucy?"

"We've gone over that. I told you I'm different."

"But could she not have been rescued from the darkness?"

I took his hand in both of mine and looked long at him until I knew he was under my influence. My emotions were high; I had to fight to keep myself level so as not to injure his mind. "Art, when she returned she was no longer the Lucy you loved. You know that. We all saw it. Remember your loathing? That *thing* just wore her form."

Tears quivered in his eyes. "Yesss . . ."

"You did right. You are not a murderer. Don't ever think otherwise. There was no other path. Dracula was the one to take her from you. It was by your hand you delivered her soul to God. I know she's with the angels and watching you now. Don't give her cause to grieve by tormenting yourself with doubt."

He bowed his head. "I'm sorry."

I let him go, putting a hand on his shoulder. "It's all right, old partner. I know it hurts."

He recovered some and swiped his sleeve over his eyes. "I wish you'd been there to tell them. You have a way of making it all right. I got very upset, and by then I'd had a lot to drink. I asked Van Helsing if he knew of more than one kind of vampire. He wanted to know why I would ask such a thing, but I wouldn't say. Then he and Jack started speaking over me as though I wasn't there and that made me angry, and I thought the devil with them and went upstairs. Jack followed me. I had some idea I might be able to reach him. I was babbling by then, couldn't seem to stop. My nerves haven't been the best of late. . . ."

"I'm not holding it against you. You had a lot to look after in too short a time, so be easy about it."

"Be easy? I'm embarrassed as hell. I was positively ranting; don't know how I shall face either of them. They must have thought I was right off my head. No wonder they put me away."

"Now, I can't believe that Jack Seward would agree to having you trussed up like a turkey and locked in with the loonies."

"Neither can I, but he's taken Van Helsing's side for this."

"Not any more. He and I had a long talk on the ride over here. He knows all about me, now, same as you."

"Really? How did he react?"

"A sight surprised at first, but he got used to it. When I left here to go to ground for the day, you were in a room upstairs and Jack was trying his best to bring the professor around on me. It all seemed safe enough, but I suppose the old buzzard never listened. He's got this place locked up like a fort with crosses all over the windows."

"What?"

"Just as I said. There's a cross painted on every piece of glass in this whole pile."

"But how did you get in?"

I gave him a look. "We went all over that the other night."

"I meant past the locks."

"Oh. That little disappearing trick of mine is mighty handy. A shut door is nothing to me."

"Well, I'm damned."

"I think not. I wonder now if Van Helsing didn't serve Jack the same as you, only kept him closer to hand."

He sat up. "Something's afoot! We must find him!"

"*I'll* find him. You rest up, and I'll bring him here."

His eyes flashed fire. "I'll do no such thing! I'm not staying in this hellhole a moment longer!"

I made a hushing gesture lest he bring the professor down on us. "Very well, old partner. We've been in tighter spots than—" I broke off, thinking I'd heard something. The sound—a voice—came again. Someone frantically shouting Art's name. It was from one of the other cells farther along the hall. My knees turned to jelly for just an instant, then I snapped around to the near-forgotten student. "*Where is she?*" I roared.

He flinched at the force of it, as though I'd struck him.

I grabbed his keys and tore my way to her, heart in my throat.

"Arthur! Are you there? Arthur, come help me!"

Following her voice, I found the right door and fumbled to get the right key in the lock. There was a flap over the window grid, but I didn't waste time with it. Instead I managed to fling the door open. This padded chamber was pitch black.

Bertrice shot from its horror like a bullet, nearly knocking me over when we collided.

"Quincey? Oh, God!" Her face crumpled, and she threw her arms around me.

"It's me, little girl. Don't you worry." I held her shaking body close and snug.

I'd wondered if anything could ever daunt her, but heaven forbid that it should become a reality. Being locked up in a padded cell in a lunatic asylum had done just that, though. She fought down a sob or three. I kept her wrapped up until the worst of it passed.

"It's all right," I told her, stroking her hair. It smelled of her spice scent. "We'll get you out of here."

"Yes, yes, but I heard Arthur. Take me to him."

There was no need. Arthur had recovered enough to shamble toward us. He looked like I felt, aghast and outraged. "Bertie, dear God! What—how—?"

I released her to go to him. They clung together a long while, seeming to take strength from each other. He eventually looked over her shoulder at me, his face grim and eyes cold. "I will kill that bastard for this," he stated.

No need to gainsay him, I was ready to do the same.

Bertrice pushed away. "You will *not!* Not until I've had *my* turn!"

He twitched a smile. "Whatever you want, Bertie."

We three walked back to the alcove where the student was starting to look too alert for my peace of mind. Without reinforcement or further orders they can wake up all on their own. I told him to resume whatever he had been doing and to forget about us. He obligingly went back to his studies, ignoring our presence.

Art and Bertrice, of course, could not ignore what I'd just done. Questions rose on their faces, but I put a finger to my lips, and motioned for us to leave. We shuffled toward the demarcation door; I unlocked it with the keys I'd kept, ushering us through.

"What was *that?*" Art demanded.

"Just something I can do," I said. "It's like hypnosis, only stronger."

"But how can—oh, bother, later. We'll work it out later. Bertie, how in God's name did *you* come to be here?"

"Quincey and Dr. Seward telegrammed me that you'd taken seriously ill, and I came as soon as I could. Thank heaven you're all right. You are, aren't you? You look awful."

"I suppose I do—but you're not surprised Quincey's alive?"

"Um, our paths crossed in London a few days ago . . . he told me everything, Arthur."

Already pale, he blanched even more. "H-how much of everything?"

"All of it. Including what that *bastard* Van Helsing put you through in regard to poor Lucy."

"Oh, I say!" Art stared at me.

I shrugged. "Not settling for anything less, she deserved to hear all. Besides, she'd already figured out about my change. I had to make a clean breast of it. Your sister's a real Sherlock Holmes."

"Loveday Brooke," she corrected.

"Who?" asked Art.

"Never mind."

"But how is it you even guessed about Quincey? How could you have heard of vampires?"

"Really, Arthur, one hears *everything* in London, you know that. Is there someplace else we may talk? I'm cold."

We tried doors, taking over an empty examining room that had a fire laid and ready for morning rounds. I put match to the kindling and stood back as they crowded close to warm themselves.

"I'd murder for some tea," Bertrice muttered.

The brandy bottle had found its way into my pocket,

and I offered that instead. She had no complaint for the substitution.

It took us a short while to get ourselves caught up on each other. I explained how Art and I had come to be here, then Bertrice had her turn. She'd sent several telegrams asking Seward for information on Art's condition, but received no replies.

"So when I could get away I took the early train and hired a trap to bring me here. When I arrived that Dutch professor greeted me. He was polite, but I don't think he liked my walking clothes. He tried to put me off, saying Arthur was too ill for visitors, even family."

"Wrong thing to say to you," muttered Art, shaking his head.

I agreed. "Art would have been confined to the lunatic wing by then. Van Helsing could not let you know that."

"I'd suspected something was wrong," she said. "His odd behavior confirmed it. Then all the servants were starting to leave, which was very strange. When I asked to see Dr. Seward I was told he'd been called away on an emergency case. Now I've not been on stage for very long, but I know a false performance when I see it. He'd have been booed from auditions for that reading, but I pretended to accept his lie, and said I'd wait. He didn't much like that, but I put on my 'high lady' act—you know the one, where I impersonate Aunt Honoria—and there wasn't a thing he could do to budge me."

I chuckled. "I'd have paid good money to have seen his face."

"It was beyond price. As we were at an impasse and stuck with each other, he seemed to try to make the best of it. He did readily answer my questions about you, Arthur, and appeared to be honestly worried, but he refused to let me even look in. Then I made a mistake. I asked if your collapse might have had anything to do with Lucy."

Art shrank in on himself a little. "Why on earth did you do that?"

"Because sitting there, pretending to be oh-so-civilized, I was quietly losing my temper with him. He was insufferably high-handed. My brother is ill and this *stranger* is keeping me at bay like I'm some invading army. And after what Quincey told me about him I was ready to believe the worst had happened." She snorted. "Had I but known the worst was yet to come."

"What did he do?"

She sighed. "He rang for tea, my great weakness. I think it was a ploy to shut me up. I had begun to ask questions about Lucy that he would not answer. I asked why there were crosses painted all over and about the garlic smell, pressing him. He got very red about those, I must say, and I pressed even more. I suppose I can thank chivalry that he didn't knock me down then and there. He hides it well, but he has a very ugly temper, especially toward anyone who disagrees with him. If I'd been a man we'd have been brawling like drunken Irishmen on the consulting room rug. He certainly looked ready to explode. Then he wanted to know how I'd come by my knowledge, so it was my turn to play the sphinx. When the last servant brought in the the tea cart I think by then the professor had made up his mind I was a dangerous liability."

That, or guessed that she'd had contact with me. Anyone I'd spoken to would be suspect in Van Helsing's imaginings. God help us all if he found out about our intimate liaison. Happily, Bertrice had on a high, concealing collar.

"Well," she continued, "I poured, and he distracted me with some nonsense about the windows, claiming he saw a bat flapping against them. It was still light out, so that was absurd, and I'm most embarrassed to admit that it was successful. He had to have slipped something into my cup when I turned to look. I suppose when one works with mad people one learns to be very sly, for I quite missed it. I thought he was trying to test my reaction to bats, perhaps use that as a means bring up the topic of vampires. He struck me as being very unsubtle, but my interpretation was off. I drank my tea and almost immediately realized what had really happened. My bones went all heavy, and I couldn't keep my eyes open. When I next became aware of anything it was my waking in the dark in that frightful padded room."

"He will pay for that," said Art.

"We'll nail his hide to the barn door," I promised.

"It was alarming, but I *am* unharmed."

Art fondly brushed back a strand from her hatless and rather tousled hair. "Oh, Bertie, no need to be brave, you were scared to death."

She pursed her lips a moment, then finally nodded. "Yes, I was. I didn't know what he would do, and he could have done anything, commit me, make me disappear, slip more sleeping draughts into my food—if he even bothered to feed me!"

"God! I shall *strangle* him."

"Arthur, I'm *fine* now. I just had a few bad hours in a dark room. When I heard your shouting I knew things would be all right. I didn't expect Quincey, though I should have since I knew he might be here."

"Yes, he's the hero for finding us."

I shrugged. "Well, I didn't exactly expect to find either of you. Not in that part of the house. I just wanted to talk to one of the staff. . . ."

They wouldn't hear any of it and elected me champion of the moment. Art thumped my back a couple times, and Bertrice kissed my cheek, which caused that pleasant humming between my ears to return full force.

But now wasn't the time to give Art any hint that I was planning to marry his sister. After all, Bertrice had the right to hear it first.

"We still have to find Jack," I reminded them, which dampened the celebration.

"And have a few words with the professor," said Art. "Do you think he'll still be in the consulting room?"

"It's a place to start."

"No, Jack's study is the place to start," he insisted.

"I've been there, it's deserted."

"I must go, anyway. It's important."

"We can try, but if we run into Van Helsing you two duck low and let me do the talking. My guess is he's hiding in wait somewhere for me to show. He's liable to go off like a hair-trigger, so I do all the parley."

They allowed the sense of that, but Art led the way out. Bertrice lingered a few steps behind, long enough to take my hand and hold it tight. The brightness of her eyes warmed me better than any fire. "Quincey . . . I adored the roses."

My abrupt flush of pleasure at this news was such that I broke into what must have been a wholly foolish grin. It was still fastened in place when we tiptoed into the hall, hand-in-hand. My heart was singing so loud I couldn't hear myself think. All was right with the world, or would be soon.

We silently traversed the house, taking a side stairs to the upper floor, and managed to avoid running into anyone. That was a relief, for Van Helsing was absolutely serious in his game. To have gone to the horrendous risk of locking up Art and Bertrice and done who-knows-what to Jack smacked of desperation. I thought of my warning to Jack about not pushing the professor into a corner, but what to do when he created the corner himself?

We passed the door to Van Helsing's room along the way. I paused and listened, then shook my head when it was clear no one was there. How simple for us had he been within. Pressing on to Jack's study, we eased inside and Art went straight to the desk. He rooted through one of the drawers for a set of keys then went to a tall oaken cabinet built into one wall and unlocked it. Propped at attention on individual brackets were the very Winchester repeating rifles I'd brought along on our Continental journey. They'd been well cared for, the barrels clean and oiled, the stocks buffed and shining.

"I'd wondered where those had gotten to," I said, delighted.

Art grinned. "I kept one as a remembrance and thought Jack should have the rest. I was afraid the professor might have armed himself. Thank goodness he did not. "You'll have them all back again, of course, and this as well." He drew out a box, opening it, but cried out in dismay upon finding it empty.

"What is it?"

"Your six-shooter was in here."

So that's what had become of it. "Jack might have it in his room."

"Never. He always keeps his firearms locked in this cabinet. With his patients he can't afford to be careless. Van Helsing must have taken it."

"To use against me?"

"You and I daresay anyone else who disagrees with him. He's quite capable of violence, Quincey. After the way he treated us . . ."

"But—"

"He may hesitate shooting me, but not you. I'll wager he's blessed each of the bullets. He once said they would kill a vampire in his coffin or something like that."

I suppressed a shudder, remembering. Dracula had told me a different tale I was more inclined to believe, but it was cold comfort at present. The thought of that crazed Dutchman lurking downstairs . . .

Art took out one of the Winchesters and began loading it from a box of cartridges.

"Just what do you have in mind?" I asked, eyebrows rising.

"Oh, not to worry, I won't wave it recklessly about; I only want it handy in case there's more trouble than we anticipate."

"Art, you and I both know that whenever a man decides to heel himself with any kind of shooting iron, then he *will* meet up with trouble."

"This is only insurance, a preventative. After what Van Helsing's done to us—"

"I agree," said Bertrice. "The man should be locked up in one of those damnable cells. He'll not be one to go quietly."

"You're right," I said. "But hear me on this, he's going to be more nervous than a ginger cat at a fox hunt. I don't want to give him an excuse to make either of you into a bull's-eye. Besides, wherever he is, I'm going in first. I will talk to him the same as I did that fellow down in the dungeon."

"Hypnosis?" asked Art. "Such as what Van Helsing did with Mrs. Harker?"

"A deal more effectual and a lot faster, I promise. Give me a few minutes and I'll have him on all fours baying at the moon if you want."

"I'd rather dangle him by his heels from a cliff, preferably over a pit of crocodiles."

"Using a very frayed rope," Bertrice chimed in.

What a bloodthirsty family, but I could understand why and side with them. "Sounds fine to me, but let's think of Jack Seward. This place is only as good as his reputation. If there's any shooting here he couldn't get a job selling snake oil in a medicine show for the scandal."

That made them stop and think. If there's one thing the English have a respect for, it is scandal. It's an entertaining thing to gossip about at a club or party, but only from a safe distance. Jack was practically kinfolk.

"Very well." Art reluctantly unloaded the rifle and put it back. "Mustn't tempt fate. I should feel better with some sort of weapon, though. Jack has a cricket bat in that cupboard, I think."

As he locked up, I tried the cupboard and found a very battered flattish paddle a couple of feet long that must have dated from Jack's university days. He and Art had taken me to a few cricket games, and I'd found it to be a surprisingly pleasing summer diversion. My friends had been kind enough not to disturb me while I caught up on my sleep.

This time I took the lead. We made it to the lower landing of the main stairs without meeting anyone, but I heard some activity in Jack's consulting room just off the central entry hall. It was there he usually received patients or spoke with their families. If luck was with us, then Van Helsing would have taken it over.

We eased slowly up to its closed door to listen. Whoever had been speaking was silent now. Even my keen ears heard nothing more than the vague suggestion of someone's presence. I leaned close to whisper to Art and Bertrice.

"I'll go outside and have a look through the windows. Stay here until I'm back."

They nodded agreement.

I hurried through the entry. The front doors were locked, but proved to be no barrier as I dissolved into nothing to get outside.

No orderlies stood guard this time, and just as well. I struck off to the left, ducking through an arched opening in a high hedge that enclosed Jack's private garden. It was bare now from winter, but showed signs of tending, the paved walk being swept of leaves. A table and chairs usually stood in the center, allowing him to enjoy his tea outside when the weather permitted. Those were stored away now, removing any cover I might have made of them as I approached the tall windows of the house.

They were of the kind to open out like doors, locked now, each pane embellished with a white cross. I sniffed. Even from here the garlic smell was pronounced on the cold air. Jack would be weeks getting rid of it.

The window curtains were drawn back. Once close enough I could see the whole of the room, though the crosses and reflections from the pale sky confused things. All was dim and dark. A single small candle illuminated the desk in the center. Seated behind it was Jack Seward. He was slumped forward, eyes shut as though asleep.

A gag was tied around his mouth and his hands were fastened to the chair arms by leather straps, the same ones used to restrain the more violent patients. A necessary evil for them, but an utterly barbaric violation of my poor friend.

I resisted my initial angry urge to charge in and free him. My time in India hunting tigers had not been wasted. I knew a tethered goat when I saw one.

Searching the shadowed corners of the room, I was able to spy a man-sized shape standing just beyond the door. Had I come through it, he'd have been able to bushwhack me neat as neat. As it was, I stood well silhouetted in the window frame, just as easy a target.

I fell back and faded away, then sieved inside. Guessing the distance, I crossed the room until certain I stood behind him, then materialized, arms out to seize.

But instead of Van Helsing, I captured an artfully draped coat tree.

Even as I realized my mistake, piercing light caught me square in the face and there was a loud, flat explosion, very close. A giant's fist smashed into my body, flinging me hard against the wall. I dropped to the floor, heavy as a brick, and just as unable to move. A terrible fire seared deep in my shoulder, tearing a groan from me.

The light splintered into my eyes, blinding. I heard a distant confusion of sounds, shouting, pounding. The light was turned away, allowing me to see. I squinted up into Van Helsing's face.

To think I'd once thought of him as kindly and good.

All I saw there now was steel, bitterly cold and hard.

He looked long at me, then made the sign of the cross and in Latin called on God to bless what was to come.

"There's no need for this," I said, my voice thin as straw.

"Yes, there is, my poor friend, though you know it not." In one hand he carried a new electric lantern, in the other, what looked to be an old muzzle-loading pistol. He'd probably had the bullet blessed. That would have helped him against Dracula, maybe even killed the old warrior; for me it hurt like hell, which was more than enough.

I lay on my back, in agony from a wounding such as I'd not felt in years, even from a bullet. High on my chest, barely a hand's breadth from my heart, a slender wooden shaft was solidly imbedded in my flesh. It was like a short arrow, but without feathers. Here was the source of the paralyzing pain. I could not understand at first how it had gotten there. How had he fired an arrow from a gun?

"Professor . . ."

"Hush, you will soon be free. A moment of the bitter waters to reach the sweet."

He'd prepared himself well. He put the pistol and lantern on a table and exchanged it for a knife—wicked, sharp, and heavy—the kind used to carve through joints.

This Dutch butcher would use it to cut my head off.

Art was banging on the door, throwing himself against it from the sound of things; Bertrice shouted my name. At the desk, Jack Seward had raised his head, his eyes bleared and dull, but waking to awful alarm. There was no help for me but that of my own making.

I struggled to vanish, but the wood in my body prevented that.

Van Helsing knelt, raising the knife high. He would shear right through my neck with one blow.

Absolute terror roused me to movement. In blind panic I surged up and threw off his aim. Weak as I was, I had a small edge of strength, and overbore him. We rolled across the carpet, ending with me on top. Bringing the knife up, he gouged a cold furrow along my ribs. He tried a furious stab, but I fixed my grasp on his arm. I couldn't hold him for long. The damned thing in my shoulder was drawing the very life from me.

With an effort born of desperation, I raised away enough to do some good and plowed my right fist as hard as I could into Van Helsing's belly. Bereft of air, he lost all ability to fight, buying me a few precious moments. I pried the knife from his fingers as he lay gasping, his eyes wild with loathing.

Crawling away, I made it to the door, turned the key, and collapsed. I caught some bruises as Art forced his way in. He nearly tripped over me in his forward rush; Bertrice was in his wake, carrying the cricket bat. She made a rending wail of anguish as she called my name and threw herself down next to me.

"Stay from him!" Van Helsing ordered, breathless, but harsh and angry.

"You murderer!" she screamed.

Sounds of a scuffle. Art yelled something. A crash.

Van Helsing grunted and cursed coarsely in his own language. Art must have won.

Bertrice held her shaking hands out to me, palms up, wanting to help, but not knowing what to do. "Arthur, find a doctor for God's sake!"

"Jack's right here. Let me get him out of these beastly straps."

"*Hurry!* Quincey? Oh, do be still. We're getting help."

I tried to catch hold of the damned *thing* in my shoulder. My fingers twitched uselessly, merely brushing it. My strength flowed from me as swiftly as my blood. Too much and I would swoon away and perhaps never come back. "Please . . ."

"Quincey?"

"Take it out," I managed to croak.

"You'll bleed to death."

That was already happening. "*Out!*"

"What are you doing?" Art called from behind her, alarmed.

"He wants me to pull this—"

"You'll kill him!"

"*Please!*" I rasped. "*Now!*"

She must have understood better than he about my nature, perhaps from gossip at Lord Burce's house. Before Art could intervene, Bertrice used both hands and pulled hard on the arrow, her cry and my own merging as one as she dragged it free.

The hurting didn't altogether cease, but retreated quick, thank heaven. I slumped and moaned out relief, then had to fight to remain solid. My body wanted to flee into healing nothingness. This was *not* the time. I *must* keep control.

Bertrice holding me helped. I was sorry she was forced to do and see such fearful things, but for all of it she showed a rare bright courage. Her pale face burned like the sun. I basked in it, smiling and squeezing her hand to ease her.

"Better," I said.

"Quincey?" Art peered down at me. He looked deathly, perhaps afraid of losing his friend all over again.

"It's a'right, ol' pard. She di' th' right thing by me."

"Please God, I hope so," said Bertrice. She blinked tears. One splashed my cheek.

"You sweet English rose," I murmured dreamily, forgetting my pain.

"What?"

"Hm?"

"Arthur, is he—?" She looked to her brother. He was struggling with the last bonds on Jack.

"I'll be all right," I quietly assured her, squeezing her hand once more. For her sake I had to stay conscious and corporeal.

"But you're bleeding!"

"No, it's closing already. I heal fast." I was weak, though, lightheaded, and suddenly famished, my corner teeth extending in reaction to my need. I had to have blood to replace what I'd lost. Lots of it. Soon.

"Lie still," she ordered.

"Where's the professor?" I didn't want him to renew the fight just yet.

She shifted so I could see the room. Van Helsing lay on the floor next to the toppled coat tree, moving a little, in recovery himself from whatever damage Art had inflicted.

I smiled, lips closed, and winked at my now-trembling friend as he came over. Not that he was scared, but his dander was up and all that dash had to go somewhere. "Now there's a good night's work. How's Jack?"

"I'll live," Jack answered for himself. Free of his bonds and successfully fighting to rouse himself from his stupor, he seemed otherwise unharmed. He found his feet and came around to look me over. "You need to lie down, though."

"I'm fine. Just a scratch."

"From *this?*" Bertrice sounded incredulous. Well she might. In her hand was the instrument of my wounding, the wooden rod with one end sharpened to a point. It was all over with my blood, the scent hanging heavier on the air than the garlic.

"What is it?" Art wanted to know.

"It goes with that pistol of his," I said, with a nod toward the professor. "Looks like an old dueler. That's what he used to ram the powder and ball down the muzzle, only he left the rod in when he fired at me. Shot it out better than an arrow."

"It could have exploded in his hand, the fool! Quincey—?"

I waved him down. "I'm fine. The Dutchman might could use some smelling salts, though."

"To the devil with him," Art snapped.

Van Helsing picked himself up, becoming the focus for us all. For a very fleeting moment he seemed strangely bewildered with the four of us ranged against him all-accusing. He raised his hands, as though to tear his hair, fingers like claws in his frustration. *"Mein Gott!* Can none of you *see?*"

"Very clearly," said Bertrice, all ice. Face like a thundercloud, she surged from my side, marched up to him, and gave him a resounding slap. "That's for what you did to me!" Another slap. "And that's for what you did to my brother in poor Lucy's tomb!"

Now was he truly shocked, but his surprise instantly transformed to rage. "Blind! You know nothing! That poor child was imprisoned by the darkness. It was a blessing to her that Arthur was the one to set her free."

"If it was such a blessing, then why didn't *you* do it yourself? And who are you to speak of dark prisons? Have you *any* idea what it was *like* for me to wake up in that pit?"

"It was for your own safety, young woman. To save you from the harm beyond your imagine did I there put you. All that I did, my misled friends, was to protect you!"

"Then God spare us from more of your protection!" She turned on her heel and came to stand over me like a lioness.

Van Helsing glared, very unused to being spoken to in such a manner. Certainly being slapped was also an unpleasant novelty for him. His near cheek was red from the force of her work. Next his gaze fell upon me, and it flared with righteous malevolence. "You it is who has taken them over, corrupted their better nature, making them to be in your godless army of Un-Dead. You have used their love of you to bring them to this betrayal of all they knew was right."

At my quiet request, Bertrice and Jack helped me up. My head went light again, and the room dipped, but the spell quickly eased.

"I have done *nothing*," I said, very softly. "But you keep talking, and I just might turn you inside out."

Some hint of my suppressed anger must have gotten through to him. I still had that butcher's knife in my fist. Or maybe he saw my teeth. I didn't try to hide them. He shut himself up fast.

"Professor," said Jack wearily, "it is time you listened. We *know* you're trying to help, but it is misplaced. Quincey is a vampire, yes, but he is not the same breed as Dracula. I've told you this a hundred times, and here is the proof. Were he evil, do you think he'd have spared you? I saw your fight. At any moment he could have killed you, instead I saw him doing his best to avoid harming you."

"He has plans of which you know not."

"Please, don't embarrass yourself with that vague threat of what might happen. Quincey? *Have* you any plans?"

"Well, I'd not mind a wash and change of clothes since these are all ruined. Beyond that, I'd be pleased if the professor would only live and let live."

Van Helsing positively sneered. "That will never happen. Vampire." He said the word like a profanity. To him it was.

I sighed, worn beyond words by the man's foolish stubbornness. Though the bleeding had ceased my shoulder and ribs ached miserably. If only I had a chance to vanish . . . "Would someone please light the lamps?"

Art did the honors, recalling, perhaps, that I'd wanted plenty of light at our first meeting.

The professor watched, frowning, knowing something was up, but uncertain what it might be. He shot a glance at the open door, but Bertrice darted there first and locked it, taking the key away. Her smile was grim with triumph. He looked to Jack next, but his former student and colleague had taken charge of the cricket bat and stood guard by the windows.

Every lamp and candle now burned, the place bright as a ballroom.

Not relishing what was to come, I paced slowly toward Van Helsing. I'd have preferred for us to be alone, the better to concentrate, but didn't trust my ability to control him without Jack and Art close by.

I paused a short arm's length from the old man. He glared hatred strong enough to wound. I fixed my gaze hard on him. He dropped back a step.

"Quincey . . ." began Jack.

"Stay where you are," I said, keeping my voice even. "All of you. Don't move an inch." I eased forward, getting closer. Still holding the knife.

God knows what was in my expression, but it must have been bad. Van Helsing kept backing until forced by the wall to halt. His heart thumped loud, but you couldn't tell by his face. He showed defiance, not fear, but I could smell it on him all the same. He slid side-ways. I followed. He reached a far corner and again had to stop.

Jack and Art held themselves ready just on the edge of my vision. Bertrice was there as well, by the door. Good. Very deliberately, I turned the whole of my attention on the task to hand. I had to hold all my attention upon Van Helsing, hating it, wanting to run myself. I got close to him, raising the knife even with his throat.

"Professor Van Helsing. Listen to me."

He stared at the blade. "You would murder, yes. It is in you now to kill, just as I have said. Friend John—"

I stopped his appeal, gently putting the steel edge against his throat. He sucked in air and went still, eyes popping. "Not another word. You listen to me or I'll cut you in two."

"I say, Quincey . . ." began Art. Someone shushed him. Bertrice maybe.

The room was so quiet I could hear all their hearts thumping away, filling the silence. "You listen very carefully to everything I . . ."

"*Nein,*" Van Helsing snapped. Then he pulled my own Colt six-shooter from his frock coat pocket and fired point-blank into my heart.

The sound of Bertrice's shriek was louder than the booming report of the shot.

Arms flailing, I staggered back with a short surprised cry.

He fired again. Another deafening boom. Fire in my chest. Blood poured out.

The floor came up and grabbed me hard.

Through the haze of smoke I saw Art leap at the professor and drag the gun from him. There was no further struggle. The damage was done.

Bertrice and Jack were suddenly with me, she holding

my head and weeping as he tore my shirt open. I fought to stay solid against the appalling burst of pain blazing through my core like a comet.

For a dreadful black instant I had a cruel return to my dying on that mountainside in Transylvania. Instead of Mina holding me it was Bertrice and hers the beautiful face twisted with grief and fear as my life bled out.

But this time the dying was absolute agony.

These were terrible wounds seared into my chest, right through it. Blood poured out above and beneath, stealing the last of my strength. Any man with a beating heart would be dead. Soon I'd be unable to . . .

But I *had* to hold on, just a little longer.

Bertrice sobbed out my name. Looking at her helped. I took her hand, squeezing it one last time.

"It's all right," I whispered. "Over now . . . wait and see . . ."

Van Helsing came within my line of view. What a remarkable change in him. Gone was his hatred for me. His stern features had softened into compassion.

Art stood next to him, staring down in helpless horror. He began to round on the professor, and there was murder in his eye.

"No!" I managed to call out in time. "Jack, don't let him—"

But there was no need for Jack to interfere. Art abruptly broke away and dropped to kneel by his sister, a comforting arm around her shoulders. "Quincey, I'm sorry."

"Don't be. I'll see you by-and-by, old partner. You too, Jack."

Van Helsing loomed over us all, his hand extended toward me in a gesture of benediction.

"Requiescat in pace, in nomine Patris, et Fili, et Spiritu Sancti," he somberly intoned, making the sign of the cross.

To Bertrice I gave my last smile, winked, then grate-
fully laid my head back in her cradling arms, breathing out a last great sigh, closing my eyes. Utter stillness
for a moment, then sweet gray oblivion stole over me,
releasing me at last from the painful bondage of a
mortal body.

Epilogue

That night, at Jack Seward's chill insistence, Van Helsing departed from the asylum, to return to Amsterdam. He expected no less. In striving to save Jack's soul from the dark influence of the Un-Dead, he had destroyed their friendship.

The same could be said for any fellowship he'd had with Arthur Holmwood.

Bertrice had simply removed herself, being unable to abide the sight of the man. She would accept no apology from him about her mistreatment, responding to his contrite overture with a promise to blow his brains out if he ever approached her again.

"She is yet young," said the professor, as she hurried away. "Soon she will realize it was for the best."

"I think not," said Arthur. He went after her.

Van Helsing turned to Jack. "Friend John, I will call you that still for the sake of what was past for us. For the future I do not hope the absolution, only that someday you may wake and understand."

Jack made no reply, his face like stone.

The professor concluded it was past time to go, went upstairs, packed a travel bag, and departed. With the staff gone no pony trap was readied to carry him; he had an ignominious walk back to town, there to finish the night out at a hotel. Jack would send the remaining luggage on later.

He locked the front doors of his house, then tiredly plodded to his consulting room to put the lights out. Only when he drew the curtains did I let him see me. I faded fully back into the solid world again by the door.

I did *not* mean to scare him half out of his skin.

He gave a terrific start, putting his hand to his breast, then sagging. "God, Quincey!"

"Sorry."

He laughed once. "Not a ghost."

I shook my head. "Afraid not, old partner."

"I don't care," he said, putting a hand on my shoulder as though to prove to himself my reality. "You're back, thank God. And you're all right?" He peered at my chest, then shoulder and ribs.

"Right as rain."

"The wounds are closed; it's as though you'd never been injured."

"Would that were the truth. I may have to borrow one of your coats to cover this mess." My clothes were in a sad state from all the bloodstains, holes, and cuts. My body was in considerably better shape. Once vanished, I'd taken myself straight to the stables in the back, there to restore that which I'd lost and more besides.

Physical healing was near-instantaneous. My spirits were somewhat slower.

I tried to repress a shudder, the latest in a series that overtook me at irregular times.

"Quincey? You don't look well."

"I'll allow that I've got the shakes worse than a drunk on Sunday morning. This has been a sight too exciting, even for me."

"Sit down then, for heaven's sake, and let me examine you." He led me to a chair.

"It'll pass. Just nerved up. I've been like this before after a shooting fight. Happens when I think too much. It's a hellish thing to face a man like that, to push him into killing. Then to stand there cold and *let* him do it . . ."

"Yet you managed. You'd convinced me—and I had some idea of what you were about."

"You did?"

"Because of your warning not to back him into a corner. To say that and then carry it out yourself—in a most literal sense. Why?"

I shrugged. "It occurred to me that the only way I could win was to let him think he'd won. I knew he had that shooter of mine on him, felt it when we were fighting. All he wanted was a chance to use it. I gave it to him."

He shook his head. "You're quite mad."

"No better place for it. But I got the job done. He won't be looking for me, will he?"

"I don't think so, though your vanishing surprised him. He thought a vampire as young as you could not do that. I stepped in with one last insistence about you being a different breed. For the first time he seemed to accept it."

"Let's hope so. I don't want to go through that again. Jack, I'm sorry to have busted things up so badly between you."

"No, I won't hear your apology, for you did nothing. If there is a fault, then it is the professor's own stubborn nature that must be blamed. If you had truly been a threat, then might we forgive him . . . but as things are . . ." He lifted his hand in a gesture of futility. "I can't forgive him, drugging me, tying us up like . . . like . . . and poor Art and his sister . . ."

Before Jack could wind down to plain speech, something hurtled through the door.

"*Quincey!*"

Bertrice flung herself bodily on me.

It's an ill wind . . .

Art was with her, and he did not seem overly surprised by the intensity of his sister's greeting. She must have mentioned something to him. Jack raised both eyebrows, though.

Talk was fast and furious for the next little while as we confirmed to one another our continued good health, and I again apologized for what I'd put them through. Like Jack, they wouldn't hear it.

"Some army of the Un-Dead," said Art. "Van Helsing created it himself, by driving us together against him."

"And I am most grateful that the three of you figured out I was going to try something." I eased into a chair. Recovered or not I felt shaky on my feet.

"Not I," said Bertrice. "I thought he'd—that you were—why didn't you *tell* me you were part Cheshire cat?"

"No time. And I am sorry, truly."

She'd taken hold of my hand and didn't seem to be in any hurry to let go. Not a bad set of circumstances. "Arthur told me out in the hall. I don't know who to be the more angry at, you or the professor. I only thought you were going to hypnotize him, and wondered why you just didn't get on to it."

"I had to scare the man up so he'd react the way I wanted. But more importantly, I had to make sure none of you was behind me in his line of fire. Blessed or not, bullets would go right through my body. Couldn't risk any of you catching one."

"How did you *know* it wouldn't kill you?

Dracula was my source for such odd knowledge, but I couldn't say aught of him. "Just a little accident I had in my travels. But don't think I wasn't worried." The shuddering took me again. I tried to suppress it for Bertrice's sake. She missed none of it and fell onto my lap, embracing me hard, as though to ward off my inner cold.

"God, I thought I'd lost you," she whispered.

"Never."

"Well," said Jack brightly. "I'm a bit peckish. Anyone else?"

"Me," said Art, after Jack thoughtfully nudged him.

They'd read the signs aright and departed for the kitchen.

"I like that Dr. Seward," Bertrice murmured.

"He's a corker, he is. Real perceptive. Sometimes."

Art would give her away, and Jack would be my best man, and it would have to be in the evening, if that was permitted. The English seemed to favor morning marriage services; I didn't know if that was custom or law.

"You're really all right?" she asked.

"Yes. Much better. Our bad patch is over and done, I have my friends back, and I've got the prettiest gal in the world sitting on my knee. What man could want more?"

"The rest of that world, perhaps?"

"Let it take care of itself."

"At least until tomorrow. Then must I get back to my troupe or 'Lady Godalming' will dismiss me."

"Can't have that. I'd be pleased to see your next show again as soon as may be." Then afterwards I could properly present her with a ring. A nice one with diamonds in it to match the brightness of her eyes.

"Actually," she said, sounding reflective, "I would very much like to introduce you to the rest of the players. There's been talk that we really do need some males in the cast so as to achieve quicker acceptance in the—"

That brought me around quick. "Whoa, there, *what* are you on about?"

"Quincey, you're a positive *natural* for the stage. I've never beheld a death scene played better. You simply *must* come and read for us."

I had plans for her, but hadn't even remotely dreamed she'd form plans for *me*.

Oh, Lord have mercy . . .

When it comes to the best
in science fiction and fantasy,
Baen Books has something for *everyone!*

IF YOU LIKE . . .
YOU SHOULD ALSO TRY . . .

Marion Zimmer Bradley . . . . Mercedes Lackey,
Holly Lisle

Anne McCaffrey . . . . Elizabeth Moon,
Mercedes Lackey

Mercedes Lackey . . . . . Holly Lisle, Josepha Sherman,
Ellen Guon, Mark Shepherd

Andre Norton . . . . Mary Brown,
James H. Schmitz

David Drake . . . . David Weber, John Ringo,
Eric Flint

Larry Niven . . . . James P. Hogan,
Charles Sheffield

Robert A. Heinlein . . . . Jerry Pournelle,
Lois McMaster Bujold

Heinlein's "Juveniles" . . . . Larry Segriff,
William R. Forstchen

Horatio Hornblower . . . . David Weber's
"Honor Harrington" series,
David Drake, "RCN" series

The Lord of the Rings . . . . Elizabeth Moon,
The Deed of Paksenarrion

IF YOU LIKE . . .
YOU SHOULD ALSO TRY . . .

Lackey's "SERRAted Edge" series . . . . . . Rick Cook,
Mall Purchase Night

Dungeons & Dragons™ . . . . . . "Bard's Tale"™ Novels

Star Trek . . . . James Doohan & S.M. Stirling,
"Flight Engineer" series

Star Wars . . . . Larry Niven, David Weber
The "Wing Commander"™ series

Jurassic Park . . . . Brett Davis, *Bone Wars*
and *Two Tiny Claws*

Casablanca . . . . Larry Niven, *Man-Kzin Wars II*

Elves . . . . Ball, Lackey, Sherman,
Moon, Cook, Guon

Puns . . . . Rick Cook, Spider Robinson
Harry Turtledove, *The Case of the Toxic Spell Dump*

Alternate History . . . . Gingrich and Forstchen, *1945*
James P. Hogan, *The Proteus Operation*
Harry Turtledove (ed.), *Alternate Generals*
S.M. Stirling, "Draka" series
Eric Flint & David Drake, "Belisarius" series
Eric Flint, *1632*

SF Conventions . . . . Niven, Pournelle & Flynn,
Fallen Angels
Margaret Ball, *Mathemagics*
Jerry & Sharon Ahern, *The Golden Shield of IBF*

Quests . . . . Mary Brown, Elizabeth Moon,
Piers Anthony

Greek Mythology . . . . Roberta Gellis, *Bull God*